NIGHTS OF THE ROAD

Midi Berry

For Sienna, Jim and the Marks

CHAPTER ONE

California

"What a scorcher, eh?" The Australian twang had given her identity away, so I continued fastening the top of my convertible without turning my head.

"Wait a minute, Jane, and I'll be with you." Balancing papers and purse, I emerged from the Mustang to embrace my neighbour. Grimy and dishevelled after spending less than eight hours in an air-conditioned office, I wondered how she could still look fresh in a Qantas uniform after coming off a fourteen-hour flight.

Our footsteps echoed in unison as we crossed the underground parking lot toward the apartment elevator. "Is it always this warm in L.A. in May?" I asked. "The ad for Mariner's Village promised a cool lifestyle. I feel like asking for a rebate."

"I don't remember it this hot by the ocean so early in the year. Climate change, I guess." Jane replied. "I'm glad of the heat, though. That cold northerly set my teeth on edge. And it's still baking hot, back home in Sydney."

She pressed the elevator button and continued, "Anyway, you'd better get used to it, girl, if you're moving across town. You'll find it warmer over there."

I groaned. "Don't start again, Jane. I've told you I've no plans to move in with Bob." Jane laughed. "Be careful then, sweetie. You've lived in this town long enough to notice all the lonely women on the prowl. Unmarried hunks with his charm are a catch for hungry cougars."

We had exited the elevator at the first floor to collect our mail and I spoke over my shoulder while bending to open my box. "I'm no hungry cougar and I'm not looking to live with anyone again. How many times do I have to tell you I came to Los Angeles to get away from all that?"

"How many times do *I* have to tell *you* that you've had long enough to brood over a dead marriage, especially one in another continent? For

"

Heaven's sake, Sarah, you had a fall in the water. Get back in the saddle again and get a ring on your finger."

I straightened. "You do mix your metaphors. Wild cats one minute, horses the next. If you think my aim in life is to persuade some hunk to marry me, so I can retire to wedded bliss in Beverly Hills, well..."

Jane laughed. "You got it, girl."

I sorted through my mail. "In case you didn't know, I am still married. John's dragged his heels about putting in our divorce papers and he's in better spirits lately, so I'm not pressing him."

We re-entered the elevator. Jane pressed the button, turned and winked at me. "That needn't prevent you and Bob living together. You know you're crazy about him. Your marriage is over and your ex has to let you go, eventually."

I pushed back. "And which of those dashing airline captains I keep bumping into outside my apartment are you planning to waltz up the aisle with – oh, that's odd!"

As I gazed down at the postcard, my heart began to thud and my ears rang.

The scene took me back to school holidays spent in coastal Dorset. Given its wide-angled view, the photo was modern, but the sepia effect gave an appearance of antiquity to match the subject. The castle lay in ruins at the top of a steep, grass-covered mound. The photographer had captured both the surrounding morning mist at sunrise and the spirit of the castle's ancient past.

"What just happened? Did you see a ghost?" Jane grabbed my shoulder and turned me toward the mirrored back of the elevator. "Look at you. You just went as white as chalk. Are you OK?"

I found it an effort to respond. "... Yes... I'm fine. I was just surprised to receive this."

"Show me." Jane pulled the card from my hand. "Wow! That's spectacular. Do you know this place? Who sent it you?" She was turning the card over as she asked the question.

"Hey, it's meant for me!" I held out my hand. Jane moved out of reach and continued reading.

Since I was not about to manhandle her for the card, I responded, "Yes, I know it well. My father used to take me there when I was a kid. But I had no idea Bob had been to Corfe Castle. It's off the beaten track and the last place in England I'd expect him to visit. And he's not the kind of person I'd expect to send a postcard. Snail mail isn't his usual style."

"What did I tell you? He's an old-fashioned guy under that Mr. Big in the fast lane disguise." Jane returned the card. "Romantic message too. Sorry. I can't resist reading other people's mail – and males."

"You're impossible!"

"Maybe, but I'm giving you good oil. If you have an ounce of common sense in that over-intelligent head of yours, you'll get Bob's ring on your finger, before someone else beats you to it." Against my will, I laughed. Jane often got in my face, but I could never remain annoyed with her for long.

At adjacent apartments we fumbled for our keys. Jane patted her airline bag. "Come in and crack a bottle. I've got Jacob's Creek already in the fridge and plenty of duty free in here."

I shook my head. "Tempting, but I've been fighting a headache all day and I need an early night. I'm booked up all week and have a mountain of paperwork to catch up on. If you're free on Saturday, though, perhaps we could do lunch? Your turn to choose where, and my turn to treat."

"Sounds good to me. Let's go to Figtree's. Say hi to the hunk from me when he calls." Jane opened her door and disappeared.

Inside, I dropped papers, purse and mail on the multi-patterned modern table that was my only prized piece of furniture in an otherwise sparsely furnished apartment. I turned on the air-conditioning, poured water from a jug in the fridge and freshened it with lime. The landline blinked. Number out of area and whoever had called had left no message. But when I opened my desktop computer, I found three emails from Bob.

Two were identical and terse. "Call Me," read the subject line and the body of the message was blank. The third had a subject line "Stand and Deliver" and I opened it up to find a cartoon of highwaymen naked from the waist down, in suggestive pose. I looked at my watch. With the eight-hour difference, it was already 2 a.m. in London. Not a good time to call Bob, and I needed a bath. I refilled my glass and headed for the bathroom.

I had just shed my clothes and was stepping into the tub when the phone rang. Shaking water and bubbles off my legs, I returned to the living room.

"What are you wearing?" The velvet voice caressed my ear. My heart did its customary flip. The banality of Bob's favourite opening line had yet to wear on me.

"Something I think you'd like."

"That red dress with the front buttons that pull undone quickly?"

"Try again."

"The scoop-necked black thing that shows every man in sight I'm the luckiest guy in town?"

"No, you smooth talker. You'd probably like this one even better."

"Better wear it when you meet me at LAX, then, babe."

I chortled. "I'd be arrested before you cleared customs."

"Don't tell me you're talking to me naked, at six in the evening? OK. I'd like a little talk with whoever is there with you."

"Not guilty, your honour. I'm alone but I was just climbing in the bath when you called." I switched subjects. "Bob, when did you visit Corfe Castle? You've never mentioned it before."

"Oh, my card got there already? That was quick. I haven't visited it, babe. I just saw the postcard and thought of you."

"I don't remember ever mentioning Corfe Castle to you."

"I don't remember you mentioning it either. The card caught my eye, it looked like a heap of old stones you'd like, and so I got the concierge to mail it for me."

"My dad used to take me there when I was small. But where did you find it? I thought you were staying in London."

"I am. I found the card at a newsstand in the street at the back of my hotel, where I go for my morning Starbucks. You know the kind: British flags, old-world kitsch and other tourist trivia."

"It's weird that you would have singled out a card of Corfe Castle from all the English beauty spots on display at a London newsstand."

"Have we talked enough about this card now?" I heard rising irritation in his tone. In our few months of dating, I had learned that Bob did not dwell long on any subject that did not centre on music, the media or him.

"Yes, quite enough about castles. Tell me how your tour is shaping."

"It's nearly complete. I've got one more trip lined up. Heading to Bristol today and staying on the South Coast overnight. Then I have a couple of days back here in London to tie up loose ends. I'm booked on an early Sunday flight out of Heathrow. Can you pick me up at the airport about mid-afternoon?"

"Give me your flight details and I'll be there. Are you still planning some time off when you get back? I've cleared my client schedule for the whole of next week. The weather's turned hot. It would be good to get out of town."

"Sounds great, babe. Yes, I can manage a few nights away before the tour starts. Palm Springs would be perfect. I need somewhere relaxing but not too far to drive. We can go straight on from the airport if you book a hotel. I'll call you tomorrow with the flight time. Oh, by the way, did you get my email?"

"The cartoon? Yes, it made me laugh."

"One of the guys from my old band sent it. He's the reason I'm going down to Bristol. He wants us to put the old band back together and ride on the back of this tour. I think it's a non-starter, but I promised not to kill the idea without hearing him and the guys out." Bob's voice rasped on his final words.

"You sound tired."

"Yeah, I spent last night in a dive with a man from a band I used to represent. I thought smoking had been banned in London but the air there was thick. Anyway, I'm bushed, and I'll need to get on the road early for Bristol. I'll call you after my meeting, OK?"

"I'll be waiting. And I can book us that hotel we like in Palm Springs, although I do wonder if it won't be too hot there."

"Check the forecast first. We could go down to La Jolla, if you prefer. Desert or ocean, I'll leave it to you."

"OK. Desert, unless the forecast says otherwise. Have a good day in Bristol."

I headed for the bathroom again and added more hot water before stepping back into the bath. Bubbles frothed and burst gently against my ear as I eased back into the soothing heat. I closed my eyes and stretched out. As I did so, an image of Corfe Castle invaded me, a rushing sound drowned out all other sensation and my watery world gave way to darkness.

CHAPTER TWO

England 1611

"What are you doing? How dare you try to scare me? Go away."

Fear made her voice shrill, but Frances was imperious.

The boy did not move. Instead he narrowed his eyes and looked down his nose. "What are *you* doing, little girl? Why don't *you* go away? Clear off. I was here first. I don't share my favourite place with a snotty-nosed child playing where she shouldn't."

Drawing herself up to her full eight-year-old height left her still at a disadvantage. Undeterred, Frances enunciated each syllable slowly and succinctly. "I can have you thrown out of here if you don't leave."

The boy sneered. "You and whose army?"

The set of the girl's chin became more pronounced. "My mother's guards will throw you out or put you in the dungeon, if I call. And I will, if you don't go away."

"Your mother's guards? Pull the other leg. Who do you think you are?" The boy remained immobile, but scorn had given way marginally before curiosity.

"This is my mother's castle. And you are treppssissing."

Condescension laced his voice. "I suppose you mean trespassing. I'm not. I came with my uncle, who has important business here. And you're telling lies, little girl. Women don't own castles. Corfe Castle belongs to Sir Edward Coke. He's a powerful man and his guards will have *you* thrown out if I call them."

"I never tell lies. It's wicked to lie. This *is* my mama's castle. Papa doesn't own it, even though he orders everybody here around as if he does. It makes Mama very cross. She's come here now to put things back the way she wants them." Her face crumpled and Frances added, in a small voice, "My parents don't like each other at all."

The boy fidgeted. "God's teeth, don't tell me you're going to cry." Frances stiffened. "Of course not." She sniffed. "It's just that I love them both and I want them to be happy together, but Papa gets so nasty when he is angry, and Mama says you must stand up to him and mustn't ever show him how upset you are, or it makes him worse."

"You women get upset over nothing. And scared off by the least little thing."

Frances stamped her foot. "Mama doesn't. She's never scared of anyone. She wouldn't even take Papa's name when they married. She said he wanted her for her Hatton wealth and conniptions, so he must accept her with her Hatton name."

"I suppose you mean connections. Is Sir Edward Coke really your father? My uncle came here to meet him today. He'll be furious if it's only his wife here instead."

Frances shook her head. "Papa isn't here. I don't know why your uncle expected him. He hardly ever comes to the castle. He worries about being too far from Court, and hates leaving London to go anywhere, except with the King or to our home at Stoke."

The boy's forehead had creased in a frown. "Damn it. My uncle will be in foul humour if he's had a wasted journey."

Frances felt instantly sympathetic. "I'm sorry if your uncle is cross. Perhaps our steward can help him. Or Mama. Why did he want to talk to Papa?"

"He's looking for backing for one of his projects. Uncle William plans to get a proper port made at Kimmeridge. Building out the harbour can make the Isle of Purbeck wealthy and, if Sir Edward gets behind his idea, everyone else round here will agree."

The idea of a bigger port made little sense to Frances. "How would building up an old harbour make Purbeck wealthy?"

The boy rolled his eyes. "Don't you understand anything, little girl? A proper harbour will open up trade. My uncle already has a rope-making business and alum works here. There's lamp oil at Kimmeridge too. We extract it from the cliffs. I'm not sure we'll find many buyers for the oil, because our own lamps smell quite foul. But Uncle doesn't like being contradicted, so I don't say anything."

Frances wrinkled her nose. "I hate smelly lamps. They make me feel sick. Where's your home? Can we see it from here?"

"No. I live in the Mansion House over at Glanville's Wootton, a long way from here. Papa doesn't live with us. My parents don't like each other either, but I don't care. When I'm not at school, I usually come to stay with my uncle. I'll show you where he lives. Come on."

They had been standing in the lee of the castle's lower wall in the west bailey, between an octagonal tower and a disused hall. The boy grabbed the girl's hand and pulled her up a steep slope toward the main castle complex. Beneath the bulwark he stopped and turned. "Look over there. Can you see that hill? The long flat one? It's got woodland on either side."

Panting from her exertions to match the boy's long-legged stride, Frances twisted and followed the line of his pointing finger. "I can see the hill but I can't see any buildings."

He nodded. "That's because Kimmeridge is down the other side. I often climb that hill to sit and look out to sea. It has an amazing view. You can see along the coastline for miles." The boy returned his gaze to Frances. "Why haven't I seen you here before, when I've ridden around Corfe Castle with Uncle William? I'm his heir, so he likes to take me places with him." He puffed out his chest.

Frances countered with questions of her own. "Is your uncle rich? What will you inherit?"

"He's always trying to get other people to invest money in his projects, so I'm not sure how rich he is. I suppose I'll inherit all the land and houses he owns here but, when I'm a man, I'm going to be so wealthy that I never have to ask anyone for money. I've seen how it puts my uncle in a bad mood."

Encouraged by the boy's confidences, Frances opened up. "My parents are rich. Mama especially. But having wealth doesn't always make people happy. Mama is very angry at the moment." She sighed and sank down on the grass. As she smoothed her full petticoats, she noticed a torn hem. "Oh no! This must have happened when you were pulling me up the hill. Now Nurse will be cross and she'll complain again that I behave like a hoyden when I'm in the country."

The boy squatted, pulled a blade of grass and sucked it between his teeth. "Why isn't your mama happy?"

Frances picked at her skirt as she replied. "Well, she says she was only truly happy in her first marriage. Sir William was old, but Mama liked him because he was kind and let her do what she wanted. He left her this castle and our house in London and many other homes as well. Mama says she never liked Papa and now she won't sleep under the same roof as him ever again."

"Why did she agree to marry him then?"

"I'm not exactly sure. Nurse says she had many offers of marriage after Sir William died. I do know Uncle Francis Bacon wanted to marry her, because he told me so himself. He's her cousin and a very clever man. Mama likes him a lot, so he often visits, but Papa hates him."

"I've heard of Sir Francis Bacon. If she likes him, why didn't she marry him?"

"I think Grandpapa Cecil encouraged her to marry Papa because he had just won an important legal case for our family." Frances pondered, then added, "I did ask Mama once about Uncle Francis. She said she prefers a real man."

"What is that supposed to mean?"

She giggled. "I don't know. He seems real enough to me."

"If you ask me, your mama is one of those tiresome women who are impossible to please."

The boy's scorn broke the conciliatory mood and Frances flared. "I'm not asking you and I won't listen if you say nasty things about Mama."

He continued as if she had not spoken. "My uncle says Sir Edward Coke is the greatest lawyer England has ever known. Uncle wants me to be a lawyer. You should feel proud to have such an important papa and your mama ought to feel grateful to be married to him. She must be very stupid."

Frances jumped to her feet. "You don't know anything about her. She's the most wonderful person in the world. You're just an unkind and nasty boy."

He pulled at her skirts. "Sit down and don't take on so. I didn't mean to upset you. You're a sensitive little thing, aren't you? I only meant that any woman ought to feel honoured to be married to Sir Edward."

Frances sat again but continued to argue. "You don't know Papa. He can be cruel when he is vexed. Mama says he never forgave her for insisting on marrying him privately. They got told off for marrying at Grandpapa's house without the right papers."

"I don't understand. Why did your Mama insist on them marrying privately? I thought females like big weddings and being the centre of attention."

"Mama says she didn't want the world to see her marrying such an old man, but the Archbishop made them do it again anyway, in St. Andrews. It must have been quite funny." Amused by her own story, Frances giggled again, and momentarily forgot her indignation. "Everybody teased Papa for being the First Lawyer of the Land and not knowing about the laws of matrimony. Mama laughed so much she cried, when she told me the story."

"It sounds as if your mother takes pleasure in making your poor Papa uncomfortable. What a vixen she must be."

Frances erupted. "You're only taking Papa's side because you hope he'll give your uncle some money or speak on his behalf to the King. You're just like people at Court. They flatter Papa so he'll help them, but they're spiteful to Mama because they are jealous of her."

"I'm not jealous of anyone, and certainly not of your Mama."

"I know lots of people who are, and they say unkind things about her like you just did. One of the Queen's Ladies of the Bedchamber even told me that my Mama was obliged to marry Papa."

The boy looked blank. "How was she obliged?"

"Oh, it wasn't true. Nurse said my sister was born after Mama and Papa had been together long enough to make a baby. Mama tells me never to show I care, when jealous people say things like that." Her tone became wistful. "I wish I could be strong like her. She never takes notice of what people say."

The boy shook his head. "Look, I'm not jealous but I don't understand your mama. I'd be happy all day long if I owned this castle and lots of other homes too." He looked up at the ramparts and then back at Frances with a measuring expression. "How many brothers and sisters do you have?"

"Only one." Her face clouded. "Elizabeth is four years older than me. She tells me I'm a pest. And she says Mama treats me as her favourite, but I don't think that is true. I do have half brothers and sisters but they're all older even than Elizabeth. Papa was married before to a lady who gave him lots of children before she died. My favourite is Clem. He's closest to us in age."

"So Elizabeth and you are your mother's heirs?"

Frances nodded.

A luminous smile transformed her companion's features. "Well, that's splendid. If you can just make sure your part of the inheritance includes this castle, I will marry you. Then we'll live here together and we'll both be very happy." He leaned forward to study Frances. "You're very pretty. I like the colour of your hair. It shines in the sunlight. And your eyes are very big. They sparkle in that way that poets write about. I'm going to write poetry when I grow up. I haven't had much to do with girls until now, but I shall need a beautiful wife and you will do very well."

Frances drew back, lifting her chin in a gesture that mixed challenge with a small girl's coquetry. "Perhaps I won't *want* to marry you." Then the clouds descended again. "I may not want to marry anyone. I'd hate to squabble like Mama does with Papa."

"Girls have to marry when they grow up. It's the law."

"Girls don't have to. Not if we don't want to."

"You do have to. You must get married, so you can have babies without shame. Don't worry. You and I won't quarrel when we're married. You'll be happy with me. I'll teach you to ride. We'll go hunting and have adventures together."

"I can ride and hunt already, silly. The King loves hunting and he says I have a very good seat and safe hands. I do wish Mama wouldn't make me sit side-saddle, though. I want to ride like boys do."

Her companion grinned. "You can ride astride whenever you're out with me. You can even dress up as a boy when we're out on adventures, if you like." Frances clapped her hands. "Yes, I'd love that. I hate wearing skirts, especially here in the country. What adventures will we have?"

The boy's eyes gleamed. "We'll go out at night and watch for shipwrecks above Kimmeridge. There's a secret place I know up on the cliffs, where we can hide from the wreckers and smugglers. They don't like to be spied on, you see."

Frances shook her head. "I don't want to be a spy. And I've never met a wrecker, but I think they must be brutes, to want people to drown just so they can get rich."

The boy laid his hand on hers. "Don't worry. They won't hurt you if I'm with you. My uncle actually owns the rights to all the wrecks on this part of the coast."

His assurance failed to win Frances over and she pulled her hand away. "No, I'm not staying out in bad weather, waiting for people to drown and hiding from men who don't like to be spied on. Anyway, how could we know in advance whether ships were going to get wrecked?"

"If you're in with the right people, you always know when wrecks will happen. You can leave all that side of things to me."

Frances did not bend and the boy yielded first. "Oh, very well, if you prefer, we can become highwaymen instead. We'll rob the rich and give whatever we steal to the poor people of Purbeck."

She still hesitated. "I'm happy to help the poor, but I'm not certain I'd like being a highwayman. It's not very kind to rob people just because they're rich. I'm sure Mama wouldn't like it, and Papa would be angry."

"We could always sail out of Kimmeridge Harbour and set off to see the world together."

The idea of foreign travel held more appeal for Frances. "Where would we go if we did sail away?"

The boy gestured toward the coastline. "Wherever we want. There's a globe in my uncle's study. You can come to Kimmeridge and look at it and help me decide where we'll go. We'll search for treasure and then I'll be rich and can give you beautiful jewels and dresses and things. You'll have to promise not to scream if pirates attack us, but I'll keep you safe."

He peered into her eyes. "You really are the prettiest girl I've seen." Frances felt her cheeks grow warm. "Am I really prettier than any other girl you know?" He nodded and dazzled her again with his smile. She edged forward and touched his face with one finger. "You have a dimple, just there. Mama told me once that men with dimples make good lovers."

"Mistress Frances! Mistress Frances! Where has that child got to now?"

The distant, high-pitched voice sounded harassed, and its effect on Frances was electric. She scrambled to her feet and peered anxiously round the edge of the bulwark toward the castle keep. "That's my nurse. She'll scold me terribly if I don't go in. I'm not supposed to leave the inner keep on my own."

She turned and caught the boy's hand as he was rising, which caused him to lose his balance. "Can you come again tomorrow? Mama never stays anywhere long, so we may go back to London soon."

He jerked fully upright. "Yes, I'll ride over at about the same time, unless Uncle needs me for something. Are you called Frances? That's my mother's name, and my sister's. Shall I ask for you at the gatehouse, or should I wait for you here?"

"Go to the inner gatehouse. I'll tell the guards to expect you and then they can tell me when you've arrived. My name is Mistress Frances Coke, but you may call me Franny, like my friends."

The boy shook his head. "No. I shall call you Frances. I'm going to be your husband and that is quite different from being a friend." He leaned down and pecked her cheek. "Until tomorrow then, Frances?"

She nodded, picked up her petticoats and raced toward the keep. As she entered, she gave silent thanks that Nurse had not reached the duty guards. Explaining about her future visitor, she included a description of the dimple.

"And the young gentleman's name, Mistress?" The older of the two guards addressed her respectfully, while the younger seemed to be caught up in a sudden coughing attack.

Scarlet stained her cheeks as Frances realized her omission. "Oh no! I forgot to ask. Please keep Nurse here, if she comes for me. I'll be back in a moment."

She retraced her steps at the run, but the boy had already vanished. Frances bit her lip as she looked down toward the outer castle wall and gate. She was already in hot water and to spend more time searching would further anger Nurse. She berated herself as she re-entered the keep. The description of the boy would surely be detailed enough for the guards to recognize him on sight. But would Mama take this marriage proposal seriously if Frances could not name her suitor?

CHAPTER THREE

California

The sky was a cloudless cobalt blue and heat from the noonday sun had begun to penetrate my baseball cap as I walked. To my left, the tide had turned and fondant-frosted waves fringed the length of the beach toward Malibu, as far as my eye could see. They curled gently over on themselves, collapsed and seeped back into the ocean.

Far ahead, near Venice Pier, clustered figures moved like matchstick men. Since leaving the Channel path at the southern end of the Marina beach, I had enjoyed the company of an occasional seagull, but had yet to meet another human being. The beach lay at the western edge of a sprawling metropolis numbering more than sixteen million people, and so finding it almost deserted at midday surprised and delighted me.

Beneath my feet, under a thin film of water, dark deposits of natural tar discoloured the sand. I picked my way barefoot between oily patches, clumps of seaweed and ink-coloured jellyfish stranded by the turning of the tide. My lungs inflated with ozone-rich air and my morning tension began to ease.

When I had arrived at my office just before eight, the red blinking light of my voice mail system heralded client messages. Three cancellations hit me in the solar plexus, and sent me in reflex action to the ocean, as soon as I had cleared my early appointments. Since childhood, the limen-land between sea and shore had been my sanctuary. Treading its ever-shifting yet ever-constant line helped me process stress. Today was my first experience of client dissatisfaction since arriving in L.A., and my self-confidence had received a jolt.

Had my three women callers compared notes before calling me? I had no way of knowing which clients knew each other, unless they mentioned their friends by name. But I knew many did socialise together and I could hardly complain about that, since it had contributed to my early success.

A chance meeting with an actor, seated next to me during my trans-Atlantic flight to California, had led to counselling sessions for two of his Los Angeles friends, within days of my arrival. These two satisfied clients had provided immediate income, and their generosity in spreading the word meant that my presence in the city became known at head-spinning speed. Requests for sessions poured in so fast that I was obliged to look for office space before finding somewhere to live. My client list multiplied by word-of-mouth and I found myself established as a Westside counsellor without having spent a cent on promotion.

I wiggled my toes, making light imprints in the sand and interrogating myself as I walked. Three dissatisfied clients in one day felt too many for a professional practice. Had I been clear in contracting with each one about ground rules for time out? Yes, and I had kept to the contract, by giving all clients the two weeks agreed notice of my intention to take a vacation.

My three Friday clients had recorded their telephone salvoes within minutes of each other, early on the morning of their appointments. Each talked of betrayal and feeling uncertain if they could rely on someone who was not available when needed. Three women, who had shown no compunction over re-scheduling at a moment's notice, signed off by declaring that they would not pay late cancellation charges, since I had given short notice of my intent to abandon them. It felt like a stitch-up.

From childhood, I had been prone to assume responsibility for communication breakdowns. Therapy and subsequent training revealed the pattern and its source, yet unexpected stress could still knock me off centre. Today I determined to draw a metaphorical line in the sand. The longer I walked, the more certain I became that I had nothing with which to reproach myself. But the experience had given me a wake-up call. I was still wet behind the ears about the dynamics of my adopted city. And I had no professional supervisor.

Bob introduced me to a therapist friend, soon after we met. The man seemed wise and willing to supervise me, but then he opted to take a year's sabbatical. While he wandered around sub-Saharan Africa searching for ancient ruins, I was left searching for his substitute. State law did not require me, as a registered counsellor, to have a supervisor but conducting client debriefs solo by the Pacific Ocean felt inadequate, given my confidence level.

The further I walked today, the clearer I became that, after a whirlwind first year in L.A. – setting up a client practice and home in an unknown continent, and embarking on a new personal relationship – it was time to stop and take stock of my life. I needed our coming break out in the desert air. Physical distance from the city would recharge my batteries; psychological space could help me gain some perspective on my work, and decide how to build on what I had achieved. Perhaps I might also find answers to some relationship questions, past and present.

I emerged from my walking meditation to check my watch. Time to get back to the office, before Friday traffic madness set in. I turned to retrace my steps. The view of the coastline south of the Marina was spectacular. Catalina Island stood out, purple and prominent. Those northerly winds that had irritated Jane had blown all hint of low cloud away, and the heat wave had yet to build and generate the haze that can envelop Los Angeles in summer.

Why were so few people out and enjoying this glorious weather, I wondered? Many people living in the Marina kept relaxed working hours, and lunchtime joggers usually swelled the ranks of casual walkers. Whatever the reason, it was my gain to feel alone and at one with the elements. Lazy calls of seabirds rising and falling in a limitless sky interwove with the muted lapping of waves. Oystercatchers ran in and out of the ocean. A breeze brushed my face, offsetting the heat of the sun.

"Caw! Caw!" A solitary crow — or was it a raven? — interrupted my reverie. It stalked and strutted along on the sand in front of me, then stopped, turned and barred my path, as if daring me to pass. The bird looked out of keeping with its environment, but it may have held the same opinion about me, for it glared as I approached and shifted sideways a few complaining paces.

As I drew alongside, a loud and sudden sound made us both jump. Somewhere a mobile phone rang. I laughed as the crow cocked its head, cawed in evident disapproval and flew off in a flurry of ruffled feathers.

I agreed with the bird. The sound was intrusive. I looked around to see the source of the disturbance. Then stopped, puzzled. I could see nobody within a hundred yards of me, in front or behind, and still the ringing continued, close and persistent. Belatedly, I realized that the sound was emanating from my own back pocket.

I never brought my mobile phone to the beach. Bob had chastised me often for leaving it in my car or apartment, and thereby missing many of his calls. "For God's sake, Sarah, you must carry your phone with you at all times. You should also have Mace whenever you're out walking alone."

Bob would not listen to counter-arguments on the subject of personal safety. I attributed it to our different cultural origins. Even in a post-9/11 world, I found it curious that such a big man could feel the need for a handgun in his secure Beverly Hills apartment. But I had grown up in an England where the police had to request a special licence to carry firearms, and weren't always granted one.

OK, so L.A. was not leafy, suburban Surrey, but I did not want to feed any spiralling US culture of violence, by buying into an armoured mentality. Why carry a mobile phone on a beach regularly patrolled by police and where, on many days, the sound of the surf drowned out the sound of incoming calls? And why not savour natural beauty, without the pressure of 24/7 communication access?

Yet today, for some reason, I had brought my mobile phone with me. And today, on an all but deserted beach with the ocean in gentle voice, I heard it ring.

"You took your time to answer. Guess where I am!" He sounded upbeat.

"Hi, Bob. I didn't expect you to call this early."

He chuckled. "Ah! I've caught you. What are you doing and whom are you doing it with, babe? I don't know why you aren't expecting me. I left three messages on your office line, telling you to call me as soon as you got free."

"I'm not at the office. I had a bunch of cancellations and headed for the ocean. I hope you're impressed I have my phone with me."

"Listening to me at last? That makes a pleasant change! Next, you'll be learning how to text."

I laughed. "Never. Call me a cave-woman, but I'm not intending to join the ranks of people married to iPhones. Maybe you were influencing me subconsciously. I wish you were here. The beach is beautiful and the weather is amazing."

"It's kinda beautiful here too. I'm having dinner in a neat place. Guess where I am and what I'm looking at?"

I tried to imagine a Bristol scene that would make as cosmopolitan a traveller as Bob sound like an excited kid. "Are you on the terrace of that hotel up in Clifton, overlooking the Suspension Bridge and the Avon Gorge?"

"I'm miles from Bristol. But you do know this place. I'll give you a clue. I'm looking at an old building in a lousy state of repair. Someone knocked the roof off and the walls need attention. No glass in the windows, either."

I felt a strange tug at my heart. "Are you at Corfe Castle? What are you doing there?"

"You can speak to the guy who brought me here in a minute. He'll explain. Remember Nights of the Road? Well, here's your chance to say hi to one of the boys from the band."

"Oh no, don't do this to me, Bob. I hate it when you expect me to chat to complete strangers." But his iPhone had already changed hands.

"Is that Sarah?"

I grimaced into the phone. "Yes. I'm Sarah. And I'm so sorry. Bob is always passing me over to friends of his that I don't know. I end up talking to people who haven't the least desire to speak with me."

He laughed. "You'll 'ave to train 'im out of that 'abit then. But you're wrong, luv. I 'ad every desire to speak to you. Bob's been telling me all about you. 'E says you're luvly and a very smart woman."

How to respond to that? I changed the subject, trying to sound casual. "Why are you at Corfe Castle? I thought Bob was in Bristol today."

"Yeah. We were both there this morning to meet the rest of the guys. I'm taking 'im back to me own place for the night. 'E's buying me a nice meal at one of me favourite local restaurants. Don't worry, luv. I'll make sure 'e's back in London for 'is flight. 'E says you know this place. I've a nice little pile not far from 'ere. Do you know Kimmeridge?"

"No, but I used to visit Corfe Castle as a kid, with my dad."

"Don't know Kimmeridge? Oh, sweet'art, we'll 'ave to change that. It's just the place for a woman with a sexy voice like yours to come and cheer up a lonely old rock musician like me."

His style of speaking irked me. His voice did not match his words and I was ready to bet that his flirtatious manner covered an awkwardness equal to my own. His accent sounded artificial, too. Some successful bands in the early British rock scene had hailed from London's East End and, even today, some musicians born far from the sound of Bow Bells coined a Cockney accent for effect.

A voice was remonstrating in the background. Bob had tired of his own game. "Hey, that's enough of chatting up my woman."

"Bye for now, Sarah. We'll speak again soon." The phone changed hands and there was Bob. "Honey, this castle of yours is great. There's a full moon too. Magic. You and I must come here together some time. This old hotel we're eating at is quaint."

"It feels odd to stand here under a midday sun on the Marina beach, listening to you talk about a full moon shining over Corfe Castle. Bob, your friend said you're staying overnight at his home. Are you going back to London in the morning?"

"If we make it to his place alive tonight! These narrow roads are quite something. And everyone seems to drive like a maniac."

I felt a pang of disquiet. "Who's driving?" Bob was airy in response. "He is. He has a sweet car. A Ferrari. You should have seen us this morning. London to Bristol in no time. I'm surprised we didn't get stopped. But there are speed cameras all along the freeways here, so the fines may catch up with him later."

"Your friend sounded drunk to me. Please be careful."

Bob lowered his voice. "Oh, so you got that? You don't miss much. Don't worry. It's safer after dark, because you can see oncoming headlamps. Gotta go now, babe. I'll have to call you tomorrow with my flight time for Sunday. Sorry, I forgot to make a note of it before I left this morning. Did you choose Palm Springs or the ocean?"

"I checked with La Valencia, but it was full, so I opted for Palm Springs. It's supposed to cool off after tomorrow. According to the forecast it won't go over a hundred in the desert, but the coast will have May Grays by mid-week."

"Desert it is then. Love you."

"Love you too, Bob."

I put the mobile phone back in my pocket and stood staring at my bare feet. The call had thrown me. Was it the surprise of having my phone with me? Or the uncomfortable exchange with his friend? Perhaps it was simply disorientating to hear a man six thousand miles away talk about moonlit dinners while I was standing by the ocean in midday heat.

I shook myself mentally and walked on a few paces. Then I stopped. Bob had just said he loved me. And I had said I loved him too. It had been quick and spontaneous, almost throwaway, on both sides. Yet we had each so carefully avoided the 'love' word until now. Had Bob taken note of what he said? If so, how he was feeling now? How was I feeling?

Disturbed.

I glanced at my watch again. If I left all my morning paperwork to the weekend, I could squeeze another half hour on the beach. Moving across to a patch of sand where wind and water had joined forces to scoop out a hollow, I settled into a natural armchair facing the ocean.

The rhythmic motion of the waves lulled me and I was adrift in a surreal haze when a burst of movement caused me to jump up and jerk round. Behind and above me, wings flapped as a flock of birds rose in the air. A high-pitched collective whistle accompanied the murmuration and echoed like a tribe of Bedouins giving tongue across the heavens.

Lying down again, I craned my neck to watch the dark silhouettes wheel and dart. I had never seen so many seabirds in a single formation. The blanket of birds twisted and sped upward on a near vertical path. I observed the avian cloud become a shadow, growing smaller and more transparent, until it blended into the blue background and disappeared.

My eyes felt strained now, but I could not take my eyes off the space where the birds had been. Then I blinked and felt, rather than saw, my peripheral vision disappear. A drumming sound filled my ears and, although I knew my body was still supported by the sand, I experienced the same sensation as the previous evening. I was falling backwards again and into darkness.

CHAPTER FOUR

England 1616

Birds swooped and soared in the clear midsummer sky. Engrossed in following the zigzag paths of their whistling flight, the girl paid no attention to her companion. They were in their favourite spot, between the Buttevant Tower and the Old Hall, where they had first met five years before.

He repeated himself. "Here am I saying how much I've missed you, Frances, and you take no notice. Do you care at all about me? Why didn't you reply to my last letter?"

His sulky tone caught her attention. Frances turned, looked at the youth by her side and smiled before returning her gaze to the birds. "Please don't be cross with me. You seem to find it easy, but I hate writing letters. I can never find the right words." She pointed upwards. "Look at the swallows and swifts. Or maybe they are martins."

"If they're martins, they have a white underside. And if they're swallows, they have much deeper forked tails. If they're brown and ordinary like me, they're swifts."

"You're brown from the sun but you're far from ordinary. Apart from anything else, you know all about birds."

He shrugged. "There's little else for me to do than watch birds, stuck down here in the depths of the dreary old country." The youth kicked at a loose stone and glared at the girl. "It's not fair. I'm not lucky like you, Frances, living in London and going off on adventures with the Court. I've never even travelled out of Dorset, except to visit my father in Somerset. And that's no thrill. Tell me again about all your grand houses in Town and other places. And what you've been doing and where you've been since I saw you last."

"There's nothing much to tell." She continued to gaze at the birds.

"Hey, pay attention to me!"

Frances sighed and turned to give him a quick hug. "I'm sorry. I don't mean to annoy you. Our grand houses? I've told you before that Mama and I love Hatton House, but Papa prefers Stoke, when he isn't in his Chambers. It's very handsome and it must have been so lively, back when Queen Elizabeth stayed there. But my sister and I always have to be quiet, so we don't disturb Papa at his work."

Her eyes had turned upward again. He tugged at her sleeve. "Say more. You've never described your London home properly to me."

A twinge of compassion shot through Frances. "I'm sure I did, John, and you must have forgotten. Hatton House is huge. It was built for the Bishops of Ely and Mama says they want it back but she's keeping it. The Queen gave it to Sir Christopher Hatton as well as Stoke Manor, and the Bishop of the time was very cross, because he was allowed no say in the matter. You remember I told you that Mama's first husband was Sir Christopher's heir?"

"Yes, and that's how she came to own Corfe Castle. I do remember that."

"Perhaps you'll visit Hatton House one day. The banqueting chamber is amazing. Mama gives the grandest dinners and our guests all enjoy coming to them, but I like the gardens best. There are roses everywhere and the strawberries are just coming into season. I love the hay meadows behind, though I'm not supposed to wander in them, because thieves hide out there. I feel safer there than at Court, though, with all the gossip and clacking tongues that want to hurt one."

"Who would ever want to hurt you?" The youth's tone was sharp. Frances looked at him and pondered how much she should reveal. "Nobody yet, but life at Court is not all fun, John."

He went back to kicking stones. "It must be a lot more interesting than having to live here. Thank God, I won't have to remain in the Isle of Purbeck forever. Uncle William has promised to send me to his old college, and then I'll be able to come and visit you. Oxford must be much closer to London. I can't wait. This place is so boring." John scowled as he stared around him.

Frances frowned. "I thought you loved it here. You've never complained before. I fear you may be sadly disappointed by London and Court life. It may seem glamorous from a distance, but horrid things can happen." She shivered and shut her eyes.

John moved closer and took her hand. "You're in a strange humour today, Frances. I so wanted you to be pleased to see me."

"I am pleased to see you. And I'm particularly pleased to be away from London just now."

He traced the outline of her fingers; smooth and elegant by comparison with his own chapped and nail-bitten ones. "Why? What's going on?"

She shrugged. "Everybody is at each other's throats because of His Majesty's new favourite. Mama is convinced that Steenie will turn King James against all his closest friends and advisers. Even Papa has to be careful, although he's always had to watch his step with the King."

"But Uncle William says Sir Edward is one of the King's most important servants."

"Yes, and he works hard for the King, but he also stands up for Parliament and the Common Law. He wants to limit the King's spending. He says Steenie is bringing out the worst in King James. He fears His Majesty will squander all the wealth that Queen Elizabeth built up for England." Frances regretted the words as soon as they were spoken. "Oh dear, please forget I said that. It could get us in trouble."

"Who can I repeat it to? My uncle never listens to me, and I hardly ever see Papa. Steenie is an odd name, though, Frances. Who is he?"

"His real name is George Villiers. Haven't you heard of him? The King nicknamed him Steenie. He said such angelic looks made him think of Saint Stephen. Now everyone uses the name, but they don't say it in quite the same way, or else His Majesty would think people are making fun of his Scottish accent. The King is very sensitive about that."

"What's this Steenie like, apart from looking like an angel?"

Frances grimaced. "Witty and charming, in a sly way. Most people seem to think he is wonderful. At least, they pretend they do. When he wants something, he can be all over you, until he gets what he wants. If you cross him, you soon see the other side of George Villiers. I don't trust him. Neither does Mama. She says Steenie is insidious, because he sows doubts about people in the King's mind."

"Why do people let him get away with it?"

The girl shook her head. "People are either taken in by his charm, or they are afraid of him because his influence with the King is growing. Somerset's jealousy has made things much worse. It's all a nasty mess."

"Where does Somerset fit in?"

"He doesn't, not any longer. He's shut up in the Tower because his wife murdered a man, and he may have helped her. The Earl of Somerset wanted to marry Frances Howard, and Mama told me they were madly in love, so he shouldn't have minded Steenie becoming the King's new sweetheart."

He let go of her hand and scratched his head. "Your story makes no sense. Who's Frances Howard? Why is the Earl of Somerset jealous? And why do you call Steenie the King's new sweetheart?"

Frances looked at her companion with a worldly-wise expression. "Oh, John, do I have to spell it all out? You must have heard that the King likes men better than women. The Earl of Somerset married

Frances Howard. She poisoned Sir Thomas Overbury, because he tried to stop Somerset from marrying her. And Somerset used to be His Majesty's lover, his special boy, if you like, before Steenie."

John recoiled. "Ugh! I certainly don't like. Men liking other men that way makes me sick. It's not natural."

"Isn't it? I don't know. I'm not a man. It's how things are with many of the gentlemen at Court." Frances frowned again. "The Queen likes Steenie well enough, and doesn't complain at the King's liaisons. Why should not men love each other, as long as people don't get hurt? Uncle Francis has his favourites. Mama often teases him that he has a soft spot for Welshmen. He just laughs."

John flushed. "Frances, I refuse to talk with a lady about such disgusting things. Let's talk about you and me instead. Will you come riding tomorrow? Uncle William gave me a new falcon for my birthday. He's magnificent. Much finer than those little birds you have been gawping at, all morning."

"Yes, of course, if Mama says I may. But don't get upset with me, John. I can't help but think about these people since they are so much a part of my world. The Villiers family, in particular."

He dived on her last comment. "Why the Villiers?"

Frances bit her lip. She hadn't intended to speak of it, but her mouth seemed to be running away with her today. "Steenie's elder brother, Sir John Villiers, made an offer for me. Mama says their horrid mother and Steenie are egging Sir John on, because they want to get hold of her fortune. And she worries Papa may be encouraging the suit."

John looked horror-struck. "Is he?"

"He's says not, but he told Mama the money and property proposal was still not to our advantage. He said 'still,' as though he might be willing to agree if the price was right."

"What money and property? What properties will you have?" John had pounced on her words again, and his focus on the details of her inheritance rather than her feelings about the match hurt Frances.

She became regally cool. "You may be sure that Mama does not discuss such vulgar things with me, John. And she says Papa agreed with her that I am too young for us to have to talk of marriage yet."

Her tone of censure dissolved when she saw John flush again, and she resumed her normal voice. "She doesn't entirely believe him, since Papa insisted that Mama's step-daughter marry when she was just fifteen. That's why she's brought coach-loads of plate and silver and furnishings with us this time, to make the castle more comfortable. She says we're going to stay longer than usual. Out of sight, out of mind."

"That suits me. I hope you can remain here for months."

Frances nodded and shuddered in the same moment. "I can't imagine marrying Sir John. It's not that he is so very old, and I do believe he would try to be kind. But one never knows what sort of humour one will find him in. He can be miserable one moment and dreadfully excitable the next."

"I'll kill him if he tries to marry you."

John looked so fierce that Frances smiled. "It's sweet of you to be protective, John. And Mama will take care of me too." Her voice wavered. "Still, I have to accept that Papa will look to marry me to someone who can help his situation."

John's face contorted. "If your papa ever tries to marry you to anyone but me, I'll kill him and them, I swear it. Goddammit! I can't wait to be a man. I will come to London then and ask your father for your hand."

Frances shook her head. "Stop swearing! And don't keep on about killing people. Stay away from Town as long as you can, John. It's a dangerous place. His Majesty has a way of changing his favourites with his clothes, especially since Steenie began whispering in his ear. Oh, but don't repeat that either, please."

"This Steenie sounds a complete menace. I will start by killing him."

Frances stamped her foot. "Enough! Stop this wild talk right now, before someone overhears you. Don't you realise that people have found themselves in the Tower for less?"

"You're exaggerating."

She raised her eyebrows. "You think so? What about Somerset? The King's former lover is in prison now, thanks to careless words being overheard. Papa conducted the trial and he told me so."

He sneered. "All these plots and people I don't know or care about. What does any of it matter?"

"Matter? The Overbury murder and trial is only the biggest scandal of our lifetime since the Gunpowder Treason. When Mama and I left Town, people were laying bets on whether the Somersets will be executed or pardoned."

"Well, I told you I don't hear much about anything down here." John hesitated. "Although, I do believe it may have been the Somerset trial that my uncle was talking about the other day. I didn't pay any attention since I have no interest in these people."

He puffed out his chest. "But don't think I'm afraid of the King or of Steenie, or of being shut up in the Tower. No one else is going to have you. You and I agreed when we met that we'll marry one day."

Frances turned her gaze to the distant hills. "I seem to remember you did the deciding for us both then, John. And it had everything to do with me inheriting Corfe Castle. Since you can't abide the boring old Isle of Purbeck now, there's no longer any point in you marrying me."

The youth glared down from his superior height. He growled, "Frances, stop teasing. You are mine. Your father must let me marry you. I meant what I said about killing anyone who gets in my way."

The boastful tone that Frances had come to know well permeated John's words as he added, "Remember how lightning quick I am with my sword? My fencing master told my uncle that nobody around these parts could match me for speed. I'll hazard I'm faster than anyone you know in London."

She laid a hand on his arm. "Let's stop being so serious. I'm only thirteen and Mama has promised me I can marry for love."

She pirouetted away and out of his reach, but the youth tried to catch hold of her as he asked, "You have explained about us to Lady Hatton, haven't you? She must be happy with me, since she's always willing for us to be together here. Perhaps I should see her now and ask for her support with your Papa for my suit."

Frances stopped twirling abruptly. "John, we shouldn't have talked about any of this. We won't do so any more. Let's go on being children just as long as we can." Now she was the one to take his hands and entwine her fingers within his. "Tell me all about the new falcon. I'm longing to see it."

"Frances, you do still love me, don't you?"

For answer, Frances stretched on tiptoe to kiss him on the cheek. A smile played on her lips. "Don't wear such a long face. You have to take care of that dimple if you mean to be a good lover."

"I'm not interested in just being a good lover. I am going to be your husband, Mistress Frances Coke. And you are going to be my wife."

CHAPTER FIVE

California

We had arrived early enough to secure a table at Figtree's right next to the Boardwalk.

A few paces away, two swarthy members of a Latin American trio strummed string instruments in accompaniment to their companion's panpipes. The music fed a festive atmosphere. Sun and heat had brought local residents to the beach, where they intermingled with stall keepers, ball players, entertainers, homeless itinerants and selfie-snapping tourists.

I tried to conceal my mood, but I felt out of tune with our surroundings. At first Jane divided her attention between her meal and the musicians, but before long she gazed at me and said, "Girl, your smile's gone walkabout. You've hardly touched your food. Want to tell Auntie Jane all about it?"

"It's nothing." But my attempt at a smile failed. "You're right. I am blue. I guess because Bob isn't coming back tomorrow." I could feel my eyes grow moist, which irritated me. I blinked several times, tried and failed again to smile. "I know it's stupid to feel so upset, but I was really looking forward to going away. You'd think I'd have learned by now that his plans can change without warning."

"Give yourself a break! You're so hard on yourself, Sarah. Yeah, quite a habit with Bob, isn't it? So what made him move the goal posts this time?"

"I'm not entirely sure. He was in a vile mood when he called and didn't want to go into details. Something about a misunderstanding with a group he'd signed for his tour."

"That sounds vague. What do you think happened?"

I shrugged. "I don't know. I'm not involved in the minutiae of Bob's world, any more than he is in mine, so I don't ask for details. All I know is he flew to Germany today to talk with some band on tour over there. When we spoke, he was boarding a flight to Berlin. He doesn't know when he'll get back to London, let alone L.A.."

"Perhaps he'll fly back direct from Berlin. He may only be delayed a day or two."

"Maybe, but I'm not getting my hopes up again. I'm frustrated, because I cleared my schedule and annoyed several clients in doing so. May even have lost them."

"Why should you have lost any?"

"Because they identify me now with people who weren't there for them when needed. The big A. Abandonment."

Jane rolled her eyes. "Strewth. Do you mean you're never supposed to take a vacation? No wonder these clients need counselling."

I laughed. "No. I contract up front with clients about giving notice. Except these three seem to have forgotten that. It's not so unusual to get some kind of a reaction. People can come to feel needy about their sessions. But this was three clients in a row, all using identical language, so I felt stitched up."

"God, I don't mean to knock what you do but, to be honest with you, Sarah, I've never understood why anyone goes to counselling or therapy. What is the point of all that moaning and spilling their guts out on your floor?"

I shrugged. "The point varies. Some of us just need help in a crisis. Others keep recreating chronic patterns from deep-seated unresolved issues. There are so many different benefits from therapy." I stopped as I felt myself colour. "Sorry, that probably sounds like a lecture, Jane. Therapy isn't for everybody, and I need to get off my soapbox."

Jane smiled. "No worries. I invited it. At least your soapbox is here on the Boardwalk now. Before, you were away with the pixies. See how good I am for you? I may have to start charging you for my services." But she stopped joking and laid down her fork as she read my expression. "Do you really think your clients won't come back?"

"Three of them have left messages saying they are re-considering."

"Do *you* want clients like that back?"

I had not asked myself the question. "It depends on what happens next. Yes, if we can use what's happened between us to look in the mirror more closely. That takes courage and a real intention to change. It's a key stage. You reach a crossroads and then you have to make a choice: be willing to go deeper or leave."

"I bet your clients will be back. I've met a couple that sang your praises. I could tell they just love unloading on you. I don't know how you stand it. I'd never have the patience to sit listening all day to people whine about their problems, and how it all started with Mum and Dad. I've locked all my gnarly stuff up in a cupboard and thrown away the key. Let someone else deal with my psychological trash when I check out."

I laughed at her comical face, but it occurred to me that our situations were equal and opposite. "Backatcha, Jane. I would never have the patience to deal with carping and complaining passengers on a long-distance flight. You've been doing so cheerfully for years."

"But they don't all complain. Especially not the ones I treat extra well. Know what I mean?" Jane winked and finished her wine.

She changed tack. "Leaving clients aside, sweetie, I feel for you and Bob, struggling to run two busy lives in sync. That's been a problem in my relationships." She leaned back in her chair and looked out toward the ocean. "Yeah, that was what broke things up between Frank and me. I really cared for him, but his operating theatre schedule and my changing flight times did not make for happy bedfellows. And it's why I've gone back to dating within the business since him. Airline people tolerate disrupted plans because we all suffer them."

I nodded. "Your schedule does change a lot. I'd hate that. I have to admit it's an issue between Bob and me. I don't mind at all if there's a genuine problem, but I do sometimes wonder if he's changing things to suit himself." I sighed. "We also have such different expectations about sticking with agreements. It seems to be a cultural thing."

"Oh my God! Don't choose a native Angeleno, if you want someone who'll stick with prior plans, girl. Or perhaps that's exactly why you have fallen for one. Perhaps Bob will help you loosen up and you can invite more order in his life. From what I've seen, he's a bit chaotic and careless, and people probably let him get away with it. He has more charm than is good for him, so he's used to getting people to do what he wants. Still, that's L.A., and the music business too. What can you expect, girl? Sex, drugs and rock 'n' roll! A playground for bad boys and girls."

Jane stretched bronzed arms high behind her head then lowered them and pointed toward the distant water. "To me Los Angeles is like the ocean. It stays in one place yet it's always restless and on the move. Quite different from Sydney, which is busy yet stable. It's odd, since both cities are on the Pacific. Different coasts and countries, different vibes, I guess. Nothing seems to stay fixed in L.A. for long. I like that, myself. Keeps you on your toes."

The waiter brought our bill and I waved aside Jane's exaggerated attempts to take it from me. "Hands off! I've already said it's my treat. And you've earned it today for putting up with me. I'm sorry to have been such poor company."

"No worries. I enjoyed my crab and Chardonnay. I like this music too. Nothing better than a free lunchtime concert with musicians who know their stuff. Can you wait for me, while I check out the CDs those guys are selling?"

"Go ahead. I'll join you as soon I've signed the check."

When I caught up with Jane, she was handing over a ten-dollar bill in exchange for a brightly coloured CD. The man who took her money was the player of the pipes. As he looked sideways at me, I noticed that one of his eyes was blue and the other brown. I smiled spontaneously. The man did not return my smile, but he continued to stare at me.

"What?" I asked. His scrutiny unsettled me.

"Difficult times ahead for you, lady. Be careful." I felt a chill at the unexpected words.

"What do you mean?"

"Take care, lady. People coming your way not what they seem. Trying to make you pay for past."

"Hey, nick off trying to spook my friend!" Jane's tone to the musician was light-hearted, but she took my arm and steered me determinedly away. I looked over my shoulder. The man with the odd-coloured eyes stood motionless, watching me.

"What do you suppose that was about, Jane?" I could hear my voice wobble.

"No dramas, girl. You know these Boardwalk musicians. He wanted you to think he was a shaman from south of the border so you'd grease his palm with silver. Betcha he was born in La Puente or somewhere equally exotic." I continued to look back and Jane spoke more sharply. "Leave it alone, Sarah. He just wanted an extra buck. He heard our accents and thought we were a couple of tourists ripe for fleecing."

She dropped my arm and quickened her pace. "Come on. The meter must be up on the car. Do you want to go with me to Third Street this arvo? Or over to Nordstrom's? I saw in the L.A. Times they've some good deals on cozzies."

I made a strong effort to switch moods. "Yes, I do need a new bikini. Perhaps I'll go to Palm Springs on my own for a few days. I'm going to be liable for hotel cancellation charges otherwise. And I could do with a break. I've been having dizzy spells lately."

I regretted the words as soon as I had uttered them. Jane stopped, turned and stared at me. "What kind of dizzy spells?" Her voice held concern. I shrugged. "I used to get them when I was a kid. I went to hospital for tests several times, but nobody ever found anything wrong that they could put a name to. I thought I'd long since outgrown them, but they seem to have come back again."

Jane probed. "Exactly what happens during your dizzy spells?"

I felt embarrassed. "It'll sound bizarre to you. Everything around me goes dark and it feels as if I'm falling through a hole in space or time. Except I know I'm not actually falling. It's as if someone or something triggers me subliminally, then my world goes distant and surreal and I start hallucinating."

"Hallucinating?"

"I don't know what else to call it. It's almost as if someone else has entered my body or is talking to me. I'm aware it's happening and yet, when I come to, I don't remember anything. Perhaps the blood supply to my brain gets interrupted, and then rights itself. Like a fuse switch that blows and automatically resets? Or maybe it's a chemical reaction brought on by an allergy."

Jane grimaced. "Look, you've got some of the best doctors in the world right here. Go and get yourself checked out." I shook my head. "I spent enough time in hospitals as a kid to last me a lifetime."

As we headed for the car again, Jane persisted. "Things have changed a lot since you were young. The quality of diagnosis is good here in the States, even if the admin systems can be a shambles. Sarah, don't take chances with your health, sweetheart. It's too important. Does Bob know about this? I'm sure he'd agree with me."

"I haven't mentioned it. I didn't have any reason to. The dizziness only started after Bob went to Europe. If it continues, I'll tell him when he gets back. I'm sure it's nothing to worry about. I probably won't get any more."

But I did, that same evening. And when I came round again from the latest turn, my body ached and my eyes felt as sore as if I had been crying for days. I dragged myself to bed, still sunk in the depths of an ancient sadness, the source of which I could not place.

CHAPTER SIX

England 1617

Tears fell on the letter. Frances exclaimed in distress and dabbed at the parchment and then her cheeks with her handkerchief. She sat alone in the small withdrawing room of her half-brother Robert's house in Kingston. Only Theophilia knew what she was doing. It had felt risky to involve her sister-in-law, yet Theophilia had oozed sympathy, and her complicity was essential for the letter to be sealed and franked.

Frances had written other letters in different places during the summer, but those had been dictated to her, first by Mama, and later by Papa. Today, the freedom to choose her own words only exacerbated her misery. What message could serve in a situation fraught with peril? Frances must try to save her childhood friend from unnecessary pain, while also seeking to ensure that John would not act intemperately. And, since her letter might be intercepted, she must avoid anything that could unleash fresh violence upon her.

She continued to dab at her tears as she checked the smudged text for errors. The words reproached her with their inadequacy. She laid aside her quill and leaned back in the chair. Her gut twisted and ached as her inner debate continued to rage:

I've been too cool and reserved.

No, it would be dangerous to be anything else.

I must explain everything, so John understands the situation is hopeless.

No, to include details of all that has happened to me would be folly.

I should have told him my parents would never countenance our match.

But that would have ruined our happy times together.

Frances had known, immediately after meeting John Clavell, that her family would never contemplate his suit. She cast her mind back to that first day when she had run to her mother and blurted out details of her new friend and his marriage proposal.

Lady Elizabeth Hatton was at her *toilette*. Eliza had given the faintest of frowns, turned from the mirror and waved her two ladies-in-waiting away. Drawing her daughter onto her lap and smoothing the girl's wayward dark mane, Lady Hatton asked one or two questions. Then she spoke her mind.

Eliza was delighted if Frances had found a little playfellow to keep her company when they were at Corfe Castle. His enthusiasm sounded charming and his taste in appreciating her daughter was impeccable. Yes, Franny might be allowed to see him again, if she promised always to show decorum in his company. An innocent friendship was one thing, but Frances must take care to avoid all talk of an alliance with – ah, how can we put it, darling? – a country child.

Frances had nodded when Eliza asked if she understood that it was not the thing to encourage advances from people of different circumstance. Still, she did wonder if she had done an adequate job in describing her new friend. So she tried again. "He has a lovely dimple, Mama. And you have said that dimples are a sign of a good lover."

Laughter tinkled around her ears. "My sweet girl. Your boy-with-no-name might have a thousand dimples, and grow up to become the world's greatest lover. But, from what you have said, he is only the heir to a local Purbeck squire." Lady Hatton frowned, as she added, "Moreover, I fancy he must be connected to that meddlesome man who keeps bothering Sir John Foyle, in hopes of my backing his harebrained schemes. I'm told the fellow is both pushy and a dead bore. I'll tolerate the boy's presence, if you find him amusing, but only if the uncle can be kept at bay. Now, Franny darling, I need you to listen to me carefully."

Eliza leaned sideways to examine her reflection in the mirror again, before she continued, "Your father irritates me beyond bearing, but he is a great man and advisor to monarchy. And I am friend and confidante to both the King and the Queen. Never fear, my sweet. You shall have a husband of high standing, when you are ready to be wed. I promise I'll find one whom you can love. Just not the nephew of a common squire, my darling."

An eighteen-year-old determined to push her lover's suit might have remarked that her mother's Cecil family credentials, however much they had acquired the patina of recent royal favour, were rooted in the ranks of commoners, while her father came from merely respectable barrister stock. At eight years old, Frances never argued with Lady Hatton. To earn Mama's approval was her paramount desire.

Lady Hatton had found it amusing to indulge her daughter in the local friendship, during their infrequent visits to Corfe Castle. Frances had latterly suspected that it gave Eliza more latitude to conduct her own liaisons but, whatever the cause, John Clavell had been welcomed at the castle, and the uncle had kept his distance.

For a member of the nobility, her mother permitted Frances remarkable liberty to explore the lanes of Purbeck on her little grey pony, trotting along beside the boy's sturdy chestnut cob. Eliza even allowed her daughter to don doublet and breeches, and ride astride. Mama laughed that tinkling Hatton laugh, whenever Nurse expressed tight-lipped disapproval, which was often.

John shared his favourite haunts, where one could tickle trout in streams and spy on snakes sleeping on rocks in the sun. Together he and Frances hawked and hunted, often alone but also occasionally in the company of Lady Hatton and any friends who had particular reason to remove themselves for a while from Court cobwebs and conspiracies.

For five years, the Dorset castle and its environs cocooned the children in make-believe. John's flamboyant flights of fancy entertained them both. He elaborated on the audacious adventures they would share when they were grown, and Frances enjoyed adding her finely embroidered stitches to his daring designs.

It had only been during that last extended visit to Purbeck in the previous year that John talked again of marriage. Then, Frances had sidestepped the conversation with him on her own account as much as for her parents. After knowing John for five years, she could no more envisage herself married to him than to old Sir John Villiers.

Plenty of time for her to think about marriage later.

But that later had come sooner than either Lady Hatton or Frances could have predicted, accompanied by such violence as neither mother nor daughter had anticipated.

Frances stood up and walked to the window. She looked out over late-flowering summer blooms that offered splashes of cheerful colour amid the haze of a drowsy August afternoon. But she did not notice the flowers, for her gaze on the garden was unseeing.

She dragged her feet back to the bureau and sat down again.

She stared at the letter. Its words taunted her in their circumspection. If it had not been so risky, the act of sharing her story in writing with John might have offered her a catharsis. As it was, the constant internal replaying of the last two months of her life continued to tear scabs off her emotional wounds before they had time to form.

She could barely yet admit to herself that this very morning she had told her visitors she liked Sir John Villiers better than anyone in the world. For her summer of resistance had come to an end in the moment she took the note from her father's hand and read Mama's perfumed words.

How long ago now seemed that mild June evening, when she and Mama first stole away with her sister Elizabeth in a mood of light-hearted adventure, to join their Withipole cousins for what was expected to be a summer of pleasure.

Her parents had lately been enjoying an extended truce. Frances had felt proud of Mama for standing by Papa and coming to his public defence, when he fell from the King's good graces and was dismissed from the Privy Council. Her heart had warmed when Papa responded by using a softer and kinder tone with Mama.

During the intermission, her parents only engaged in one shouting match: when Papa spoke of re-opening discussions with the Villiers family about a betrothal for Frances. Mother and daughter both realised that Sir Edward was entertaining the notion only as a desperate means to restore himself to the King's favour. The row blew over quickly, with Mama reiterating her promise to Frances that it would all come to nothing.

"All the properties that interest the Villiers are mine, so they would have to secure my agreement to any marriage settlement, darling. And that, you may rest assured, I will never give." Nonetheless, Lady Hatton had judged it might be wise to distance themselves from Stoke for a few weeks through the summer. "Out of sight, out of mind, Franny, remember what I always say?"

Papa had retired to bed early on the night they left, as was his custom in the country. While he snored, Sir Edward Coke's wife and younger daughter made their exit. When they climbed into the waiting coach, arranged without Coke's prior knowledge, it had seemed like just another of Eliza's harmless practical jokes. Frances had felt a moment's qualm at their subterfuge but reassured herself that, free of his family of chattering females, Papa would enjoy the peace and quiet he demanded at Stoke.

Oatlands was less impressive than Hampton Court, yet Frances preferred its gentler charms to the regal grandeur of its neighbour. And for a time, their sojourn in the Duke of Argyll's rented palace had been like an unfolding fairy tale. The Withipoles were good company and Mama added to the holiday atmosphere with some funny and fantastical plotting. She had decided they would remind Papa when they returned home at the end of summer, that Frances could not marry Sir John Villiers because of her long-standing engagement to Henry de Vere, Earl of Oxford.

When Eliza explained the prior arrangement between mothers, supposedly made during Frances and Henry's infancy, it had sounded plausible. The Earl had left England immediately after his mother's death, and long before Frances entered her teens, so it would have been improper for him to declare himself to her in person at that time.

Elizabeth's warning that Mama was making the story up should have alerted Frances. But her sister had also described the Earl of Oxford as a debauched and riotous young man. Her sour comments sounded less like truth and more like jealousy, born from Frances leapfrogging without intent over her elder sibling to become the centre of matrimonial discussions. After Mama waved a letter that arrived for Frances from Henry de Vere, even Elizabeth's scorn and scepticism had been silenced.

Eliza insisted on composing the reply that Frances must send, and waved aside her daughter's concerns that its language and style were excessive. To please her mother, Frances copied it out word-for-word:

I gyv myselfe absolutely to Wyffe to Henry Vere Viscount Balbroke Erl of Oxenford to whom I plyghte my trothe and inviolate vows to keepe myselfe till Death us do part: and if I even brake the leaste of these I pray God Damne mee Bodye and Soule in Hell fire in the world to come: and in this world I humbly beseech God the Erth may open and swallow mee up quicke to the Terror of all faythe breakers that remayne Alive.

Once the florid missive to her betrothed had been sealed and sent, Frances began to wonder aloud what her future as Countess of Oxford might be like. Unlike sister Elizabeth, she preferred to remember Henry as darkly handsome and dashing. Mama agreed with this and declared, to the vociferous accord of the Withipoles and visiting friends, that marriage to a young, debonair and wealthy de Vere must be so much more delightful than one to an old, mad and impoverished John Villiers. Frances began to spin teenage girl daydreams.

The summer turned sour without warning.

The stupefaction of the Oatlands house party had been total when Papa stormed into the palace with a dozen men at his rear, including his sons. Sir Edward Coke smashed glass, beat down doors, and threatened violence to any that stood between him and his daughter. Mama immediately took up a position as human shield, but Sir Edward flicked Lady Hatton aside, much as he might an irritating fly. In front of horrified onlookers, he carried Frances out of the palace and handed her up into the saddle and arms of her half-brother Clem.

There followed the most embarrassing and ungainly ride of her life back to Stoke Manor, where Papa tied Frances to a bedpost in an upper room, and bellowed that she would remain there until she agreed to marry Sir John Villiers.

Her situation deteriorated with the arrival of Lady Compton, mother of John and George Villiers. Mary Compton had never wavered in her determination that her firstborn should marry Frances. The only question from her to Coke now concerned the size of the child's dowry. The girl's own wishes? Irrelevant. Beat her into seeing sense, if need be, Sir Edward.

Tied to her bed in that upstairs room, Frances still summoned extraordinary resolve to resist her father. Until, egged on by Lady Compton, and sadly unrestrained by Clem, Papa committed the unthinkable.

Frances had always been aware of her father's temper. His battles with Mama were legendary and often involved the throwing of heavy objects by both parties. The former King's Chief Justice was renowned for easily losing his cool in court and, over the years, Uncle Francis Bacon had taken a perverse pleasure in whispering tales to Frances of Sir Edward's visits to prisoners in the Tower, where he was reputed to enjoy watching the more inventive torturers wring confessions from the recalcitrant.

Through all those years, faith in her father as her ultimate protector had remained intact in Frances. She might not always be able to rely on his good humour, but she was Sir Edward's cherished youngest daughter. He would never raise his hand to her.

On a July day, when she had shaken her head yet again to the proposed marriage, her father demonstrated how hideously her trust in him had been misplaced. Frances Coke's world fractured. She neither screamed nor cried out. Innocence died without a whimper as her father lashed her back and shoulders over and over and over.

Her spirit remained remarkably whole. Frances would have died rather than submit to brutal bullying on her own account. Nonetheless, as she now lay bruised and traumatised in the bed to which she had lately been tied, the recognition that her father had lost his self-control through falling victim to his own terror of social and political oblivion gave her pause. Frances had fathomed a secret that Coke would not admit to himself. Beneath the whip-wielding exterior, Edward Coke was half crazed with fear that he had become the latest card on His Majesty's permanent discard pile.

With her beating, Coke must have overreached his own limits, for he laid the riding whip aside. But he did not hesitate to use other weapons in his arsenal, including verbal abuse. Frances must know that their King stood ready to banish her mama, should Steenie's desire be thwarted. If Lady Eliza Hatton continued to obstruct the marriage against the express desire of her King, she would be finished forever at Court. Had Frances forgotten so quickly the fate of the Somersets? Did she know what could happen to a woman who has forged love letters from an Earl?

Forgery? Oh, Mama.

Out of the blue came rescue. Lady Hatton had succeeded in getting Francis legally ordered away from her father. But the victory was only partial. Eliza had made frantic efforts through Francis Bacon to get her daughter back in her custody but, somewhere in the process, his personal support buckled. When the Council duly ordered Frances to be removed from Stoke, it was Bacon himself who stipulated that she was not to go back to Hatton House and her mother. And the half victory turned out to be temporary and uncomfortable.

Bound initially into the safe keeping of the Privy Council's Clerk, Frances found herself besieged from all sides. Sir Clement Edmondes' home became overnight a magnet for family and friends of the disputing clans. Half of London seemed suddenly determined to have its personal say in the Villiers-Coke affair.

King James, back in his native Scotland and enjoying his first visit home in the fourteen years that Frances Coke had been alive, was kept daily apprised of the situation, always by those with particular fish to fry in the royal fat. Tongues clacked the length of His Majesty's kingdom.

Had she inherited her mama's attention-seeking disposition, Frances might have taken strength from finding herself at the centre of a *cause celebre*. Introverted by nature, physically bruised and emotionally battered, she shrank from notoriety. She knew a brief respite, when the Council ordered her to the much less accessible home of Sir Thomas and Lady Elizabeth Knyvett in Staines. The quiet kindness of her hosts offered Frances momentary healing balm, as did the visit of one of their young kinsman for whose company she had long entertained a partiality.

But, within days, her father's machinations saw her bundled again into an escorted carriage and taken to another home. Once Sir Edward's eldest son became the watchdog for his father's interests, Frances was no longer in neutral territory. Mama received the right to visit Kingston Manor, but Lady Hatton seemed far from her usual ebullient self during their tearful reunion, and Robert Coke refused to leave her alone with her daughter.

Shortly afterward, Robert reported to Frances that, on returning to Holborn, her mother had become indisposed. Fears for Eliza weighed the young teenager down. Her sister-in-law sought to be gentle but, while Lady Theophilia oozed empathy, she supported her husband in advising Frances to accept the inevitable. Yes, it was an unfair and unhappy situation. It could also be fatal for everyone in the family, Robert and herself included, if Frances continued to oppose Sir Edward, Steenie *and* His Majesty.

Robert Coke soon had more disturbing news. Lady Hatton had suffered a nervous collapse, which necessitated her immediate care in the London home of Alderman Bennett. At Kingston, Theophilia agreed with an anguished Frances that this was code for an involuntary confinement, but she expressed confidence that Eliza would come to no harm, if her daughter would act instantly to do what was needed.

Still Frances clung to a final thread of hope. "Papa, I will marry Sir John, but only if I know that Mama agrees."

The letter that Sir Edward dictated for his daughter to send to her mother lacked the dramatic flair of that which Lady Hatton had prepared for Frances to send to Henry de Vere. Yet Coke's subtle prose was couched in a similar bed of lies and parental self-interest:

Madam

I must now humbly desire your patience in giving me leave to declare myself to you, which is that without your allowance and liking, all the world shall never make me entangle or tie myself. But now by my father's especial commandment, I obey him in presenting to you my humble duty in a tedious letter, which is to know your Ladyship's pleasure, not as a thing I desire: but I resolve to be wholly ruled by my father and yourself, knowing your judgments to be such that I may well rely upon, and hoping that conscience and the natural affection parents bear to children will let you do nothing but for my good, and that you may receive comfort. I being a mere child and not understanding the world nor what is good for myself. That which makes me a little give way to it is, that I hope it may be a means to procure a reconciliation between my father and your Ladyship. Also I think it will be a means of the King's favour to my father. Himself is not to be misliked: his fortune is very good, a gentleman born. So I humbly take my leave, praying that things may be to everyone's contentment.

Your Ladyship's most obedient and humble daughter for ever.
Frances Coke
Dear Mother, believe there has no violent means been used to me by words or deeds.

Reaching again under her petticoats, Frances pulled out Mama's reply. Holding it to her nose once more, she ingested the scent of Elizabeth's favourite perfume. At least, in confinement, Mama retained access to her creature comforts.

Frances peered at the note. Her sore eyes were unequal to the task of deciphering each word. But their overall import was clear: Lady Hatton had conceded the fiercest and most public battle of her married life to Sir Edward Coke. Her efforts to block the marriage were at an end.

What else might Frances have done then, after reading Mama's message, than acquiesce in becoming betrothed to a man of uncertain disposition, more than twelve years her senior, and whom she did not love? May God at least forgive her for having put her name to so many half-truths and untruths.

Frances dropped Mama's note back into her hidden pocket, re-arranged her petticoats and looked again at what she had just written. Would John Clavell, in far away Dorset, gain any inkling from it of what she had endured during two shock-ridden summer months that had brought her to today's unhappy pass? Her letter contained neither the scented sentimentality of her mother's prose, nor the minutely measured distortions dictated by her father. She judged her words as wholly inadequate to the occasion, but at least they were her own, and every one of them was true.

Frances dipped her quill in the ink, then signed and dated her letter:

Dear John,

It is arranged. I am to be married to Sir John Villiers. The marriage licence will be acquired this day and the wedding will take place as soon hereafter as it can be arranged, likely on the day of St Michael's Mass. My father is in good health and expects to be recalled to the Privy Council. Papa assures me I shall like being wife to Sir John. Mama does not visit me, for she is indisposed and remains in London, while I stay here in Kingston with my half brother, Robert. I have received her note this morning, declaring that she is in agreement with Papa and with the desire of His Majestie, who wishes me to marry Himself. I am still only a child, and so must submit in this matter to the desires and wisdom of my parents. John, it will not be seemly for me to receive your letters once I am married. I pray you to suffer no further inconvenience on my account. I commend you to our Lord's safekeeping, in recognition that this is the last letter that shall pass between us. I shall remember all our times together when we were children with much affection. I hope you can retain a happy memory of me as
Your once dear friend,
Frances Coke
Kingston Manor, this fourteenth day of August 1617

CHAPTER SEVEN

California

I was still debating whether to leave town alone the next day when I walked into my office. The hotel had agreed to defer cancellation charges and drop them if we occupied the room within the next week. I decided to hold my decision until speaking with Bob. I was taking advantage of my empty Sunday to catch up on office admin. If I left, it would be with an empty desk and a clear conscience.

The office building was empty and silent, an ideal environment to complete client notes, sort bills and write cheques. I was done by late afternoon and, just as I stood up to leave, the office phone rang. It was Bob. I held the phone away from my ear, while he stormed down the line. "This whole fucking tour looks like it's falling apart, unless I can pull something out of the bag. It's like baby-sitting, with these bastards. A bunch of demanding kids, all with outsize egos."

I broke his rant with a question. "Where are you calling from, Bob?"

"I'm still in Berlin, but I've gotta go back to London now and start over." He returned to his grumbling, although in a lower key. "That fucking idiot. I should never have listened to him."

"What idiot are you talking about?"

"Johnny Clavylle. He always was impossible to deal with. Unpredictable. Ego the size of a hot-air balloon. I don't know why I thought he might have changed. Even so, I didn't expect him to go making trouble with all the other bands behind my back."

"Who's Johnny Clavylle?"

"He's an irresponsible troublemaker, that's who. You spoke to him by phone the other night, remember? I was having dinner with the bastard, by that old castle." Before I could make any response, Bob checked himself and his angry tone morphed into one of resignation. "Oh, forget it, Sarah. I'm sorry to sound off at you. It's too long a story for me to explain now. I just have to get things sorted out here as best I can."

"I guess you can't have any idea how long it is going to take?"

"No. I do have to get back to the States as soon as possible, or I'll be facing a bunch of other problems. But it looks like Thursday at the earliest before I can leave. And before you ask, no, I'm not sure I'll be able to take any time out then, thanks to that smart-ass muscling in on my patch."

I felt leaden with disappointment, but tried to keep it out of my voice. "I'm so sorry you're having a bad time, Bob."

He sighed. "I'm sorry too, for ruining your plans."

"Don't worry about anything here. Perhaps I'll take off on my own for Palm Springs. I really don't want to waste this week, now I've put off all my clients. Do you mind me going alone?"

"Mind? No. Why should I?" He sounded both relieved and surprised that I would ask.

"Then I'll stay at Ballantines for a few nights and hang out by the pool. I can drive in to meet you at the airport on Thursday or whatever day you come into LAX. Or, if you get back in time, perhaps you can hire a car and come straight out to Palm Springs to meet me there?"

"I don't know, babe." He was edgy again. "Let me play it by ear and see how things work out."

I backed off. "Look, there's no pressure. It's just that you've often said it's impossible to get anything done in the music business on a Friday in L.A.. So, if you get back here by Thursday, coming out to the desert might help you get over your jet lag before work on Monday."

His voice cleared. "You may be right, honey. Anyway, whatever happens with me, there's nothing to be gained by you suffering too. You go on out to Palm Springs and have a good time. I'll call you again as soon as I know how things are shaping up. Drive carefully and have fun. But remember. I have my spies in the desert. No talking to any strange men – or women – while my back is turned, promise?"

I giggled. "I hope things sort themselves out for you soon, darling. And I promise to keep my cell phone by me, so you can reach me anytime." I replaced the landline and set the voice mail, switched off my desk light and picked up my purse. At the door, I turned and gave a last glance to check that all was in place before leaving for the week.

I was already thinking about calling the hotel as I opened my outer office door. And almost bumped into a man whose hand was poised on my bell.

He was tall, fair-haired and rangy.

I drew back and said, "Hello, can I help you?"

"I certainly hope so. I'm your new client."

"Excuse me? Have we met before?" I stared up at him. A wisp of familiarity clung to his spare frame, but I had never met him and would have remembered any new appointment. Especially one made by an Englishman.

"Almost. I got your name and address from a friend of yours." He continued quickly, before I could ask the name of the friend in question, "You come highly recommended, even though I know you haven't got your therapy licence here yet. I don't care about that. I need to talk with someone who's British. I've got to have someone in this crazy city who can understand me and where I'm coming from."

The stranger looked to be in his early fifties. He must once have been strikingly handsome, but dissipation had taken a toll of his looks. His skin sagged and, even in the shadows of the passage, I could see that his complexion was unhealthily sallow. His blond hair may have been expertly cut and dyed, but the effect was spoiled, for it had not seen a brush or a comb recently. Dark rings under his eyes suggested a period without sleep and his clothes, although expensive in fabric and cut, were heavily creased.

Yet the man's appearance contrasted with his bearing. His clipped English accent held a tone of command and his confidence bordered on arrogance. Intuition told me that I was looking at a casualty of the British private education system. Yes, I thought, I'm willing to bet you were sent away from home to boarding school and obliged to put a lid on your feelings at an age when no child should have to.

I said, "Look, I'm sorry, but I don't commit to taking people on as new clients until I know a little about them and can assess whether I'll be of any use. Not even if they know my friends. By the way, who was it that recommended me to you?"

His smile was brilliant. It transformed his face and his next words knocked me off guard. "Bob. Bob Howard."

"Bob? How do you know him? And what's your name?"

"I'm Antony Makepeace. Bob has surely spoken about me to you?"

I shook my head slowly, as I sifted through my memory. "No, I don't think he has." I hedged. "But Bob talks of so many people that I can't always recall names."

He was still smiling. "It doesn't matter. He's told me a lot about you and that's what counts. From everything he said, I know you can help me. Bob's away in Europe just now, isn't he? We're both in the music business. Won't you see me, please? I really do need someone to talk to, or I'm going to go mad."

I hesitated, pulled in opposing directions. I was not looking for new clients. And something warned me to reject his request. At the same time, the man did sound as if he might be in need of immediate support.

I spoke neutrally. "Do you feel you are in crisis, right now?"

His laugh was jagged. "You could say that."

I fought a brief internal battle. "If it's an emergency and you have no doctor to advise you, you could present yourself at a hospital for crisis treatment. I can suggest one if you like."

"God forbid."

"Then an alternative would be to seek counselling at a community health centre. I can refer you to one of those if you prefer."

"Can you guarantee they'll provide me with someone who is British?"

"No, I can't guarantee that, Mr. Makepeace."

"*Please* see me."

I hesitated again. "I'm sorry. I have a full client list and I'm leaving town tomorrow for the week. I can fit you in for a preliminary session the following week, if one of my regular clients doesn't show. I may have some space coming up on Fridays. But, given what you say, you won't want to wait that long. So the best way I can help is to find a couple of numbers for private therapists you can contact right away."

"British?"

"I don't know any, sorry."

"No dice then. What happens in your preliminary session?"

"Think laying down foundations for a building rather than starting construction. We focus on agreeing the contract. You tell me what's happening with you and what you feel you need. I explain how I work with clients. We decide mutually if working together might be useful. If so, we agree terms and ground rules, then set our first date."

"Sounds perfect. I need to get going. Let's do this contracting thing right now and we'll start tomorrow before you leave. OK?"

I shook my head. It wasn't just that the man had ignored whatever he did not want to hear. Something else was troubling me. I felt a need to get another point of reference on Antony Makepeace before accepting him as a client. I would call Bob. He was street smart and a good judge of people.

"I'm sorry, Mr. Makepeace. I'm just leaving my office, as you can see, and I'll be leaving town early in the morning. Give me your number and I'll call you a week on Monday by the end of the day, to let you know if and when I can be available. I'll need to check in with other clients first."

"Please call me Antony. Mr. Makepeace makes it sound as if I am booking into the dentist. God, how I hated going to the dentist when I was a kid."

I smiled. I too had hated visits to the dentist. He must have felt he had created an opening, for he pressed again. "Next Monday is more than a week away and you are not even committing to see me then. Can't you see me sooner, pretty please? Look, I'm really in crisis, or I wouldn't be pushing you like this. I need to talk with someone so badly."

I hesitated. The man's expression held a pathetic appeal. Beneath his pushiness, something had touched me. I had no doubt that Antony Makepeace was a wounded soul. And again I felt that sense of familiarity about him.

A voice in my head said, "Stay clear." The voice in my heart said, "He's suffering." I relented. "Very well, Antony. I'm leaving town early, but I'll see you at eight tomorrow morning for a preliminary half-hour. If we suit each other, I'll give you first option on my next opening."

"You're really sure you can't spare half an hour to see me now?"

I shook my head, determined to stand my ground. Antony Makepeace shrugged. "OK. I guess it'll have to be tomorrow then. Eight o'clock? I'll be here on time, I promise."

But he was not.

As I waited for him, I felt annoyed with myself. I had put myself in this situation, by overriding reason and succumbing to inner pressure. And I had not heard from Bob again since yesterday, so had been unable to verify Antony Makepeace's story.

Why would the man make such a push to see me and then not turn up? Had I been duped by his hard-luck tale or had something serious happened to him? In the flurry of our first encounter, I had forgotten to note down his contact number, so had no way to follow up.

I waited until eight-thirty, in case he had been delayed in traffic.

Makepeace did not come.

I picked up my keys, locked my office door and exchanged a brief greeting in passing with a therapist neighbour whose consulting rooms were adjacent to my own. As I took the elevator down and emerged on ground level, I told myself to let go of my frustration or my day would be spoiled.

I climbed into the car and fastened the seat belt. Let go and move on, Sarah. I sat staring at the steering wheel. Something clicked inside. Makepeace had triggered me because of a superficial resemblance to my ex. In which case, I should not be surprised at his no show. During our marriage, John had rarely been where or when he promised to be, although he had demanded punctuality and reliability from me.

In moving to the United States, I had promised myself to be done with a lifetime habit of giving in to others. I had spent too much time in places and activities of little intrinsic interest to me. I determined to stop being the wounded healer who could not heal herself.

I had chosen a culture that prided itself on individualism, and was living in a city where narcissism had been developed to a high art form. My new situation obliged me to become self-reliant and my new relationship with Bob supported this. In him I had a role model for the independent, self-assertive person I wanted to become. He pursued his agenda wholeheartedly and urged me to do likewise. I had been doing well, until yesterday, when I allowed an unknown Englishman to pierce my defences.

I lowered the hood of the Mustang. The sun was already hot and I took my baseball cap out of the glove compartment. I looked at it, and laughed aloud. Its message remained as current today as when I had found it, lying discarded in the middle of the Boardwalk and waiting for me to pick it up, the day after my arrival in Los Angeles. On one side of the cap was embroidered the name *John*. On the other was the embroidered silhouette of a foot; an emblem used by my ex as his company logo. The insignia read *55th Rescue Squadron*.

I had kept the cap to remind me of the role I intended to drop from my life. Remember the lesson now, Sarah! I laughed again. Frustration shed, I fixed the cap on my head, pulled back my hair and secured it through the hole at the back, then checked my appearance in the sun visor's vanity mirror. I started the ignition, put the gear into drive and eased slowly out of the office parking lot.

As I waited to turn on to Barrington, I noticed a shiny black S 500 Mercedes with tinted dark glass glide silently up behind me. Nice car, I thought, but I'm happy with my trusty white second-hand Mustang. Here I am, about to head out on vacation into the Californian desert under a cloudless sky. Time to relish the freedom of the open road.

CHAPTER EIGHT

England 1617

Nine grand carriages commissioned to transport Sir Edward Coke's entourage carried a miscellany of family, friends and political cronies, out to reap every advantage from their place in the public moment.

It promised to be a grand affair. A wedding in the Chapel Royal of Hampton Court was an event at which anyone who is anyone must be seen, my dear. And the likelihood of emotional fireworks at this particular wedding had been fuelling the imaginations of the chattering classes since the betrothal had been announced.

Throughout the jolting three-mile ride from Kingston to Hampton Court, Frances struggled to keep tears at bay, if only to avoid smudging her make-up. She stole occasional sideways glances at her father. From the smile on his face, it seemed clear that Papa had no inkling of her misery in this moment. She preferred to assume that it was insensitivity rather than cruel intent that led him to press jocular comments upon her as their destination drew near. Sir Edward had won his victory. He could not wish to continue to be unkind, or could he?

Did one ever place trust again in an abusive parent?

Frances bit her lip and turned her head away. She gazed unseeingly out of the carriage window and wondered whether Papa had selected Michaelmas Day for her marriage or if the choice lay with the impecunious Villiers family? Frances knew it as a day when debts were settled throughout the land, when annual rents came due and when merchants sold their wares. An appropriate date, she thought, with a burst of inner gallows humour. Today Sir Edward Coke is selling his daughter to save his political skin.

The front carriage came to a halt in the courtyard next to the Chapel Royal. Handed down by her father, Frances stood shivering in a late September wind, while Sir Edward stood back and swept a critical gaze over his daughter's immaculately clad person. He moved closer to straighten her heavily jewelled outer coat.

"Beautiful, my child. I am proud of you. Now stop shaking like a leaf and stand up straight, so all of us can see your lovely self, on your special day."

Frances stared up at Sir Edward. There was no trace of irony in his voice. Papa was in love with the moment, and believed she must be too. Catching sight of her own image in the reflection of her father's eyes, it occurred to her that she was an over-dressed lamb about to be led to the slaughter. She flinched when offered Papa's arm. She could not yet put aside the memory of it raised against her.

Coke patted Frances's hand and tucked it inside his own. Side-by-side they passed through the doors that led into the chapel. At first sight of the crowd squashed together within, Frances caught her breath and shrank back. As she hesitated, Sir Edward pulled his daughter forward. "Don't be shy, child. Remember this is your day. Eyes ahead. Shoulders back. Smile, girl, smile."

Frances thought, but did not say, Papa, this is your day, not mine.

Her father handed her to two men waiting by the inner door. As Coke bowed, Frances acknowledged each in turn. She curtseyed and managed a watery smile for Charles, Prince of Wales, but her head went down and she stared at the floor while making a perfunctory bob before the man about to become her brother-in-law. She was obliged to accept George Villiers as an escort, and must rest her hand upon his arm during her walk to the altar. But nothing was going to make Frances look into the Earl of Buckingham's eyes.

Favouring Prince Charles as much as she dared, Frances watched her father stride forward toward the Royal Box with his head held high and his chest thrust forward like a well-stuffed turkey cock. Sir Edward's grey beard bobbed up and down as he surveyed the noble congregation with a gimlet gaze. He passed between tightly packed pews, acknowledging acquaintances with a nod as he went.

He was searching for someone in particular. Who?

Before she spotted the man in question, Frances had guessed his identity, and the flash of vindictive pleasure illuminating her father's profile affirmed it. Today's victory over Sir Francis Bacon must be at least as sweet for Sir Edward as that of nearly twenty years before, when he took Lady Elizabeth Hatton as his wife.

In contrast, the look that Frances directed toward Uncle Francis held doubt and sadness in equal measure. Mama had assured her, in a whisper, during their meeting at Kingston, that Uncle Francis had tried his best to save her from the marriage. He had even written to the King, enumerating the many reasons he considered it an improvident match.

But, if all that was true, why had the Lord Keeper of the Great Seal changed his position? What or who had obliged Bacon to recant support of his beloved Lady Hatton, which must have surely hastened the collapse of Mama's resistance to the marriage? Frances doubted she would ever receive a satisfactory answer to these or other questions that had been gnawing at her, in the unhappy weeks since her betrothal.

Bacon turned and caught sight of the young bride at the back of the chapel. As their looks locked, his expression became in turn wry, comical and apologetic. It made Frances want to cry. It also reignited her resentment toward her father.

Papa, enjoy your mastery in this moment. You have vanquished Mama and me, and perhaps Uncle Francis too. But what will this victory bring you, when today's pomp and circumstance is yesterday's dream? You'll have your place back on the Privy Council this weekend, for having delivered me to Sir John, yet how long do you expect the fickle favour of your King to endure? And, if it does, will it have been worth the sacrifice of my life's happiness?

As she thought of the future extending before her, victimhood threatened to swamp Frances. Her chin came up. She willed herself to assume an impassive mien. Looking at the congregation, she saw many of Mama's enemies, who would love to see her daughter crumble in front of them. Spiteful gossips must not be allowed to profit from watching Mistress Coke cry, as she awaited her royal summons to the altar.

Sir Edward had reached the elevated Royal Pew and stopped. He bowed. A brief distraction ensued, as stragglers in the Coke's wedding party filed noisily into the chapel, thereby earning their patriarch's ire. The scramble to find places in densely occupied pews took several minutes of pushing, rustling and muttering, before the Chapel congregation again fell quiet.

Doors on the lower floor behind the Royal Pew opened. A trumpet sounded and the congregation rose. His Majesty, King James the First, appeared at ground level. He ambled toward Sir Edward, stopped and acknowledged Coke's second bow with an amiable smile and an extension of the royal hand to be kissed.

Sir Edward was now obliged to adjust his stride to that of the King. Together they meandered the short remaining distance to the altar. His Majesty gave no hint to an expectant Chapel Royal that he wished to reach his destination. The two men walked as if out together for an afternoon stroll. Their slow pace derived from the King's bowed and spindly legs, which were causing an aging James to grow progressively fainter of step.

Now His Majesty had turned and was beckoning the bride and her escorts to join them at the altar. Flanked by the Prince and Buckingham, Frances fixed her eyes forward on the painted artwork decorating the exquisite glass front behind the Mass Table. A figure moved in front of it, and she caught sight of her future husband. Frances gripped the Prince's arm and raised her head heavenwards in an effort to blink back fresh tears. The opulent fan-vaulted ceiling of the Chapel Royal towered above her. Gold stars twinkled in the lofty firmament of Henry the Eighth's fabled blue ceiling. Coy Renaissance boys trumpeted down from their gilded pendant vantage points.

The trio reached the King and Sir Edward. The Prince handed Frances to her father with a practised bow, while Buckingham stepped sideways to join his brother. After more words of mutual congratulation, Coke passed his daughter to the King. Frances felt her inner tensions ease. Something in the benign quality of His Majesty's smile dispelled her bitterness that her marriage was taking place by royal command.

As Frances took the King's arm, she found much to hold onto. James was neither especially tall nor fat, but his costume was cut full and easy. She leaned on his richly jewelled sleeve and he reciprocated by squeezing her hand.

Frances had enjoyed His Majesty's casual affection since babyhood. Growing up around his Court and used to playing with the royal children, she had known James less as her monarch than as a kindly, erratic and often smelly man. Her nose wrinkled as it was borne in upon her that, even for her wedding, the King of England had not washed. Moreover, as he smiled over her, his breath revealed that James had been at the bottle.

None of these shortcomings dimmed the gratitude Frances felt in the moment for her King's good-natured and rickety presence and she only gripped him the more tightly. James Stuart patted her hand and bent to whisper in her ear. "Happy, my pretty one? See how all eyes are on you today. Such a day as every maiden dreams of, eh, lassie?"

His Scots brogue was still thick, in spite of years of southern living, so that Frances was obliged to guess at certain of the King's words but the benevolence in his voice made her want to cry again. "Ye—es, Your Majesty." Frances hoped James would attribute her wavering voice to bridal nerves.

She dropped her head toward the floor. Oh no. Her nose was threatening to drip. She sniffed and looked up again. In front of her, the Villiers brothers, John and George, stood side-by-side facing the altar. Wishing to look anywhere in this moment but at their backs, Frances turned to her left and searched beyond the detestable Lady Compton for her mother, who must surely be in the front pew.

Lady Hatton's natural beauty was so striking, her *toilette* so painstaking, her dress sense so unerring and her spending upon her wardrobe so lavish that she could be relied upon to stand out in the most dazzling of assemblies. In today's glittering gathering, Frances Coke's mother was conspicuous only by her absence.

Mama, why are you not here?

Papa had told Frances that His Majesty himself had required in writing that his dear friend Elizabeth grace the wedding with her presence. Was her mother indisposed or had Lady H. elected to demonstrate that she did not come running when Majesty crooked his royal finger?

Mama, I need you here.

Frances gazed around the congregation. For the first time it came to her that none of her mother's Cecil relations were present, not even her grandfather, the Earl of Exeter. This could be no accident. She knew a sudden sinking sense of having been abandoned in an enemy camp.

A loud sob escaped her.

One hundred heads swivelled in rapt attention. Two hundred eyes were just as swiftly averted, as the King frowned and Court discipline asserted itself. A gentle smile replaced his regal glower. The tongue that seemed too large for its mouth lolled aimlessly over the monarch's lips and dipped toward the stringy beard that made a poor job of covering the royal chin.

James leaned forward and whispered again in the bride's ear. "Courage, my child. Few of us marry where we wish. We still can find love where we will." Frances blinked in surprise. Had she misheard or imagined his words? The bride looked up into the bloodshot gaze of King James and observed his eyes seize upon the younger Villiers brother.

No, she had imagined nothing.

Alerted perhaps by his lover's stare, George Villiers chose that moment to turn and survey the King and Frances. As Viscount Buckingham received the full force of His Majesty's naked desire, he responded with a graceful inclination of his head. The congregation held its delighted breath, and a *frisson* of collective voyeurism swept through the Chapel Royal.

A guileful grin spread slowly across Viscount Buckingham's angelic features as he acknowledged the public's recognition of his unrivalled place in his monarch's affections. The gesture was artful, even humorous. Yet it evoked in Mistress Frances Coke a surge of fury. Here, in the moment of her own sacrifice, the author of her woes was laughing and freely demonstrating his influence over the King of England. Buckingham and his mother's greed had already crushed Frances's hopes of marital felicity, and now George was relishing his role in her public immolation.

On her wedding day, Frances Coke felt, for the first time in her life, visceral hatred toward another human being. It set every cell of her being on fire. The burning sensation passed, but not before she had revealed its intensity to the object of her fury. Pale and tearful as Frances had been seconds before, her face beneath her veil was now aflame. And, as George Villiers' attention slid from the face of his lover to that of the girl-woman on the King's arm, he must have felt the blast of her blaze.

For a fraction of a second, George's smile froze. It was replaced in the next instant by a look of contempt. George Villiers turned away, but not before Frances had received his return salvo. *You, my sister-to-be, will learn that any who fail to worship at my shrine are de facto my enemies.*

Frances felt faint.

"Here we are, my wee lassie. Your matrimonial moment has arrived. And here's the bonnie young man who has the good fortune to share it with ye." The King kissed Frances and handed her to Sir John Villiers. Wordlessly she took her place, struggling to avoid physical collapse.

In any other circumstance, Frances might have felt moved by Sir John Villiers' tentative smile. Kindness, perhaps even seeds of a genuine love for her, animated her bridegroom's hovering, anxious gaze. But, rather than reassure, it made her more uncomfortable in the moment. She would have preferred to hold on to hatred than be tugged into sympathy toward her betrothed. She must *not* cry again. How to get through this ordeal?

Frances lowered her eyes and studied her shimmering ivory gown. A plethora of pearls and a dusting of diamonds adorned the richly brocaded and farthingaled wedding overdress. *Fit for a princess, my Lady,* the royal dressmaker had said, while making adjustments at her final fitting. It was no exaggeration. Frances was exquisitely attired. But the bride derived no comfort from her finery, for the ties of her *supportasse* bit into her neck, and she was obliged to lift her head again.

She saw that another figure had joined the little cluster before the altar and was bowing low to His Majesty. James Montagu, Bishop of Winchester, Dean of the Chapel Royal, religious mentor and personal friend of King James, smiled to the bridegroom, beamed at the man's brother, and belatedly acknowledged the bride. The Bishop cleared his throat.

"Ahem. Dearly beloved, we are gathered together here in the sight of God, and in the face of His congregation to join together this Man and this Woman in holy Matrimony; which is an honourable estate instituted of God in Paradise in the time of man's Innocency."

Innocency?

Where, wondered Frances, did Innocency figure in this elaborate and cynical charade into which she had been coerced?

As fourteen-year-old Frances Coke knelt beside twenty-six-year-old Sir John Villiers at the feet of the Bishop, she had a fleeting flashback. Innocency had reigned once, long ago, on a sunlit day when an eight-year-old girl and a ten-year-old boy met in the grounds of a Dorset castle.

Today, in the Chapel Royal of Hampton Court Palace, Innocency was dead.

Long live Innocency.

CHAPTER NINE

California

The hotel had changed owners and staff since I was last here with Bob. A new receptionist confirmed that our favourite Movie Men room was free, but offered me a smaller alternative, when I explained that I would be here alone for several days. I went with my original choice. It was beside the swimming pool, where I planned to spend most time and, if Bob did get here for the weekend, I would not need to change rooms.

I laid my purse on the Eames surfboard table and unpacked my case. The yellow and navy blue swimsuit that I'd bought with Jane lay at the top. A swim before lunch would wash away the dust of my drive. Minutes later, I emerged from the pool, refreshed and invigorated. I showered and slipped into a sleeveless cream linen dress with matching low-heeled sling-back shoes, then set off to choose a restaurant.

The thermometer in the reception lobby showed the mercury at just under one hundred. Hot, but not too hot to walk. I grabbed a wide-brimmed straw hat from the boot of the Mustang, and soon felt glad of its protection, even during the brief distance to Palm Canyon Drive.

Memories of wandering here with Bob assailed me as soon as I entered the main street. We both loved Palm Springs. The desert city was slow-paced and small-town in character, yet its history and celebrity associations gave it a certain cachet and style.

I blushed, feeling childishly pleased, when the staff at our favourite Mexican restaurant welcomed me warmly. I was accustomed to people hailing Bob by his first name wherever we went. A big man with an extravert and playful personality, he tended to leave a powerful and pleasurable impression on people and places. Reserved with strangers, and inadequate at small talk, I had no such track record.

I felt self-conscious initially at finding myself the only customer in the restaurant eating alone, but soon relaxed. One margarita and two soft fish tacos later, I felt as if I had been away from work for months. I ordered a double espresso while studying, and then rejecting, the dessert menu.

My espresso arrived. As I sipped I reflected that, in one regard at least, my taste remained stubbornly European. Cloyingly sweet and already cold, this coffee bore no resemblance to the piping-hot, rich dark roasts served in France and Italy. Images of Parisian cafes frequented with John during the early days of our marriage drifted into my mind.

Could I at last look back on my life with him and recall moments of shared happiness? They were the more precious for being so few. A sigh escaped me as I remembered how John and I had become trapped in stifling bonds of co-dependency that brought neither of us the marital joy we had anticipated when making our vows.

I shook myself mentally. Sighs for the past were redundant. I had sprung the trap. Here I sat, a continent away from my former life, having enjoyed a pleasant lunch alone in a city where I had no friends and was far from all usual points of reference, yet feeling content in my own company. For the next few days, I could please myself entirely how and where I spent my waking hours. What a gift.

I paid the check and sauntered back to the hotel. Entering the inner courtyard, I noticed a man and a woman stretched out on sun loungers in the shade, outside the hotel's quirkily appointed Fifties lounge. Engrossed in each other, neither glanced up as I passed on the other side of the pool. Their stillness and the empty silence of the hotel had me feeling I had walked in on an Edward Hopper painting.

My bikini had dried in the sun on my private patio during the time I had been at lunch. I shed my dress and stepped into it again. Armed with a towel, suntan lotion and a bottle of water from the fridge in my room, I returned to the pool and selected a sun lounger facing the San Jacinto Mountains. I adjusted the umbrella and lowered myself onto the soft cushioned fabric.

On the far side of the pool the man and woman looked up and half-waved. I returned their gesture, with an inner grin. *I know just how you feel. Now you're reassured that I'll keep my distance, you can afford to acknowledge my presence.*

Closing my eyes, I stretched out and prepared to soak up the peace of a poolside afternoon. My mind immediately began to spin and turn over a palette of themes: my practice and how to develop it; my relationship with Bob and what it meant in my life; my marriage and how to lay my life with John to rest. I tried to still my thoughts. On this first afternoon in Palm Springs I desired nothing more than to luxuriate for a couple of hours in the sensuous feel of sun on my skin.

It was not to be. However much I sought to relax, my mind continued to race. None of my usual methods of emptying my mind proved effective. I began to chew over my work concerns. Those three cancelled appointments still rankled with me in ways that I did not fully understand. I could already hear Bob taking on the role of devil's advocate. He would surely tell me to blow any issues with clients off and move on.

Bob had already remarked that, as a recent immigrant working on the fringes of a crowded Californian profession, I would do well to stop constantly looking my gift horses in the mouth, let alone trying to pull their teeth. He had consensus reality on his side. The walls of my consulting room echoed with tales of newcomers to L.A. facing loneliness and fear of failure or financial ruin. And not only newcomers. I had been lucky to land on my feet, in a city whose calloused underbelly featured often in clients' stories.

My immigration lawyer had once remarked that one of L.A.'s guardian angels must have been watching over me. She had referred to the speed with which my training credentials and visa application were processed by the national accreditation body and US immigration. Yet her comment could have been applied to my general situation since arriving in the city.

Still, I wanted more. Allergic to quick fixes and flavours of the month, I wondered if this was what I had inadvertently become. I wanted to support people committed to make real change in their lives, instead of surfing the waves of an image-obsessed culture, feeding and fed by endemic narcissism. Colluding to maintain the status quo felt neither useful nor fulfilling, however remunerative this might be. But perhaps I needed to focus inward rather than on my external situation. Why had some snippy messages and unjustified innuendos from three clients got under my skin?

At the moment I asked myself this question, I felt as if a curtain had covered the sun. I opened my eyes. No cloud could be seen. Just a large bird of prey – an eagle perhaps? – circling above my head, like a mirror for my cycling thoughts. I shivered and felt myself being sucked down again, back into that familiar darkness from which I felt powerless to escape.

CHAPTER TEN

England 1617

Entering the Great Hall behind His Gracious Majesty and his brother, her husband led Frances to their place of honour at the Royal Table. Sir John Villiers pushed in her chair then took a standing position behind her.

Hampton Court's Great Hall was long and wide and measured sixty feet up to its cathedral-like hammer beam ceiling. Yet for all its imposing scale and size, the hall filled fast and soon became overcrowded and stuffy.

Her clothes did Frances no service. Why must the fashions be so heavy and inconvenient for a woman to wear? At the start of what was always going to be a day of torment, Frances had been grateful for garments that provided her with a protective armour. Yet, with only a part of the ceremony behind her and the worst yet to come, her wedding finery had become a sweat-filled, tight-fitting prison. As soon as she sat, she knew fresh agony, for the bodice whalebones bit into her sides.

The new Lady Villiers was also soon burning with embarrassment at the nature of the attention that came her way. Strained and shouting voices bombarded her from all sides. False compliments mixed with coarse quips, which became more cutting as wine flowed and tongues loosened.

The banquet itself was a waking nightmare, for rich dishes and strong liquor were constantly presented to the bride. Lady Compton and her father had previously primed Frances that His Majesty had ordered the best and grandest of fare be served at the wedding feast. She must show her gratitude by eating heartily. To refuse to taste any dish, they told her, would cause great offense to the King.

Frances hated the taste of goose and wished she might disappear under the table, when His Majesty insisted on coming over to serve her copiously with meat from a large bird on a golden platter, complete with its own huge egg.

"Wee Franny, ye must observe the ancient Michaelmas custom, if ye wish your marriage to prosper."

Under her King's bleary-eyed watchfulness, Frances cut into the meat. Fat shot from the goose and stained the front of her jewelled bodice. A couple sitting near the Royal Table tittered and pointed, drawing the attention of their neighbours to her plight. The sober-faced young man seated to her right passed his red-faced companion his napkin and pressed her hand lightly.

Frances wiped her front and murmured her thanks. Charles was the only comfort and support she could rely upon in this chamber of tortures. Sir Francis Bacon had been given the seat to her left, but Frances felt resistant toward his obsequious overtures. How could she repose trust again in one who had professed himself her mother's dearest friend, then backtracked at a crucial moment, and played an active role in delivering Frances to her fate?

Sir Francis Bacon was not now and maybe never could again be her confidant. Frances needed someone steadfast. She had known the Prince of Wales since she was an infant, and before his brother Henry's death had left him as the King's only remaining son and heir. Only three years separated them in age, and they had wandered and played together frequently at a Court which, thanks to the fun-loving nature of King James, opened its doors freely to children and granted them many liberties.

Frances felt closer to Charles than to any of her half brothers. She felt sympathy for him too, because he was so often sick. She appreciated his manners, fastidious by comparison with many of the uncouth children who appeared at Court. Dark and intense, Charles tended to keep to himself, for the combination of his stutter and that frequent scorpion-like sting disconcerted many. But Frances liked that the Prince was so unswervingly honest and direct. She felt safe in the presence of a boy who could read her mind yet respect her secrets. In a blabbermouth Court, the heir to the throne of England and Scotland spoke only when he had something to say.

There was no need for polite cover-up between them today. Frances knew the Prince had observed her red-rimmed eyes beneath her make-up and veil, from the moment she had arrived at the Chapel Royal. She trusted Charles to do all he could to ease her suffering, while she endured the unhappiest public occasion of her life.

Yet for all the Prince's silent strength, Frances continued to feel lost, as she sat between Bacon and Charles and watched the scene before her unfold. Ever since the betrothal, she had woken each morning to a sinking feeling that her father and mother had consigned her to a life of permanent menace. Here in the Great Hall of Hampton Court, on her wedding day and under the magnifying glass of an ogling and prurient crowd, Frances was receiving her first public taste of what that life would be like.

It might have helped if she could have found a way to connect with the stranger standing behind her chair. Sir John Villiers was neither ugly nor unkind. Frances recognized that, like the Prince, with whom as Groom of the Bedchamber and Master of the Robes he was on intimate terms, Sir John was currently doing all he could to shield her from unwanted attention. She felt grateful that he tried to deter his drunken youngest brother from pawing her. She guessed, from all his fidgeting, that Sir John liked the peep show in which they were principal players as little as she. But still he remained an alien being to Frances, with jerky gestures and unexpected laughs.

And Sir John came so heavily laden with family baggage. His Villiers kinfolk were everywhere she looked, including the odious Kit who, in spite of all his brother's efforts to ward him off, kept reappearing, to leer over her with his alcoholic breath. Everything about the party manners today of this extended family into which she had married confirmed to Frances that the dread she had been feeling about her future was merited.

Frances read dislike from her new sister, Susan, and coolness verging on animosity in the critical stares from her mother-in-law. All contact between them leading up to this day had forewarned her that Lady Compton would not hesitate to crush any who threatened her ambitions for her favourite middle son and herself. Her position now, on the other side of the King from Steenie demonstrated the height to which she had climbed in royal favour.

Buckingham was pointedly ignoring Frances. In the moment she felt grateful, but their earlier wordless clash had given her a hint of the relations she might henceforth expect to enjoy with George Villiers. She shivered and sought the Prince of Wales' hand under the table. He turned toward her, made an ironic face and smiled.

Bless you, dear Charles. For your kindness and protection of me this day, I will love and be loyal to you as long as I shall live.

As if he had intuited her silent oath, the Prince remained with Frances throughout the wedding feast and its subsequent entertainment. Long after Bacon had risen and wandered off to gossip with cronies, Charles maintained a watchful eye around the Hall. He nudged Frances unobtrusively when well-wishers visited the Royal Table, and brought her out of her reveries to acknowledge toasts being made throughout the Great Hall to the nuptial pair. Unusually, he filled several awkward silences between her and individual wedding guests with well-chosen words, spoken without a stutter or a sting.

Now Charles was touching Frances again on the arm and indicating with his eyes. His royal father was on his feet, wobbling on those weak legs, and supporting himself by leaning on Steenie. King James raised his ornate gold goblet to propose his umpteenth inebriated toast to the health and happiness of the bonniest bride in his kingdom and her fortunate lord.

This time the King followed his action with a belching proclamation: "Let the masque commence!"

The noise level went up an octave as chairs and benches grated, guests shouted at each other across the hall and a stampede began to make full use of the twenty-eight seats at the Great House of Easement before the evening's entertainment began. Minutes passed before the cacophonous crowd resumed its seats and came to order for attention to focus on the stage opposite the Royal Table.

Frances cast another apprehensive glance at Charles. The seventeen-year-old Prince of Wales shrugged and squeezed her hand again. The wedding masque was about to begin. Who knew what entertainment was in store?

CHAPTER ELEVEN

California

"It is Sarah under that hat, isn't it? Oh, I'm so sorry, my dear. I didn't mean to startle you. I saw your name in the register and guessed you'd be over by the pool. I was wondering if you were ready for a wine or a beer? You're alone, I hear."

I struggled to emerge from some dream that sought to hold me captive, the events of which were lost as soon as I opened my eyes. I sat up, rubbed my eyes and looked around. The young couple had disappeared. The sun had dropped behind the mountain. Disorientated, I blinked up at the round-faced woman who was beaming down on me.

Belatedly, I recognized her.

"Hi, Cathy. I wondered if you were still working here. Is it already six? I must have been sleeping for hours. Yes, I'd love a white wine. Do you still have that Italian Pinot Grigio from last time we were here?"

"I think you're in luck, my dear. Come with me."

I stood up and pulled on my bathing wrap. Stretching chilled and cramped limbs, I followed Cathy across to the poolside bar. The hotel had changed hands several times in its life, but the original owner's cocktail hour endured, offering guests an opportunity to enjoy a free drink beside the pool at sundown.

As I sat on a stool and sipped my wine, Cathy confided that she would be leaving the hotel and Palm Springs soon. Her youngest daughter had just finished college and, with single-parent responsibilities at an end, Cathy planned to explore parts of the world that she had long dreamed of and never visited.

"That sounds adventurous. Where will you go?"

She reeled off the names of a dozen countries on her list.

I was impressed. "My, it sounds as if you'll be travelling non-stop for the next few years. I seem to have lost my wanderlust since arriving in L.A.. I travelled so much while living in Europe, but Palm Springs is as far as I get these days. And this evening I'm only going as far as that

Italian restaurant on Indian Canyon. I want to go somewhere I know I'll enjoy the food."

I waved away her offer of a refill. "One glass is enough, thanks."

Cathy nudged me. "Go on, take advantage of the moment, Sarah. You may have to fight to get to the bar, tomorrow evening. A group is coming in for a two-day business meeting. Every room in the hotel will be booked."

I shook my head. "Thanks, but I'll take my chances."

"Well, enjoy your Italian meal then, and do make the most of tonight's peace and quiet. They're a nice enough bunch, but quite high-spirited."

I drove to the restaurant and found a convenient parking spot.

"It's such a pleasure to see you again, Signorina. Are you eating alone tonight or will your friend be joining you?"

That staff here also remembered me came as a bigger surprise than my lunchtime greeting. Bob and I had only eaten twice at the restaurant.

"You have a good memory."

The Neapolitan waiter who had served us on both previous occasions bowed: "It is easy to remember such a beautiful woman as yourself, Signorina."

I glowed. "Thank you. You are very gallant."

"I am truthful."

Once again I was the only person eating alone. From a secluded table in an alcove, I could people-watch without being seen. It suited me perfectly. I sat in solitude, enjoying the relaxed ambience, and reflecting on what a good turn had I done myself by striking out for a new life in the USA.

I could not remember having received a casual compliment from a waiter or, indeed, having been encouraged to think well of myself by anybody in England. Throughout my childhood, I had been discouraged from thinking about myself at all, in a family where *being selfish* was considered a cardinal sin. Nobody had suggested that I was beautiful, even in my adolescent years, when men began to invite me on dates, or even when one particular man became persistent in his advances.

As at lunch, so at dinner, I found my mind drifting back again to a world that I had left behind and thence to my marriage. John had been dilatory about applying for the divorce but, if I was honest with myself, I too had been holding on to some residue of my life and identity with him. Revisit the past, Sarah. But revisit it this time, with a view to letting it go.

I sat musing on how, from the outset, my parents had actively encouraged our courtship, although John was twelve years older than me. They must have fallen under the charm of his title, his Eton education and his apparently perfect manners. John had been a man in a hurry then. When he proposed that I leave college early to marry him, nobody recommended me to wait and complete my studies.

By falling into marriage with a man who had a prominent public profile, I took a path of least resistance, like that trodden by many young women before me: our path in life mapped out for us by prevailing mores and expectations of parents, friends and society at large. At nineteen, eager as I was to buy into the fairytale and make everybody around me happy, I had not yet connected enough with the person known as Sarah, to discern whether she might want anything different from life.

Our wedding had been a grand affair, covered by Tatler. My mother-in-law presided over every decision, from guest list to honeymoon location, although my father paid the bill. Initially, life with John was a buzz of international travel, business dinners and glamorous social and political events, at which I was expected to look pretty and say nothing controversial. I floated along in a romantic bubble, feeling special and cared for.

We had not been together long before the bubble burst.

John began to display odd moods, that included demeaning and belittling me in public and then, increasingly, in private too. I endured growing unhappiness for several years, convinced that behind my husband's acts of unkindness lay a goodhearted person trying to escape from the prison of his rigid and impersonal upbringing. Stuck in my own conditioning, I accepted responsibility for all the difficulties that developed between us, and clung to a belief that things would improve if I could only learn to be a more appropriate wife.

Childless still after a decade, though not through choice, and increasingly bored with the meaninglessness of my life, I began an Open University degree in psychology to try and complete my studies, but soon received reprimands from John that my coursework clashed with the demands of his social calendar. I bolstered my flagging spirits, by reminding myself that, on his good days, John could still be sweet and charming.

The good days became fewer and John's mood swings became wilder. When he turned physically violent, I colluded with him, by concealing my bruises from parents, friends and even our family doctor. I tried to talk with John on his calm days, but he always denied there was a problem. He ignored my pleas that we seek expert counselling and, if I tried to persist, became menacing.

I had not wanted to worry my parents with my problems but, after a particularly brutal battering, I felt desperate enough to turn to them for help. They expressed astonishment that I could have been experiencing distress for so long and my father declared that the physical abuse must stop immediately. However, they also worried that a formal separation might create a scandal for the family. In particular, it might adversely affect my father's position in the community, at a time when he was planning to run for senior political office.

My parents decided they must take me to talk with John's family and see if something could be sorted out between us. But an emergency political meeting came up for my father on the day agreed, and my mother felt unwell, so they urged me to keep the date and go alone.

I hit a brick wall of denial. John's mother looked put out, said nothing and left the room. John's father looked through me, as he recommended that I be careful, if I intended spreading lies about his son. My situation created its own solution, for the visit triggered my nervous breakdown.

My parents paid for me to enter a private clinic where, for the first time, I received objective support and practical advice. My dark night soul journey helped me understand unconscious effects of my childhood and address issues in my relationship with John. For some time after I came out of the clinic, he seemed eager for us to work on our marriage together and resolve our differences. The violence stopped.

I had begun therapy to address my own issues, but I became so fascinated by the process that I decided to train as a therapist. It was a long training but when, as an intern, I began to work with clients, I knew that I had found my calling. I had natural empathy and my intuition was strong.

Two things happened just after I received my diploma. First, a well-meaning friend suggested I might have difficulty establishing my practice and getting clients. She revealed that John's parents and siblings had for some years been using the fact of my time in the clinic to put it about that I was mentally unstable. I challenged John. He defended his family's actions and hit me again. It was the push I needed to leave him.

Second, I had a strange and powerful dream that I must go to Los Angeles. It stayed with me on waking and for weeks thereafter. One day I shocked my parents and friends – and myself as well – by announcing my intention to emigrate, if I could secure resident status in the USA. It had turned out well. I was making my own way in the world, no longer reliant on a husband, parents and long time friends. My newfound pleasure in my own company seemed proof that I was on the right path.

So, let go of the past and all that drama, Sarah. You are free. Write to John and say that you propose to initiate divorce proceedings. Do it tonight.

In confident mood, I paid my bill and drove back to the hotel.

I let myself in by the side door and glanced across at the reception area in passing. The front desk remained lit but was empty, as it had always been after 9 p.m. on our previous stays. The pool area was also illuminated, but the hotel bedrooms lay in darkness. All except for my own room, where a dim light flickered behind the curtains. How careless. I must have left the TV on when I left for dinner.

Unlocking the door to my room, I entered, locked it behind me, turned to switch on the main light and froze. Antony Makepeace lay sprawled across the bed, apparently engrossed in a television program.

"What are you doing here? Who let you in?"

"Hello!" He looked up, switched off the TV with the remote control and waved a room keycard at me. "I'm waiting for you, Sarah. Patiently, too, since there's nothing to eat or drink here, and not a thing worth watching on this stupid box."

I stood transfixed, unable to think. Makepeace stretched and sat up. "I do hope you enjoyed a good meal while you kept me waiting."

I exploded at his sarcastic tone. "You're a fine one to talk about being kept waiting, Antony Makepeace. Where were you this morning at eight, when I waited for you in my office? How did you get a key to my room? My God, did you follow me all the way here from L.A.?" My gut contracted at the thought.

"Don't worry. I cased the joint. Lucky I did. If I hadn't waited until that old bag Cathy left, she might have blown my story. The new girl at reception was thrilled. The kid thought I was your boyfriend, just arrived from London. You'd said that Bob might be arriving later in the week and you didn't tell her he's American. Thank you for that, sweetheart."

For a moment I forgot to be frightened. "You posed as my *boyfriend?* How dare you!"

Antony Makepeace grinned. "Don't get all huffy. I was going to say I was your brother, but she assumed I was Bob, so I went along with it. It was quite touching how pleased for you the little thing was. Empty-headed creature, but nice to look at."

My heart thudded and I felt faint. "What makes you think you have a right to enter anyone's room without an invitation?"

"Now don't get upset, there's a good soul. I can't stand a fuss, particularly with my nerves in their fragile state."

Again I exploded. "Fragile? I'd say you've got nerves of steel, Antony Makepeace. You tell me a hard-luck tale and persuade me to give you an emergency appointment, for which you never show up. You follow me to Palm Springs and impersonate my boyfriend to gain entry to my room. That seems to be more than enough nerve. I need you to leave. Now."

"Sorry to disappoint you, Sarah, my sweet, but I don't intend to do that, at least not without you. You see I want that talk we were planning to have."

"Forget it, Mr. Makepeace. I have no intention of talking with you as a client, now or ever. Clients who want to work with me do not play cat-and-mouse games. They turn up as previously agreed, or call to rearrange. No show, no talk."

Behind what I hoped sounded like a firm rebuttal, I felt sick with apprehension. For the first time, I realised the drawbacks of staying alone as a woman in a hotel with no overnight staff on the premises. I wondered which room the young couple had taken and whether they might hear if I yelled. I wished the rowdy group were already in residence.

There was an emergency number and phone to contact hotel management in reception, but I'd never make it that far if Makepeace intended to detain me. My mobile phone lay in my purse, which I'd dropped by the door in my shock. Could I find a way to get it out and dial 911 without being detected?

Antony Makepeace rose from the bed. "Sweetheart, we *are* going to talk, and for much longer than the paltry half hour you offered me. We're going to do it at my place and on my terms, not yours." He was still grinning, but with no humour in his eyes. "I didn't like your office. No offence, Sarah, but it didn't feel like home. Not the kind of place to share all my dark and difficult secrets. And I don't intend to tell you my story against a ticking clock."

As if he had divined my intention about the mobile phone, Makepeace moved quickly, picked up my purse from the floor and held on to it. "We're going to take a little drive to my place. It can get quite cool at night where we're going. So get a jacket and anything else you may want to slip into. You'll be staying a while, so you might need fresh undies."

I continued to stand with my hand on the door.

"What makes you think I'm coming with you, Mr. Makepeace?"

"You have no choice. Once you know me better, you'll realise that I take what I want and when I want. So give us both a break, by doing things my way and without arguing."

"What *do* you want from me?" I was shaking with fear now, but hoped he had not noticed.

Makepeace manhandled me away from the door. "You'll learn that soon enough. Do as I say and stop stalling. Grab what you need, and we'll be on our way."

I made one last stand. "If I refuse?"

"You won't do that."

As I stared at the knife that had materialised in Antony Makepeace's hand, I had to agree.

CHAPTER TWELVE

England 1617

The stage had been constructed so that His Majesty and his companions, including the newly weds, might enjoy an uninterrupted view.

The masque had been commissioned and composed expressly for Sir John and Lady Villiers' marriage. Its theme was innocuous enough: the poesy and many pleasures associated with a loving union. But the mood for this evening was set early by the vulgar music and impropriety displayed during the opening dances.

Intended only as a foil to the sublime show that would follow, as in other masques created by Ben Jonson, on this occasion the tone and tenor of the anti-masque coloured all subsequent proceedings. Several members of the Coke family and the new sister-in-law were among those performing the more provocative moves, as well as others whom Frances would never call friend again. Tableaux that had been meant, and in other circumstances might have been received, as subtly sensual and soulful were greeted on this occasion by catcalls, cheers and hysterical laughter.

Meanwhile, offstage, a competition developed, to create capital out of the bride's evident discomfort. In her seat of honour, Frances had no means of escape. Looking up from beneath her lashes, she realised that someone was orchestrating the sideshow. Seated with his arm casually draped around his royal lover's shoulders, George Villiers was engaged in catching the eye of cronies, then nodding his head toward Frances. His asides were not loud enough for her to hear, but she observed that they caused others within earshot to snigger and send off-colour remarks in her direction. Even a usually benign King James appeared to be completely in his cups, his laughter braying and out of control. Derision marked the few glances that Buckingham sent directly at the bride.

Had he known Frances better, the Earl might have called an early halt to his tormenting. It was what his new sister-in-law needed. Raising her chin in a characteristic gesture long known to her family, Frances set her face into a deadpan mask. From this moment on, if the effort killed her, none present in the Great Hall should have sight of Lady Villiers' private misery. Let her husband, now seated beside her, be the one to giggle in embarrassment and grow red in the face, as a result of his brother's baiting.

Beside her, Prince Charles continued to watch the stage unsmiling, but he murmured softly, "Well done, dear Franny, well done."

While it was being performed, Frances wished the masque would end. When it was over, the last revel danced, the *aubade* sung and the supper consumed, she wished all might begin again, to delay the inevitable ritual to come. The clamour in the Great Hall built as guests began to clap and stamp their feet and whistle and point. At a signal from King James, the wedding celebration for Sir John Villiers and Mistress Frances Coke moved to its public climax. The crowd received His Majesty's blessing to swoop upon the bridal pair, then lift and propel them across the hall.

Borne high on a human tide headed by His Majesty and directed, at his own erratic pace, toward the rooms in the Royal Palace that had been designated and set aside for the wedding night, Frances fought to keep calm. Aloft and at her side, Sir John Villiers clasped her hand, while staring about him and snickering. His grip was clammy. For the first time, it occurred to Frances that her husband might be feeling as nervous as she.

A figure came between the newly weds, her hand was pulled from Sir John's and Frances shut her ears against the overbearing voice. "Come, brother. Leave the ladies to prepare your real wedding feast, while we fortify you for the task of eating it."

Grotesque shadows flickered and fuelled the bride's apprehensions, as Buckingham and Kit Villiers led their brother along the passage in the King's stumbling wake. Bawdy comments and laughter echoed after them along torch-lit and tapestry-hung stone walls.

Frances was bundled through a door and into a small candlelit chamber, the walls of which were covered with mirrors. She stared at the mirror, unsmiling, while her fourteen-year-old body was bared, prodded and adorned to titillate her husband. She longed silently and in vain for Lady Hatton's presence. Eliza was self-centred and quarrelsome, but she also possessed an inherent refinement that influenced others around her. Mama would never have allowed Frances to be treated in such a callous and coarse manner.

But Mama was not here.

Lady Compton had deputed her daughter Susan to supervise proceedings, while Elizabeth Coke led the ladies of the court who physically undressed Frances. Her sister avoided all eye contact and her expression was as tight-lipped as it had been from the start of the day. Frances sighed. She could not find it in her to blame Elizabeth, older by four years and still single, for taking offence that this wedding had been held before her own. But her sister's coldness meant that she had neither sympathetic friends nor warm-hearted relatives to turn to for support. Apart from Susan and Elizabeth, the crowd of ladies who prepared Frances for her marriage bed with raucous shrieks and innuendos were as inebriated as the men attending her husband.

Minutes later, she sat shivering in a huge canopied bed in the adjoining chamber that had been prepared for Sir John and his bride. The main door burst open, causing the fire in the grate to sputter and smoke, as the King, Buckingham and Kit Villiers entered in a gust of alcohol. Still flanked by their tide of courtiers, they propelled a nightgown-clad John Villiers before them. The groom tripped toward the bed and climbed in beside Frances.

The King winked at her as he came forward and pawed her hand. His words were slurred and his Scots brogue pronounced as he drooled, "I've brought ye your man, Franny. May he be all ye ever dreamed of." His Majesty leaned over and nudged Frances in the ribs. She shrank back, feeling naked and exposed in her gossamer fine shift.

"Now remember, lassie, ye mus' nae rise in the morning before I visit ye both. And be sure tae have those sheets ready for me tae inspect." Cheers and laughter accompanied the monarch's proclamation that he intended to bear royal witness that the marriage vows had been fulfilled. More jokes accompanied His Majesty's exit, as Steenie led a limping King James from the nuptial chamber.

The door slammed shut and the echoing cries of the Court diminished. Silence filled the room as two all but total strangers found themselves alone together for the first time in their life.

The hours that followed were long and sleepless for Frances Villiers. The King did not come until well past noon on the following day. By then she had learned much about Sir John Villiers. Some things that Frances anticipated did not happen. Some things happened that she had not anticipated. Some she was surprised to find she liked. And some of them she did not.

CHAPTER THIRTEEN

California

We were out in open country when Makepeace braked and pulled up at the side of the road. He switched on the interior light and flashed me a false smile. "Sorry about this, sweetheart, but it won't be for long. I can't keep this knife in my hand while I drive. It makes me too tense."

Makepeace leaned across me and placed the knife into the glove compartment of the Mercedes as he spoke. He removed a thin nylon rope, turned toward me and pulled my wrists together.

I flinched but did not struggle as he bound me. I watched his fingers and noted, as in a dream, that they were long and fine with well-manicured nails. He was deft and, in the circumstances, surprisingly gentle. He leaned forward again, withdrew a scarf from the glove compartment and folded it into a blindfold.

"Turn your head. Away from me a little. Yes, that's perfect." He placed the blindfold over my eyes, checked its position and tied it in a knot behind my head. "Very good, Sarah. Turn back toward me. Excellent. Now we can be comfortable."

I felt anything but comfortable.

The wheels of the Mercedes spun on loose gravel as Makepeace put his foot down hard. We were off and driving fast into the night.

Locked in a visual prison, I had no hope of recording our route. We turned, and turned again and I became disorientated. Makepeace's erratic driving threw me from side to side. Fear coursed through my veins. I tried to breathe deeply and slowly. Focusing on breathing brought some relief.

As I grew calmer, I became aware of Makepeace's physical presence. The aura and magnetism of the man affected me, even when I could not see him. It was as if he knew a way to bind me psychically as well as physically. Now, as well as fear, I was feeling resentful of his hold over me.

Makepeace began to hum softly. Against my will, I strained to identify the melody. I had heard the tune before. Perhaps he had read my mind, for he said, "Recognise it? Would you like to hear the original? One of your favourites, I bet."

I could hear the cat-and-mouse tone again and I did not want to play.

"I don't know what you're talking about."

"I don't know what you're talking about." He mimicked me exactly, then, "I'm talking about the original version of this song, woman. Who sang it? What are the lyrics? Come on, Sarah, you're not dumb. It was his last record before he left the band."

I felt him fumbling in a box compartment between our seats, while the car swung from side to side. "Here we are. Just a minute." Now he was fiddling with the stereo system.

Music filled the car. Yes, I knew both the song and the singer.

The volume was painfully loud. Makepeace bellowed, "Know who it is now, don't you?"

I wasn't about to tell him that Bob played me this song the first time I visited his apartment:

Riding through the night
Chasing moonbeams of delight
We will be forever free
Just as long as you're with me
Riding through the storm
We won't stop until the dawn
Then the life we've left behind
Will be gone and out of mind

"A pleasant enough little ditty. Bob wrote it, not me. Dull, but quite appropriate for our present situation, isn't it?"

Behind the blindfold I was crying. Hearing Bob's voice had broken my resistance. I yearned for him to arrive and scoop me up and out of this nightmare. But Bob was in another continent and no knight in shining armour was about to swoop in and rescue me. I would have to rely on myself. I squeezed my eyes together, leaned forward to wipe my nose on the back of my bound hands and set myself to try and think clearly.

Bob had left that band thirty years ago. Makepeace evidently knew of Bob's past musical career. How well did he know him now?

Bob rarely talked to me about his performing past, for his energy was focused in his present work and promoting other bands. I pressed him once about his reasons for quitting when his career was at its height. Initially he was reticent but, when I persisted in probing for an explanation, he spoke of fights that had begun during an exhausting series of back-to-back international tours. Conflicts developed, cycled and seemed incapable of resolution.

For Bob, once personal relationships in the band were poisoned, the magic went out of making music. He left England, where the band was based, and returned to the United States. He'd made a lot of money during his time with the band and, unlike some of his peers, had managed it wisely. He was under no financial pressure to do anything but, after a year of hanging out with older brothers and childhood friends in his native Los Angeles, he became bored and went into the business side of rock music.

Bob declared himself fortunate among his contemporaries. Many had died. Too few survivors had found fresh and fulfilling outlets for their creativity. Even fewer succeeded. Only a handful of classic rock musicians could still count on performing regularly. Some drifted into lethargic, over-weight retirement, dulled by drink and drugs. Others became caged tigers, pacing the plush carpets of their luxuriously appointed homes, disenchanted with the monotony of their lives.

Sporadically, a need for cash or a yearning for the old adrenalin rush sent some out in search of deals that might get them back on the road. When they got there, they found that the business had changed. Technology had democratised the music scene. More music was being made than ever, but few bands made a good living for long. A corporate gig might earn a fat cheque, and festivals provided an occasional fillip, but public concert tours were increasingly hard to come by, as well as often hit-and-miss financially.

The glamour of performing had also faded for many middle-aged bodies that complained at late night shows, sandwiched between awkward travel schedules. Business class air tickets on scheduled airlines, a well-sprung tour bus and ageing, if loyal fans were a lame substitute for the good old days of private jets, stretch limousines and screaming hordes of excited youth.

At home or on tour, substance abuse still lingered in the rock music air. By now the piper was calling in payment. Barely a month passed without the media reporting on a musician, retired or still performing, whose body had called a halt to its chronic misuse and neglect.

In the current climate, Bob had every reason to count himself among the favoured ones. His health was excellent and his reputation solid. He had kicked his own early excesses, and was internationally known as a promoter with original ideas for concerts and festival line-ups, together with a talent for judging when and what the market would bear. He knew the business inside out. Colleagues found him dependable and enjoyed working with him.

Makepeace's voice intruded on my thoughts. "Not bad, but the stuff the band got into after Bob left was the real deal. Don't you agree?"

I heard his desire to bait and replied as neutrally as I could, "Don't ask me to judge rock music. I'm no expert. I didn't even know that band existed before I met Bob."

"One of the best known British bands of all times and you didn't know it existed? Were you hiding under a rock during all those years, sweetheart? Or under some other rock star, perhaps? That's funny. I bet it must have dented Bob's ego to learn that his English rose didn't know his band." Makepeace sounded genuinely amused.

"On the contrary. He finds it refreshing to be with someone who likes him for himself."

Makepeace's hoot was disbelieving. The brittle sound made me want to slap him. "Oh, he may have said that, sweetheart. We all do, when we want to get into a woman's knickers. But I'll lay a large sum that our Bob felt positively piqued when you told him. Hah! I love it. The great man's girlfriend didn't know him when he was strutting his stuff on stage."

The car lurched again, as Makepeace scrabbled around once more in the box compartment between us. "Oops. Ah, yes, here we are. Now you can hear what that band got into, after the high-and-mighty Bob Howard got out of the way and let it play what it was created for."

The sound of heavy rock burst and reverberated through the car.

Makepeace evidently knew the CD by heart for he was word perfect, if sometimes off-key, when shouting out the lyrics to each track. The Mercedes rocked and bucked like a kangaroo, as his foot slid on and off the accelerator. He was still driving faster than felt safe to me. Physical jolting and fear that we might crash made me nauseous again. I could feel a scream building inside me. Was the man unconscious of his effect or deliberately pushing my buttons?

Without warning, we veered off the main highway. Makepeace made no concessions to road surface as we bounced at high speed over a heavily potholed dirt track, touching bottom often. Ominous grating sounds emanated from the car's undercarriage and I was jarred each time we made contact. Then we turned a sharp bend and the car skidded so violently that I fell against him. Jerking myself upright, I turned toward the passenger door and scrabbled with my tied hands for an armrest or something else to hold on to.

"Having a bumpy ride? Sorry about that. I thought Bob's woman would be the kind to like it hard and fast."

I said nothing. Makepeace repeated his comment, his voice developing a rising edge. An instinct for self-preservation told me to react in kind. I twisted in my seat and yelled at him, "Slow down and turn this damned music off!"

To my relief, Makepeace reduced speed and turned off the CD. For some minutes we drove in silence. I listened to the tyres reverberate on the dirt road and wondered how far we had come off the beaten track.

"Here we are." Makepeace braked. The car slithered to a halt. I jerked forward, but the seat belt held me in place. The car engine died and my captor's manic mood appeared to evaporate with it, for he said conversationally, "We're home, sweetheart."

I sat motionless, my body still feeling as if I was flying forward at high velocity. Antony Makepeace breathed in and exhaled loudly. "I love it here. Nobody around for miles. Just you, me and the desert."

I heard his door open. "Listen, Sarah."

Disorientated and dizzy, I strained my ears. Nocturnal sounds filled the desert air. Cicada wings vibrated close by. Somewhere in the distance a night bird spoke to its mate and was answered.

I felt Makepeace turn and lean toward me. His lips brushed my ear as he spoke again. "I love this place. Nowhere on earth like it. You'll love it too, darling. You can leave all your worries behind. And help me leave mine behind."

He leaned across me and I flattened myself against the seat, terrified that he was about to kiss me. Makepeace only laughed lightly, turned my face away and untied the blindfold.

I blinked and looked around. Initially, I could see nothing, for the car headlamps had been turned off. As my vision acclimatised to the night, the startling beauty of our surroundings revealed itself. Out here in the desert, the sky knew no interference from artificial city lights. Stars loomed close and bright. Stunted trees surrounded the car like lurking silver ghosts.

A large boulder blocked our path, inches from the Mercedes' front grille. Looking sideways and to the left, I saw that we had parked parallel to a long and low building.

It looked like a large log cabin.

"Come, my sweet."

Makepeace climbed from the car and pulled me out via the driver's seat. Negotiating the gear selector with tied hands was a challenge. I swung my feet out onto the ground, stood up and staggered. Makepeace caught and held me tightly. I had no choice but to accept his support as he steered me toward the door of the building. Once, I stumbled against a stone and righted myself again with his help. His voice was at once amused and patronising. "Careful, sweetheart. You're not a country girl and we don't want twisted limbs out here. No doctors for miles around."

I watched without speaking while Makepeace produced a bunch of keys and opened three different locks. When the door yielded, he slid a hand inside and switched on a light. Opening the door wide, he quickly turned off an alarm system, then turned toward me and bowed theatrically. "Welcome to my humble abode, sweet Sarah." This time there was no inflection of irony. He might have been welcoming an honoured guest into his home. He stood back to let me pass.

Inside, I looked around and heard myself gasp. The cabin was luxurious and modern beyond anything its rustic exterior had led me to expect. The room was long and rectangular. A misted glass wall separated off one half of the large main living area. Beyond the glass I could see a massive music console, guitars and a miscellany of other musical equipment. The recording studio spoke of significant financial outlay.

"I expect you'll need the bathroom." He was right. "Let me show you the geography. It's through here." He propelled me along a passage. I entered the door he indicated and turned quickly to shut it, but Makepeace had already put out his foot.

"Sorry, but I must ask you to leave this open. I don't intend you to do yourself a mischief or try and leave by a window, although they are all locked. Don't mind me, my dear. I won't peep. I'm not kinky. At least, not in that way."

He turned his back. I used the bathroom awkwardly, and then followed him back into the main room again.

"Watch this." Makepeace moved across to one corner and pulled a concealed lever. A king-sized bed unfolded from the wall with a creak and a snap. It was already part made up. Makepeace pulled brightly coloured pillows and a matching duvet out of a large chest of drawers in a corner, shook them out and laid them out on the bed.

He looked at me and smiled. "Neat, eh? Don't worry. Everything is clean and dry. Whenever I shut the place up, I leave everything ready for a possible late night arrival. You'll be very comfortable on this. But I am going to have to tether you for a while."

I drew back as he advanced on me. He laughed. "It's OK, really, Sarah. Come and sit down here, so you can test the bed."

I sat on the bed. He untied my wrists but immediately pulled two sets of handcuffs from the top drawer of the chest. He attached one to the tubing that surrounded the bed's headboard and took my left wrist.

I screamed, "Don't tie me up. Don't hit me again!" I did not recognize my own voice or what was prompting my words. They seemed to surprise Makepeace too, for he took a step backwards and stared at the shaking heap I had become.

Uncertainty reflected in his eyes. "I haven't hit you. And I won't, if you do what I say."

Still terrified, as Makepeace secured my wrist, I begged him again, "Please don't." Now my back stung as if I had been burned or lashed.

Makepeace said nothing and attached my right wrist to the headboard with the other set of cuffs. My back felt as if it was on fire and I screamed louder.

Makepeace pushed me back against the pillow, yelling too, "Shut up and calm down, you stupid bitch."

His face and body blurred as I felt myself fall back into darkness.

CHAPTER FOURTEEN

England 1620

"Your servant, sister."

The tone was contemptuous, as always. Frances choked back the bitter response that rose to her lips, as her brother-in-law exited the room with Lord Purbeck.

Left alone with her thoughts, as she was so often these days, Frances reflected that George's mocking face stayed with her even after he had left. Not only did he dominate every public and private social occasion she attended, and saunter without announcement into the rooms she shared with her husband at the Prince's Palace, as he had done this morning to bear John away for the day. Lately, George Villiers and his difficult mother had even begun to invade her dreams.

Frances could not and would not display the sycophantic gratitude toward George that so many of her acquaintance recommended, although she had learned to stay silent, when told that she was beholden to Steenie for all her good fortune.

She did not deny that George had arranged with His Majesty for his brother to be made Master of the Horse and Keeper of the Prince's Palace at Denmark House. That George had selected the sumptuous furnishings for the suite of rooms in the palace enjoyed by the Villiers. That it was Buckingham who had prevailed upon the King to entitle John as Baron Villiers of Stoke and Viscount Purbeck of Dorset, when he was created Marquess, and his mother Countess, of Buckingham.

George was also the prime reason why the young couple kept company with the King and his entourage, whenever Lord Purbeck's state of mind permitted them to hunt, dine, perform in masques, travel with the Court, and generally engage in such pleasure as His Majesty had invited dear Steenie to devise for the royal circle's entertainment.

To many, it must have appeared that Buckingham's position alone had accorded Frances entry to this charmed inner circle. They may have forgotten – the *parvenus* had presumably never known – that her mother's connections had privileged Lady Purbeck to move in that circle from infancy. Few guessed, and even fewer cared, that the lonely young viscountess would have gladly exchanged her married state for a return to the identity of Mistress Frances Coke, free to mix with royalty, yet also at liberty to ride the lanes around Corfe Castle, in the carefree company of a local squire's nephew.

Frances understood what so many who were dazzled by Buckingham's charm did not, that he intended her no personal favours through the honours he engineered for his brother. And further, that George would take personal pleasure in doing Frances down, if he could find a method that would not create a backlash on his family.

He had already deprived her of the material means to maintain her household alone in Town during her husband's absences, by taking hold of the management of his brother's funds. Buckingham's withholding of her marriage portion became so blatant that Frances finally summoned courage to write to the King herself. That action at least had led His Majesty to drop a gentle reminder in his favourite's ear, concerning what James knew could only have been an oversight, resulting from George's preoccupation with all the vital affairs that he managed on the royal behalf.

Lady Hatton waved away her daughter's predicament as of little account, relative to her own suffering. "I've had to put up with far worse behaviour from your father throughout my marriage. Just don't pay Buckingham any attention. It's disgusting if he only allows you one thousand marks a year. But I've always told you, Franny, it only makes a man behave worse if he thinks you are scared of him."

All very well for her mother to say. Frances would have felt more secure if she could feel certain that Mama herself would not eventually buckle under the relentless Buckingham pressure. Eliza Hatton's record in that regard had been catastrophic once for her daughter, and it was a poorly guarded secret that the Buckinghams did not intend to stop until they had obliged Lady H. to transfer inheritance of all her properties to her son-in-law.

Thus far, Eliza had used her years of practice in countering the property-grabbing pretensions of her husband, as well as sage counsel from her confidante, Sir John Holles – whom gossips loved to hint was more than just her secretary – to stay one step ahead of the rapacious Buckingham mother and son. To the surprise of many, she turned up her elegant nose when the King, at George's prodding, suggested that his sweet Eliza might enjoy the title of Countess of Purbeck, in exchange for signing over her interests in the Isle of Purbeck and elsewhere to Sir John Villiers.

Eliza's reply had been succinct. She would keep her properties and forego the new title, thank you.

George had not forgiven the lady her refusal, or the private tittering that it had induced in some Court circles. Lady Elizabeth's wealth and standing with the King and Queen, together with her own well-honed powers to charm, inveigle and persuade, made her a worthier opponent than most. Unfortunately, Eliza's supreme lack of concern for the Buckinghams' displeasure left Frances more exposed than ever. While George and the Countess of Buckingham continued to search for a way to secure the coveted Hatton fortune, they deflected their anger toward the thick-skinned mother onto her vulnerable daughter.

It had to be acknowledged that Frances also exasperated George in her own right. That, from the day of her wedding, she would not massage his ego fuelled their mutual animosity. But there was more to it for him than personal pique.

The stakes against Frances rose when George's mother awoke to the realization that her daughter-in-law might constitute a danger to their dynastic dreams for her favourite middle son. The Buckinghams became aware that the last thing they needed was for Frances to present the eldest Villiers brother with a baby boy. Unless George himself could beget an heir, a Purbeck child might yet inherit Lady Hatton's wealth *and* all the titles and vast estates that the Buckinghams were striving to consolidate and augment.

Once George and the Countess became alert to this danger, they leaped into action. George began to use any means at his disposal to keep his brother out of the marriage bed. His main obstacle was his brother. John made it clear to all that he worshipped his lovely young wife and his fondness showed no sign of abating. He spoke often to her and others of the joy his life's treasure, as he called her, brought him.

Next, Frances learned that the mother and brother were spreading rumours of her husband's insufficiency far outside their usual circle. Since her own waistline still showed no signs of thickening, her lord's performance, or rather his lack thereof, had become the subject of crude jokes fed to the Court by his nearest and supposed dearest.

It had shocked Frances in the early days of her marriage to realize that John Villiers was as much a puppet in his family's self-aggrandising schemes as she. Frances felt devastated by such unkindness. She was coming to know her husband as a man of sweet disposition, when in his right mind. And she knew more about him than his mother or brother did. John was gentle and courteous with her in the bedchamber.

Their lovemaking never induced particular pleasure and, from her limited understanding of the procreative process, seemed unlikely to produce a child, but nor did it create the fear or pain that so many women endured, for which Frances felt grateful.

Still she could not anticipate when Purbeck's frenzies or depression might rock their marital world. Within a month of her wedding, Frances was packed off to stay with a minor Buckingham relative in the country, until John's latest episode of mania had passed. None of the physicians consulted had come up with a satisfactory diagnosis, let alone a cure. Some of the highly regarded, like Richard Napier, were stalling on the Buckinghams' requests to take Lord Purbeck on as a patient. No doctor felt equipped to advise George and the Countess whether John's condition affected his virility, just as none could predict if his condition might prove hereditary, should Lord Purbeck succeed in fathering a son.

The Viscount was penitent whenever a manic episode had passed. He would weep over her bruises and assure Frances that he had never intended to lay a finger upon her. She had every reason to believe this, for he was the only person in whom she had found comfort within the family she had married into. But Lord Purbeck's erratic moods had side effects for Frances beyond his occasional violence toward himself and her.

The King insisted John be removed from Court whenever his distempers threatened, and at such times the Prince also required his Keeper to vacate his palace. Those of the Court outside the Buckingham clan preferred to keep the couple at arm's length, and many gave the permanent cold shoulder to Lord and Lady Villiers. Frances felt the stigma of an unsympathetic society toward Purbeck's little understood condition, as well as suffering from the fact that it give the Buckinghams a legitimate excuse to keep her away from John.

George's marriage had provided a momentary distraction, and Frances did enjoy friendly overtures from her new sister-in-law. But she also realized that sharing confidences would put Kate Buckingham in an invidious position, and it would be too easy for a misplaced word to reach the wrong ears.

A younger Frances would have shared her personal problems with Lady Hatton. That likelihood died on the day she realised that Mama had so massaged her perceptions of past events as to deem the central, indeed the only, injured party in the whole marriage saga to have been Eliza herself.

Lady Elizabeth had been at her dramatic best when she announced publicly at her first dinner with His Majesty after the Villiers' wedding that she was ready to forgive her little puss of a daughter for having gone against a mother's dearest desires. Frances was struck mute by Mama's theatrical gall.

The Frances Villiers who listened to Eliza's performance that evening had lived through months of personal hell and was a different adolescent from the Frances Coke of half a year before. Seeing her mother with new eyes, she knew a sense of rising resentment and felt no inclination to exchange kisses of forgiveness with such a self-centred Eliza. At the time, the King mistook little Lady Villiers' reticence for contrition. Ever anxious that everyone make up and be friends, he ambled across to escort Frances to receive the Hatton embrace. To deny her mother's kiss then would have been to deny her King.

But mother and daughter's meetings since that night had been few and cool. They typically began with a cascade of complaints from Eliza about her own situation. Only when that subject had been exhausted, would Mama offer outspoken comments on what Frances was doing wrong in her marriage and what she should do differently.

Incapable of harbouring resentment for long, Frances accepted and even forgave her mother, but she was not Eliza. She had not sought this match but, once married, she desired to be a caring and dutiful wife. No longer blind to her mother's caprice, she had no interest in emulating Lady Hatton's husband-belittling tactics. Enough people were engaged already in that regard with Lord Purbeck, and she felt it was not John's fault that he was so afflicted.

Frances therefore learned to keep her own counsel. Covert attacks from George, his mother and her sister-in-law Su wore her down. Life at Court, with politicking and junketing that offered her little pleasure, was interspersed with periods of marital separation and even banishment, when Sir John's excesses sent him into seclusion. Frances became increasingly lonely and isolated, whether with or without her husband.

She had no illusions. She had been sighted, selected and snared for her dowry. The Buckinghams' profligate lifestyle had already eaten the large up-front sum delivered by her father. Lady Purbeck would henceforth be kept from her marriage bed, and her presence in the family tolerated only until the whole of the Hatton inheritance was in their hands. Thereafter she would be discarded.

The King's lazy affection for her provided no safeguard against the Buckinghams' intentions and manoeuvres. For years Frances had watched Steenie play James like a violin. And recently she was noticing how the Prince of Wales, once the model of an independent spirit at Court, was being wooed by a man adroit enough to have discovered a way to defuse the risk of Charles viewing him as a rival for his father's affections. George had opted to fill the hallowed place vacated by Prince Henry. As caring substitute for a dead older brother, he had positioned himself to weave the Buckingham web of intrigue around Charles as surely as he had already woven it around the King.

Alone each day in the Prince's Palace, Lady Villiers had prayed for patience and fortitude in her trials. She also prayed that she might know a little joy in life.

Be careful what you pray for, Viscountess Purbeck.

For, after three years of marriage, Frances had just begun to know happiness.

It came during slivers of stolen moments for which she knew she might, soon or late, have to pay a high price. Already a guilty conscience was adding to the weight of her other cares, and it sent Frances all too easily into a downward spiral of self-blame. Occasionally a small voice within spoke in her defence. But still she was left with the same uncomfortable and unanswered questions.

In an England where only a third of noble marriages saw regular co-habitation among spouses, was it a sin for young Lady Purbeck to have found pleasure outside the arms of her alternately manic and melancholic, as well as often absent, husband?

Had Fate tempted Frances away from the path of marital righteousness, or simply offered her a means of making that path bearable?

What was the path of righteousness for an adolescent girl, who had been beaten and sold by one parent and abandoned by the other; who was in danger of physical attack from her husband whenever he fell into one of his fits; and who was under constant mental and emotional assault from the most powerful man in the realm and his mother?

Frances knew only one person in the world with whom she felt safe even to voice these questions: a man she had known since infancy as a friend and whom she had lately discovered to be a loyal and passionate lover.

CHAPTER FIFTEEN

California

I opened my eyes and looked around, feeling heavy-headed and nauseous. I must have dozed off.

A large cardboard carton lay in the centre of the room. The writing on its side indicated that it originally contained twelve bottles of whisky. The brand was Scots: famous, old and expensive. The top of the carton had been ripped. Twisting sideways on the bed, I could see a bottle across on the kitchen counter, open and no longer full. There was no sign of a glass. Was Makepeace a drinker? I had not detected alcohol on his breath when we first met or while we were in his car.

I looked around the cabin. The door was open. He must be unloading the Mercedes. Clothes flung in the car during our hasty departure from Ballantines were now lying folded on the chest of drawers next to the bed where I was bound. Next to the clothing was my purse and, as I stared at it, my mobile phone inside began to ring. Could I reach it? I struggled to work a cuffed hand down the side of the tubular bed head, but the other cuff was restraining me. My heart beat hard. Only three people in the world knew my number.

Makepeace entered at a run. "Oh good! You're awake again. Shall we see who that is?" He bounded across the room. Pulling the phone out of my purse he opened it before it stopped ringing, lifted it to his ear and spoke. "Good evening, Bob. Or good morning, as it must be in London. I assume you're calling from London? Business going well, I hope?"

Makepeace nodded at me with a grin. Exaggeratedly, he pointed to the phone and mouthed the words, "It's him."

He listened briefly, then laughed. "I bet it's a surprise. No, I'm not clairvoyant. Far from it, I promise you. I can't predict the future, though I'm really good at remembering the past. But it wasn't hard for me to guess who was likely to be calling Sarah at this late hour. Not if she is as faithful to you as you believe. I do compliment you, Bob, old son. She is every bit as beautiful as you described. Thanks for arousing my desire to meet Sarah in person. The experience is proving an even greater delight than I could have hoped."

Makepeace listened again, then, "No, not possible now. She's too tired. She's sprawled here on the bed half asleep, She's got that tousle-haired and inviting look, I'm sure you know it well." He shook his head. "Don't worry. She's quite safe. And when you call us tomorrow, I'm sure she'll be up to speaking with you again."

He transferred the phone to his other ear as he looked at his watch. "Now let's see, dear boy, I just need to work this out. Ye–es. You will call us next at four o'clock in the afternoon, your time. That gives Sarah a chance to catch up on her beauty sleep, as well as any other activity she and I may decide to indulge in. What's that, Bob?"

He was silent again, then, "You really shouldn't speak to me like that, old friend. She still has all her clothes on – at the moment." Another brief pause and, "I promise you there's no point in swearing at me. Sarah's not hurt. Not yet. You understand? Not – hurt – yet. She's just a wee bit confused, that's all. She doesn't know where she is or who she's with, whereas you and I both know, don't we?"

Makepeace laughed hard, as if he had just made a joke, but his mood changed quickly as he snapped down the phone, "You're trying my patience now, Bob. God, how many times do you need me to repeat myself? Just accept the situation. There really is nothing you can do about it. We'll speak tomorrow. At 4 p.m."

Makepeace lowered the phone as if to end the call but, as an afterthought, he raised it to his ear again and his voice was harsh, as he said, "No point in ringing before four, Bob. The phone will be turned off until then. I'm sure you won't be late. Remember how much I hate waiting around? Good." His final words sounded teasingly bland. "Thank you so much for calling, old man."

Antony Makepeace giggled to himself as he pressed the disconnect button. My mouth dropped open as he pulled my phone charger out of his pocket. He caught my expression. "Yes, smart of me, wasn't it? That's the kind of man I am. Attention to detail. I was sure you'd forget the charger, so I pocketed it before you got back to the hotel."

Makepeace turned off the phone, plugged it in to a wall socket to recharge and moved back to perch on the end of the bed. In the cabin light, I saw his eyes shine bright and blue. "So convenient that Bob can call us on this phone of yours, isn't it? We don't have to go in for cloak-and-dagger phone box calls, like they do in old movies. Which is fortunate, since there are no phone boxes within miles. We're lucky to be living in an age of advanced technology, don't you agree?"

I said nothing. Had he realised the police could trace my mobile phone? I wondered what would be going through Bob's head at this moment. Would he report the call? Makepeace had not identified himself by name, but Bob must have recognised his voice. Did he know the man well enough to guess where I was being held? Everything I had heard and seen suggested that Makepeace had brought me to a hideaway that he owned. If they were close, Bob might even have visited this cabin. I hoped so.

"You're not sulking because I didn't let you speak to him, are you, my sweet?" The cat was taunting the mouse again. It irritated me, for which I was grateful. I preferred feeling angry to being consumed by fear. It was a struggle to remain expressionless, but I gazed at Makepeace impassively, and stayed silent.

"I do believe you *are* sulking. Sarah, I wonder what it will take for you to accept that I know best. It won't help for you and Bob to chat. Not until I can trust you and we've agreed what you are going to say."

He was edging up the bed toward me and I tried not to shiver, as he patted my captive hand. He ran a finger around the steel of the handcuff then stroked the inside of my wrist. The intimacy of the gesture scared and incensed me in equal measure.

Makepeace laughed. "The lady is not amused. You know you are prettier when you are angry, Sarah? I'm sure you do. You women know how to drive us men crazy. OK, so let me explain something now." He sat beside me and continued, "You probably think of your Bob as a dear fellow. But he has a short fuse and a nasty temper under that easy-going exterior. So we must stop him landing us all in trouble. Big men who are used to getting their own way can be such a problem."

While he was speaking, Makepeace had slipped his hand toward my shoulder. "Do stop thinking the worst of me. You'll speak to Bob when he calls, if you have been cooperative. I'm sure you will be, won't you?" Now he began to massage me gently while he spoke. I shuddered. He shook his head in mock resignation and withdrew his hand. "You are going to have to work a little better with me here."

I only glared and he became brisk. "Very well, just tell me who else might want to call you on that cell phone over the next day or two."

I could not think straight and my hesitation made him impatient. I needed him to stay calm, for my own safety. "Bob and my parents know my number. Mum and Dad are in England and never call me, except in an emergency. I don't give my mobilel phone details to clients and friends use my home number or office voice mail."

"Perfect, my dear. You're someone after my own heart. I don't give out my cell phone number either, although I might be willing to make an exception for you." Makepeace stood up. "Excuse me for a minute or two, then, while I finish what I started."

He went out through the front door and returned with the last of my belongings. He laid them with exaggerated care in the drawer from which he had earlier pulled the pillows. "This shall be your space while we're here. You'll enjoy yourself once you've settled in. You must admit it's cosy for a pad in the boondocks."

"Where will you sleep, Mr. Makepeace?"

He raised an eyebrow. "Concerned for your virtue? My dear, I promise you will find me quite the gentleman. I've never needed to force my sexual attentions on any woman. No bed sharing for us until you're quite ready."

"No bed sharing, then," I replied. The smile flickered and faded. It returned, but lacking its former spontaneity. "I shouldn't be entirely sure of that. Now, I'm going to unload the rest of the food from the trunk and make myself a little something to eat. Will you join me? No?"

Makepeace brought in three large bags of groceries from outside which he unpacked into cupboards and a large fridge. He locked the car and triple locked the front door, then returned to the kitchen, where he began to pull cooking utensils out of a drawer.

He gave the appearance of being a practised cook and talked all the while he prepared his food. "Don't take it personally, but I'm giving myself the luxury of leaving you tied up for tonight. I'm overdue for a little shuteye, and I'm a wee bit nervous about your intentions. You haven't done anything to boost my confidence, Sarah. It doesn't feel as if we're singing off the same song sheet yet. Don't worry. I'm sure it's only a matter of time before we find ourselves in perfect harmony."

Makepeace walked across the room to the opposite wall, where he opened a cunningly concealed wall cabinet above a ledge and took out two large glasses. Ignoring the open whisky bottle on the kitchen counter, he pulled a second from the carton on the floor and waved it at me inquiringly. I shook my head.

"Wise girl. A silly habit." Makepeace opened the new bottle, poured himself a full tumbler, and placed the bottle on the ledge.

I turned my head away. Stretching out on the bed as fully as my handcuffed hands would allow, I lay back against the pillows and shut my eyes. I wriggled, searching and failing to find a position that came close to feeling comfortable. My irritation increased as the physical limitations of my situation became apparent.

"Would you like me to sing you a lullaby?" I stiffened. Makepeace had approached the bed so silently that the first intimation of his arrival was whisky-laden breath on my face. He laughed in my ear. Close. Too close.

Willing myself not to show the fear that I felt, I kept my face turned away. My captor sighed, straightened again and moved away.

For once, I welcomed the sensation of falling backward into darkness.

CHAPTER SIXTEEN

England 1620

He stood before her, feathered hat in hand.

In four years he had grown tall and filled out. A smudge of a moustache adorned his upper lip. Only his bright blue eyes and silky blond hair remained just as when they were last together. His clothes were extravagant and expensive. "Oh Frances, you are beautiful. Even more than I remembered. My God, how I do love you. I've never stopped thinking about you."

John Clavell fell to his knees and feverishly kissed her hand.

Frances gasped and jumped back, pulling her hand away. "John, get up at once. You must not speak in such a way. My husband or brother-in-law, or even the Prince, may return and come in upon us at any moment. I've only agreed to receive you because I feared your continuing attempts to see me would put us both at risk. You must know that your behaviour is unwise?"

"Unwise? I always told you that, after I went up to Oxford, I would come to you. You've kept me at arm's length long enough. You never responded to my letters, even before you told me to stop writing to you. Why did you turn your back on me, Frances? How could you forget our promises and give yourself in marriage to that disgusting old man? I hear he's not only soft in the head but impotent as well."

Frances stood twisting her hands. She had no idea how to respond to his accusations and insults. A sneer twisted John Clavell's mouth as he looked around him and continued, "I suppose you had to remain part of that in-crowd? Living in splendour in the Prince's Palace. A country boy like me holds no interest for one as grand as the great Lady Purbeck has become."

She took a deep breath and tried to stem his noxious flow. "John dear, please don't torture me or yourself with such unkind words. You know we were never promised to each other. If it brings you any relief to hear it from me again, the marriage I made was not of my personal choosing."

"Whose choosing then? The idiot's?"

Frances bit her lip. "My husband is neither soft in the head nor an idiot. He is a kind man and I try to be as good a wife as he deserves."

Clavell scoffed. "John Villiers is kind? Hah. Oh sorry, I suppose you would prefer I call him Viscount Purbeck, since the King gave him a title for a place he has never bothered to visit in his life. Anyway, whatever I choose to call him, all the world knows Lord Purbeck is crazy."

"All the world is wrong then and needs to mind its tongue," Frances snapped, then repented as she saw the stricken look that invaded John Clavell's face. "Please let's not fight. I beg your pardon if my marriage has caused you pain and disappointment, but it cannot be undone. I don't know why you even wanted to see me again. You must understand the impropriety of this situation. I so wish you had never come."

John Clavell grabbed her hand again and covered it with kisses, while Frances struggled once more to free herself. "I have come to take you away from here. I have the means to care for you at last."

She stopped struggling, momentarily diverted. "Did your uncle die, John?"

A sneer twisted his face. "No, nothing has changed with my family. My uncle is alive, in rude health and likely to remain so for many years, more's the pity. His humour does not improve. Papa is in the suds, as always. His latest fancy woman is a costly little number and Mama refuses to support him any more because of her. But he's doing fine now, ever since he managed to rope my sister's husband into paying his debts."

Frances flinched at John Clavell's story and the contempt in his tone. How hard it must be for John to have so little respect for his father. She remembered her own feelings, when confronted with Sir Edward Coke's weakness. She shuddered. It was not a memory of which she wished to be reminded.

She changed the subject, hoping to lighten the exchange. "Well, you must be in receipt of a handsome allowance, for you are looking very splendid."

John Clavell's face creased into a momentary smile before the scorn returned. "Actually, my uncle makes me a pathetic allowance, but thank God I don't have to depend only on that old bore any longer. I have found a capital way to make an independent living. I was determined to find the means to take you away and now I have."

"Are you no longer up at the university?"

Clavell gave a high-pitched laugh. "I'm still up at Brasenose, but I also have a great little affair going on the side, here in London. So, let me tell you what I have decided to do. I'm going to set you up in a cosy little place in Oxford, where nobody will think to look for you, until I have completed my studies. Then afterwards we can go wherever you like."

Something in his tone gave Frances misgivings. "What exactly is this great little affair?"

He laughed again and released her hand. Twirling his hat, he threw it in the air and caught it. "Least said soonest mended, my darling. You have no need to worry your pretty head. All you need know is that I've put enough put by already that we can leave right now. I can buy you dresses and anything else you may need. And, once you are installed in Oxford, I shall find you a maid."

"John, are you out of your mind? My brother-in-law has me watched day and night. Buckingham would find me and harm us both. Your life would be forfeit and I would be cast out of my home with no means of support."

Clavell moved forward again to take both of her hands, but Frances backed away from him.

"John, please put all such childish ideas out of your head. You must leave. Now. You truly put us both in grave danger by remaining. Please let's say farewell and content ourselves with memories of the happy times we shared as children."

A pink flush stained John Clavell's face. "I am disappointed in you, Frances." His hand moved to his smallsword. "I am not afraid of that pervert, Buckingham. It's common knowledge that he seduces our King and bleeds our country dry. And you are wondering about my business dealings? I assure you they are as honest as the day is long, by comparison with the kind of crimes committed by your Buckingham and his toadying Court cronies."

Frances flinched again but she spoke forcefully, "Lower your voice, if you value your life and mine. It is a brave man or a very foolish one who speaks thus in the home of the Prince of Wales. These walls have ears. I must require you to leave now, before I am obliged to call for help and we are both compromised by your presence."

At last, her words had penetrated. John Clavell bowed stiffly and his feathered hat brushed the floor. He marched stiffly to the door, where he turned and bowed. "Don't think I have given up my claim on you, Frances. We are meant to be together. Your servant, Madam. Remember what I have said. You shall be mine. It is only a question of when."

CHAPTER SEVENTEEN

California

The sun was beating in on my face. I opened my eyes. Closed them again. Opened them and blinked several times. As my handcuffed wrists came slowly back to life, other parts of my body began to complain. I moved stiff and swollen finger joints one by one, to stimulate my circulation, and felt the stabs of myriad pins and needles.

Light poured in through windows that I had not noticed during the previous evening. A scraping sound suggested that Makepeace was pinning shutters back outside. Framed by the nearest window, on the wall behind my head, a dark silhouette obscured much of the sky. A gaunt man appeared to be standing close, with his arms outstretched toward the heavens, as if in supplication. I twisted round as far as I could to get a better view and realized that the man in question was only a yucca.

I suddenly remembered a legend Bob had told on our first trip out into the desert, of pioneers heading west across the North American continent. When they first gazed upon a tree like this, they believed that ancient Joshua had appeared to guide them on the way to their promised land of milk and honey.

I pulled myself upright on the bed. My wrists were sore and, in the light of day, I examined my handcuffs more closely, wondering if it would be possible to remove them without a key. I twisted and turned, but my mobility was limited and efforts to slip the cuffs proved ineffective. I succeeded only in depleting my energy and further hurting my wrists. Weak and frustrated, I lay back against the pillows, trying to take comfort at least in my newfound conviction that I had identified our location.

Hinges squeaked as shutters at the studio end of the cabin opened and other yuccas came into view. Beyond the low trees, I could make out large granite rocks glinting yellow and orange in the early morning sun. The landscape was distinctive and it confirmed my initial impression.

Makepeace had driven us out into the Mojave Desert and, judging by the length of time we had travelled in the car, we must be in or near Joshua Tree National Park.

I recalled something else. The first time he drove me out to visit that park, Bob had told me that several of his contemporaries had built cabins out there. Several well-known musicians lived in the area year round. I wondered how close was our nearest neighbour.

The door swung open.

"Good morning, Sarah. How do you like our view in daylight?" Makepeace spoke brightly.

"I'd like it better if I could go outside and look around. When are you going to take off these handcuffs?"

"That's in your hands as much as mine. Hah! In your hands! Get it?" Makepeace closed the door, still tittering at his pun. I was not amused but at least, in full daylight, I no longer felt the fear that had gripped me in the night.

I tried to sound matter-of-fact. "I can bring charges against you for kidnapping. I need you to take me back to Ballantines immediately. Once you've done that, Mr. Makepeace, and as long as you then agree to stay out of my life completely, I won't report you."

Makepeace looked at me with his head on one side. "Sarah, my sweet, you do look attractive when you try to sound in charge. Especially after having slept in your clothes. That rumpled look becomes you. You're lucky. Most women look a sight in the morning. Let's get you something to eat. I'm sure you must be hungry."

He began to hum as he went to the kitchen. He poured himself a large tumbler of whisky and raised it toward me. "I'm partial to a liquid breakfast. Cheers, my dear." He drained the glass in one lingering gulp, then wiped his mouth and spoke again. "You must appreciate that I'm not releasing you until I feel certain that you don't intend to leave. I'm only thinking of you. We're miles from anywhere. People die in the desert if they travel alone and without the right gear. You're a city girl and, if I may say so, you're singularly ill-equipped for solo trav—"

In mid-word, Makepeace stopped and stared out of the window beside me. "Oh, look. Can you see it?"

He moved forward slowly and pointed. Reluctantly, I followed his gaze.

It was about fifteen inches long. Its head was square and dark. On its face, strategically placed pale patches created a comic moustachioed effect, but its dark hooked beak was unlikely to amuse potential prey. Alert eyes scanned the landscape for the slightest movement.

"It's an omen!" Makepeace sounded joyful. His eyes shone as blue as the sky on which he now gazed. I stared at him, attracted and repelled in the same moment. A distant bell rang in my mind. Somewhere and sometime in my past, whether in a movie or dream, I had watched eyes like these gaze with the same rapt intensity upon a bird of prey.

The falcon must have found something worthy of its investigation for it launched itself into flight and, with a single flap of its powerful wings, disappeared from view.

Makepeace looked back toward me. "Do you know how lucky we were to get such a close-up? They live here all year round, but that's the first time I've seen a prairie falcon this close to the cabin. They usually stay much higher up in those rocks, away from people. Amazing, although I'm glad he's gone. I've got Scott's Orioles nesting in that tree over there." He pointed toward another yucca further away. "I'm sure there's a nest hanging under the crown of that tree. Can you see where I mean?"

Moving quickly across to the bed, Makepeace seized one of my hands between his own. He did not seem to notice me wince. "You *are* glad to be here now, aren't you? This is the best time of year to be at the cabin, before it gets too hot. Once I can trust you not to run away, we'll take hikes together."

I gazed at Antony Makepeace, mesmerised. He sounded less like a ruthless captor and more like a boy on vacation, elated to have a new friend with whom to share his country passions. It was hard to believe that this Antony Makepeace intended to harm me.

As I watched him, he emerged from his own trance. "Right. I must get you some breakfast, unless you prefer a liquid diet like mine? No? I didn't think so. So I'll get you some food and then–" he consulted his watch, "and then we must decide exactly what we are going to tell our dear Mr. Howard when he calls."

"That part is easy, Antony." I decided to go for a friendly approach. "I'll tell Bob that you were playing a practical joke last night. I'll say there's nothing for him to worry about. He needn't try and join us out here at *Joshua Tree*, because you'll have taken me back to my hotel long before he can get a flight."

Makepeace's sudden stillness, when I emphasised the name of our likely location, spoke volumes. He narrowed his eyes. "Aha. So you think you know where you are, do you?"

"It wasn't difficult." I embroidered and pushed my guess to the limit. "I know how long we were on the road. I have a good sense of direction, even in the dark and I counted our turns. The blindfold actually made my job easier. Concentrated my senses, I suppose."

Gauging his reaction, I felt I might have succeeded at last in upsetting the balance of power between us. I attempted to consolidate any gain.

"So, take me back to Palm Springs as soon as we've had breakfast, Antony. Then we can say goodbye, with no hard feelings."

Makepeace stared through me. With what seemed like an effort at concentration, he brought his gaze back to my face. It was another moment or two before he replied, "A nice try. Quite courageous too, Sarah. But you don't imagine I went to all this effort just to hand you back to Bob Howard on a plate, do you? Sorry, I won't, not without getting what I want from him first."

"What exactly *do* you want from Bob?"

Makepeace offered me a beatific smile. "Oh, we can't spoil the surprise. I'm going to keep you in the dark until I tell Bob himself. It's more fun that way. Still, now that you *think* you know where you are, I have to revise my plan to let you speak with him. I expect that will make Bob cross, but it can't be helped. It's your fault, after all."

He returned to the kitchen, opened the door of the refrigerator and peered inside. "Tell me what you would like to eat. Cereal, toast, bagels, eggs? I do a great line in breakfasts. I've even got bacon in here. A good old English plate of bacon and eggs can be a perfect way to start the day out in the desert. You never quite know when you may eat again."

He took primary-coloured plates from a cupboard and French-style enamelled flatware from a drawer, then looked up. "If you promise to be well-behaved from now on, I'll make you some pancakes, Sarah. I make the best pancakes in the world. I saw a recipe with cottage cheese once, years ago on a Martha Stewart show. Just before she got busted."

He opened a cupboard and pulled out a packet of pancake mix. "I've been using it ever since, with this. I watch the food shows all the time when I'm in the USA. Best thing on American TV. Most of their stuff is such crap."

Without waiting for any comment from me, he turned back to the fridge. "Yes, I'm glad I remembered cottage cheese. I shopped early yesterday. Had to be up with the lark, so as not to miss you at your office. I was so well organised that I even remembered ice for the cooler. Everything was still cold when I unpacked last night."

I felt bemused. My mercurial kidnapper had now become the archetypal genial cooking show host, spreading breakfast ingredients out on the counter while he chattered and radiated fake charm. "I'm going to make you a wonderful breakfast. Now tell me you're glad you're here."

Unable to find words that might adequately express my feelings of the moment, I turned my face back toward the wall.

CHAPTER EIGHTEEN

England 1622

Closed curtains concealed the carriage's occupant and storm clouds looming over London offered further protection for the woman's identity. Reaching home before the heavens opened took priority for passers-by over wondering whom else might be out and about in the Strand.

The coach-and-four turned and passed through the ornate four-storey stone gateway of Suffolk House, before coming to a halt in the huge quadrangle outside one of its self-contained apartments adjacent to the river.

Frances descended into the hands of her smiling coachman. Mann had shown himself discreet and protective toward his mistress. He must be aware of what might happen to them both if Lady Purbeck were discovered here alone, where she should not be, by any who wished her ill. But the coachman gave no sign that he had been asked to transport his mistress anywhere out of the ordinary.

Her unaffected and courteous manner toward her servants had reaped dividends in terms of staff loyalty for Frances during her years at Denmark House. Many eyes observed and silently judged the injustice of Lady Purbeck's treatment at the hands of certain relatives although, within the army of servants at the Prince's Palace, some were in the pay of George Villiers to keep him informed of her movements. Frances would stake her life, did stake her life, on Mann not being among the latter.

She wrapped her cloak more tightly about her person and spoke in a low voice. "Thank you, Mann. I'll check whether he is in and, if so, I will want you to leave now and return in an hour. The carriage may draw attention, if you linger."

Mann nodded and bowed. "As you wish, m'Lady. I'll send word via the footman of my return." He stood watching until the door to the apartment had opened and Lady Purbeck had been received within.

Then he climbed back onto his seat and retrieved the reins from his young groom.

"So it's round the 'ouses and through the parks and back again for us, m'lad. Let's 'ope we don't get a soaking along the way." Mann cracked his whip. Four bays with matching white socks sprang into synchronised action. Lord Purbeck's carriage wheeled around the quadrangle, out through the gateway and turned left toward the Mall.

The apartment Frances entered was handsomely furnished. The political influence of the Suffolks had plummeted during their differences with the King but, by the time Steenie had persuaded His Majesty to strip the Earl of his wealth, the cupboard belonging to the head of the House of Suffolk was conveniently bare. The Countess of Suffolk rivalled the Buckinghams in her scheming and, thanks to his wife's foresight, Lord Thomas had already signed away most of his vast fortune.

"My Lady?" The footman bowed.

Frances loosened her outer garment. "Where is Sir Robert? Would you tell him he has a visitor, please?"

"I'm here, Frances."

The man stood framed in his library doorway, with his arms opened wide to receive Frances. Ignoring all proprieties before his servant, she dropped her cloak and rushed into them.

"Thank God you are here, Robert. I was so afraid you might be away from home. Forgive me for bursting in upon you like this, unescorted and without notice. I hate to put you and your family to embarrassment on my account, but I could stand my situation no longer and have nobody else to talk with."

"Hush, my dear. My father and Theophilus are out of town and only Thomas and Edward are in residence this week. It is nobody's business but ours if you visit me and, even were it unwise, I would count it well worth the risk for the joy of seeing you."

Sir Robert guided Frances into his library. "My sweet, you're freezing. Come in and warm yourself by the hearth, and then you shall tell me what has upset you." Seating her by the fire, he took chilled hands within his own and kissed her pale fingers one by one. "My poor darling. You are icy. I had no idea the day was so cold. Now what has happened, to put you in such a pass?"

"George has insisted my Lord should stay with him at Wallingford House during this last week, while his latest distemper has been growing upon him. He said that he wished to act before the Prince felt obliged to order Purbeck out of the palace again."

Robert rubbed her hands. "Well, it's happened several times before, hasn't it?"

Frances shook her head. "Not like this. John insisted that he wanted me with him, yet I was barred even from accompanying him to Wallingford House. I am only allowed to visit him now by day, when either his mother or George is present. They pretend it is safer for me, but they just want me kept out of his bed. It's stupid, for John becomes more upset when forcibly separated from me."

"I sympathise with Purbeck. I hate every moment I am separated from you. But go on. This has happened previously, so why are you so overset this time?"

"This morning I went to visit. John was awake, but not dressed. He descended as soon as he heard my voice. He entered Kate's withdrawing room and smiled at me, with that vacant expression he wears when all seems in order and yet is far from well. You know?"

Robert nodded.

"He sat with Kate and me so calm and sweet and good-humoured. Then all of a sudden, he jumped to his feet and shouted, 'You shall never detain me against my wish or in any religion against my will,' and then he ran out of the room."

"Was anyone threatening him, at the time?"

"No, but Kate told me afterward he had been in a physical scuffle with Buckingham, just before I arrived. Anyway, Purbeck rushed out of the front door and ran up and down outside Wallingford House. People stared, because he was in his nightclothes. Then he screamed for the whole world to hear that we were all converting and nobody should stop us."

"Oh, Dear Lord. What happened next?"

Frances shuddered as she recalled the scene. "Buckingham quickly had him brought back inside and taken upstairs by the servants. But George flew into a frenzy with me. He said I was inciting John to Papism to embarrass his family, which is untrue. He swore that John had been quite relaxed until I came, which according to what Kate said must also have been a lie."

Her companion shrugged. "It's widely known that the Countess of Buckingham has threatened to convert. She's only recanted now from fear of being sent away from Court," Robert hugged Frances close as he continued, "George need look no further than to his own mother for any religious influence on Purbeck. And your father and mother are such staunch Protestants that nobody will believe misplaced talk against you."

"But there's worse than that, Robert. George said he has proof I have consorted with sorcerers to place evil spells on John, and has witnesses who will swear to it. He called me a second Countess of Somerset. He said I share Frances Howard's name and nature and I am another evil whore just waiting my time to commit murder."

Sir Robert disengaged abruptly, rose and paced the room. When Frances saw his face, her hand flew to her mouth. "I'm so sorry, my love. I should not have repeated those cruel words about your own sister."

As fresh tears spilled down her cheeks, Robert resumed his seat again, and held her tight against him. She could feel the tension in his body.

"It's unacceptable that George submits you to this continual bullying and that his family colludes in it. You will have to leave Purbeck and that whole cursed brood of Buckinghams, my darling. I must find a means to take you away, or else I shall end by calling the man out."

She raised her head and sniffed. "Dearest, where can we go? You have no property expectations and my portion barely covers my pin money. I cannot stay here or at Audley End. Your father would be compromised and things are difficult enough for him already."

"If only Eliza could be prevailed upon to help."

Again Frances shook her head. "Mama already blames me for being indiscreet. She disapproves of us and will never sanction our living together outside marriage. We can't blame her. Even if, by some miracle, she would allow us to live quietly at one of her more distant manors, she would only be pursued by George and quite possibly confined again."

She searched for a handkerchief before continuing, "Buckingham intends me never to be alone with John again, for fear I fall with child. Yet, unless the inheritance issue is settled with Mama, he will not allow me freedom to leave and live my own life. So I am caught in his trap."

Robert grimaced. "I curse the day His Majesty allowed that devil to get such a hold over him and the affairs of our nation. You're right, Frances. We can't embarrass your mother and it would take only one slip-up with the King at present for my parents to find themselves back in the Tower."

He stared into the fire. "It's ridiculous that one man and his conniving mother can run roughshod over us all. I feel so useless that I can offer you no protection."

Concern for her lover pushed Frances to regain her composure. She took the handkerchief Robert had offered her and blew her nose vigorously.

"Kate suggested today that my Lord and I might go abroad again to Spa, to take the waters. She reminded us how it seemed to help his condition a couple of years ago. But George bade her be silent in such a rough way that I could see he had quite wounded her. She is right though, Robert. John is always calmer when he is away from London and his family. I swear his mother and brother are the ones who distress him, not me."

"I've heard Richard Napier is of the same opinion, at least about the effect of his mother on Purbeck. Having treated her benighted husband, it is one reason why he has been so loath to take the poor fellow on as a patient."

"You would have thought it would be in everybody's interest to use my influence to have John as calm and well as possible. My Lord is forever telling them that I am his best tonic. We must just pray that Kate will give George a son, and then perhaps the pressure on Purbeck and me may cease."

A gust of wind whistled down the chimney and smoke blew back into the room. It brought tears of a different kind to Frances's eyes. The couple sat together in a dejected silence. Too soon for them both, a tapping heralded the return of the young footman. Frances's cloak was in his hand.

"Excuse me, my Lady, but your carriage has returned. Since it's very close to raining now, your coachman thought you might wish…"

His voice tapered off at sight of his master's face, but Frances rose and held out her hand for the cloak. "Thank you. Yes, if it is going to rain, I should leave now. Please go and tell Mann I will be with him directly."

The footman bowed and withdrew.

"Must you go, my sweet? The storm may pass. With Purbeck at Wallingford House, your absence will surely not be remarked at the palace. Doesn't the Prince spend most of his time over at St James's instead of Denmark House these days?"

Frances turned back to Robert who had also risen. She pressed his hand to her cheek. "My dearest, I've courted danger enough for us both today, by coming here so openly. I cannot leave the carriage outside as a visiting card, and I will not ask Mann to drive around in the rain."

He took her in his arms. "May I come to you this evening via Isabel Peel?" He sounded plaintive, as always when parting was upon them.

Frances shook her head and sighed, feeling obliged to be strong for them both. "It is too dangerous for you to come to Denmark House at the moment, with George making such open threats against me."

His voice broke. "It is agony to live a lie, when we are neighbours and thrown together so often at public gatherings."

Fresh tears streamed down Frances's face and Robert tightened his hold. She wrenched herself away. "No more, please. I cannot bear it."

Pulling her cloak around her, she hurried from the library. Robert Howard sat heavily back on the couch and groaned as he placed his head in his hands.

CHAPTER NINETEEN

California

The mobile phone rang at eight o'clock sharp.

Bless you, Bob, I said silently.

Makepeace paced the room, with my phone held to his ear. "Good morning, Bob. Or rather, good afternoon. What's the weather like in London today?"

He winked at me, but then his expression changed. His voice wavered, before becoming once again forcedly jocular. "Are you really? Marvellous what they do on aeroplanes these days, dear boy. The line is so clear, isn't it?" He pointed at the phone and mouthed at me, "Bob's speaking from a plane," then continued, "I can't imagine why you had to go running back to L.A., old man. Such a pity. You have no idea where your delicious girlfriend and I have shacked up together. Hawaii? Vancouver? Cabo?"

He listened, then shook his head violently. "Bob, you're making things unnecessarily difficult for yourself and me. A natural knee-jerk reaction, but you should have stayed put until you got my orders." After another short pause, he spoke again. "No, that won't be possible."

Now I could hear Bob's voice raised and agitated. Makepeace held the cell phone away from his ear and gesticulated with a wry expression. I said nothing as he put the phone close and spoke again. "Keep your hair on, old man. I know what I said last night. But it's not my fault. You can blame Sarah. She thought she knew where we were. She's wrong and it doesn't help to feed you wrong information. Anyway, you're making enough of a mess of things on your own today."

He drew breath and it was my cue. "Bob, we're at his cabin in the desert. Joshua Tree." I yelled as loud and clearly as I could.

Makepeace whirled and turned his back. "Bob, I'm afraid you must ring off and call back in ten minutes. Sarah and I need a little talk. Ten minutes should be enough for me to put her straight."

He pressed the disconnect button, stood for a moment then turned and walked slowly across the room toward the bed. I lay still and stared up at the knife that had appeared in his hand.

Bending over me, Makepeace spoke into my face. "Try – anything – like – that – again – and – you – are – dead – meat. Do you understand, bitch?" Dry-mouthed and heart thudding, I nodded. He breathed heavily and stood back. "Let's go over some ground rules. You will stay handcuffed to this bed. You will not speak to Bob when he calls back. If you try to shout at him again, I – will – harm – you. Got it, Sarah?" I nodded again. Makepeace's voice remained bitter. "You stupid bitch. I can take you places far more remote than this, and much less comfortable. Remember that. You see a couple of yuccas and think you know where you are? Don't be so bloody quick to jump to conclusions."

He turned abruptly and walked across to the table next to the kitchen. He put the mobile phone on the table, threw himself into a chair, and brooded. I lay, silent and shaken. Makepeace spoke in a carping tone. "God, what a hopeless pair. You jump to wrong conclusions. He jumps on a plane." He stared at the phone as if it were somehow to blame for our transgressions.

I found my voice. "What did you expect either of us to do? Sit back and wait for you to pull our strings like marionettes?" He looked up and frowned. Against the odds, I suddenly found myself wanting to laugh. Makepeace had the air of a petulant child deprived of a treat. It was hard for me to believe that the same man had threatened me with a knife just moments before.

Was Makepeace capable of following through on his threat to harm me? I did not think so, but I was not about to test the theory. I tried another route. "Antony, you said when we met that you wanted to talk. Let's do that, while we're waiting for Bob to call back. What did you want to share with me?"

Makepeace looked up and through me again. He did not respond.

"Did you want to talk to me? Or were you just trying to get at Bob through me? Is holding me a way to persuade him to do something for you?" Silence. I shrugged. "If and when you do want to talk, really talk I mean, I'm ready to listen."

Makepeace stood up and came back over to the bed. He stood looking down at me. "I can't talk to you properly when you're tied up. It won't work." His voice was almost conversational again.

I forced myself to respond with a laugh. "Well, if that's a problem, untie me. I won't object."

Makepeace shook his head. "I'm disappointed in you and Bob. I expected better from you both." The fretful note was back. But as he turned, something caught Makepeace's eye and his expression changed.

"Look. There they are. Mr. and Mrs. Scott's Oriole, sitting over on our yucca." I followed the direction of his pointing arm.

The birds were on separate limbs of the yucca. The male, resplendent in a coat of black and gold, sat several inches above his smaller, greenish yellow companion. "If I can just open this window a fraction without disturbing them, you may be able to hear his call. Keep listening. After he sings, she may answer." He opened the window gently as he spoke.

I was becoming as curious as I was apprehensive of these abrupt and frequent changes in attention and mood. Makepeace now seemed absorbed again in the birds. My professional interest was aroused. I began to review aspects of his behaviour since we met. The process had the additional advantage that it released me from feeling like a victim.

Before Makepeace had succeeded in fully opening the window, the phone rang again. "Damn him. What a moment to call. Now he's scared them off." He shut the window and grumbled his way back to the phone. "Damn you, Bob. Your timing always was bad." His complaint quickly turned to laughter. "Well, your timing is way out there, too. If you will go junketing around in a plane, what do you expect?"

Makepeace sat back down at the table and stretched long denim-clad legs out in front of him. He picked casually at a piece of lint on his knee and continued in light-hearted vein. "Man, have you never received lessons on how to behave with a kidnapper? I can do something nasty to your girlfriend here, if you make me lose my temper. Or maybe I'll do something *nice* with her instead. Serve you right. You once told a journalist I was Mr. Excessive Incarnate. Remember how pissed off I was? See, I don't forget those things."

I was mystified. Makepeace spoke now like a kid, out to settle playground scores. But I had not imagined the knife. And I had not dreamed his earlier fury. My captor was a volatile enigma of a man. He continued. "Look, Bob, you're no slouch. You must know what I want." A longer pause. Then, "Well, you're not completely off course. But I'm thinking bigger than Nights of the Road. I've developed my original idea. Let me run it by you."

He made an expansive gesture with his free hand. "A full-scale new British Invasion, but this time with all my bands and me on the one bill. What do you think?" He listened then grimaced. "No, you don't get my drift. Instead of concentrating on old stuff, we take one band from each decade and then bring things up to date with Jax. Isn't that a clever notion?" Makepeace put his hand over the mouthpiece and whispered to me, as if I was a fellow conspirator, "He's slow on the uptake. It'll take him a moment or two to catch up with us, but he'll love the idea to bits, when he does."

Apparently Bob did not love the idea to bits, for an edge returned to Makepeace's voice. "Ah, but you don't have any choice. If you want Sarah back safe and sound, you'll do what I tell you." He drummed his fingers on the table. "How do you know I've even got Sarah? Come on, man. You heard her yell at you earlier. Would I go to all this trouble if I had nothing on you? If I didn't have her, how would I have her mobile phone? Bob, do us both the favour of putting your mind in gear before you speak. Wait a minute, though."

His eyes narrowed. "Didn't you hear her shout earlier? No?" A grin stretched from ear to ear. "I'm *so* sorry you didn't hear her. Listen, I'll tell you what–" Makepeace changed hands with the phone as he turned to face me. "I won't have her talk to you because she isn't cooperating. But I'm a reasonable man. I can understand you need to know the bitch is alive. If she was already dead, she'd be less of a bargaining chip, wouldn't she?"

Again I heard a raised voice from the phone. Makepeace giggled. "Sorry, dear boy. I didn't mean to call her a bitch. Now listen. You can ask me a question for which only she could know the answer. I ask her. She tells me. I tell you." He listened. Then, "Fine. Sarah, what is the name of your ex and when did you leave him?"

I itched to ignore the man and his puerile behaviour. But I wanted Bob to know I was OK. "My ex is John Villiers. We… we have been separated for – for more than two and a half years."

Makepeace mimicked my tone, including the way I fell over my words. Then, "What? Oh, for God's sake, man." He made a face. "Sarah, that wasn't enough. Bob wants to know when and where you last talked with John Villiers in person."

"It was in October, more than two years ago. I don't remember the exact date. It was a Sunday. We went for a walk by the Serpentine."

"Oh that is precious. October, eh? Seasons of mists and mellow fruitfulness. Listen, Bob, I'll sing you a clue, like on the quiz shows." Makepeace warbled in a high-pitched falsetto the words of a song I recognised. "Take me to a park all covered with trees. Tell me on a Sunday please." He followed it up with, "The falling leaves drift by my window."

Smirking at me, he spoke into the phone. "Get it, Bob? Park? Autumn leaves? October? Sunday? And she said Serpentine too. Satisfied now?" Makepeace laughed at the answer, but his voice became business-like. "Now let's cut to the chase. You've got a lot to organise. I don't mind if you line up a '60s band as an opening act. In fact, yes, let's get some tired, old men of rock to open up for me. They deserve that, after treating all the rest of us like shit, when we started out."

He stood and walked to the window where he had looked out on the birds, still alternately listening and talking. "Why? Well, that's tough. Get 'em back. It would be good for any of that bunch to have to eat humble pie. You know the rest of the line-up. What?" He listened again. "Yes. Moonlight Jax headlines. Road Agents next on the bill and Toe-bee Men, if we can get the guys together, all along for the ride. Nights of the Road will have yours truly as lead singer, just in case you had any doubts. Ah, what a night of the road it's going to be."

Makepeace was talking fast now. "OK. Go to it, Bob. I don't want to hear from you again until you've got a twelve-gig US tour sewn up. No, on second thoughts, you had better call me at this time each day on Sarah's number with a progress report." He consulted his watch. "So, if you're in L.A., that will be at... eight-thirty Pacific Time tomorrow morning. Be punctual, please. Gotta go now. Sarah and I are bird watching. Good-bye, dear boy."

He turned off the mobile phone and replaced it on the table. Humming a tune that he had sung to Bob, he went to his drink cupboard, took out a clean glass and poured a tumbler of whisky. He turned, raised the glass to me and swallowed its contents. "Cheers, my dear. I wonder how quickly your Bob will get his act together. Or rather my acts together. Want a drink?"

I ignored his invitation. "So I was just a lever to get Bob to jump to your bidding? You want him to set up a tour for you. But why create this elaborate game of kidnapping me? You've only made trouble for yourself."

Makepeace shrugged. "I guess we knights of the road just have to flex our muscles sometimes, Sarah. Stand and deliver! Get it? In this case you'll stand and Bob will deliver. Oh, I forgot. You can't stand at the moment, can you? Well, later maybe I'll let you get up off that bed for a while." He refilled his glass and raised it once more in my direction.

"By the wa–ay," his voice had begun to slur, "smart you may be, but you're wrong. You're more than a lever to get at Bob. I've got some questions for you, pretty lady. I'll ask them. When I'm ready to stand and deliver."

CHAPTER TWENTY

England 1624

"The man is a brute. Damn Buckingham. Damn Robert Howard. Damn your father. Damn Coke especially, for all that he has put me through these many years."

"Please, Mama!"

But Lady Hatton was already in full flood. "I should never have married him. I've never had a moment's peace since my wedding night. He steals my property and beats my child, and then will not raise a hand to help her, when she is in trouble of his making."

"Mama, there is no use blaming Papa. Only the King would be able to stop George now, and we all know he won't. I cannot find it in me to condemn Papa when I go in such fear of Buckingham myself."

"Franny, you always were too nice for your own good. And you've always made excuses for your father. You exasperate me, child. No wonder Buckingham always seeks to get at me through you. He knows you are my Achilles' heel. I'm the only one to try and stand against him. I sacrifice my peace of mind and suffer all kinds of unpleasantness, just to safeguard you and your inheritance. Was ever anyone more put upon than me?"

Elizabeth Hatton's reproaches plunged Frances into a torment of guilt. Once again, she was being held responsible for her mother's suffering. She had lately begun to wonder if Lady Hatton used the theme to avoid any self-criticism. Certainly, Eliza had never suggested to anyone, least of all to her daughters, that she was a less than perfect mother. Frances quelled the rebellious train of thought and chastised herself silently for being mean-spirited. Her mother was giving her a much-needed roof over her head.

Eliza was off again. "I think the less of Charles for letting you to be thrown out of the palace. I always knew that boy was sly. To think he will be our King one day. It does not bode well for our nation. Well, I'm obliged to have you stay here, now George has had you put out in the street, for where else can you go? A mother as caring as I could hardly shut the door upon her own daughter. Even one who has brought this on herself."

Frances flinched. She had known no alternative than to seek help from her mother. All doors in Town had shut on her, from the moment that Buckingham secured her eviction from the Prince's Palace, in spite of Lord Purbeck's protests.

John had been kindness itself to Frances during these last months. His health had been stable since his extended time with Sir Richard Napier. He had been calm while his brother was overseas and had fulfilled many of George's responsibilities at Court, while Buckingham was in Spain with Charles, trying to secure the Infanta in marriage for the Prince. Even so, John had been powerless now to prevent his wife's eviction.

Eliza returned to the mirror and studied her reflection, talking at the same time. "Of course, I do run a serious risk of incurring His Majesty's displeasure, by taking you in, Frances. Oh well, if I am confined again, I dare say I shall find the strength to bear it. God knows I have already put up with so much, through all these years of protecting you."

After applying a beauty spot to porcelain skin, Eliza turned to her daughter, her eyes sparkling. "Franny, I have the solution. We'll go to Stoke and insist that your father take action on your behalf. He hides away in my house with his law books, while I am left to suffer the slings and arrows hurled at me by Buckingham and Society, in my efforts to protect you. It won't do."

Lady Hatton expanded upon her intent to share the parental load of their daughter's problems. Frances voiced doubts at the likely success of such a venture but, back at the mirror, her mother was not to be deterred. "You need sound advice, Franny. Does George have the legal right to separate you from your husband? Coke is not going to sit there, squandering my hard-won wealth and refusing to lift a finger to help you. It's time for him to earn his keep."

Privately Frances reflected that her mother's wealth had been won through Lady Hatton outliving her first husband; an unremarkable achievement, given the gap in their respective ages. Aloud she said, "Mama, we know George will do anything to avoid me giving Purbeck an heir. And he gets the King's full support to ignore the law, whenever it suits him."

Eliza shook her head. "Well, your father's stupid ambition and his carelessness with the King got us into this dreadful alliance. We will remind him of that. Now, how shall we manage things?"

Apparently satisfied at last with her appearance, Lady Hatton turned from her mirror and began the arduous task of juggling her social calendar. "We can't leave today. It's too late and I am promised to Holles for the play this evening. Tomorrow I am to picnic with Gondomar. The day after – is that free? Yes, the day after tomorrow will serve. We shall go to Stoke and tell your father he must make things right. What do you think of that, Franny?"

Before Frances could respond, another question presented itself to Elizabeth. "I wonder about our escort?"

"Do we need an escort, Mama? Stoke is not so far. We can be there and back in daylight, if we leave early."

"With the roads as they are, travelling without a man is unthinkable. And unspeakably dreary too." A gleam lit Eliza's eyes again. "Edward cannot stand Holles, so we'll take him. Dear John is always such diverting company and he'll be a perfect protector. I'll tell him tonight, at the play. You'll see. He will enliven our journey. What fun we shall have!"

For Frances the visit was far from fun. Sir Edward Coke could not bar his wife entry to her own manor. He did, however, refuse to engage with Eliza, as soon as he understood that she intended him to take responsibility for his youngest daughter's plight. Bluntly he announced that Frances had brought her misfortune upon herself. She had always been a hoyting girl. Now she was become a hussy and a Jezebel, and must bear the blame for having given Buckingham a lever to secure her downfall. She was ruined in the eyes of the Polite World and His Majesty, and also a severe embarrassment to Coke.

"You were a brazen little fool to encourage the advances of another man. You were doubly a fool to imagine you could engage in clandestine meetings with one of Suffolk's cubs without being discovered. My God, Frances, what were you thinking of?" Sir Edward paced the room and his beard bobbed up and down. The sight reminded Frances of her wedding day. Her misery deepened.

Coke spun round and glared at his daughter. "Why couldn't you keep your nose clean, my girl? You should have stayed at home and attended to being a good wife to your maniac of a husband. And what a weak fool he's turned out to be, letting his brother push him around."

Something snapped inside Frances when her father spoke disparagingly of John Villiers. "You married me to my maniac of a husband when it suited your purposes, Papa. I can assure you my Lord is far from weak when he hits me, although not as strong as you. Did you mean to sell me to a wife-batterer? Have you reaped the reward you hoped for from that transaction?"

Frances stopped, horrified at her own outburst.

"Bravo, darling." Eliza Hatton clapped her hands.

Sir Edward's eyes blazed and he took a step toward his daughter, his hand raised and his fist clenched. Frances's heart fell into her soft kid boots. It was here in Stoke that she had received the beating of her life.

The tall and elegant frame of Sir John Holles inserted itself between Frances and Sir Edward. "It's one thing to refuse to help a daughter in difficulties, Coke. I may condemn that privately, but it's your own affair. It's quite another matter to raise your hand against a young woman who has already suffered enough at your hands. Do you expect me to stand by and let you beat Frances in my presence? You and I have been reared in different schools, sir. I've shot a man for less."

Elizabeth Hatton clapped her hands again and cheered loudly. "Bless you, Holles, you darling man. What a good thing we brought you with us."

Lady Hatton moved forward and took her daughter's arm. "Come along, Frances. Let's consign this pathetic old man to his law reports. How could I have imagined we might secure justice from a former Lord Chief Justice? We'll leave your father to hide away in the home he enjoys through my generosity."

Eliza's evident high spirits at the latest humiliation of her husband took no account of the fact that her daughter's situation remained unresolved. Frances sat white-faced and silent in the coach, as Lady Hatton replayed events. "Franny, aren't you glad now that I insisted we bring Holles? Depend on it, your father will be in agonies, wondering what we will tell the world about our visit. He'll skulk away in Stoke for months. Oh darling, try and look a little more cheerful. I can't think why you are so glum."

Frances said nothing. Eliza shrugged and turned her attention to Sir John. "Look, Holles. Over there. I swear that must be the ditch we turned over in, on our way to rescue Frances all those years back, when Coke was beating the poor child black and blue." Lady Hatton stroked their escort's arm. "Remember how we had to put up at a poky little post house until the wheel could be fixed? And how you kept me cheerful, when I was out of my mind with worry for my darling girl? And here you are, our rescuer again, defending Frances against that savage brute. Such a perfect way for Coke to get his comeuppance, don't you think?"

What John Holles thought would not be known, for the coach shuddered to a halt and its occupants fell against each other. Amidst neighing horses, a cursing coachman and creaking timbers, a voice shouted, "Stand and deliver!"

With a terse ejaculation, Sir John Holles was out of his seat and fumbling for his pistols. The two women stared at each other and turned to the carriage door, as it swung open and a voice boomed, "Descend, ladies."

Sir John pushed himself back into the shadows, put a finger to his lips and gesticulated that his companions should descend. Lady Hatton stared and frowned. In Frances, light of understanding dawned. She spoke quickly, in a high, clear voice. "Come, Mama. Do as the man says or he may shoot. Oh dear, you and I should never have travelled without an escort today." So saying, Frances stepped down and out of the carriage, straight into a drawn pistol.

The masked man appeared to be alone.

Lady Hatton had evidently caught on too, for she was talking as she descended. "What do you want, you knave? Jewels? Money? Can't you find a better way to scratch a living than to frighten two poor and defenceless women alone on the King's Highway? Shame on you, sir!"

"Defenceless, maybe. But I never heard anyone call you poor, Lady Hatton. Don't worry. You can keep your jewels. Except for the priceless one."

The voice was familiar and unexpectedly cultivated, but it took Frances a moment to recognise her masked assailant. As she did so, a single shot rang out from within the coach. Blood spurted over a hand that, seconds before, had been holding a pistol. Their assailant clutched at his wounded wrist and swore. "Goddamn it! I'm hit!"

"You're lucky. I was tempted to put a ball in your head. However, I prefer to see ruffians like you brought to public justice. Making an example of you may deter others." Sir John Holles had swung from the carriage as he spoke, exhibiting agility and speed for a man nearly sixty years old. He wrenched Clavell's unmarked arm high up behind his back and called up to the coachman, who still sat as if glued to his seat. "Have you a rope or spare harness, man? Lend me a hand to tie up this rogue. Jump to it!"

The coachman scrambled down to do Sir John's bidding.

"Please don't tie him up, Sir John. I know this man." Frances giggled. "You know him too, Mama."

"What can you mean? I am quite sure I don't know any thieves. Especially not cowardly curs that hold people up on the road."

"Mama, it is John Clavell. Remember the boy I used to ride out with when I was a child at Corfe Castle? He always talked of becoming a highwayman, but I never thought he meant it."

Holles ripped off the mask. Exposed to view, John Clavell's face was pale and screwed up in pain. He glared at his captor. "Damn you sir, for spoiling everything. I am only out to recover what belongs to me."

Lady Hatton stepped forward and tapped John on his wounded wrist, which elicited a shriek of pain. "I can't think what you are talking about,

John Clavell. None of us has anything that belongs to you. What an impertinence. What do you think you are about, playing such a trick on us? Does your uncle know how you spend your days?"

Clavell scowled. "If you had allowed me to marry your daughter, Lady Hatton, I would not need to spend my day holding up your coach. Frances was promised to me long ago. If you and Sir Edward Coke had honoured that commitment, she might today be a happy woman and you a contented grandmother, instead of mother-in-law to a sterile madman."

Frances spoke sharply. "John, how dare you speak of my husband like that? And you know I made you no promise."

He swung toward her. "You lie, Frances. And I won't support your lies any more."

Sir John Holles spoke. "You young fool, this is no way to go on. Do you imagine the way to a woman's heart is by accusing her of lying? Did you expect to carry Lady Purbeck off into a lifetime of bliss with such sensitive wooing? I wonder how you were planning to dispose of her lawful husband. And how far you think you would have got before being arrested for kidnapping. You're lucky to escape with no more than a grazed hand."

John Clavell reddened. "I don't know who you are, sir, but I don't like you or your interfering ways. Nor do I appreciate your patronising tone."

"Well, that is altogether too bad, sir. I happen to know exactly who you are, now that Lady Purbeck has furnished us with your name. You're that young scoundrel Lord Loftus baled out of trouble once, for stealing your college's silver plate. You don't seem to have learned much since your student days."

John Clavell looked down at his wrist. "It won't stop bleeding."

"Use this. Bind it tight. And stop your damned fuss about a flesh wound. You're not dying. Yet." Sir John Holles passed Clavell his handkerchief, and turned back to the women. "Eliza, Frances, what do you propose we do with this fellow? Shall we deliver him into custody and press charges? Or is the stupid young fool to be let loose in the world again? My inclination is to get him locked up, before he does some serious damage, but it's your choice."

Frances stared at her childhood friend. "John, I told you, when you saw me at the palace, that I would not come with you. Nothing has changed."

He responded hotly. "It has. I've kept watch on you. The Duke of Buckingham has had you thrown out of the palace. You and Lord Purbeck are separated. One of your mother's maids tells me all your movements. That's how I knew you were going to Stoke. The stupid girl didn't tell me this fellow would be with you, though." Clavell glared again at Holles.

"One of *my* maids? Tell me her name. I'll turn her off on the instant." Lady Hatton looked and sounded furious.

Frances held up a hand. "Mama, please be quiet for a moment. John, listen to me. However things stand between my husband and me, I will never live with you. I have the strongest possible reason for saying this."

Clavell clenched his jaw. His voice became gruff. "I know you have been consorting with another man, but I'm willing to forgive you for that. I can understand you must have been lonely."

Frances took a deep breath. "John dear, I've known that man since my childhood, much longer than I've known you. I love him and my love is reciprocated. We may never be able to be together but, because of my feelings for him, I could never go away with you."

John Clavell stared at Frances. The remaining blood drained from his face and momentarily it looked as though he might collapse. Then he stiffened, gave a little bow and half turned toward Sir John Holles. He spoke in a clipped voice. "Do what you will with me, sir. It does not matter any more. If you choose to let me go, I give you my word that I will not trouble you or either of these ladies again."

Holles looked at Frances with an inquiring expression. What he read in her face led him to drop Clavell's arm. "Be on your way, then, and look for a doctor to patch up that scratch. I'll give you a hand to mount."

"I don't need your hand." John Clavell pushed the older man aside and picked up the reins of his horse. He mounted with difficulty and gathered the reins awkwardly. He bowed to Eliza and Sir John. "Excuse me for having detained you, Lady Hatton. Your servant, sir."

He turned in the saddle, looked at Frances and, in a tone heavy with reproach, uttered a single word. "Good-bye."

John Clavell wheeled and rode away into the deepening dusk.

Silence reigned.

Holles grunted. "Ladies, I suggest we resume our journey before it is entirely dark." He nodded to the coachman, now standing expressionless at the head of his lead horse. "Come on, man. Let's get going." He opened the carriage door and invited his companions to enter. Climbing in behind them, he slammed the door shut and rapped on the roof from within. The coach lurched forward.

Lady Hatton was the first to break their silence. "Well, what a to-do. So here we are, beholden to you twice in one day, Holles. My darling privy councillor, I am going to have to reward you handsomely. I wonder how?" She laid a hand upon Sir John Holles's sleeve and smiled up into his eyes. Holles looked at her with a hint of a grin playing at the corner of his mouth.

Frances averted her gaze and stared out of the coach window. Her face was wooden. She prayed that her mother and her flirt would ignore her for the rest of the journey. Lady Purbeck wanted neither of them to guess how deeply affected she had been by two such painful encounters with men who had each occupied an important place in her heart.

CHAPTER TWENTY-ONE

California

I came to with a start. And with a scream stuck in my throat.

A whiff of whisky announced Makepeace's presence, even before I detected the outline of his hunched body in the darkened cabin. He was only inches from me, leaning forward on a chair that he must have placed beside the bed while I slept. I assumed it was the middle of night, but I had no way of knowing, since all the shutters were closed and the lights were out.

Once again, I had been obliged to sleep with my wrists handcuffed and suspended above my head. Afraid to make a noise, I shifted my weight and exclaimed involuntarily as pain shot up my arms. As my senses returned, I became aware that the energy now emanating from my captor was in stark contrast to that of the previous day.

After the call from Bob, Makepeace had assumed the role of an attentive host, and responded with courtesy to almost all my physical needs. He checked that the cabin's air conditioning was set at a comfortable temperature. He cooked meals. He let me take a shower and even washed out by hand the crumpled dress from which I had changed. He appeared to enjoy domesticity.

Throughout the afternoon and evening, ignoring the fact that he still held me captive, Makepeace was a pleasant, even a charming, companion. He watched for birds; he read, and he spent time in his music studio. The one thing over which he remained intransigent was keeping me cuffed to the bed.

Now everything had changed. I could feel his gaze burn into me. Without warning, he shone a flashlight in my face. I turned my head away.

"Why did you do it, Frances? Why wouldn't you wait for me?"

Shock ran through me. Makepeace had just called me *Frances*. How did he know my middle name?

"Nobody calls me Frances."

He continued as if I had not spoken. "I wouldn't believe it, not when you first told me. I thought you were telling lies, to try and make me forget you. As if I ever could."

"What lies was I telling?"

"Don't play around with me. I saw through your act from the beginning. You know who I am and I know who you are."

"Why did you just use my middle name?"

His response was to shine the flashlight on me again. I felt confounded. Until now, Antony Makepeace's moods had been volatile, but I would not have described him as delusional. His mental condition must be more fragile than I had assumed, unless he was trying some convoluted mind game on me.

I racked my brains. Could anything in my purse have given him the clue to my middle name? My driving licence had my middle initial, but it was a stretch from seeing a single letter F to matching it with Frances. I tried to dissolve the tension. "Please turn on the light. It's so much easier to talk when we can see each other."

Makepeace ignored my request. His voice was high-pitched and jagged. "I refused to believe you, Frances. Not until you stood by and allowed me to be shot. Then I knew you must be happy to have betrayed me. Did you always mean to break my heart, even when we were children?"

"For God's sake, switch on the light!" I yelled. To my relief, Makepeace got up and did so. Returning to his chair, he pulled it closer and leaned forward until our faces were nearly touching.

"OK, pretty little blue-eyed Frances. Now you can see me. It makes no difference to me. I hear your lies as easily in the dark as in the light." He sat back and his voice dropped a notch. "Just do me a favour and tell the truth. Starting with why you married Villiers, when you were promised to me."

"Antony, what *are* you talking about? I was never promised to anyone before I married. I didn't have time to be. I was still in my teens on my wedding day. You must be mistaking me for some other woman. My name is Sarah James."

"Your name is Frances Coke and well you know it."

What was Makepeace talking about? "My last name is James. My second name *is* Frances, but I never use it. Nor does anyone else in my life."

"You lie. I always call you Frances. And so does *everyone*. Except when they call you Franny."

I shook my head. "Antony, remember we met for the first time on Sunday when you appeared at my office?"

"You can stop calling me Antony. It isn't funny."

My head was spinning. Was I losing my grip on reality? I strove again for calm. "What do you want me to call you, if not Antony?"

"John. Johnny Clavylle. You've known that all along. Don't try and pretend otherwise, you scheming bitch."

"Johnny Clavylle? You – are *you* Johnny Clavylle, Bob's musician friend from England?"

"Who the hell else would I be?" His face was livid, as he yelled at me. I scrambled to make sense of what I had just heard. This was apparently the same man with whom I had spoken on the beach, when Bob called me from Corfe Castle. Was it possible? Throughout all his mood switches, I had never heard a trace of a Cockney accent in Makepeace's cultivated English. But I now remembered having sensed artificiality during the phone call with Johnny Clavylle. And perhaps that conversation had fed the impression of familiarity, when he and I met face-to-face at my office.

I tried again. "Antony – John, I mean – if you're Johnny Clavylle, then we had already spoken by phone before we met. *Was* it you in Corfe Castle with Bob?"

"Yes," he nodded.

"Well then, I'm confused. Let me try and work this out. That phone call took place on my Friday at midday, which would have been a Friday night in England. You were in L.A. by Sunday. You must have travelled the next day, after dropping Bob off in London, unless you came straight to my office from a Sunday flight. But why didn't you say something about flying to the USA that weekend, especially since you said you wanted to meet me?"

He spoke in an ordinary voice. "I didn't know I was coming, until Bob refused to play ball with me about the tour. I don't know why you are confused. I flew on Sunday morning from the UK and got to L.A. on Sunday afternoon. I knew there would be at least one free first-class seat on Bob's flight, once I'd sent him off on a wild goose chase to Berlin. I just had to make sure I got it. It helps to have contacts. I do. And yes, I came straight to your office from the airport. No mystery there."

Bob's words, during our Sunday call, came back to me: "Johnny Clavylle. He always was impossible to deal with. Unpredictable."

I breathed deeply. "OK, so now I'm getting part of the picture. But you used a false name with me. Why? You're not really Antony Makepeace. Make peace? Hah. I suppose that's another of your jokes."

To my surprise, he sounded offended as he replied, "It's not a joke. I don't see anything funny about it. I *was* christened Antony, and my surname *is* Makepeace. But I'm also Johnny Clavylle. Just as you were named Sarah James but you're also Frances Coke. The same Frances

Coke who agreed to marry me when we met at Corfe Castle. You were eight years old. I was two years older than you. We were happy for years until you betrayed me."

Acid returned to his tone. "You double-crossing bitch. You had to go and spoil it all by agreeing to marry a half-wit. I suppose you were lured by the promise of a title. I bet you enjoyed being married to Sir Manic-Fucking-Depressive John Villiers. Did you get all the attention you wanted at Court, along with your prize of a lunatic husband?"

The viciousness of his words sent pain shooting through me. I tried to ignore my physical reaction and focus only on the content of Makepeace's words. There was mystery and confusion enough in these to have me reeling. I had indeed married a Sir John Villiers. Where could Makepeace have learned about John's mental health issues? What was this conundrum about us having known each other as children at Corfe Castle? I must have been about eight when I first visited the castle with my father, but I had no memory of meeting a boy of ten there.

I shook my head. "You're going to have to explain. I still can't make all this out. You say I agreed to marry you when I was eight. That's crazy, since Monday was the first time I set eyes on you."

"Says you," was all Makepeace would offer.

I decided to offer more, in the hope of getting more out of Makepeace too. "Maybe my head *was* turned by John's title. I was young. My parents liked having a titled son-in-law, just as John liked wealthy in-laws, and my father investing in his business. But I married John because I fell in love with him. What do you know about my marriage, and why should it matter to you?"

Makepeace glowered but said nothing. My wrists were throbbing. I twisted on the bed; tried and failed to find a more comfortable position. Frustrated, I lay back and continued. "John does suffer manic-depression. How do you know this? Have you met him, or did Bob say something? I don't appreciate you calling John a half-wit or a lunatic. Neither is true."

Makepeace remained silent and sulky. I returned to my original question. "I'm still curious how you discovered my second name. I can't remember ever mentioning it to Bob. My driving licence has the letter F on it. But so many girls' names begin with F. What made you light on Frances?"

"Let's stop going round in boring circles, bitch."

"Please stop calling me bitch. I find it offensive."

"Hah! That makes two of us offended, then. I find it *offensive* that you pretend not to know me or what we once meant to each other. I find it *offensive* that you rejected me for a lunatic half-wit of a husband. Yes, and

I find it *o-fucking-fensive* that you rejected me a second time to run off with goody-two-shoes Robert Howard and have his kid."

I gasped. Robert Howard. What now? Was he talking about Bob? Bob's last name was Howard but nobody I knew called him Robert.

"Robert Howard? A kid? Antony. John. Antony. Whoever you are. This has to be a case of mistaken identity. I have no kid. I've never been pregnant. I don't know a Robert Howard. I only know *Bob* Howard. I've known him less than a year and I haven't run anywhere with him. Ouch!" My captor had moved so abruptly that I pressed back on the bed and, as I did, the handcuffs bit into my wrists again. I saw stars. Pain blotted everything else out.

Coming to again, I felt drained. "Antony, John, I need you to release me. I know you're upset about something you think I've done, but you've mistaken me for someone else. I promise not to run. Once I'm free, we can sort out whatever it is that you want Bob to do for you."

With an exclamation of suppressed violence, Makepeace jumped to his feet. His flashlight and the chair fell as he pulled the knife from his pocket. For a moment I feared he was about to slash me, but it was only his voice that lashed me. "You stupid little bitch. If you think I've done all this just to hand you back to smart-arse Robert Howard, you've understood nothing. The two of you have fucked up my life and it's payback time."

I groaned, from pain and frustration. "How can we possibly have fucked up your life since I didn't know you before we spoke by phone on Friday?"

"Didn't *know* me? I stole that silver for you. It was your fault that I took to the road. Thanks to you I festered in jail for months. You and fucking Robert Howard went off together and destroyed my dreams. Time for you to dance to my tune now, Lady Innocence Purbeck."

Makepeace picked up the chair from where it had fallen behind him and hurled it across the room. It bounced off the table and crashed to the floor against the recording studio wall. Fortunately, the soundproofed glass held. I closed my eyes. Seconds later I was being grabbed and kissed. I struggled to push him away and he released me with an exclamation of disgust. Bruised and shaken, I went internal and silently willed the man to move away from me. Then I went blank and let go of wanting anything at all to happen.

Makepeace left my side and turned off the light. His footsteps sounded heavy and dragging as he went down the passage. The bed in the room at the far end creaked as Makepeace threw himself upon it.

For a time thereafter the silence between us was loud.

Makepeace spoke once into the darkness. "Sleep well. If you can. After ruining my life, you don't deserve to sleep well ever again."

CHAPTER TWENTY-TWO

England 1624

His eyes were purple, large and unfocused as he stared up at his mother. Their future colour could not yet be predicted with confidence.

"He looks just like you, Robert."

Sir Robert Howard bent over the swaddled babe and peered. He straightened and stared at Frances with a puzzled expression. "Are you sure? How can I tell, when he averts his face and refuses to say a word? What kind of greeting is this, for a father who has stayed up into the small hours to greet his firstborn?"

Frances pulled back the shawl, so that the baby's head was exposed to full view. His tiny face puckered when he encountered the light, and he mewled in protest and closed his eyes tight.

"Do you think he might be willing to acknowledge my existence, if I address him by name?"

Frances laughed. "That obliges us to agree on what it shall be."

"I still favour Thomas. It is my father's name and it was at the home of dear Uncle Tom Knyvett, God rest his soul, that I realised I loved you."

A shadow crossed Frances's face. "I question whether your father will welcome having his name bestowed on a bastard grandson."

Sir Robert Howard winced. "Don't say that, Frances."

She shrugged. "A few of our tender-hearted friends may say love child, but bastard is the word that those who wish to hurt him and us will call our son. The House of Suffolk cannot formally acknowledge him. He will not bear your family name, but let him at least have a part of you. I wish him to be Robert."

The baby's father bowed his head and turned away. His voice became thick. "That could be construed as provocation by your husband's family."

She groaned. "I came here to escape the pressure of my husband's family, if only briefly. They should not be allowed to dictate how we name our son."

When Robert's gaze returned to Frances, his expression had cleared. "Very well. Robert he shall be. And, when father and son are together, which I intend to be often, he shall be Robin, so that we know to whom you speak." Robert bent and kissed Frances on her lips, then lifted the infant from her arms. Holding him with great care, he walked across the room.

"So what do you think of the great wide world, Master Robin?" Robert held his son up to the window of the Manning's garden house. "You will see it all more easily by dawn's light. May it treat you kindly, my sweet boy."

Tears began to course down Frances's cheeks as she watched father and son silhouetted against a moonlit October night sky. The birth of a healthy child should have been a moment of unalloyed happiness and Frances did feel joy. Yet it was already shot through by her fears of the challenges that must lie ahead for them all. The physical effort of giving birth did not fully account for the present churning in her stomach and the ache in her abdomen.

Frances had known intermittent terror since the day her monthly flux, usually so regular, failed. As soon as they had confirmation that she was with child, Robert had insisted that she remain in London with her mother, but visit Purbeck and stay with him in private, whenever she could succeed. In this way, Robert reasoned, Buckingham and the Countess would never be able to prove that the baby Frances carried was not her husband's child.

Robert had drowned all her doubts with his certitude. He declared himself primarily concerned for the baby and Frances's well being. If, God forbid, some misadventure should befall him before he could arrange his affairs to offer her his protection, Frances would be safe and their child would have a place in society.

Lord Purbeck, when told of the pregnancy, had reacted exactly as Robert hoped. He entertained no doubts about the paternity and refuted all aspersions that the child Frances carried was not his. When his brother and mother repeated their former comments about impotency, Viscount Purbeck faced them down with unusual vigour. His wife's condition proved him capable of begetting a child, he declared, and he would listen to no slander against her sweet name. Furthermore, Frances should no longer be kept from living with him at Denmark House. His brother must use his influence immediately with the Prince to allow her return.

Frances had felt grateful and guilty.

Fate smiled briefly on Lady Purbeck then, for George and his mother fell ill at the same time and remained indisposed during May and June. But by July both were back and applying renewed pressure on Purbeck to disown the pregnancy. Their arguments visibly destabilised him, whereupon the Countess insisted that her eldest son be escorted to the country for an extended period of seclusion, to calm his poor nerves.

The day after Purbeck's enforced departure in early August, a terrified Frances found herself under direct bodily assault. Her mother-in-law demanded physical proof that she was with child. The examination forced on her had not been gentle.

As she watched her lover now, cradling their newborn, Frances's recall of what she had endured on that day fed her fears of further possible assaults to come. She braced herself to speak. "My love, I feel the only course open is for me to return to Purbeck permanently and have him claim our son as his own. Maybe then his mother and brother will accept the situation and leave us alone."

Robert whirled and stared at her. The baby mewled afresh, as his father's abrupt movement rocked his tiny world. "Hush there, my little one. Did you hear, Frances? Your son cries out against the very idea."

She struggled to sit up straight. Her body ached and so did her heart. "Robert, please listen. There is still no sign of your affairs being completed. Your poor brother is dead more than two years, God rest his soul. Surely you should have been able to claim your estate by now? What kind of a life can our son expect, if I am estranged from Purbeck, but cannot live with you?"

"I only need a little time to settle Charles's estate. The settlement was complicated, but I have already assumed all his official responsibilities in Shropshire. Can you not go back to your mother for the short time I still need to finalise my affairs?"

Frances shook her head. "Mama says she cannot have a love child living in her home. Do you imagine either my father or yours will recognise their grandson? Purbeck is our boy's only hope."

"Frances, your exertions have laid you low. After all we have been through together, you cannot believe I will let you or my son go. I would flee the country with you both, sooner than allow that to happen."

"You would be a fool to do so, now you are elected to Parliament and will have a comfortable inheritance eventually."

Robert returned to the bed and stood by her. "Please trust me, my darling. Charles's widow has slowed progress on settling the estate, with her demands and her temperament, but we are near agreement. I need only a little more time. I have promised I will give you a home. If Eliza will not help, then Purbeck must be your protector. But be clear that the situation is only temporary."

Frances managed a half-hearted smile as she took the baby back in her arms. "Forgive me. I must indeed be tired, or I would not have talked so. Some evil maggot made me doubt in our future for a moment." She kissed the top of her son's head. "Our baby must be christened quickly, though. If he cannot be known for who he is by the world at this time, at least he can be acknowledged in the eyes of God."

"I had ample time to think that through, during all those interminable hours that you were at your travails, my love. I've spoken already with the minister up the road at St. Giles's. He is paid and will perform the baptism here, as soon as you are strong enough to leave your bed. In the morning, perhaps, when you have slept?"

"Did you also think through *what* our son is to be christened? We need Purbeck's protection for him, but the idea of him carrying the name of Villiers fills me with sadness."

Howard stroked her cheek. "Yes, I've thought of all that. You are registered here as Mistress Wright, wife of John Wright, gentleman, of Bishopthorpe in Yorkshire. It cannot be sensible for me to be present at the ceremony, so Manning will deal directly with the minister on our behalf. For now, our boy shall be christened as plain Robert Wright. We'll go on from there and make all things straight anon."

Her voice was flat again. "This is only the beginning of our troubles, isn't it, Robert? I fled here for the birth because those who examined me were so brutal. I know my mother-in-law intended me to miscarry. She would have harmed us both, if I had allowed midwives of her choice to attend his birth. Purbeck would not have been able to protect me. Now Robin is born, I ask myself how long will George and the Countess allow him to remain alive?"

"I have arranged a wet nurse and a place of immediate safe keeping. She will take Robin where I can keep a watch on him. I know it will be difficult for us all, Frances, but we must be resolute. Immediately after the baptism, you must hand the baby to the nurse, then return to Denmark House, and advise Purbeck that he has a healthy son, who is currently with a wet nurse. Confide your fears for the boy's safety to him and explain why you are keeping him hidden, not in a dramatic way, but enough to arouse your husband's protective instincts. That will buy us time."

"My Lord will surely want to see the baby he believes to be his son."

Howard nodded. "Certainly, but you must first ensure that Purbeck understands the need for extreme caution and subterfuge. Fortunately, George has just accompanied the Prince of Wales to Royston, for the King is reported to have taken ill. There is also talk of George going to Paris as soon as the King has recovered, to bring back the Prince's young French bride." He chuckled. "You may depend that Buckingham will wish to make that trip as soon as possible, given his own romantic interests there. And he will insist in going in a style calculated to impress, so there will be much for him to oversee for the journey."

Frances sighed. "Poor Kate. It's so hard for her to deal with all the gossip about her unfaithful Duke."

"Poor Kate indeed, but lucky for us, if Buckingham's preoccupation with the French Queen leads him to ignore you. With all he has to arrange for France as well as organising naval support to the expedition to recover the Palatinate, I warrant George will have his hands too full to worry about you and our babe. Time is all I need now, Frances, to secure our own future."

"I'm tired of feeling so continually afraid."

He nodded again. "It's natural, my sweet. You are exhausted. The wet nurse will be here at any moment. As soon as she arrives, you shall hand Robin over to her and rest. Believe me, sleep will restore you quicker than all else."

Robert leaned across and dropped a kiss on the head of their newborn. Holding them both close, he murmured softly, "I am so proud of you, my brave girl. Thank you for our son."

Nestling in her lover's embrace, Frances shut her eyes and knew momentary relief. It began to dissipate, as soon as she felt Robert disengage, but she took heart from his parting words. "My darling, believe me when I promise you that we shall win through."

Her head was bowed over the baby, so that she did not observe the expression that creased Robert's features as he exited her lying-in chamber.

CHAPTER TWENTY-THREE

California

Morning brought daylight. Waking out of a fitful sleep, I found myself wondering if my extraordinary interchange with Makepeace had taken place in a nightmare. First sight of my captor's face told me otherwise. He exuded anger, as he stomped into the cabin after fastening back the shutters. Crossing to the kitchen without a glance or a word in my direction, he poured a large whisky and began to prepare food.

I cleared my throat. "Should I call you Antony or John?"

Makepeace shrugged. "Please yourself."

I hoisted myself up awkwardly in the bed, flinching as steel cut into my swollen wrists. The skin was breaking in places.

"Antony, then. You said things during the night that made no sense to me. Can we talk about them? And won't you take these cuffs off me? My wrists are becoming infected."

Makepeace brought over a bowl of cereal and placed it down on the chest by the bed so heavily that milk spilled onto the wood. He studied both my wrists, unlocked my right hand and transferred the bowl to my knees. "I'm putting this back on again as soon as you've eaten. The other one stays. You're not leaving this bed except to pee and brush your teeth. I was lenient with you yesterday, Frances, and you took advantage."

I steadied the cereal bowl, then took the spoon he had handed me.

"You're calling me Frances again. Why?"

Makepeace scowled. "Oh God, we're back at that silly game, are we?"

I responded. "Antony. John. Whoever you choose to call yourself, I truly have no idea why you call me Frances."

He pointed to the cereal bowl. "Shut up and eat."

But I persisted. "I want to understand how my marriage could have affected you. You said things about Bob and me during the night that make no sense. I was dating him months before I met you. I don't see how I can have done anything to ruin your life. And just in case you missed it earlier, I have no child and have never been pregnant."

The mobile phone rang. In a couple of paces Makepeace had picked it up and was speaking fast. "Where the hell did you get to, Bob? Are you in Los Angeles?" The reply appeared to wrong-foot him, but he made a quick recovery. "Really? You're obviously better at sleuthing than singing. Yes, we're at the cabin. You'd better get here as soon as possible. But come alone. Unpleasant things will happen if you bring anyone."

I listened, anxious and hopeful, as Makepeace gave instructions. "I don't want you getting lost, like last time you came here. When you reach Yucca Valley, stop and call me. I'll direct you in from there. You'll park a couple of hundred yards back from the cabin. No funny business. If I get a hint that you've involved the cops, I'll have your girlfriend's guts for garters."

Something in his last comment made me want to laugh. Each time Makepeace spoke to Bob, I felt I was watching a third-rate actor play the stereotypical kidnapper in a movie becoming more far-fetched by the minute. But the knife was no laughing matter. Nor were my memories from the night.

Makepeace pocketed the phone and turned to me. The amiable conversationalist returned. "Smart man, Bob, I'll say that for him, even though he's a lousy musician. He's followed your trail to the hotel in Palm Springs. I need to get things ready, so hurry up and finish your cereal."

"Antony, forget cereal. Before Bob gets here, please tell me why you created this elaborate charade. At first I thought it was simply that you want to force Bob's hand over a music tour. But then you spoke about a score to settle with us both and this Frances. What are you really after?"

"Hah. I've got you guessing now, haven't I? The smart psychoanalyst has begun to understand I'm not such a simple case. Good." He was grinning as he went on, "I'll give you one clue and it's a big one. You owe me for the way you and Robert bloody Howard patronised–" Makepeace broke off and moved to the window. He opened it stealthily and stared out. He turned back to me. "Can you hear the birds? They're back again."

I shook my head and gave up trying to make sense of a man who could seemingly switch personalities before my eyes. Dissociative identity disorder, the DSM manual might call it, but I had always hated labels and I had no clue as to what was going on between the two of us, since the strange events of the night.

Makepeace hung by the window a while longer, then took my empty bowl back to the kitchen. "I need a little something." He stopped at the whisky bottle and poured himself a tumbler full of the light golden liquid.

"Cheers, Frances. Don't look so worried. We don't need to say anything more just now. All will be revealed as soon as your precious Robert arrives."

I sighed. "Could you turn on the air conditioning?" My limbs felt leaden. Hours spent lying attached to the bed were taking a cumulative toll and the temperature was rising, as hot desert air poured in through the open window.

"No, I don't want to miss the sound of his car. Or anyone with him."

Makepeace moved to open another window next to the door. He peered outside, chewing his lip and drumming his fingers against the wall. He topped up his whisky, then sat down at the table. Minutes passed in silence.

As our wait for Bob dragged on, we both grew more tense. "Come on Robert. Where the hell are you, man?" Makepeace drummed his fingers again. I could feel him growing agitated. This time, when he rose, he went to the door of the cabin and opened it. At the same moment, the cell phone rang. He pulled it out of his pocket. "It shouldn't have taken you this long to get to Yucca Valley. Are you messing with me?" He listened. Then, "A flat? Are you kidding me? Is it fixed?"

Makepeace swung out of the cabin, with the phone still in his hand, and disappeared beyond my restricted line of vision. I could still hear his voice but his words became indistinct as he walked further away. For the first time I began to wonder what might happen when the two men met. Bob was large-framed and tall, and he possessed a temper in direct proportion to his size. On the only occasion I had seen him roused to anger, his physical intensity awed me. He had never lost his self-control in my presence, but these were combustible circumstances.

Makepeace re-entered the cabin at a half-run. He threw the phone on the table, went into the recording studio and unlocked another concealed cupboard set in the wall. My pulse rate rose as I watched him take out a hunting rifle with a box of cartridges. He loaded the gun, looked at me and smirked. Holding the rifle half-cocked, he picked up the phone and exited.

I strained my ears but for several minutes I could hear no sound. Then a low humming vibration gradually grew louder until it became identifiable as an approaching vehicle. I heard tyres brake on gravel, an engine cut out and a car door open. Makepeace spoke loudly. "Get out slowly and put your hands in the air. Don't try anything. That's right. Now go inside."

Two sets of footsteps approached the cabin. I stopped breathing. As a familiar form filled the doorway, I cried out. "Thank God."

"Honey."

With the single word, Bob was at my side and had folded bear-like arms around me. I knew profound relief, combined with excruciating pain from the pressure on my wrists.

"The bastard!" Bob muttered under his breath, as he took in why I had exclaimed in pain. He began to examine the cuffs but a voice commanded him from the doorway. "Sorry to interrupt the touching reunion. Get up and move away from her." Makepeace stood with his rifle levelled at us both.

Bob hesitated, then turned and rose slowly to his feet.

"Sit down over there in that chair." Makepeace jerked the barrel of his gun in the direction of the table.

As Bob sat down facing me, I had my first chance to study him. His features were haggard, and I guessed he must have slept little, if at all, since his first phone conversation with Makepeace. I had been yearning to see him, for my security and comfort. Now, as I registered his exhaustion and anxiety, I felt gripped with a desire to reassure him.

"Thank you for coming so quickly, Bob. I'm so sorry about this mess. I still don't know exactly what Antony wants."

"I still don't know exactly what Antony wants." Makepeace mimicked me in his jeering tone. "Well, let's just see if your boyfriend can guess what Antony wants then, shall we, bitch?"

Bob stiffened. "Johnny, you're big and you're strong and you have a rifle in your hand. You don't need to call Sarah names as well. Let's keep things pleasant. It'll be easier on us all. Why don't we begin by you telling me exactly what you need from me?"

I relaxed. Bob was taking a conciliatory line.

"I'm glad you understand which side your bread is buttered, old chap." The sneer was strong in Makepeace's voice.

Bob replied wearily, "Johnny, I've just flown halfway round the world because of you. You're in control here. Would you please just tell me what's up? And take those handcuffs off Sarah?"

Makepeace's answering giggle was so high-pitched that both Bob and I started. "Don't take me for a complete fool, Bob. Sarah has disappointed me. I don't want you to do so as well. She's staying in those handcuffs. Your girlfriend is not as trustworthy as you may think." Makepeace pulled another chair from the studio out into the main room, positioned it where he had us both in his sight and sat down, with the rifle at the ready.

Bob yawned and stretched. "OK, Johnny. We'll play this whatever way you choose. God, I'm tired. Could you begin by telling me what you want?"

"That's better, old chap. I know it must be hard for an arrogant bastard like you to have to eat crow. But I'm calling the shots here and can do so quite literally. I have a score, a very big score, to settle with you both."

Bob shrugged. "I don't know which score with me you're referring to. You and I go so far back together that there are a million and one things we can hold against each other, if we wish. But I'm damned sure that you can have nothing at all to settle with Sarah."

"With Sarah, no, that's actually true. But with Frances, yes. And with the two of you together, oh yes, indeed. Remember? Our history goes way, way back and far beyond just you and me."

Bob rubbed his eyes, blinked and stared at Makepeace again. "You always loved riddles, Johnny. What are you talking about?"

"Surely your memory isn't that short?"

"My memory? My memory got lost somewhere over the Atlantic Ocean, along with most of the rest of my brain. I've been operating on autopilot for forty-eight hours and it can't surprise you to know that I'm feeling like death at the moment. Could I have some water? Johnny, please just tell me what it is that you want. I'll oblige if I can."

I spoke. "Antony Makepeace – or Johnny Clavylle, as you call him – seems to think we all knew each other before."

"Before when?" Bob turned and looked blankly at me.

Makepeace chortled. "My God, you both should have been actors. You never could sing, Robert. You'd have done the world a favour to stay away from music. You and Frances would have been perfect on stage. You could have done your amnesiac routine as a double act."

Bob swung round in his chair to stare at Makepeace again. "Why do you call her Frances?"

"Tell him why, sweetheart." Makepeace waved the rifle toward me.

"I can't tell him why, because I don't know. Actually, my middle name *is* Frances, Bob. I probably never mentioned it to you."

"So why tell him?"

"I didn't tell him. I have no idea how he knows or why he calls me Frances. I may not have been on a trans-Atlantic flight like you, but believe me, after the last couple of days here with Antony Makepeace or Johnny Clavylle, I'm so confused that I'm feeling jet-lagged myself."

"OK, game over. I've had enough." Makepeace stood up abruptly, then seemed to change his mind and sat down again.

"Since you both want to act the injured innocents, I'll refresh your memories. Settle in, children. Are you sitting comfortably? Good. Then

I'll begin. I'm going to tell you a story. A story of everyday country folk who lived four centuries ago."

CHAPTER TWENTY-FOUR

England 1625

The alderman sounded embarrassed as he raised his voice and endeavoured to be heard above the baby's screams. "Lady Purbeck, I am sure we both hope that this arrangement will be of short duration. Be assured that I will do everything I can to ensure the well being of you and your infant. I wish that your stay here may be as comfortable as possible in the circumstances. Your servants will also be found space in my staff quarters."

"Thank you, Sir Edward. I do understand that you did not order my detention and are simply fulfilling the orders of the Council. Please forgive our noisy invasion of your home. My child does not understand why his routine should be upset and he is hungry. Could someone show his nurse where she may feed him?"

Sir Edward Barkham summoned a servant and Robin left the room, in the arms of his wet nurse, still complaining. His wails reverberated along the passage until a door shut. Then, for the first time, quiet prevailed between Frances and her jailer. It gave each the opportunity to study the other.

Frances knew that she still looked wan and painfully thin, although her face remained blessedly unmarked by the smallpox that had laid her low four months before. She had no idea what Sir Edward Barkham might be thinking about her but, observing his diffident smile, she decided to take the initiative.

"Sir Edward, I would like messages delivered to my mother, my husband and Sir Robert Howard. I need to assure them all that my son and I are safe and being treated kindly. Will you be able to arrange this for me today?"

The draper coloured. "My Lady, as to your husband and your mother, this can be arranged. However, I understand that Sir Robert Howard is also being held against His Majesty's pleasure. I am doubtful that a message to him would be in accord with the Council's wishes."

Frances's chin came up. "Is it the Council's wishes that concern you, or those of his Grace, the Duke of Buckingham?"

She stared unblinking at the alderman.

Sir Edward's colour grew more pronounced but he returned her gaze squarely. "Lady Purbeck, we do not know each other well, or else you would understand that I do not keep company with those who jump to the whims and wishes of his Grace of Buckingham. My interest lies today, as it always does, in upholding the laws of our land."

"As Sir Edward Coke's daughter, it heartens me to hear that you are concerned to uphold the laws of our land. So will you need to take advice from the Council, Sir Edward, or can you allow me to set my friend's mind at rest, concerning my well-being and that of Lord Purbeck's son?"

Her chin was still held high.

Sir Edward Barkham bowed low. "If you understand that this is not to be a regular occurrence, my Lady, I will arrange for a message to be sent to Sir Robert Howard, as well as to your husband and mother."

"Thank you. You are most gracious. I have come sadly ill equipped, so I must ask you to provide me with writing materials. I assure you that I will then make no other awkward demands of you."

She smiled. The alderman caught his breath and blushed for a third time. Frances wondered why. It would be the next day before she would receive an answer, when she passed an open door and overheard Sir Edward Barkham within confessing to his wife that Lady Purbeck's smile had enabled him to understand why a son of the House of Suffolk would incur such inconvenience on her behalf.

"My Lady, you may write your letters in my study. I will have them sealed and delivered to your husband and mother. I will also confirm where Sir Robert is being held. I believe him to be at Alderman Freeman's home." Sir Edward led his charge along the passage to a room that lay beyond oak double doors. It smelled of dust and leather-bound volumes. Frances knew Barkham's business to be in leather. The appointment of his mansion suggested that it was a profitable one.

Sir Edward settled her at his desk, and bustled around to provide her with quill, ink and parchment. When he had left the room, Frances took up the quill and immediately began to write:

Robert,

I am in the custody of Sir Edward Barkham. He detains me in the name of the Council. I know not for how long this may endure, as I have yet to hear details of charges against me. I am quite unharmed, and indeed Sir Edward shows himself most gracious toward us. My child is safe and well and I hope he will settle in these strange surroundings. May God be with you and keep you safe, dear friend.

Frances Villiers, Viscountess Purbeck

Frances looked around the study. She stared up at a portrait that dominated one wall of the room. In it, Barkham carried badges of office and wore his full regalia as Lord Mayor of London with evident pride, but she observed his expression in the portrait to be quite as sweet as at his reception of her today. One of Nature's gentlemen, she reflected. If she had not misread him, Sir Edward Barkham would prove a thoughtful and kind jailer.

Her mother had also once been held in the home of a former Lord Mayor, who had behaved with kindness and courtesy toward his charge. How many years had elapsed since Mama had been confined, first by Alderman Bennett and then Sir William Craven, for trying to prevent her marriage? Seven or eight? Today, that part of their story seemed a lifetime away.

Would Lady Hatton be able to pull strings at Court, to extricate her daughter from her present predicament? Frances suspected not, although she knew Mama intended to make another appeal to Sir Edward. Her father would not involve himself, of that she felt sure, for he had denied her once before and now had too many fish frying in Parliament to be distracted by the needs of an errant daughter. And, although her husband must be distraught at her detention and willing to speak on her behalf, Frances entertained no expectation that Lord Purbeck would find the strength and resources to countermand his brother's move against her.

What of Robert? He would surely wish to move heaven and earth to have Robin and her freed, but could he do this, when he was detained himself?

The second message Frances wrote was to her mother and the third to Purbeck. They were both longer and less restrained, although differing little in content, than her note to Robert.

She had completed her final signature and just laid the quill aside, when the door to the study opened again. A liveried servant bowed before Frances. "Sir Edward wishes to know if you are ready to send your messages, my Lady. If so, you are to give them to me for his seal. A carriage is on hand to deliver your letters, and Sir Edward particularly wishes you to know that all three will be delivered today."

"Thank you so much. Everyone here is most amiable." Frances handed over the three sheets of parchment and received another blush at her next smile, this time from a servant rather than the master of the Barkham establishment.

Only when the door of the study had closed behind him did she bow her head and give way to the tears that had been threatening from the moment she and Robin had been seized.

CHAPTER TWENTY-FIVE

California

It was growing dark and the temperature had begun to drop. The air in the cabin felt less oppressive. The three of us had been silent for at least fifteen minutes, since Makepeace had finished his story.

I lay limp on the bed. Bob slumped across the table with closed eyes. The only movement came from Makepeace, who lounged back in his chair, swinging the loaded rifle intermittently on his knee and whistling through his teeth.

"OK, kids. Time for some liquid refreshment." Makepeace rose to his feet. Still holding the gun, he switched on a light and went to the counter where he poured himself a whisky.

"Want a drink, either of you?" Makepeace pointed at the bottle and looked around the room inquiringly.

"Water, please." Bob spoke hoarsely, without looking up. His head remained pillowed in his arms.

Makepeace laughed. "The man wants water. What a sober-sides you've become. What happened to the wild man from the Seventies? Have you ever told your woman what you got up to when you were young? I remember a quaint expression you used to use. I wonder if you've told her about the pipe you laid when you were in the band. Maybe I'll enlighten her."

I shifted position and raised myself with difficulty. Makepeace's crude taunts grated on my nerves as much when directed at Bob as when I was on the receiving end. I cleared my throat. "Antony, I can't take in any more stories just now. I'm still trying to make sense of the one you told us earlier."

Makepeace looked at me and raised his glass. I ignored the mockery behind his gesture and continued, "We've both told you we know nothing of this story. I have to agree that some names seem to fit, and there are other strange coincidences. But to believe that we all knew each other in seventeenth-century England? Don't *you* feel it is far-fetched?"

"Far-fetched or not, Sarah, that's how it was." Makepeace raised his glass again. "Cheers, my dears."

Bob lifted his head. "So, what if we suspend disbelief? Let's assume for a moment that this tale you've told us happened exactly as you say it did. What then, Johnny? We're here in a cabin in the desert, in twenty-first-century California. What do you want from us right now?"

"Retribution."

"*Retribution?*" Bob yelled. "For what? If your story is true, seventeenth-century Johnny was just as responsible for his own fuck-ups as the one living four hundred years later. He didn't need any Frances Coke or John Villiers or even a Robert Howard to make a mess of his life. And you haven't needed Sarah or me to make a mess of yours. For God's sake, grow up."

I could hear from his tone that Bob's self-control was slipping. Even as I watched, he stood up and pushed past the rifle levelled at him. Ignoring Makepeace, he reached across and grabbed one of the many used whisky glasses that lay scattered along the counter. Bob walked into the kitchen. Moving slowly and deliberately, he washed the glass out and opened the fridge. He found a bottle of water, filled the glass and downed its contents in a single, long gulp. After he had refilled it and put the bottle back in the fridge, he turned back to Makepeace, who had been watching him with no discernible reaction.

"Look man," said Bob, "let's just stop fucking about. When we were in Bristol, I offered to organise an opening slot on a new tour for Moonlight Jax, if you would go into rehab first and dry out. That offer still holds."

Makepeace sat immobile and silent. I held my breath. The balance of power between the two men seemed to be shifting as I watched, but I did not trust the situation. At any moment, Makepeace might erupt and he was the one with the gun. Bob wandered back to the table and sat down again. Without looking at either of us, he continued. "Apparently, you didn't take kindly to being called an alcoholic and my offer didn't satisfy you. Did you really have to show it by destroying my tour, through spreading lies and ill will all over London?"

Now he stared up at the other man. "You ruin my tour and then you pull me halfway across the world on a crazy kidnap stunt. I find you in your cabin here in Joshua Tree, drinking yourself senseless, after keeping my girlfriend tied to a bed for two days. You cap it all by waving what I have to assume is a loaded rifle at Sarah and me, and telling us a tale that's all in your mind. Sorry to say it, but you're off the wall, Johnny.

Seriously off the wall. You need help, man. It's time to wake up. This thing has gone way beyond being a silly joke between old friends."

The reaction I feared came. Makepeace leaped to his feet and brandished the barrel of his rifle wildly at Bob. He bellowed, "Yes, it's gone beyond a joke. It never was a joke for me. And it's you who needs to wake up and realise that *you're* the one who needs help here, you arrogant bastard." He paced the room, then swung around at Bob again, with the rifle pointed at him. "Who the bloody hell do you think you are, to tell me that you'll organise an opening slot in a tour for me *if* I stop drinking? Who appointed *you* to be the behaviour police on my parade? Shut your fucking mouth and stay sitting at that fucking table until *I* tell you when to get up. Otherwise you will find out whether this gun is loaded or not."

Bob seemed impervious to the outburst. He shook his head slowly. My heart was in my mouth as he replied and I hoped he knew the man better than I did, by continuing to stand up to him while facing the barrel of a loaded weapon. "Johnny, personally, I don't give a sparrow's fart whether you drink yourself senseless or not. It's your life. Or death."

The other man half screamed. "So why interfere in what I do?"

Bob's tone sounded wearier than ever. "I didn't interfere. I only recommended you dry out when you said you wanted to tour here in the USA. I've told you I think Moonlight Jax can do well if the band is positioned and promoted properly. But I won't sign you guys for a US tour unless you get clear of the demon drink. American audiences don't love addicts any more. The days of rock musicians running wild are gone."

"Such a Mr. Squeaky Clean, aren't we?" Makepeace sneered and looked at me. "Sarah, I bet you'd enjoy some stories I can tell you about how your boyfriend used to get fucked up on coke and Jack Daniels." He turned back to Bob. "How are your sinuses these days, Robert?"

I spoke quickly. "I've already said I don't need more stories, but it sounds to me as if Bob did go halfway toward offering you something you want. What else were you looking for?"

"As a matter of fact, Madam Psychotherapist, I am getting a lot of what I was looking for, just by standing here and making the two of you sweat. I know what you're both wondering, Sarah. Is he crazy or drunk enough yet to pull this trigger?"

"For God's sake, cut the crap, Johnny!" Bob slammed his fist down on the table.

I intervened again, fearful and eager to neutralise the situation. "You're right, Antony. At least you've read me right. That is just what I've been asking myself, ever since you pulled that rifle out of the cupboard and loaded it. And before that I wondered if you would really use the knife you kept pulling on me." I hoped Bob would pick up on my comment about the knife as well as the loaded rifle.

I continued by expressing openly how I felt in the moment. "I still don't know the answer to either of those questions. Sometimes I feel terrified of you and wish I could run and hide. Other times I feel that I could actually enjoy hanging out with you, Antony, if you'd only take these handcuffs off. I really am scared that my wrists are going to get infected, you know."

I saw his eyes flicker toward my wrists. Good, I did have his attention. I went on, "And I want to understand what you need, so I can help you get it, if possible."

"Oh no. We're not in your office now, Madam Psy. What I don't need is any of your sympathetic shrink-with-addict routine." Makepeace's tone was still surly but he sounded calmer.

I kept going. "Yet, when we first met, you told me that you needed to talk with someone in L.A. who was British. I believed you, enough to make an appointment to see you. Was all that you said then just a line? I don't think so."

"Fuck you, Sarah. Get off my case." Makepeace strode over to the counter and grabbed the bottle, spilling its contents. He strode back to his chair and threw himself down on it, still holding the rifle.

Bob spoke, conciliation back in his voice. "Johnny, you and I *do* go back a long way and I know life's been tough for you recently. I can forgive most of what's happened these last few days. But I can't tolerate you speaking rudely to Sarah. *You're* the one with the gun, remember? You don't need to act the bully. And, for the love of God, please unlock her cuffs."

"One more word from you and Sarah gets it."

In spite of the threat, Makepeace sounded again like a posturing schoolboy. His rifle was aimed at me now and I needed to remember that armed school kids sometimes killed people. Yet, in spite of this, I was beginning to feel curiously hopeful. Since he had finished telling us the story of seventeenth-century Frances Coke, Makepeace had addressed me as Sarah.

I had no idea how to defuse our current situation. I only knew that his attention must be kept in the twenty-first century. And he was not the only one who needed to stay anchored in the moment. When he had related his story, I had felt an inner tug. Makepeace's tale had touched more in me than I felt comfortable to admit. As he talked, I had also recalled my dizzy spells. Some strange and swirling universe lay close to the edge of my awareness. If we could work our way out of this present standoff, I would need to learn more about the world on which his narrative had opened a door.

The sudden movement shocked me, but it must have shaken our captor even more. I wasn't sure how it had happened, but Bob had moved with lightning speed and was holding the rifle that seconds before had been balanced on Makepeace's knee and aimed at me.

"Get up." Bob spoke tersely but without menace. Makepeace rose to his feet. Like me, he looked astonished at the unexpected turn of events.

"Get those cuffs off Sarah. Now."

"I can't remember where I put the key." His tone was now a mix of whining and truculent.

"Then remember. Before I smash your face in."

If I had nurtured any doubts about Antony's capacity for violence, I felt none at all with regard to Bob's. Nor, it seemed, did Makepeace. He went to the kitchen and pulled a set of keys from a drawer. He swayed across the room and sat down beside me on the bed.

As I looked in his eyes, I knew a heart-stopping premonition. "Bob, he has a knife too." Makepeace swore as his hand moved. Bob flew across the room with a remarkable turn of speed. He caught the hand holding the weapon and squeezed. The knife fell to the floor as Makepeace exclaimed with pain. "Fuck you, Bob, you've broken my wrist."

"No, just bruised it, and that's nothing compared with what you've done to both of Sarah's wrists. Make one more move like that and I'll gladly break every bone in your body. Give me those keys and get back over to the table."

Makepeace stood up and handed over the keys. He rocked on his feet and dragged himself unsteadily across the room. The bottle he picked up was empty. He made for the half empty carton of bottles.

"Stop where you are."

"I need a drink."

"There's water, if you are thirsty."

"I want whisky."

"Get over it."

Bob kept one eye trained on Makepeace, while he unlocked my handcuffs. He exclaimed at the extent of the chafing and bruising.

"I'm so sorry I let him do this to you, sweetheart. I'll kill him, if he makes one false move."

Bob's arms went round me. As my release registered in me, my body began to shed the physical and emotional tension of my captivity. My head was empty in the moment, but I felt safe for the first time since entering my hotel bedroom in Palm Springs to find Makepeace on my bed.

CHAPTER TWENTY-SIX

England 1625

"My God, Frances, the tale is being spread all over Town? Were either you or Robin harmed? I came as soon as I could get away. Tell me what happened." Sir Robert Howard sat by Frances and put his arms around her.

"I don't know what tale you may have been told, Robert, but George must have employed a footman, called Worley – whom I'd turned off before I was arrested – to do us harm. The fellow tried to gain an audience with me here in Stepney. Mr. Elwick turned him out, but later he was spotted carrying arms outside Bowler's Tavern in the Strand, together with one of Buckingham's servants. Then he spoke too freely for his own good inside the tavern, when he and the other fellow were in their cups."

"That matches the story I heard. I was told that Worley talked of having a purpose that might earn him as much as thirty or forty pounds, and when he had fulfilled it he was to go into France, to await the Prince's pardon. Buckingham must have been going to arrange an amnesty for him when the deed was done."

Howard stood again and clenched his fists. "So we were right to fear George would attempt reprisals, once you were granted bail. I shudder to think of it, Frances. You and Robin could have been killed."

In the face of his evident distress, Frances hastened to reassure her lover. "Robin and I were never actually in personal danger. Mrs. Wingfield first discovered Worley inside the house and alerted Mr. Elwick, who had him removed immediately. Can you believe the wretch had the gall to send me a complaining letter that Mr. Elwick had prevented him from seeing me to ask for a new position? As if I would take him into my service again, after those lies he spoke against me to the Commission. He must have already been spying for Buckingham, when he worked for me."

Sir Robert Howard looked around him and went over to the window where he studied the latch. "We need to strengthen security here. I believed this little house out of Town with Mrs. Wingfield would be safe for you and Robin when Barkham released you. It concerns me that Worley could gain entry so easily. We owe your solicitor a debt for his quick thinking in evicting the fellow. Thank God he was here when the scoundrel arrived."

"We owe Mr. Elwick for more than that. He has since arranged depositions against the two men, and he assures me they are stopped in their tracks. So our minds may be at rest again, Robert."

He turned and looked at her. "This time, maybe. But a thousand Worleys and Dickensons are still available for hire on the streets of London. My mind will never be at rest until I can get you both to Shropshire and secure under my own roof." Sir Robert shook his head. "It's damnably frustrating to have inherited all my brother's legal duties with the Lordship of Clun, while the properties have yet to be settled. So far, I have inherited all the responsibilities without the rewards."

"Pray God that the Commission will find in my favour, so I am free to come to you, once your affairs are settled." Frances grimaced. "My goodness, what an extraordinary year of upheaval this is turning out to be, Robert, quite apart from our own personal difficulties."

Sir Robert Howard sat again. "We must pray for it all to work out in our favour. The King's death inevitably has disrupted the Commission's proceedings, God rest his soul. Now all this fighting talk over Spain is grabbing everyone's attention, with Charles wanting war and your father shouting as loud as any in Parliament in favour of it, by the way."

He took her hands in his, as he continued, "You're right about upheaval. There's the Old King's funeral to arrange, as well as the New King's wedding and coronation to prepare for." Howard's expression lightened as he spoke. "At least Buckingham will insist on orchestrating it all, so he will have his hands full, even without his love interests across the Channel. With all the goings on, there is a chance that your case will never again see the light of day."

Their conversation was interrupted by the arrival of a baby. Sir Robert leaped to his feet with an exclamation of delight. Frances was eager to show off their son's newfound proficiency in crawling, and Robin gave every sign of being thrilled to perform for his father, so personal concerns and public affairs took a momentary back seat to the couple's mutual enjoyment of their child.

After his nurse had reclaimed Robin and Sir Robert was fastening his cloak, about to take his leave, he remembered another piece of gossip. "By the way, I also heard news of some other criminal activity today. It must surely have escaped your notice, as it did mine, given all that has happened in recent months. I'm sorry to say that young friend of your Dorset days has been holding people up on the King's Highway again."

Frances stiffened. "You don't mean John Clavell?"

"The very same. Apparently he leads a gang of right ruffians. They hold men up to steal their horses and other valuables, including even the clothes off their back. Your fellow, Clavell, then takes off his mask and reveals himself to his victims, as bold as you please."

She frowned. "Why would John show himself off like that?"

"To get himself noticed, I suppose. If you can't achieve fame, go for notoriety instead. Young fool. It's only a matter of time before somebody gets shot and he'll be hunted down and caught. Then he'll get more public attention than he's bargained for. He'll swing for his crimes and I doubt even Loftus will try to get him pardoned this time."

Frances exclaimed, "Oh, the poor, silly boy! Will he never learn? Why does he try to hurt himself in this senseless fashion?"

"No doubt, if asked, Clavell would place responsibility for his life of crime at the door of that beautiful and heartless young woman who reneged on her childhood promise to him. Wasn't that his signature theme?"

Frances winced at the disdain in Robert's voice. "Where do he and his gang conduct their crimes?"

Sir Robert picked up his hat and secured it on his head. "In the general vicinity of Beaconsfield, I believe. So there's little likelihood of you encountering him again, as long as you stay tucked up here in Stepney and don't even think of visiting your father at Stoke."

"There's no danger of that, since I'm not welcome in my father's presence since Robin was born, whether at Stoke or in his Chambers. But we must do something to try and save John."

"We? Really?" Howard took her hands again. "What do you propose, Frances? If you fancy I'm going to visit your childhood love and seek to reform him, I have to disillusion you."

"If you could find out where he is living, I can visit him myself and see whether I may do something to deter him."

Sir Robert's jaw dropped. "My lover of lame dogs, would you care to remember that your situation is precarious and mine scarcely less so? The two of us are barely released from custody, and my brothers had to work hard to make that happen." He squeezed her hands. "Promise me to lie low, until it is clear that the Council is not continuing to proceed against you."

She remonstrated, "But, Robert, if I can just speak with him, John Clavell may listen to me. I owe it to our friendship to try."

Howard sighed. "Dear Lord. You really do have a penchant for rescuing people, don't you, Frances? I wish now I had never said a word about the wretched fellow. Please do us all a favour by staying focused on our own concerns. If not for me, then at least for our son's sake."

"We *must* do something." Midnight blue eyes pleaded.

Grey eyes looked unwontedly stern in response. "We *must* do precisely nothing that may bring unwanted attention on you."

Frances persisted. "Robert, if you had known John as I do, you would know that his heart is in the right place. When he used to dream of being a highwayman, he wanted to rob the rich to pay the poor."

Sir Robert dropped her hands and sounded irritated as he replied, "Frances, wake up. This is no childish dream. John Clavell is robbing the rich to pay himself and some crooked London goldsmith he's embroiled with. The poor do not benefit one jot from Clavell's particular brand of philanthropy."

Still she continued, "You don't understand. He's had a difficult life. His father was a ne'er-do-well and left his mother when he was tiny. I believe she neglected John dreadfully. It's hard for children when their parents are not on good terms and abandon them. His uncle is a stern and difficult man as well."

Robert's irritation appeared to be growing. "I reject your 'poor John' story. There are plenty of children from ruptured families who don't turn into petty criminals. Yourself included, Frances."

Unexpectedly, she chuckled. "I have to tell you that, when John and I were young, we did talk about me becoming a knight of the road with him. I was not eager at first, but he made it sound such an adventure that latterly I was almost persuaded. As children, it was so easy to create a cocoon of make believe around ourselves. We were both blind to the unpleasant realities that were waiting for us both in adulthood."

Robert sat beside her again. "Well, you *are* an adult and also a mother, so please don't even think of spinning any more cocoons, except around yourself and Robin. I'm frankly amazed at you, Frances. Haven't you had enough drama and difficulty in your life? You cannot afford to bring any public attention on yourself. Promise me to leave Clavell alone, my love."

Frances did not respond. Instead she pursed her lips and stared fixedly into the fire. Robert Howard observed her for several minutes.

At last, the silence between them must have become more than he could bear, for he grunted and said, "Oh, Frances. You are a stubborn woman. I'll see if I can obtain an address for your highwayman. If I can, I will *not* give it to you, but I will instead undertake to have a letter from you delivered to him. And that is quite as much contact from either of us with John Clavell as I am willing to countenance, as well as a great deal more than he deserves."

CHAPTER TWENTY-SEVEN

California

Makepeace sat with his head bowed. His face was part hidden but his whole aspect spelled dejection.

My heart went out to him. "Bob, he is sick."

" Yes, he's sick. Sick in the head." Bob pulled out his iPhone. "I'm calling the cops now."

"Wait, Bob. Please let's just think first about the best thing for him. Once we involve the police, there's no turning back."

Bob swung round and stared at me, incredulity written all over his face. "Best thing *for him*? The only thing to do is to get this lunatic locked up. Then you and I can pick up the pieces and get on with the rest of our lives, like two normal human beings."

"Bob, you've every right to feel furious. I would be too, if I had been pulled halfway around the world. But I'm not sure calling the police is the right move."

"My God, Sarah, have you lost your mind now, too? I know you must have been under a strain, but we need to get him locked up. You've been jerked around the parking lot by this prick, as much as I have. Your wrists bear the proof."

"I felt OK as soon as you got here."

"Yeah. And before? Don't tell me you enjoyed spending two days cuffed to a bed and ending up with your wrists torn to shreds. This man *kidnapped* you, Sarah. He's no longer just the egotistical pain-in-the-ass he used to be. He's committed a criminal act and he needs to be locked away for it."

"Bob, please listen. Apart from anything else, he's very drunk and he's sick. I don't know the source of his *malaise*, but I doubt the California State penitentiary system is the place to discover it and get him the treatment he needs."

"I can't believe I'm hearing this. You can get treatment in the prison system. And who cares where he gets treatment, or if he gets it at all, as long as he's out of our lives? Goddammit, woman, I've always thought you are too nice for your own good. Can't you see that being held hostage for two days by a sick bastard with a knife and a loaded gun and then, as soon as you're free, talking about what's best for him, is over the top, even for you?"

Bob looked nonplussed. When I did not reply, he shrugged. "Well, I guess this is what people mean when they talk about Stockholm syndrome. Please don't tell me you've fallen in love with your kidnapper, Sarah. Who are you? Patty Hearst the second?"

The sarcasm in his voice stung, but it also stiffened my resolve. "Bob, you know me better than that. I'm being practical. I don't know the sentence for kidnapping in this state, but I imagine it is a heavy one. I'm not ready to write Antony Makepeace's life off, on the basis of what he just did to me."

"Then you're as crazy as he is."

I persisted. "No, I don't think I am. Yes, he's behaved abusively to us both. But neither of us is likely to suffer long-term harm as a result. In the depths of me, I don't believe that Antony is a criminal. Locking him up for a prison term might make him one. It doesn't help us. It just sweeps him and his problems out of our immediate sight. It doesn't get to grips with Antony's issues about the past and his wish for retribution. It may make them worse."

"Who *cares*, as long as he's locked away? Retribution? Maybe you can turn the other cheek, but *I* need retribution. I need to see Johnny Clavylle get what he deserves, shut up in a place where he can't do me and mine any more harm. You haven't known the man for nearly forty years. If you had, you wouldn't be talking this way."

"You're right. I don't know him like you do. So tell me about him, Bob."

Bob shook his head wearily. "Oh, for God's sake, Sarah."

"*Tell* me about him."

Bob glared. "Woman, I don't need this from you right now."

I stared him down. Eventually he responded grudgingly. "Ever since I met him, Johnny Clavylle has coveted everything I owned. Things began to go sour with Nights of the Road from the moment he joined the band. He wasn't one of the original members, you know. The fights I've told you about began the moment he joined. He wanted me out, to take over as lead singer."

Antony raised his head for the first time since Bob and I had begun talking about him. "That's because I'm a better singer than you are. Everyone in the band but you knew that."

Bob ignored the interruption. "Johnny also only had to see a woman looking as though she might be interested in me to want to take her away from me. I can't tell you how many times that happened."

I glanced at Makepeace, whose head had dropped again, then back at Bob. He nodded. "Ask Johnny how many times he went behind my back and told lies to my girlfriends about me being unfaithful. It usually worked. Women believed him. And guess who was always waiting in the wings to mend their broken hearts, when they had walked out on me?"

Bob half turned and stared at Makepeace hard, before looking back at me, "You heard him trying to do the same thing earlier today. Johnny wanted to make trouble between you and me, by telling tales about my past. Same old pattern. At least you had the sense to cut him off, before he got started. Retribution? Hah! If anyone here is in line for some retribution, it's me."

Bob got up and wandered the room, which had seemed so much smaller since his arrival. He went across to the glass wall, stared into the recording studio, then turned and faced me.

"Look, babe, I am hungry and tired and out of patience. Let's please just get this over with now, by calling the cops."

I breathed deeply. This was hard. "Bob, I'm sorry too. I'm sorry that it's been so tough for you with Johnny for so long. But that's between you and him. You must do what you want, as far as you and Antony Makepeace are concerned. For my part, I want to try and find out what is behind all this, for his and my sake."

I stood up from the bed that had been my prison for more than two days and walked across the room. I stopped in front of Makepeace and looked down at his averted face.

"If I choose not to bring kidnapping charges against you, are you willing to follow Bob's suggestion?"

"What suggestion? The only suggestion I've heard Bob make is to call the cops and get me locked up. I'm hardly likely to say yes to that, am I?"

Makepeace's tone was as unresponsive as his expression, but he looked me in the eyes as he answered.

"He talked with you in England about going into rehab. From the amount you've drunk since we got here, it's clear to me that you do need to dry out and I doubt you can manage that without professional support. You're ruining your liver, and drink is impairing your judgment. If Bob and I keep the police out of this, are you willing to go into a residential rehab facility here in California, for as long as it takes for you to get dry?"

Makepeace did not answer.

"Antony, I want to get to the bottom of this strange story about our shared past. I'm ready to explore it with you, if you are. But you've got to get your drinking under control first. What do you say?"

Still there was silence. I looked across at Bob. "How do you feel about this?" Bob looked heavenwards and said nothing.

I sighed, feeling leaden at their lack of response. "OK. I've said all I want to for now. I'm going to the bathroom to clean up. I'll be a while."

I walked back toward the bed and picked up clean clothes from the pile in the drawer that had been washed, dried and folded by Makepeace. I made for the bathroom, intentionally looking at neither man as I went.

I spent a long time in the shower. I washed my hair and luxuriated in the feel of warm water sluicing down over my face and body. As I stood under the cleansing stream, my heaviness dissipated and the ache in my wrists eased. I exited the shower, feeling tired but purified, inside and out. After patting myself dry, and applying antiseptic ointment from the bathroom cabinet to my wrists, I dressed and found a hair dryer in the vanity cabinet.

I stared at myself in the mirror, while I blow-dried my hair. The face looking back at me was not one that I recognised. My cheeks had hollows that I had never observed before and dark shadows under my eyes accentuated their size. My recent experience had left obvious physical marks. Yet I saw a woman who also exuded new strength and resolution.

I had no idea of what I would find or what I would say when I returned to the men, but I no longer felt any nagging anxiety. I had extended a hand of forgiveness and suggested a path forward. I had promised to support Antony Makepeace in unravelling his strange story, if he wanted it. I had done what I could to explain my reasons to Bob. I had neither hopes nor expectations. It was now for the two of them, and the larger stage on which we were all players, to determine what would happen next.

Walking back along the passage, it seemed to me that the atmosphere in the main room had lightened. Makepeace had moved over to the bed, where he now lay facing Bob. The rifle had been unloaded and its cartridges lay on the table next to the knife. Both men looked drained.

I looked from one to the other. "What have you decided?"

Bob spoke. "We'll try it your way, Sarah. Johnny's promised to go into rehab. So find him a good place here in the state, and quickly, before I change my mind. In the meantime, I'm hanging on to these." He indicated the rifle, the ammunition and the knife.

I smiled. "Thank you, sweetheart." Then I looked at Makepeace. "I know a few places. Have you ever been in a residential rehab before?"

He shook his head. I said, "It won't be a picnic, Antony. Are you willing to make the effort to stay the course?" Walking over and sitting down beside him on the bed, I continued. "You're the only one who can do the work and it will take more than just willpower. You'll have to open up with people, to help you unearth what drives your drinking and your destructive behaviour."

Makepeace picked at his fingers. "I don't need a lecture, thanks. I gave my word I'll give it a go. That's all I'll say."

I pressed. "What makes you ready to give it a go? Are you only agreeing in order to get off the hook of a kidnapping charge?"

Makepeace laughed, but he did not sound amused. "Maybe."

I responded acerbically. "Then I hope you won't be disappointed. You may find that you've chosen a harder short-term path than jail." I saw the look in his eyes and felt myself soften. "But I'm glad you've decided to try."

"Know why I did, Sarah?" Makepeace's expression and tone changed.

"No, I don't. Do you?"

"Yep." He nodded. "I did it because *you* chose a harder path. In your situation, I would have been bent on taking revenge. It surprised me to hell and back again when you started talking about what I need and what's best for me. Bob's right. You're a nice woman and you're behaving better than I deserve. I appreciate it."

I felt a rush of empathy. "I actually care about you getting through this, Antony. I'll do everything I can to support you."

"There's one thing I don't understand."

"What?"

"I don't get *why* you care, given how I've treated you."

I laughed. "I'm not sure I do either. I just don't seem able to stay angry with you, in spite of you being so unpleasant at times. It may have to do with how I felt whenever you watched the Scott's Orioles and that prairie falcon. I used to watch birds with a friend when I was a child. I couldn't stay frightened or resentful, when those birds were around. And it seemed like you couldn't behave badly toward me then either."

Makepeace's features lit up. "That reminds me, I forgot to tell you. While I was waiting for Bob to arrive, I saw where their nest is. I was right. The male went down into that dead stuff just under the yucca crown. I'm sure he was taking food in to the female. She must be sitting on her eggs. We can take a look, but we'll need to be careful or we'll frighten her away."

"I don't believe it!"

We turned to Bob, who was looking from Makepeace to me and back. He threw up his hands. "I get here to find you with a loaded gun in your hand, Johnny, and you tied up in handcuffs that have ripped your wrists to shreds, Sarah. Now the two of you sit here chatting about bird watching. The world or I have gone mad. Perhaps both."

I stood up from the bed and moved over to give Bob a hug. He made a big show of fending me off, but his hands gripped mine and did not let go.

"Do you think we could focus on reality, or at least that version of it known as LaLa Land? I need to get back into town. In case you've both forgotten, I've still got a music tour to try and salvage from all that Johnny has done to wreck it."

Bob's voice sounded rough at the edges as he added, "And, given the way you two have just tied me up in knots, maybe it's time I gave up trying to promote any more British invasions of the USA."

CHAPTER TWENTY-EIGHT

England 1626

"It's done at last!" The man wore mourning clothes but his face was creased in a hundred smiles.

Frances looked blank. Robert seized her hands and pumped them up and down. "The estate finally cleared the courts today. After four years, Clun is mine and I have my own castle to offer my queen. You've often said you are a country girl at heart. Now's your chance to prove it. Shropshire awaits you in its midsummer glory. When can you and Robin be ready to leave?"

Frances shook her head. Her face puckered. "I don't know if I can leave Purbeck alone. He is having problems again. It feels so cruel to abandon him. And Buckingham would pursue me into Shropshire."

"Buckingham has been trying to drive you and Purbeck apart for years. Let him think he's won the day. Tell him you agree to separate permanently from your husband and that you will go with your son into seclusion."

"He won't believe me, Robert. George expects everyone to have a hidden agenda. He detects subterfuge at a thousand paces."

"This is no subterfuge. And he's got problems of his own, these days. He will lose interest in us, when you disappear from view. You can't do that if you continue to be seen abroad with Society's most gossip-worthy hostess. I hear Eliza is back in Town and that you and she have been seen visiting."

"I'm being discreet, but I won't turn my back on Mama. She tried to get help from Papa, during my detention, and she's kinder to Robin now. She's still upset over the Duchess of Richmond throwing the lease of Hatton House back at her. And you're wrong about George. He will hurt you as well as me if he can. People close to him told Mama he's still seething, all these months on, that you avoided the oath in the High Commission, and claimed Parliamentary privilege to get free, as well as securing my bail."

Robert chuckled. "He was even angrier when he learned the Commission could not legally fine me, thanks to your father. Funny that Sir Edward should have helped us, even though he refused Eliza, and he could not have known in advance that expunging that legal clause would assist my case. But it makes me feel somewhat less harshly toward him. As for Eliza, she shouldn't have complained that the Duchess of Richmond was cheating her."

"Mama often feels cheated over financial transactions. Anyway, I can't desert her altogether, for she's growing fond of Robin now he is talking, even though she still disapproves of us."

Robert served himself a glass of red wine. "I don't lose any sleep over Eliza's disapproval, but I must admit that, when you have needed her help, she usually tries to support you, even if with much preening and sighing over her noble sacrifices. So you may tell her she will be welcome to visit us in Shropshire, if she misses the boy."

Frances looked doubtful. "I don't think Mama enjoyed what she is now calling an agonisingly wild exile out in the Fens of Cambridgeshire. I suspect that venturing as far as Shropshire would seem like visiting a foreign land."

Robert shrugged. "Eliza can please herself. Shropshire will doubtless survive not receiving a visit from Lady Hatton. Oh, by the way, that fellow Selden wants to prove that my excommunication was an illegal act. I couldn't follow the ins-and-outs of his argument, and I'm only a stepping-stone for him to catch larger fish, but I've agreed for him to proceed on my behalf. So my dear, everything is moving in the right direction for us now."

"You make light of things today, Robert. It's natural, given your elation about the settlement, and I'm glad for you. But please don't forget the extent of Buckingham's anger that the Commission still has not pronounced me guilty. Remember how he set Worley on me? Think of the mischief he has done your family. If he believes that I want to separate permanently from Purbeck, George may try to chain me to John for life, just to punish me."

Robert only shrugged again. "Frances, I think you are allowing yourself to feel tyrannised by George unnecessarily now. I called him out last year and he would not even meet me. That's how much of a man your Duke of Buckingham is. I don't make light of our situation, but nor do I believe George's influence is what it was when the Old King was alive."

Frances disagreed. "I thought his star would fade when the old King died, but you must have noticed he maintains as tight a hold as ever over Charles."

"Yes, he still has a grip on the King, but our new Queen is not smitten and she spells trouble ahead for Buckingham with Charles. Meanwhile, Parliament is openly condemning George's recklessness. The Palatinate fiasco has made people angry, and impoverished the nation. Buckingham's failed campaigns in Cadiz and La Rochelle have emptied the Exchequer. Charles cannot buy George's way out of trouble any longer."

Frances was ready to concede one point. "You may be right about the Queen. I hear that Henrietta Maria loathes Buckingham and does not hide it. And Mama believes that Charles loves her and her influence will grow."

Robert sat down beside her. "I think the most important change for you is that George has a son at last. He need no longer feel threatened about the succession. Perhaps the Council does not pronounce sentence because it cannot prove adultery. Your staff and intimates remain loyal, so I believe you will not be prosecuted further. You are in a much stronger position, Frances."

"Worley spoke against me, and might have acted too, but for Mr. Elwick. You were not sanguine about our situation while I was in Stepney. And the adultery charge has not been dropped. George and his odious advisor may yet pull a damning enough story together to get me convicted. What if they oblige Isabel Peel to testify? You've used the passageway from her apartment to come to me. What about the nights we spent together at Ware? I don't trust Dr. Lambe not to do me harm, if Buckingham turns the screws on him. "

"By odious advisor, you mean Laud?" When Frances nodded, Robert laughed. "That reverend gentleman is certainly a Buckingham lap-dog, but I'll wager he has some guilty secrets of his own, when it comes to where and with whom he sleeps. Laud will not stick his neck out, if it puts him at risk. As for that footman you dismissed, he was obviously acting out of vengeance."

"There's Kit too. He's hated me ever since I first refused his advances, years ago. He was elated to be given charge of progressing the Commission's inquiry against me. And Robin stands between his own boy and the Buckingham estates, if anything happens to George's son."

"Our august Earl of Anglesey? Frances, you're really scraping the barrel, if you are worrying about Kit Villiers. The man's already expelled from Court for drinking and lechery. Charles won't abide the lush behaviour that went on in the Old King's time, and the Queen is as irritated by all the Buckingham relatives as she is by George. She made a huge fuss at having to receive your mother- and sister-in-law as a Ladies of the Bedchamber. You're searching for trouble where there is none now, my love."

"I don't agree," insisted Frances, "My name has not been cleared. Laud was the one who arranged your excommunication, as I am sure your friend Selden will prove. He will do anything to please the master with whom he is besotted and George still means to pin sorcery charges on me. I know it." She shivered. "People get so stirred up by talk of witchcraft. We were stupid to ask Dr. Lambe to read our future in the stars."

"Calling us stupid does not undo what is done. And, if Lambe were going to land us in hot water, he'd have spoken out by now. I suspect he has some juicy secrets to tell against George and his mother. Can't you stop being a killjoy, my love, and celebrate with me?" Robert raised his wine goblet to her.

Frances ignored the gesture and became accusatory. "It's easy enough for you to shrug all this off, Robert. You're a man and you enjoy established rank. As a Member of Parliament you are beyond so much of the law. You don't know what it is like for me, always feeling so exposed."

Robert Howard took her hands. "Let's not dispute. It's *because* your situation is exposed, and we've had proof of Buckingham's past intent to do you harm, that I want to take you away now and give you my protection." Emotion showed in his face. "I would not ask you to leave, if I thought you could be happy in London. You're a saint to have put up with your Lord's violent moods. It's time to think of your own interests. And Robin's."

Still she was doubtful. "There's Papa and Mama to think of too. I hate to bring gossip and dishonour on them."

Howard stroked her cheek. "Dishonour? Frances, you've jumped through hoops for your selfish parents. Do you intend to go on making sacrifices for them? They make their own gossip, with or without you, and their reputations are solid for good and bad. Your father is as powerful as any in Parliament and your mother has always been a match for anyone in the land. I've never known anyone more adept than Eliza Hatton at ignoring the critics, and getting what she wants, although it rarely leaves her content."

As Frances continued to hesitate, Robert became heated in turn. "Goddamn it, the situation with Purbeck and you was intended to be temporary. A lifetime of happiness awaits us, if we have the courage to seize it."

Frances stared at her lover. In the years that they had conducted their clandestine relationship, he had never made such a stand. But he had never had an estate of his own to offer her until now.

She wanted to respond in kind, but a feeling of oppression weighed her down. "Truth to tell, Robert, I'm not certain I can ever know real happiness again. Quite apart from George's enmity and poor Purbeck's continuing condition, we've suffered so much loss in these last few years. Your brother Charles and then my dear grandfather. Elizabeth leaving her baby Frances to grow up without a mother." Tears filled her eyes. "I feel so sad that my poor sister waited years for her own wedding, then had little time to enjoy her marriage and none at all to cherish her daughter. It's too, too cruel of Fate."

Her tears were flowing freely now. "The list of misfortunes is endless. John Clavell's capture and his death sentence was such a dreadful shock. His Majesty's unhappy end saddened us all. Uncle Bacon has left a hole in my life. At least he and I were reconciled before he passed. And it is only days since your dear father went to his Maker, God rest his soul."

"All the more reason for us to make a happy life with Robin while we have energy and health to do so."

Her tears subsided and she considered his words. Still, Frances felt drawn to question. "Robert, have you fully considered the effect on your reputation of living openly out of wedlock with me? You know Purbeck has converted, so will never countenance a divorce. Think carefully on this, my dearest."

"I have thought of little else for four years, ever since knowing I would eventually have a home at Clun to offer you. My brothers are fond of you and will not object. Your mother wants you and Robin safe, even if she disapproves of us. And, think how delighted she will be if our living together angers your father."

His last comment drew a reluctant laugh from Frances. Then she faltered and fell back on her earlier refrain. "But can I do this to Purbeck? He claims Robin as his son. We encouraged him to do that, remember?"

Robert groaned. "You're not living day-to-day as man and wife. What will Purbeck lose? What can Robin gain by continued association with the Villiers name? An empty title, assuming George's boy thrives. Your mother has never settled her properties on Purbeck. With Elizabeth already gone, when Eliza passes, you'll have everything of hers, and Robin will inherit through you."

Her temper rose. "Forget Mama's wretched properties! That's all I've ever heard about since I was young and it sickens me. Purbeck loves me and delights in Robin. He's always said he could bear me loving another, for he knew that my heart was never engaged when we married. But, if I leave him permanently and take Robin, he'll have nothing left to live for."

Frances stood up and paced in agitation. She turned back to Robert and put her hand on his sleeve. "When his fits are not on him, Purbeck is sweet natured and far from the fool that people make him out. He does useful work behind the scenes, serving George and the King, and gets no credit for it."

Her companion only scowled. "You're barred from living with Purbeck, and Robin is not his son. What difference does it make whether you live with Eliza or under my roof? If Purbeck is so fond of you, what has prevented him all these years from persuading his brother to stop harassing you?"

"He has tried. Do you know anyone who has had any success against Buckingham, other than Mama? And she has done so only because George still itches for her to change the terms of the wretched inheritance. It *would* hurt John to know that I am with you. There is a difference between me living with Mama or you. I must feel grateful to Purbeck for his loyalty and kindness."

Her lover pulled away. He looked upset but determined. "Frances, I'm leaving if you use the word 'kindness' about a man who has raised his hand to you. It offends me. I need you to make a choice. I am offering you my protection and my home. I cannot offer you or Robin my name while you remain married. Nor can I give you my heart."

Frances was so shocked by his last words that she gave a little cry of hurt.

Robert laughed and caught her in his arms. "You little goose! I can't give you my heart because you already have it in your keeping." He indicated the chestnut-coloured lovelock that cascaded down over his broad left shoulder. "All the world knows I wear this as testimony to our love. I've been yours since that day we saw each other again at Uncle Thomas Knyvett's home, do you remember?"

Frances nodded. "Your love has been the one constant in my life."

He stroked her face. "That day at Staines, you were being pursued by the whole world, and about to be forced into marrying John Villiers. God knows I wanted to protect you. I wish I had followed my instincts then and carried you away from Uncle Tom's. But you were so young."

A gurgle escaped Frances. "We are neither of us exactly ancient now."

"Sometimes I feel extremely old, Frances. Especially when I fear that our lives may pass without us knowing the delight of living together."

Robert took her hands again. "I mean what I say. You must choose. I will not go on living a hole-and-corner existence with you. I want my son to grow up with his real father. I feel no ill will toward Purbeck. But, if it is a question of setting his intermittent happiness against our own, well, I can be as selfish as your parents or Buckingham." His mouth set in a rigid line. "Frances, I am asking for the last time that you come away with me to Clun. Will you?"

Grey eyes were fixed on hers. Frances put a hand to her heart and breathed deeply. "Yes, Robert. And may God forgive us if we sin."

CHAPTER TWENTY-NINE

California

We travelled in silence and I sensed unspoken resentment in the air. I wondered if Bob was experiencing backlash; perhaps wishing we had not trusted Makepeace to book himself into the rehab clinic I had contacted.

It seemed better not to ask sensitive questions until our journey was over. Bob was usually an excellent driver, but nervous exhaustion and jet lag were currently affecting his reactions behind the wheel. Fortunately there was little traffic to challenge his erratic driving.

In Palm Springs, he parked next to my Mustang, sitting in the lot outside the hotel. I touched it in passing. Bob caught my gesture and gave me the ghost of a smile. Cathy was washing glasses in the bar as we entered the inner courtyard.

She oozed concern. "Well, look at you! What a relief to see you back, Sarah. We were worried when you left without a word, with your car still in the parking lot. Then Bob arrived, not knowing where you had gone, and Heidi told us about a man whom she mistook for Bob. What's been going on? Are you both OK?"

I hid my wrists. "A communication mix-up. A friend picked me up for a surprise visit out to his place in the desert and then I had difficulty contacting Bob, to let him know where I was. I'm sorry if I worried you by disappearing so suddenly."

"No problem. It's good to see you. It's a little late, but do you guys want a drink?"

Bob said nothing and kept on walking. I looked at his back and shook my head. "Not this evening, thanks, Cathy. We're both tired and Bob is jet-lagged. He's had a hard trip."

"I'll say I've had a hard trip," Bob muttered as we entered our hotel room. I responded instantly. "I know. Thanks again for giving Antony a chance. It can't have been easy for you, given his past behaviour."

Bob shut the door, turned and glared at me. "I can't think why I let you talk me into it. He'll never turn up at that rehab place. He only agreed to avoid getting arrested. He's no fool, even if he is crazy. Too late now, anyway. Who's going to listen if you try to bring kidnapping charges against him later, especially after what you just said to Cathy? And he'll deny it. Johnny Clavylle will get off scot-free yet again."

I felt myself being pulled into a fight. "I didn't talk you into anything. I left you and him together to decide what to do. We're following a recommendation *you* had already made him in England. Trying to get him to deal with his addiction."

"Yeah, but that was before he kidnapped you at knifepoint, Sarah. And before he turned a loaded rifle on us both. Johnny's lucky I didn't blow his brains out with it."

I shrugged, feeling defensive. "We've taken a risk. Life is about risk, that's what you're always telling me. I wouldn't have suggested rehab instead of jail, if I had believed that he would threaten anyone else. You and I are apparently the two people he wants to hurt, and I want to find out why."

I put down the pile of clothes I had been carrying and looked at Bob. He was clearly unconvinced by my words. "Bob, I'm sure he won't ever come after me again in that way. There was something so unconvincing about him in the tough guy role, except when he was really drunk and acting like a man possessed."

Bob threw himself on the bed, still scowling. "I hope you're right. But I should never have left him able to drive in his present condition. Talk about an unguided missile."

I felt like responding that a tired and tense Bob had not been the safest of drivers during our journey back to Palm Springs, and that he had still judged himself better able to take the wheel than me. An inner voice prompted me to defuse our conflict, so instead I said, "It's important for him to make this next step on his own. He let us take his remaining whisky and the weapons without a murmur. And he's promised not to leave the cabin until morning and then go straight to Dream Canyon."

"For all we know, he's got a stash of liquor and other arms hidden there. He can always buy whisky and another gun."

I sat on the bed beside Bob and stroked his arm. "We'll know soon enough whether he keeps his promise to check himself in at Dream Canyon. I'll call them tomorrow afternoon to find out if he's arrived. For now, let's concentrate on us? You're exhausted. Do you want to eat? Shall we go out for something? We can call and get something delivered, if you prefer. Unless you'd rather sleep?"

"Listen to you, mother hen. You're the one who was trussed up at knifepoint by a madman for two days. How about we concentrate on what *you* want?"

I laughed in relief that Bob's mood could shift so quickly. "I'm fine. I have speedy powers of recuperation in such situations."

"You make a habit of being kidnapped, do you?"

"No. But from the moment you arrived, I felt safe. I *was* afraid quite often before you came, although it didn't seem like a real kidnapping. There was something artificial about the whole thing, as if we were in a movie." I stretched out at Bob's side. "I don't know about you, but I *am* hungry. I'm up for that French restaurant on Palm Canyon, if you are. We may as well enjoy some vacation while we can, since I won't see much of you, once we're back in L.A.. Which reminds me. Will you be able to salvage the tour or has Makepeace really ruined it?"

Bob yawned and his voice mellowed. "I'll pull something out of the bag. I've never failed yet. The trip to Berlin had its useful moments. In fact, the line-up is probably stronger than before. And, if Johnny does succeed in drying out, a Moonlight Jax tour later might work. I do face a mountain of work to contact venues and get publicity changed for the new bands. And the ticket selling machine needs to be actioned yesterday."

"A tour may be what Johnny needs to stay sober when he comes out of Dream Canyon."

"*If* he goes into Dream Canyon. God, I hope he does, Sarah. He's such a pain in the ass, but he also happens to be one of the outstanding rock musicians of all time. I guess that must have influenced me not to turn him in myself."

"I'm wondering about my own motives for wanting to help him. I know you think I'm soft, but something else was driving me. It's hard to put into words."

"Try."

"Well, for one thing, I believe we've all contributed in creating a myth around mega-rock stars like Johnny Clavylle, which is hard for individuals to carry, without losing a sense of perspective. I feel we all bear a responsibility to stick with people, if the shadow side of that myth comes home to roost and people like him start behaving as if they are outside the law."

"Sounds heavy. Who are you including in this we?"

"Society and all who live in her. Starting perhaps with those of us who pinned our dreams on rock and roll to change society. For many of us, at least in Britain, the rock scene was about getting free of outmoded rules and breaking out of what felt like a prison. As a teenager I was a screaming fan, who conspired in letting ordinary young men believe they were rock gods. And there were plenty of hangers-on ready to feed the myth, in order to make money out of the machine."

"I was never a screaming fan. So are you including me in the ordinary young men or the hangers on? Am I a rock god or a leech?" Bob sounded suddenly cool.

"If the cap fits, wear it. You had a taste of the glamour and superstar status in which Antony Makepeace seems to have got stuck. But it seems you had the sense or good luck to get out of the limelight before it dazzled you into believing you were beyond the law. You came out the other side of drugs without doing yourself any long-term damage. From all you've told me, you were probably a mixture of lucky and smart."

Bob looked into the middle distance, so I continued, "And yes, I guess now you're a hard-headed business type making good money out of people like Johnny. You love the music, you have a good heart and you play fair with people, so I'm sure you give value for money. But to me we are all still part of an addictive system, that itself is a symptom of an addictive society. And I don't like to see any one person or part made into a scapegoat and carrying an unfair load as the shadow for the whole."

"Quite a speech. And much too deep for me to take in while my hard business head is scrambled." Bob's tone had become light and humorous.

I was happy to follow his lead. "We'd better let the scrambled head get some rest then, particularly if it is to be any use to Antony in arranging a tour for Moonlight Jax."

"Babe, don't get your hopes up on that score. I don't believe he's going to make it. Although, if Johnny can do the hard work of getting sober, I'll play fair, as you put it, and try to make something work for him." Bob could not help himself and I could see his mind, even in its exhausted state, already begin to turn on the possibilities. "His recent bands are known here in the US and there's a solid fan base to build on. I'm not so sure how well the highwayman image will play now. It's always a gift to special effects, but it may be too sensitive, with the mood of the country so different since 9/11."

He had reminded me of the story we had heard at the cabin. "I wonder why the highwayman theme keeps repeating in Antony's bands? It seems so much more for him than just a clever device to attract fans. I want to investigate his story and especially the coincidences between our names and his supposed real-life characters. They've quite spooked me. Did you ever hear anything about his family history that might offer a clue?"

"He said his family originally owned vast tracts of the area, the night I stayed with him down near that old castle. I assumed he was showing off and the whisky was talking. But since you've proposed yourself as Johnny's professional support through this next stage, I guess you'll find out soon enough. I can't say I like that idea. You've got me to look after."

I chuckled. "I didn't know you needed any professional support or personal looking after. Are you jealous?"

"Nothing of the sort." Bob looked and sounded offended.

I leaned over and nibbled his ear. "My mistake. You have no need to feel jealous of him or anyone. Now, are we going to go out and eat before I show you how much I missed you, or afterwards?"

Bob pulled me into his arms.

"How about you show me how you missed me before *and* after we eat?"

CHAPTER THIRTY

England 1627

"You are wrong about him, Robert. We have been friends since we were young. Charles has not always been as supportive as I might have wished in recent years, since Buckingham has had his ear, but I know the King could never actively wish me harm. It must be thanks to him that I have heard no more about the charges against me. Do you not think I must have been included in his Coronation pardon, even if I was not named?"

"I prefer you to take no chances, Frances. Power does odd things to a man, especially the absolute power of our monarch."

Frances shook her head. "You'll see. Charles is loyal and he will protect me now as King, just as he did when we were children."

"I would still be more comfortable if you and the boy would remain here. I will not be in Town for a moment longer than is needed."

"Robert dear, I pine for adult company whenever you are away. I get so lonely here in Shropshire when you leave, especially with winter drawing fast upon us. People do not know how to treat me, since I am not your wife. And I do yearn to hear all the gossip from Mama. She misses us too and has not seen Robin for more than a year."

He frowned. She pressed. "I will not put myself about in Society, I promise. Robin and I will stay quietly with Mama and visit Purbeck at York House. He is said to be well at present and longs to see the boy. We can spend time with you next door, at Suffolk House, when you are free. Other than that I will simply run a few errands in Town. I need Yuletide supplies that are impossible to obtain in the country. I want Robin to have a Christmas to remember now he is old enough to take notice. I promise I will not show my face anywhere near the Court."

When residing in Shropshire, Robert made a point of attending services in turn at each of the churches that fell within his patronage as lord of the vast estate of Clun. Today it was the turn of St Mary's Church at Hopesay and the couple were whispering together in the front pew. As the minister entered and the organ started to play, Robert stood and put his finger to his lips. "Let's talk about this later."

After leading the small congregation through the opening hymn, he sat back and chewed inwardly on his concerns during the lessons and sermon that followed. Robert Howard wished he might share Frances's sanguine attitude toward a London visit for their son and her but he believed their situation to have deteriorated since he had brought her to Clun.

Robert did not hold a rosy view of the New King and nor, he knew, did many of his peers in Parliament. He was five years senior to Charles, so was already eight years old when the Stuarts arrived in London from Scotland with their royal children. A younger son of the house of Suffolk playing regularly at Court had ample opportunity to learn from observation, and Robert watched the little prince closely, throughout his childhood and beyond.

From the first, he had judged Charles to be a difficult and moody boy. Exquisite manners showed themselves early, but Charles was also prone to tantrums. With Henry's death, the new Prince of Wales seemed to grow more arrogant and age did nothing to increase his humility. He brooded, took offence easily and never forgot nor forgave a real or imagined slight.

Robert felt despondent about the deteriorating national situation since the New King's accession to the throne. It was true that James and his spendthrift lover had so squandered Elizabeth's legacy that the monarchy was bankrupt when Charles inherited it, and that even before his death the Old King had allowed many levers of government to pass to the war-mongering Buckingham. Yet his benign and conciliating influence had kept the country relatively stable and calm for nearly a quarter of a century.

Now, his son and successor, Charles, was pursuing an avowedly militaristic course in Europe, steered by Buckingham at great expense and with a notable lack of success. The New King had inherited all the debts and obligations, but none of the peace-loving and essentially kindly nature, of his father. Moreover, while Charles's standards of personal morality had stemmed hedonistic excesses at Court – which bothered Buckingham little, since the object of his current affections lived across the Channel – the young French-born Queen was proving wilful and extravagant.

Worse still for the country, Henrietta Maria was a Papist. The large Catholic entourage that had accompanied her from France at her marriage had created divisions at Court and the conflicts soon rippled out into a land in which Puritanism was gaining an ever stronger foothold. Tension was mounting monthly, as Henrietta Maria pressed her husband to grant the leniency in laws toward Catholics that had been promised by the Old King during their marriage negotiations, and his Protestant advisors demanded the opposite.

In the three years that Robert had been representing Bishops Castle in the House, clashes between King and Parliament over religion or money had become increasingly heated. Unfortunately, Charles had shown himself more intransigent and contemptuous of Parliament than even his father before him. Costly and failed military expeditions accompanied by demands for more taxes did nothing to raise morale among the King's beleaguered subjects. Meanwhile, the mood across the country was depressed by frequent outbreaks of plague and poor harvests. England under King Charles the First was not a happy place.

Concerning Buckingham, Robert felt convinced from his recent London visits that Frances needed again to be on her guard. George's influence with Charles had not waned, in spite of his lack of popularity with the Queen, Parliament and the country at large. And he continued to punish his enemies without mercy.

Howard's antennae had twitched early in the year, when Isabel Peel and her servant Elizabeth Ash were convicted at the beginning of February, for past complicity in affording Robert secret access to Frances. He was working behind the scenes now to try and obtain their pardon, and he downplayed the matter with Frances. Still, to him it seemed clear that the women's convictions revealed George was still out for blood and would do all he could to keep the matter of Lady Purbeck in legal play.

In addition, Buckingham had lost his only son, Charles, in March. The Duchess was pregnant again, and the King had also just signed an extraordinary order that, in the event of no male heir, Buckingham's daughter Mary would inherit all her father's titles and honours. But it was clear that George nursed fresh concerns for the Buckingham succession. Kit too. That put Robin back in the spotlight and once again at risk.

All in all, Sir Robert Howard had sound reasons for wanting his little family to remain tucked safely away in Shropshire at this time.

Frances nudged him. Lost in reflection, Robert had not noticed that the service was at an end. The congregation was waiting for the Lord of Clun to take his leave, before any other person would move. He edged sideways out of the Howard family pew, turned and presented Frances with his arm.

"What were you thinking of, my dear? You seem so far away." Frances spoke softly as they walked together out of the church. He shook his head. "Later, my dear."

She took his cue and smiled to others around them, as Robert nodded and spoke to several parishioners he had recognised. The young minister greeted them at the church door and expressed his honour at welcoming the Lord of Clun to his Sunday service. Then the vicar turned to Frances. He blushed a beetroot red and fell silent. Howard raised an eyebrow.

Frances filled the awkward silence. "I enjoyed your sermon."

His colour still heightened, the minister thanked her and stammered that it was always a pleasure to welcome Lady Purbeck in his humble church.

"What does that poor young man make of our domestic situation?" Frances whispered to Robert as they walked to the waiting carriage.

Robert shrugged. "I don't know. He was certainly twitchy today. Perhaps he has received word from on high that he must try to persuade us to repent and reform our sinful ways." He chuckled. "He's no fool, though, even if he is young. He knows his living is in my keeping."

"Poor fellow. I feel guilty to be such a difficulty and a discomfort to him."

"Now don't go taking responsibility for that, as well as every other wrong that exists in our world, Mistress Frances Wright. This is my domain and we have the right to enjoy its privileges as we wish. Come, my love, enough talk. Our son is waiting."

"Very well. I promise not to take responsibility this time, but only if you allow Robin and me to accompany you, when you travel to Town."

"Did I ever tell you what a stubborn woman you are? Oh very well, my dear," Robert allowed himself grudgingly to be persuaded and Frances radiated joy during their coach journey back to the comfortable manor house at the edge of the forest, that they had chosen as their home, in preference to the part-ruined, if magnificently situated, castle at Clun.

Less than two weeks later, Sir Robert Howard was regretting his moment of weakness and wishing he had stood firm against all Frances's entreaties, when several officers of the law elbowed his protesting footman aside and entered his apartment at Suffolk House in the Strand.

Robert leaped to his feet "What in God's name do you think you are doing, entering my home without permission?"

The man at the head of the group inclined his head. "To whom do I have the honour of speaking, sir?" His courteous tone contrasted with the manner of his arrival.

"I am Sir Robert Howard, as you must well know."

The sergeant-at-arms bowed again and held out a parchment. "Your servant, Sir Robert. Written here you will find all the permission of which my men and I had need to afford us legal entry today." The sergeant nodded his head toward Frances. "In the name of His Majesty, I am required to conduct this lady to the Ecclesiastical Court of the High Commission."

He turned to look at Frances "I assume that you are indeed Lady Purbeck? We attended you at your *husband's* apartments next door in York House, but the Viscount himself advised us we would probably find you here."

"Why does the Commission demand my presence?" Frances was already standing, white-faced and trembling.

"Lady Purbeck, you have a case outstanding against you, which has been called for this very day. It is all written here on this warrant. You are charged with incontinence to your husband, the Lord Viscount Purbeck. You are called to present yourself forthwith before the Court of the High Commission and it is my job to escort you there now."

"It's nearly two years since this charge was brought. Why is it being resurrected now? I presume you are in the pay of the Duke of Buckingham."

"My men and I are in the employ of the Privy Council, ma'am."

"Which is well known to be at the beck and call of his Grace. Will you and your masters never have done with harrying me? I would have expected you to have more important matters to attend to, sir. Am I not covered by the Coronation amnesty? Why have I received no warning that such a charge is being brought in Council today?"

The sergeant's answering tone was both defensive and moralising. "You must address all such questions to the Court, Lady Purbeck. Since you ask my humble opinion, I would suggest that the harrying might cease if you decide to have done with making a mockery of the sanctity of marriage."

Robert swore. "Damn you for your insolence. Warrant or no warrant, you shall not address a lady thus in this house. Watch your tongue, sir."

"Sir Robert?" The burly man swung back toward Howard. He bowed a third time. "Read this also, if you please."

The sergeant handed over a second parchment. Robert bit his lip as he scanned the page and noted the distinctive signatures. He looked at Frances and shrugged. His anger and frustration were palpable. "My dear, I fear you must go. Damnation! It is entirely my fault for not listening to my better judgment about you coming to Town. Try not to worry. I will go to Purbeck immediately, to see if he can come to the Court to speak on your behalf. I will also do all I can to ensure you are not detained beyond today. And the boy will be kept safe, do not fear."

Howard turned back to the sergeant. "If this lady suffers any inconvenience or harm while in your care, you shall answer for it personally to me, Sergeant."

Frances incurred no physical harm during her six-mile journey along the river to Fulham Palace, nor did the sergeant and his men hold her beyond the end of the day. But the six hours she passed within its great chamber where the Ecclesiastical Court had assembled were unpleasant in the extreme.

Looking at the faces of the men brought together to listen to witnesses, and then confer and pass judgment on her case, she recognised most of the lords but only a few of the clerics. Present were the Lord Keeper of the Great Seal, the Earls of Dorset, Manchester, Montgomery and Pembroke, Viscount Grandison, five Bishops – including London, in whose residence they were gathered – two Deans and sundry lesser clerical and legal dignitaries.

Only in the soft brown eyes of Sir Charles Caesar could Frances discern a glimmer of sympathy for her situation, but that meant little, since Sir Charles was widely known as a man of courtesy and pleasing manners toward all women. Most of the judges wore neutral or stony expressions throughout the proceedings, although the churchmen seemed self-satisfied to a man.

The Bishop of Bath and Wells in particular was openly gloating. Frances gazed at William Laud for a long time without expression, then stood and turned slowly to hear the judgment read against her.

"May it be known that Frances, Lady Villiers, Viscountess Purbeck, has been found guilty of adultery and is therefore sentenced to be fined the sum of five hundred pounds, separated from her husband and to do penance, barefoot and clad in naught but a white shift, in full public view in the Chapel of the Savoy on a future Sunday to be named, where she is to seek forgiveness of her sins."

CHAPTER THIRTY-ONE

California

I felt nervous as I walked across from the visitors' car park to the clinic's main entrance. I had just reached the steps when a voice hailed me. "Hey."

I swung round. Makepeace was sitting with another man on a bench under an olive tree in a grassy garden area. He rose as I walked across and I held out my hand to him. "Hello, Antony."

He raised my fingers to his lips and kissed them with a gentle, old world courtesy. This was a different, calmer Antony Makepeace than I had met before.

"It's good of you to come and see me, Sarah. This is Jack. He's a smart guy, so the two of you will speak the same language. A university professor, Japanese history no less. He drew the short straw, getting a dunce like me as a roommate."

I shook the hand of a lean, grey-haired man who smiled. "Nice to meet you, Sarah. I understand it's thanks to you that Antony is here at all."

"I tell everyone you're my guardian angel." Makepeace chipped in.

"Hardly that." I had not known what to expect, but I had not anticipated idealisation. An inner voice told me to play it cool.

"I'll leave you both to catch up, but I hope to see you again, Sarah." The man named Jack rose and ambled away. I sat down in the seat he had vacated and looked around. In contrast to the sparse and dry mountain landscape in which the clinic was situated, the grounds immediately surrounding the main building were lush with vegetation.

There were people scattered everywhere, sitting and walking, alone and in pairs or small groups. Snatches of quiet conversation floated on the air, amplifying an impression of tranquillity. Dream Canyon seemed aptly named.

"What a beautiful place. An oasis. I've not visited this clinic before, although I've referred a couple of clients here." I turned to face Antony. "So what's going on with you?"

"Do you want me to be honest?"

"Of course."

"I haven't the faintest idea what's going on with me." Antony scratched his ear and rubbed his face. I waited for him to continue.

"The first two days I was completely out of it. They had me sedated. The next five or six days were pretty much hell. Then it was up and down for quite a while. The last couple of days have been OK, I suppose, but mostly I feel as if I'm on the edge of a precipice, and in danger of falling off, if I don't actually jump first, to end it all."

"Sounds tough. What's your daily routine?"

"Early to bed. Early to rise. I'm already wealthy, so I'm hoping that staying in this place will fill in the other two blanks. Come back next week and perhaps you will find my healthy and wise wings have sprouted."

I laughed. "It sounds as if they may be budding. The most difficult step was checking in here. That took a lot of guts."

Makepeace muttered something inaudible and looked embarrassed. I returned to neutral questioning. "Have you become involved with any groups, or are you still only meeting one-to-one with the staff?"

"Both. The group stuff isn't my favourite scene, but I'm seeing two great doctors during my individual sessions. Seen some powerful lectures too. Shit, Sarah, when they show you what happens to your body with alcohol poisoning, it's enough to turn you sober for life."

I laughed again. "That's the whole point of showing you, I imagine."

"Yeah, well it's good for shock tactics, but I don't know how long the effects will last. I don't know if I have it in me to stay sober when I leave."

"You don't need to think about leaving yet. The focus with this treatment process is different from some other addiction centres. And if you do feel a need for the ongoing structure that a programme like twelve-step offers, you can always connect with AA almost anywhere in the world when you leave."

"No thanks. I did try AA in England once and didn't make it past my first meeting. Twelve-step just didn't cut it for me. They hit me with all that stuff about addiction as a disease that you can recover from once you admit all your sins and surrender to a power greater than you. I've never bought into that crap. At least they don't push it on me here."

"Hmm. Well, twelve-step has helped millions. Still, it sounds as if you're feeling aligned with what goes on here. I'm glad if that's so, since I did try to match you to a process that I felt might be right for you."

Makepeace became suddenly animated. "One of my doctors is really great. He talks about addiction as an ally that you have to wrestle with, in order to discover its secrets. He says it can lead you to the source of your personal power, like getting a dragon to yield up its hidden treasure."

"Has your dragon yielded any treasure yet?"

"Not a lot. None really. Perhaps the trove has already been looted."

I chuckled. "I very much doubt that. Antony, when we were in your cabin, you went through a period of calling me Frances. Do you remember?"

"Of course." He sounded surprised at my question.

"Why did you do so?"

"Because that's what I always call you when I think about you. Before and after we met in this lifetime. I've already told you the story." He spoke impatiently and I saw traces of the old Antony in his irritability.

"So you do believe what you told me?"

Makepeace laughed. "Sarah, I may have been drinking more whisky than is good for my liver for too many years, but I am not actually nuts." He looked at me steadily. "Yes, I do believe we knew each other four hundred years ago."

"Tell me the main points of that story again."

He spoke patiently, as if repeating himself to a small child. "I lived in Dorset. You and I knew each other when we were children. Robert and I met much later in life. Your family was extremely wealthy and more highly connected than mine. Your mother owned Corfe Castle. You stayed there sometimes when you were a girl and that was how we met."

"What were our exact names?"

Makepeace stared down at his nails. "I've already told you that I used my own name when I began playing professionally in this lifetime, although I didn't know about my past life then: John Clavell or, as I prefer to spell it, Johnny Clavylle. Spellings varied a lot in the seventeenth century. You were Frances Coke. You spurned me and married a nobleman called Sir John Villiers. He was the Duke of Buckingham's older brother. Later he and you were made Viscount and Viscountess Purbeck by the King of England."

His story remained consistent with everything that he had previously told Bob and me. Only his style of delivery was different. His quiet tone made it easier for me to focus on the content of his tale. And something in what he said resonated with me, just as it had when I listened to him in the cabin.

Makepeace's voice developed an edge, as if he was falling back into identifying with the four-hundred-year-old character, and he began speaking quickly. "You turned me away when I came for you. Then you ran off with Robert Bleeding Howard and had his kid. He was one of the Earl of Suffolk's brood. I suppose you must have had a thing for men with position and titles in that lifetime. And this time round too."

I ignored the sting that accompanied his last remark. "I'm surprised you have such detailed recall in this lifetime."

"I didn't at first. I just used to have strange haunting-type dreams when I was a kid. Then, a few years ago, just after my wife left me, I met a woman who was into past-life regression and all that stuff. I was really sceptical, but I wanted to get her to sleep with me, so I went along to a residential workshop with her. There were some weird people there, but I didn't mind, since I was able to share her bed for the week. I ended up getting a whole load of stuff that I never expected out of the workshop."

Makepeace stared across the canyon for a while, then looked back at me. "That was when I first understood why playing with Bob Howard had always got under my skin. It made sense of so much that happened between us when we were in the band. During the regression session, I found out that he and I had known each other in my previous life, and he stole the woman I loved."

He leaned closer and his eyes bored into me. "Fast forward a few years. Bob and I meet up again years after Nights of the Road has disbanded. He tells me about you. Something in the way he talks makes me curious. Apart from anything else, he's always been a confirmed bachelor and I've never heard him so serious about any woman. Then I hear your voice on the phone. I recognise you immediately and the whole picture finally falls into place."

My heart was thudding and I shook my head. "You've got to admit it sounds extraordinary."

Makepeace stood up and his voice was curt as he replied, "Suit yourself whether you believe me or not. I need to go. I've got group therapy in a few minutes."

I stood up as well. "Shall I come and see you again? Your doctors said it's up to you, if and when I come, now you're through this period of no outside contact."

He shrugged. "It's all the same to me. Come if you want. Stay away if you'd prefer. Say hello to Bob. Tell him I still hate his guts, but I'm grateful he didn't shoot me or turn me in. I probably wouldn't have been as generous, if our positions had been reversed. Bye, Sarah." Makepeace turned and strode toward the main door. As I watched, a woman with short blonde hair, stonewashed jeans and a brightly coloured shirt, hailed him from her seat on the grass. He waited for her to join him and they entered the building together, without looking back.

I sat down again on the bench. My mind wrestled with what I had heard. Makepeace's story had stirred something visceral in me, and it was not a comfortable sensation. I shut my eyes. A figure came close, temporarily blotting out the sun, and I opened my eyes and looked up. Jack was looking at me as he passed. He half smiled, looked forward again and hurried on.

I called after him. "Excuse me, Jack, do you have a meeting now, or could I have a word with you?" Jack hovered then stopped and turned. He looked discomfited and I divined his thoughts. "It's OK. I don't want you to break any confidences about Antony. I was simply wondering, do you teach at a university here in California?"

He walked back toward me and stopped a few feet away. Wariness was in his face. "Why do you ask?"

"I wondered if you might know any historians here in Southern California who are knowledgeable about seventeenth-century England?"

The scholar's interest was caught. "Seventeenth century? That would be the Civil War period in Britain, I suppose?"

"Maybe. I don't know. I'm bad on dates and I'm ashamed to say I'm hazy about most periods of English history. But I need to find out what was happening between some people who lived in the early seventeenth century."

"It's not my period or my continent, but I do know a bright young man down in San Diego. He's British and I believe his doctorate was on the seventeenth century. His name is Dan Godfrey."

"Do you know how I can contact him?"

"You'll find his email address on the university's web site. You can use my name if you contact him. Professor Jack Rathbone from UCLA. But please don't say where our paths crossed. I'm officially overseas and on sabbatical just now."

I smiled. "Of course I won't. Thanks for the contact, Jack. Perhaps I'll see you again when I come back to visit Antony."

"I hope so. He's lucky to have you. My girlfriend left me. I can't blame her. It's not easy maintaining relationships with people like us."

I caught the isolation in his voice. "Jack, a lot of us are people like us. Most people I know have addictive processes of one kind or another going on in their lives. It's all a matter of degree. If we get stuck in an addictive state, any one of us can need help to shift and transform it. That's how I look at the process that goes on here."

"That's quite a radical view of addiction."

"Maybe. But have you noticed how many highly addictive processes are acceptable to the mainstream, and get health-stamped as legal? The less apparently socially acceptable our addictions, the more we are liable to get stigmatised for them. A few people end up carrying a shadow role for the whole of an addictive society. And people who consider themselves normal often collude with so-called addicts to keep them stuck where they are."

He came closer. "What do you mean?"

"The mainstream culture dictates what's socially acceptable. Then, for anything that falls outside the norm, it uses identified addicts of one sort or another as scapegoats. They carry the shame and blame for the whole system. That way, mainstream society can stay in denial about its own addictive nature and keep on doing what it does, without changing."

Jack Rathbone sat down beside me. "Give me one example of a socially and legally acceptable addiction in this culture."

"Workaholism must be near the top of the list in the USA. It's not just acceptable but praised and rewarded by schools and corporations. Yet look at the havoc it can create."

"Antony said you were an interesting woman. You speak the same language as some of the people running this place. So what's your own addictive poison, Sarah?"

"I have twin addictions. Most of us have. I'm addicted to freedom. It creates its own problems of isolation, but it does tend to keep me clear of substance abuse. I can't bear the thought of becoming enslaved to any particular drink or drug. On the other hand, I'm addicted to helping and harmonising relationships. So you can imagine how freedom and relationship issues get tangled up."

"Relationship? You call that an addiction?"

"It can be, for someone like me."

"I'd have thought that it was a good thing to become addicted to."

"Like anything, it's OK if you wake up to what you're doing and use the energy constructively. It's when you are not aware of harmful patterns within your relationships that you tend to repeat them unconsciously."

"Care to name a harmful relationship pattern in your life?"

"Sure. It's easy for me to get sucked into the role of rescuer. My addiction to wanting to be of service can hook me into doing things that are unhelpful to me and others."

Jack grinned. "A recovering rescuer, eh? I like it. Now I begin to get how that can conflict with your need to be free. So you could be wrestling with yourself, say, in deciding whether to stay with Antony or drop him right now? That's what my woman struggled with. She tried to help at first but couldn't keep it up. When she left, she dropped me like a stone."

I could hear from the tone of his voice that he had entered his own drama and was revisiting a personal wound.

"I'm not Antony's girlfriend."

Jack looked back at me quickly. "No? You surprise me. He said you've known each other forever. He talks about you as if you're the woman of his dreams. I assumed that you had been sweethearts since childhood."

"I met him for the first time just over a month ago."

Jack whistled. "Now you astonish me. I thought you were a long-term fixture in his life. Just shows how wrong I can be about people. No wonder my own woman dumped me. Well, gotta go. Say hello to Dan Godfrey for me, if you ever speak with him."

CHAPTER THIRTY-TWO

England 1628

The crowd inside and out of the Chapel of the Savoy was larger than usual and the air was vibrant with expectancy. Poking fun at a shivering, shift-clad and titled lady's public disgrace promised fine entertainment for a bitterly cold January Sunday morning.

When time and the service passed and still no titled lady, in white shift or otherwise, appeared to do her penance, the congregation grew restive.

"B'gad, the woman surely never means to defy the Court," Sir John Finett, Master of Ceremonies to two Stuart Kings, muttered in the ear of the man seated beside him. The pretty fellow lisped, "If she dothn't come of her own accord, m'dear, she will thoon be obliged to do tho. Look behind uth."

Sir John turned and followed the gaze of his companion. To the rear of the chapel, a sergeant-at-arms had entered, at the head of a small group of constables. Senior-ranking churchmen approached the officers. A huddled conversation took place. The sergeant stood to attention and marched out of the chapel, with his constables at his heels.

"There'll be the devil to pay now. Buckingham will never stand for being ignored. He'll have her in the Tower for this. Just mark my words." Finett's pink-faced friend nodded in excited agreement. "And Howard rithkth being thrown in there with her too."

The congregation now understood that it had been denied its morning's entertainment, but that sport of a different kind might yet be found close by. The trickle of early leavers converted into a mass exodus, which pushed as a single pedestrian body along Savoy Hill toward the Strand. Minutes later, those at the front of the crowd were able to observe the door of Lord Purbeck's apartment in York House shake to its second battering of the day from officers of the law.

The door opened. Words were spoken. The door closed.

Inside the apartment a servant reported to his master. "They've gone, my Lord, but they say they intend to return with a warrant for my Lady's arrest. They also say the house is surrounded, so none may hope to leave here without being intercepted."

While Lord Purbeck thanked and dismissed his footman, Lady Hatton spread her arms wide in a theatrical gesture. "Oh, my darling child, once again it seems I am powerless to protect you. Damn Buckingham! Damn your father too, for refusing to lift a finger to save you! Damn all men everywhere!" She turned and waved her hand at each of her male companions in turn. "That does not include you, Purbeck, or even you, Robert, although we might have been more comfortable all these years if you had not chosen to complicate my daughter's life by falling in love with her."

If and what Sir Robert Howard might have responded would not be known, since another servant interrupted them. "Begging your pardon, my Lord, but the Ambassador of Savoy has just entered by the *garden* door and desires an audience." Disapproval was evident in the footman's voice, as he reported Abbé Alessandro Scaglia's informal method of entry. "Should I admit him?"

Lord Purbeck spoke mildly. "Whatever can the Abbé be about, wandering in through the flower beds? Yes, do show him in."

The Ambassador entered. A courtier first and a churchman a long way second, he made his best bow – which was a fine one – to the four adults in the salon and tweaked the cheek of the three-year-old sitting on Lady Purbeck's lap. The little boy stared up with round eyes, as he was addressed in accented English.

"Little man, you grow bigger and more handsome each time I see you. What a glorious picture you and your dear mother make." Scaglia turned to his host. "Purbeck, your servant. We must entice our mutual friend over from Antwerp again soon, to do your wife and son justice, don't you agree?"

"This is hardly a moment to be thinking about portrait painting, Abbé."

Turning his striking countenance and dark eyes upon the speaker of the sharp words, the Savoy Ambassador nodded and bowed again. "Believe me, I do so understand your concern, dear Lady Hatton. Art is perhaps not the most useful topic to discuss when the Strand has become a moving mountain of heaving humanity."

The Abbé sighed. "Why must the English wish to behave in such a barbaric way toward their loveliest ladies? I am saddened to think that even my dear friend, Lord Buckingham, might be implicated in this reported want of gallantry toward Lady Purbeck. Do you think the time may have come for you to whisper words of restraint in your brother's ear, dear Purbeck?"

Apparently forgetting that she was not currently in her own home, Lady Hatton waved Scaglia to a chair. "Do sit and explain why you have arrived at such an inopportune moment, dear Abbé. I hope you are not merely gossip mongering. I should warn you that my nerves are to pieces today. So try to speak in plain English, I beg of you."

The Ambassador seated himself and smiled at her. "To explain, dear Lady Hatton. Several large gentlemen of the law interrupted me at my devotions. And why? They demanded that I allow them admittance to my garden. And why? It seems that they require easy access to *your* garden, Lord Purbeck. And why? It seems they intend to block any attempted escape by Lady Purbeck. And why? It seems so that they may arrest and carry her away, although they would not tell me where."

"How did you respond, Scaglia? I hope that, at the very least, you declared that you would run them through, if any of them so much as dare set foot within your perimeter?"

The Italian turned and engaged Robert for the first time. "Ah, Sir Howard. You also have come to commiserate with our dear, unfortunate friends? It cannot surprise you that, as a man of the cloth, I must always prefer a diplomatic path. I have offered the officer and his friends admittance whenever they may wish. I have even presumed to recommend the exact moment in time that could be most opportune for them to return, if they wish to be confident of effecting an arrest of Lady Purbeck."

"*What?*"

Howard and Purbeck shouted in mutual outrage. Lady Hatton gave a single piercing shriek. Robin swivelled his head from side to side and his lower lip began to tremble, as all around him began to shout at once.

Only his mother remained silent and still. And deathly pale.

The ambassador held up one elegant, bejewelled and white lace-cuffed hand. "This is indeed most satisfactory. If my dear friends are all thus easily taken in, then so too perhaps will be your good officers of the law. Yes, I have indeed recommended that they return immediately before the dinner hour."

He turned to Frances. "I hope it has not slipped your memory that you, Lady Purbeck, have begged my carriage to take you out to dine this evening." Scaglia winked at her. "Did I not hear you say you expect to enter Denmark House by way of a certain, much-used inner passageway from York House, dear Frances?"

Alessandro Scaglia chuckled as he observed stupefied expressions on the faces around him. "Now, if you are all agreeable, we shall prepare our own plan for Lady Purbeck's evening, which I suggest may run just a little differently." His voice became serious. "First, however, I must satisfy myself of one thing. Do you have a safe haven, preferably far from London, assuming we can get you away from here safely, my Lady?"

Frances looked from her husband to Robert and it was Howard who responded. "My carriage is already on hand next door at Suffolk House, to take Frances out of town. I have offered both her and the boy protection, to avoid Lord Purbeck placing himself in any embarrassing situation with his brother. But our present challenge lies in actually getting her away from York House. As you have already commented, a crowd blocks the street and the area is infested with officers of the law. We were speaking just before you arrived of trying to get Lady Purbeck away under cover of darkness, but it is going to be damned tricky."

"Just so, Sir Robert. Which is why a little Italian diversion might perhaps be of service in this moment." Alessandro Scaglia presented his scheme.

Lord Purbeck gave a shout of laughter. "How long have you been awaiting an occasion to play such a trick as this? It sounds a capital idea." His laughter turned quickly into a frown. "But have you thought that your involvement may bring my brother's wrath down upon you? You risk alienating his Majesty too, Alessandro."

Scaglia smiled. "Purbeck, my dear fellow, you of all people know how excellent are my relations with your brother and His Majesty. I could never involve myself knowingly in any project that may incur their displeasure. However, I do sometimes find it difficult to restrain the youthful exuberance of certain of my servants. I have remarked that they have particularly vivid imaginations when it comes to fancy dress and playing make-believe."

Lady Hatton gushed. "Your plan is perfect, dear Alessandro. Quite perfect. How shall we ever thank you?" The Ambassador smiled and murmured that he would be happy to hold private audience with her to discuss the possibilities. Eliza looked fifteen years old instead of fifty, as she proceeded to organise the group and assign them their various roles.

Lord Purbeck, whose only allocated task was to present an imperturbable face to any further visits from the law, was still frowning. "Alessandro, I do regard us as friends as well as neighbours, but I am unclear why you should go out of your way to perform such a kindly act for my wife, at possible risk to your own relations?"

"My Lord, as always you are too modest. It is you who are long overdue a kindly act. For you are the man who introduced and first made our dear friend van Dyck welcome in England. He and I do not forget your many friendly efforts on his behalf. By helping your wife, it is my hope to serve you."

Several hours later, a constable was admitted into the Denmark House garden of the Savoy Ambassador to the Court of King Charles. It was dusk and the dinner hour approached. The man was advised that the Ambassador was unavailable, for he would shortly be leaving to dine with a lady. However, Abbé Scaglia had left word that the constable and any of his colleagues who wished could make full use of the garden, and let themselves out when their mission was complete.

Minutes later, with much noise and show, the Ambassador's coach was driven from the Denmark House mews to his front door. It opened and out into a halo of torchlight stepped a lady dressed in evening attire, bedecked in jewellery and wearing an elaborate coiffure. As the carriage door closed upon her and the vehicle moved forward, the figure of Lady Hatton emerged from within.

"My darling, could you not wait for your mama to say farewell?" wailed Eliza. She picked up her skirts and hurried toward the departing carriage, then stopped and moaned loudly. At that moment, a constable blew his whistle and sped out of the Ambassador's garden into the Strand.

His whistle drew fellow officers of the law from diverse hiding places, but all were foiled in their efforts to intercept Abbé Scaglia's coach by its turn of speed and reckless course. A milling crowd obstructed the constables' pursuit of the coach, as did additional passers-by, who came running from all directions to discover the source of the noise and general disturbance.

Several minutes after the Ambassador's carriage and its pursuers had disappeared, Sir Robert Howard's coach slipped sedately along the Strand in the opposite direction. It drew no attention, for nobody remained in the street to pay it any notice.

"Where are we going, Mama?"

"Back to the country to live with Papa, my darling boy."

"With my real papa?"

"With your real papa."

"Will you stop crying and be happy again, Mama?"

"Yes, my darling boy. I will stop crying and be happy again."

The small round face with its lollipop eyes looked up at Frances. "Don't be afraid, Mama. My London papa has told me to look after you carefully."

His words set his mother's tears flowing again.

CHAPTER THIRTY-THREE

California

"Thank you for making time to see me, Professor."

Dan Godfrey was young, dark-haired and bearded. His handshake gave an impression of boundless energy.

"Call me Dan."

"Thank you. I'm Sarah." I sat in the chair offered and looked around his office. Three books lay on a coffee table. Each bore the professor's name on the cover.

"You're a prolific author, Dan."

He laughed and endeared himself to me by saying, "I'm prolifically ambitious, Sarah. Publishing is the name of the game in university circles. Teaching students comes in a far distant second. It's a crazy system, if you actually want to educate young people well, but who am I to challenge it?"

He sat down behind his desk and pointed to one of the books. "I got lucky early. My doctoral thesis was accepted for publication because it dealt with a trendy subject. I wrote a book on witchcraft that made a splash on both sides of the Atlantic. Sales outside the academic world, especially here in the States, exceeded my publisher's wildest dreams. Hey presto. I've never had to struggle since to get a manuscript read."

"I don't suppose that in your witchcraft researches you ever came across anyone called Frances Coke, Lady Villiers or Viscountess Purbeck, did you?"

"I certainly did."

I leaned forward. "Really? What can you tell me about her?"

"Let me see. Well, a lot of scandal attached to her. Her brother-in-law detested her. Unfortunately for her, he was a powerful and ruthless man."

"The Duke of Buckingham?"

"You know the story?"

I hesitated, not wanting to reveal the source of my interest. "I must have heard it in school."

"Really? You had a well-informed teacher, then. Not many teachers back then would have had the detailed knowledge of seventeenth-century England to enable them to say much about Lady Purbeck. Sorry, I don't mean to suggest you're ancient, but I'm guessing you must have learned your school history in a pre-Internet era." I nodded.

He continued, "Frances would have been an obscure and quickly dismissed character even in academic circles, at least until the burgeoning of feminist history, if she hadn't been the offspring of a famous father and become caught up in Buckingham's net through her marriage to his brother."

"What was her link with your witchcraft research?"

"Buckingham accused Frances Purbeck of using sorcery on his brother. It was probably at the most a case of pots and kettles. He was up to his eyeballs in black magic. He might have got further with his accusations against Frances, if he hadn't been obliged to backpedal, in order to take the heat off himself. But he made life hell for his sister-in-law in all kinds of other ways."

"What else can you tell me about her?"

"Not much. Nothing was ever established against her in terms of sorcery that I could discover. To be honest, I lost interest once it was clear to me that she wasn't a witch and didn't practise any black arts. She had a bunch of loyal friends and seems to have been well loved and admired due to her remarkable beauty. Especially by the fellow she ran off with."

I leaned forward. "Was that a man called Robert Howard?"

"Yes, you do know your history. He was a younger son of the Earl of Suffolk and brother to the notorious Frances Howard, Countess of Somerset. Now there was one woman who did dabble in sorcery or poison successfully enough to actually murder a man."

"How can I find out more about her? Frances Purbeck, I mean."

"For starters, I suggest you do a search on the Internet and see what her various names bring up. Coke, Villiers, Purbeck. You'll find a wealth of old books, original letters and manuscripts are posted online, as well as various biographies in online encyclopaedias. History is getting its own share of information overload."

The phone rang and he answered it, but signalled me to remain, when I rose to leave. He told the caller he would call them back, put the phone down and smiled at me.

"Try checking Frances out via her father and mother's names as well. That should give you plenty of leads to explore. Sir Edward Coke was the preeminent lawyer of his day and Lady Elizabeth Hatton provided all kinds of society gossip. Frances didn't do badly herself in the gossip stakes, although her lifelong affair with Robert Howard seems to have been a touching story of mutual fidelity. Come to think of it, I must have got something here that will interest you."

Dan Godfrey jumped up and searched in a bookcase for several minutes, humming to himself. "Ah yes, here it is. A little volume called *The Curious Case of Lady Purbeck*. It was written more than a century ago, and it's quaintly prim. I'll lend it to you, if you promise me on the head of your favourite child to return it safely. I should warn you that I weave my worst wizard spells against anyone who steals my books."

I giggled and took it from him. "I have no children, Dan, but I do promise to bring it back in person. I'll be driving into the desert just inland from here to see a friend next Thursday. Will that be soon enough to return it?"

"Thursday's less than a week away. Keep it longer if you need. You can always mail it back to me."

I had read and reread the slim volume twice by the time I entered Dan Godfrey's office the following Thursday. "Thank you so much, Dan. I did find the book quaint and prim but also very interesting. Now I have one other question. Have you ever come across a man called John Clavell or Clavylle? There's no mention of him in this book and I'm keen to know if he and Frances could have known each other when they were children."

"The name doesn't ring a bell. What do you know about him?"

"Only that he would have lived in Dorset not far from Corfe Castle in the seventeenth century, when Frances was a child."

Dan Godfrey opened his Mac. He entered the name, asking as he did so: "Didn't you try Google, as I suggested for Frances?"

"I didn't do too well with any of my efforts at Internet research. I turned up so many links that went nowhere. When I tried Purbeck, I kept getting sites about geology. And I did try Clavell, but that only took me to an author called James."

"Good Lord. You should have persevered. I thought by now everyone could do Internet research standing on their heads." His fingers flew over the keys. "Ah, here we are. Yes, see, you should have put his first name in as well. First item under John Clavell looks promising. Dorset. An interesting character. He appears to have been a highwayman." He clicked again.

I jumped. "A highwayman. Are you sure?"

"Yes, come take a look." I went round the desk and looked over his shoulder. Dan had found a website dedicated to British highwaymen in different centuries. He laughed as he read some text on the screen. "Lord, a pretentious fellow, your John Clavell. He obviously fancied himself as an author. He wrote something called *A Recantation of An Ill Led Life*. Let's see now."

I found it hard to view the screen clearly, so moved aside while Dan Godfrey speed-read his way through the site. He spoke animatedly. "Yes, there it is. He was actually locked up and sentenced to be executed, but he got a Coronation pardon. That's when he would have recanted, I suppose. Or at least made out that he had, in order to save his hide. There's a reference to a book on him here. Hmm. That *is* interesting. He seems to have been rather more than your average knight of the road. See?"

Dan Godfrey pointed to the screen again. This time I leaned across and read the name of the book to which he was pointing: *John Clavell, 1601-43. Highwayman, Author, Lawyer, Doctor.*

My heart beat fast. "Would I be able to find a copy of this in a library?"

Dan peered at the screen, then shook his head. "I doubt it, unless you've got a university reading ticket. It looks as if a private press produced it. Self-published by the author, maybe. I can try and get hold of a copy if you like."

"I don't want to put you to any trouble, Dan. You've been kind already."

"Happy to help and it would be no problem. Although you may be able to order it yourself from your local public library, through an inter-library lending service. It will take a while, though, if it has to come from overseas. You may actually find it quicker to search rare book services on the Internet and buy a copy, if it's not too expensive. I use Abe's. They're quick and reliable. Out of interest, let me just see…"

Dan's fingers took off again in flight as he input the book title. He exclaimed in satisfaction. "Yes, there you are. Not expensive at all. But only one copy available. Why don't you seize the chance and let me order it online, while we've got it here in front of us?"

I hesitated. "I've never ordered anything online."

He laughed. "You must be one of an increasingly endangered species in the USA. It's not rocket science, Sarah. Nothing to be afraid of. All you'd have to do is enter credit card details and an address for mailing. You needn't worry that I'll be able to do anything with your credit card information afterwards. There's a button you can press to make sure it's all deleted."

I laughed. "I'll trust you. You're obviously an Internet whizz and it would be great if we could get it straight away, Dan. The book would make a perfect gift for someone I know. But he's probably leaving the USA quite soon, so I'll need it delivered quickly."

CHAPTER THIRTY-FOUR

England 1632

The great doors of Stoke Manor swung back to admit a travel weary woman holding a child by the hand. As the pair entered the large entrance hall, their eyes were drawn to a frail figure, who was walking slowly but unaided and without a stick down a wide and sweeping staircase.

Sir Edward Coke stopped at sight of the arrivals. He surveyed his daughter and grandson without speaking. They gazed up at him, also in silence. Sir Edward continued his slow progress, until he stood at the bottom within a few paces of Frances and Robin.

"What brings you here?" His voice retained the harsh rasp that was graven into Frances's memory, although she had not heard it for nearly a decade. Coke's high-templed forehead was gaunt and his hairline had receded, but the hair that remained was thick and white. Eyes that had once been dark and piercing were now bleached and hooded with age.

Frances felt touched. Sir Edward looked every inch the ailing octogenarian that her half-sister had described. Yet her father held himself upright and had paid fastidious attention to his dress. He was the proud and self-contained man she had known, still in full possession of his faculties.

"Ann wrote to me, Papa. She suggested you might enjoy meeting the grandson whom you do not know." Instinct led Frances to confront a core issue between them without delay. She did not think it useful to mention that her half-sister, Ann Sadler, considered their father's reconciliation with Frances was needed for the peace of his soul. Or that Ann attributed his recent infirmity and low spirits at least as much to his sadness over Clem's premature death as to his advancing years and the recent fall from his horse.

Sir Edward looked from the daughter facing him to the chestnut-haired boy standing beside his mother. He met the child's open gaze. "What's your name, young fellow?"

"Robert, sir. My family and friends usually call me Robin. You may do so too, if you like. Mama says you are my grandfather and that you were once the greatest lawyer in the land. Is that true?"

Sir Edward Coke looked taken aback but gave a crack of caustic laughter. "Do you typically question your mother's word, young man?"

"I like to verify matters for myself, sir, whenever possible."

"Hmm. Well, if you like to read as much as you like to verify matters, you shall study my reports. When you have read them all, you may then give me your personal verdict on my legal record. Alternatively, I could furnish you with a list of character references. Will either of these options satisfy you?"

The boy ignored, or perhaps he did not even hear, the irony in his grandfather's voice. Instead, he looked up at his mother and then back to Sir Edward and spoke confidentially. "To tell truth, Grandpapa, I am not much of a reader. My tutor despairs of me. But I am a capital rider. Aunt Ann told Mama you still ride every day, so I was hoping I might be allowed to accompany you. And Mama says you used to keep falcons, so I was wondering if you still have them? If so, perhaps you might let me take them out with you sometimes?"

As an afterthought, the boy added, "I will try and read whatever you want me to, if it would please you, sir."

"And you, Frances? Have you also made detailed plans for your entertainment, while the pair of you grace Stoke with your self-invited presence? If I am to understand this young man, you intend a lengthy stay."

Again the irony was evident, as the man turned toward his daughter.

Unlike Robin, Frances flinched at Coke's tone. After years of estrangement, her father retained the power to wound her, if only with his tongue. She struggled with reactions that included a pain-filled memory of his hand raised against her in this house.

In that moment, Sir Edward's hand crept out toward the banister rail. His fingers closed on it tightly and his knuckles showed white. Frances saw and understood instantly how much physical and emotional effort it was costing her father to stand so erect and unbending before his daughter and grandson.

She sighed inwardly. Life did not feel fair in the tasks it apportioned. Her father's pride was such that, if their relationship was to mend, she must find a means to withstand his attacks, and open herself again to his unspoken frailties, while pretending to notice nothing.

"Papa, I'm here today to try and make my peace with you, before you or I quit this world. I for one do not wish to leave unsaid things that should be spoken of between us."

His mouth twitched but he said nothing. She continued. "I'm also here because Ann felt you might desire more company than she can offer you since Clem died." At the name of his youngest and favourite son, a shadow passed across Sir Edward's face and the extent of his vulnerability moved her. "Please believe me that your grandson and I did not come here to vex you, but rather with the hope of giving you pleasure. If you prefer that we do not stay at Stoke, we shall leave immediately."

Coke swallowed. "It seems you are also here for some plain speaking."

Frances felt amazed at the steadiness of her voice as she replied, "Yes, Papa, and I should infinitely prefer to do so sitting than standing, if it would not inconvenience you."

"It did not occur to you to send word of your visit beforehand?"

"Oh yes, Papa. It also occurred to me that, if you were forewarned, we might not be admitted to your home. If we are not welcome at Stoke, I prefer to hear it from you, rather than from a servant shutting the door in our face."

Silence. Then, two words: "Follow me." The old man turned and led them to his huge book-lined library. Sir Edward took hold of a bell pull near the large old stone fireplace with gnarled and arthritic fingers and tugged.

"You and the boy will require refreshment. We do not dine here until five. Give your orders to my man when he arrives. You know the house, so you may choose for yourself where you and the child sleep, as long as you do not disturb me."

Frances ordered tea for herself, and some cordial and biscuits for Robin. When the aged retainer had left the room, she looked around. Nothing appeared to have changed in the years since she was last at Stoke. She turned and looked at her father. Sir Edward had lowered himself into a chair by the fire. He waved his daughter into another. Uninvited, Robin had begun to explore books and other memorabilia that lay scattered throughout the room. The old man watched the boy closely but did not forbid him to touch.

He spoke over his shoulder to his daughter. "So, what is it you think we need to say, before the Lord claims one or the other of us? I wager he will take me first, Frances." He stole a sideways glance. "You look surprisingly well for one who has lived so long in sin. I notice the pox did not mark you as seriously as reported by the gossips. Jealousy on their part, I suppose."

"Papa, it is nearly eight years since I survived the pox. My face has had ample time to recover from the scars, although it is true that I did not contract it as badly as many. My husband nursed me carefully through it all."

"And what of that other fellow you have lived with since you discarded poor Purbeck? I hear rumours that Howard has beaten you and cut your nose."

Frances looked at her hands, folded in her lap, then up again at Sir Edward. "My goodness, it seems that Town gossip of the most vulgar and inaccurate kind can travel as far as Stoke. For your interest, Papa, Sir Robert and I have had but one serious argument during our life together, and that was about the advisability of me coming to visit you in Stoke. Robert feared I might be placing Robin and myself in the way of unnecessary unkindness. For your further interest, Sir Robert has never once lifted his hand against me, which is more than I can say for you."

He glared. "You think this an appropriate way for you to conduct a dialogue with a parent in front of your son?"

Frances took a deep breath. "Robin is no stranger to plain talking and difficult situations. He is a discerning child. He understands that his parents' circumstance would never have arisen if my father had not married me against my will at the age of fourteen into a family with designs upon our wealth. The fact that certain members of that family did their subsequent best to ruin me, and the whole country along with us, does not prevent him from holding Lord Purbeck in affection and still bearing his name."

Sir Edward studied his daughter with a stony expression.

"We're evidently at one in our view of the influence of the Buckinghams upon this land. I don't suppose either of us lost sleep or shed tears at Buckingham's assassination or indeed at the recent demise of his unappealing mother. But, if you have come here only to resurrect childish complaints against me, I fear our relations will not prosper, madam."

"I came with the hope that we might make our peace, but that is unlikely to happen if either of us tries to sweep truth or ill feelings under the carpet."

Sir Edward pursed his lips. "I will not tolerate unjust attack from you, Frances. I have received enough of that over the years from your mother. Anything I have done, I did with your best interests in mind. I married you into the family of one who had more influence with our late King *and* the son who succeeded him than any other man in the realm. A dutiful daughter might have deemed that an honour and a privilege. If you had played your cards right with Buckingham, my girl, you might have received all you wanted."

"Forgive me if I see things differently than you, Papa. I was the one who had to live with his violence, when my husband was in his distempers. I was the one who had to endure his mother and brother doing all they could to separate me from that husband and poison the minds of the King and Court against me. They made my married life a misery. They publicly discredited all my efforts to be a good wife to Lord Purbeck and pretended it was me and not they who so often upset him."

Frances leaned forward. "Papa, did you know that Buckingham and his mother sought to do away with your own grandson, so that Robin might never inherit? I cannot believe that you were ignorant of the legal measures taken by my solicitor to bring their armed thugs to order. Do you call attempted murder of your daughter and grandchild an honour and a privilege?"

Sir Edward said nothing.

"I'm sure you also know that the man who is still my husband testified over and again that I had been a good and loyal wife to him. Nobody has ever heard Purbeck speak a word against me. My conscience concerning my conduct is clear, Papa. I wonder, how clear is yours?"

Still Sir Edward did not respond. He stared into the fire with an expression on his lined face that was impossible to interpret.

"Grandfather, if it pleases you, what is inside these bags?"

Robin stood in front of Sir Edward, holding a black buckram bag in either hand. Frances held her breath. As she looked into the trusting face, she uttered a silent prayer.

"Has your tutor ever told you anything of the late Earl of Essex?"

"No sir. At least, he may have done when I was not paying attention, but I do not think so."

"Hmm. And what about the Gunpowder Treason? Were you not paying attention if and when he told you about that?"

"Oh, I know *all* about that. But it was Papa who told me, not my tutor. He says I owe my life to Sir Thomas Knyvett, who must have been a brave man because he arrested Guido Fawkes. And, when I get caught playing truant from lessons, he sometimes tells me he will send me away to the school that was founded with Sir Thomas's money, after he died."

"What nonsense is this about you owing your life to old Tom Knyvett?" Sir Edward looked annoyed but his attention was clearly caught.

"Mama, can you explain to Grandpapa, please?"

Frances coloured, but she looked her father in the eye. "Sir Robert told our son that it was while I was staying with the Knyvetts at Staines, just before my removal to Kingston and my marriage, that he and I discovered our love for each other. Fifteen years, during which neither Robert nor I have loved another. Our child is the fruit of a loving union, which has survived public persecution and attempted humiliation. Sir Robert wants Robin to know the circumstances surrounding his birth, so he may grow up to judge our actions for himself. We hope he may feel as proud of his parents as we are of him."

Sir Edward set his jaw, turned away from his daughter and glared again into the fire. Robin looked at Frances and his eyes had become very large and round. She shrugged. The boy stood his ground before his grandfather, still holding up the heavy bags and shifting his weight from one leg to another.

Sir Edward turned back to Robin. "Those bags contain the business of the late Earl of Essex and of the Powder Treason. Since you say you know all about the latter, there is nothing more to say. But a lad of your age should be conversant with the whole of his nation's history, beyond that of his birth and immediate family. I shall find you something about the Earl of Essex. To learn about him shall be your first reading task."

Coke rose and walked stiffly toward a bookcase. A series of unbound documents lay on the bottom shelf. He bent with a grunt, selected one and studied the handwriting on its cover. "Yes, here we are. This is an abbreviated account of the trial." He handed it to the boy and took from him the buckram bags, which he replaced carefully in their habitual place.

Robin's face was a study in childhood consternation as he looked at the size of the document he had just been given. Watching her son, Frances's heart went out to him. She wondered if Sir Edward, so precociously brilliant at school, had any idea of the reading powers of a typical eight-year-old.

"You and the boy will stay tonight, Frances. We shall see how we all rub along together from there. You, young man," Coke turned back to Robin. "I expect you to tell me the key points of that trial by dinnertime tomorrow," pointing at the document in the child's hand.

He added, as if in afterthought, "In the meantime, if you can be ready by eight in the morning, you shall accompany me on my daily ride. We'll see about the falcons, after I have been able to observe your riding prowess. Like you, I prefer to verify a man's reputation for myself."

CHAPTER THIRTY-FIVE

California

Bob called while I was driving to the clinic, and ruminating on my meeting with Dan. He was travelling with the Re-invasion tour and we hadn't connected for longer than a brief phone call for days.

I spoke first, eager to share with him the outcome of my recent discoveries with Dan Godfrey. "It was all there in the book he lent me, Bob. Well, not all, because there was no mention of Frances having known John Clavell. But everything else Antony has told me about Frances has been corroborated. She was legally married to Sir John Villiers, although her affair with Robert Howard seems to have been a marriage in all but a legal sense."

"Sweetie, I can't handle this. Not now. I don't mean to be awkward, but I am swamped in tour business and I can't take in any gobbledygook about the seventeenth century and all that cra–"

Bob stopped himself but I had understood. "You do think this past life stuff is all crap, don't you?"

"I don't know what I think. And this isn't the moment for me to worry about it. I'm up to my eyeballs in alligators. This tour is still a nightmare. My only consolation is that Johnny Clavylle isn't a part of it. If he had been, by now I would be the one locked up in a lunatic asylum instead of him."

It took an effort for me to contain the frustration and hurt that flooded me as Bob spoke dismissively about Makepeace. I stared at the road ahead and forced myself to speak lightly. "OK. Bad timing, Bob. We can talk later, when I'm not driving and you have less pressure on you."

He changed instantly. "I'm sorry, babe. Sorry I can't give you the attention your story deserves just now. When this tour is over, we'll take time out together. I promise I'll make it up to you."

"Bob, there's nothing to make up. Call me when you have space to breathe again."

"I don't know what I did to deserve you. Thanks for being so understanding. And I'm glad if your researches into all this history stuff are going well for you. I'll call you again, when we've finished here in Austin."

I switched off the car phone and drove on to the clinic.

Makepeace was sitting on his usual bench as I turned into the parking lot. He was staring up at the mountains. I hailed him and walked over. "Hey, Antony, you're looking great. The tan suits you."

His expression was wry. "The very picture of rude health, eh? If they can't save my soul, at least they're doing a great job with my body. As long as I'm here, that is. God knows what'll happen to it and me when we leave."

I sat down beside him. "You're still concerned about what happens afterwards?"

"Wouldn't you be?"

"Have you shared your feelings with the staff?"

"Oh, yes. We've even done some fun exercises. Processing our fears, they call it." Sarcasm sounded strong in his voice today.

I responded neutrally. "What happens in the fun exercises?"

"I'm invited to imagine my worst fears for the future and act them out, like in a role play. Apparently it's called *Embrace your Death*. Trouble is, when I try, I get stuck at the moment before I die and can't get beyond that."

"Maybe that's because it isn't time for you to go there yet?"

"Or maybe it's because the death I'm due to experience is too terrible to contemplate."

"Well, if it's too terrible, what shall we contemplate instead? Your life?"

His mouth twisted. "Not much of a life left to contemplate, I fear. I've fucked it up and have only myself to blame."

"Phew, you do sound down on yourself today, Antony."

Makepeace turned his head sharply away, but not before I had seen moisture glistening in his eyes. I knew an urge to take him in my arms and cradle him. Instead I sat in silence, feeling my own feelings.

"Sorry, I'm not more entertaining company for you today, Sarah."

"I didn't come to be entertained."

He swung round. "Why *did* you come?"

I pondered his question. Then, "Because I care about you and what happens to you. Because I know how difficult an experience this must be. Because I respect you for your courage in sticking with it."

He looked sceptical. I shrugged. "When I wrestle with my own demons, it sometimes helps just having a friend around. Other times I need to be alone. I can hang out with you now, if you feel like company. If you don't, I'll leave. Your call."

Makepeace looked into my eyes. His face looked haunted. "I kidnapped you and held you for two days against your will. I kept you handcuffed to a bed. Your wrists probably still bear the scars."

He leaned over and touched the fading pink marks. "Don't you bear me any ill will even for this?"

I searched my heart, then answered, "No."

He let go of my wrists. "What are you? Some kind of a saint?" His voice was hard. I looked up at the rugged mountains that lined the canyon. "I promise you I'm at least as much of a sinner as a saint."

I looked at Makepeace again. "I didn't believe you would ever have actually used your knife or the rifle on me. I trusted my instincts about that. Like I trust now that you're getting something of what you need from being here. All your struggles and reflections may be laying the basis for a new life when you leave, if you want it enough. And that new life may be more scary in prospect than when you actually come to live it."

"Is that the recovering rescuer talking?" The sneer was fleeting but noticeable.

"Sounds like someone else has been talking." I kept my voice light, but I felt my body tighten in self-defence.

"Jack said he had an interesting conversation with you." His tone had softened but I played dumb. He went on, "Actually, he said it helped him a lot with some things he was struggling with."

I relaxed. "I'm glad if it did. Jack helped me with something I was struggling with too. He gave me a useful history contact. For the record, I'm not interested in rescuing you at the moment. I want to understand my part in this seventeenth-century world we are supposed to have shared. That feels quite different from rescuing, at least to me."

Makepeace released his breath in a hiss, like a balloon deflating. "Sarah, I'm sorry. It's kind of you to have driven all this way from L.A. so many times, just to see me. Excuse me for being churlish."

I reached out and squeezed his hand. "Thanks for that, Antony. But there's nothing to excuse. So, do you want me to stay now or go?"

"I'd like you to stay." His voice was gruff, and under the tan his cheeks were suddenly pink.

"Then I'm happy to do so."

A sudden movement on a distant rock caught my attention. "What is that bird up there? Isn't it like the one we saw at the cabin?"

"Yes, well spotted. It's a prairie falcon. I've seen several of them since I came here. Do you suppose they're stalking me?"

I laughed "Perhaps they have a message for you."

"A message?"

"Yes. I read somewhere that birds of prey are considered by some indigenous peoples to be messengers from the gods."

"Maybe I should *pray* you're right." Makepeace sounded sceptical again, but his face had brightened.

I groaned and grinned. At least, I thought, he's ventured far enough out of his black hole of despair to make another of his atrocious puns. And maybe praying *will* help him find spiritual ease.

CHAPTER THIRTY-SIX

England 1634

She could not believe he was gone.

To the last, her father had eschewed medical aid and waved the doctors away from his sickroom. Sir Edward Coke ended his life and left the world as determined and independently as he had made his way through it.

And, to the last, Frances had devoted herself wholeheartedly to his comfort, which included ensuring that his final hours were free from uninvited visitors. The latter task had not been easy.

Sir Edward never knew that the King's men had appeared at Stoke and demanded entry. He was not on hand to observe his daughter's lip curl, although he would have appreciated her haughty response to Sir Francis Windebank's stammered explanation of why he had found it necessary to arrive at an old man's home in the company of so many heavily armed men.

Coke would surely have enjoyed hearing Sir Francis back down from his initial demand to be admitted to Sir Edward's presence and agree to confine the search to the lawyer's study and voluminous library. Frances made no secret of her disdain, as she recommended the men search at their leisure for any seditious materials harboured by the great legal servant of England against the interests of his King. They would be disappointed in their endeavours, since her father did not have a seditious bone in his body, but it was for them to choose if this was how they preferred to waste their day.

Frances cared for one thing alone: that her father should remain undisturbed during his final hours on earth. Robin had other concerns. The nine-year-old entered the library and observed the search with all the bristling attention of a guard dog. He moved to bar the passage of the King's men when they sought to remove two black buckram bags.

"Those bags belong to my grandfather. Hand them to me at once, or return them to their place." Robin stood foursquare in their path. One of Windebank's men attempted to elbow him aside. The child yelled, "Lay hands on me, sir, and it will be the worse for you."

The shout brought his mother to the scene.

"Robin, thank you, but these men have come here on the authority of our King to remove whatever they deem necessary from your grandfather's affairs. We may not hinder them in their search."

Robin turned and stared at his mother. "Mama, those bags contain the business of the Earl of Essex and the Powder Treason. Don't you remember? They are in Grandpapa's safekeeping. Why should they be removed?"

"His Majesty must have his reasons."

"Well, I don't believe we should let any of these things be taken away, unless Grandpapa gives his permission." Robin's face was flushed, his voice now shaky but insistent.

Frances dropped to her knees and looked up at the boy. "Robin, my darling, these documents may be important to the King and the State, in ways and for reasons we cannot understand. They can be of no use to your grandfather where he is going. And we must not disturb him now. To learn that Sir Francis and his men have been searching his possessions today would only make Grandpapa needlessly upset."

She rose and put a hand on his shoulder, smiling deep into the eyes so like his father's. "I am proud of you for wishing to defend your grandfather's property, my son, but this is a moment for us to let certain things pass. Papa would recommend it too, I feel sure, if he were here."

The boy still looked uncertain. He gazed at his mother and then turned toward Sir Francis Windebank. "What you are doing here is wrong, sir. You should not be behaving like this in my Grandpapa's home."

Turning, Robin walked with all the dignity that a nine-year-old could muster out of the room and toward the stairs. When the King's men had quit the premises, Frances went in search of her son and found him at the door of her father's bedchamber, plainly on sentry duty. He was pale and tears had streaked his cheeks.

"I was making sure they did not come up and disturb Grandpapa, Mama."

She put an arm round his shoulder. "Thank you, darling. Your grandfather is fortunate to have a guardian such as you. Let's go and sit with him awhile, now all is quiet again."

He held her back as she was about to open the door. "He's dying, isn't he, Mama?"

"Yes, Robin."

"But he's never been that word they said – seditious – has he?"

"Sweetheart, a man holding public office for so many years and through periods of great conflict cannot hope to satisfy everyone all the time. Your grandfather has occasionally displeased royalty and other powerful men, but his loyalty to God and the laws of his land have never been in question. You can feel proud to be the grandson of Sir Edward Coke, just as I know he has taken great pride in being your grandfather."

More tears fell. Robin wiped them away angrily. "I love him. I don't want him to die, Mama."

"I know. I love him too and I don't want him to die, either. But your grandfather has led a long and extraordinary life and we are blessed to have been here to enjoy its closing chapter with him. Did you know he has told me that he wants you to have one of his falcons when he is gone? What an honour to be so trusted by him, my darling."

Robin gulped and nodded. He allowed Frances to lead him inside the bedchamber. There he stayed, sitting with her in silent vigil over a supine Sir Edward, until a nine-year-old's hunger caught up with him.

By then the end was almost on them. Robin was in bed and Frances sitting alone at her father's bedside late into the following evening when, minutes before the stroke of midnight and with the lightest hint of a death rattle in his throat, Sir Edward Coke gave up the ghost. For a man who had been loud in life, he left quietly.

Frances shed tears then.

Sir Edward had not acknowledged, much less apologised, for the wrong he did his daughter in her youth. She had neither asked nor expected it of him. For her it was sufficient to have spoken her truth in his presence and to have noticed an occasional glimmer of his unspoken remorse.

Frances had also enjoyed the satisfaction of knowing she had given unstinting love and comfort to Sir Edward at the end of his life. Her act of willing selflessness had cleansed the slate of her own residual feelings of guilt about their years of estrangement. She could forgive her father because she had already forgiven herself. Thus, for nearly two years, father and daughter had been able to live together in perfect harmony.

One loose end remained that now could never be tied in life. Frances had sighed over it, but she had also long since learned that miracles did not occur to order. Mama had refused to visit Stoke once, during the two years Frances was with her father. Mama had also expressed extreme displeasure in writing that her daughter should have chosen to live at Stoke with a man who had treated them both so badly. A thirty-five year marriage had therefore ended in permanent rupture, and any reconciliation between Sir Edward Coke and Lady Elizabeth Hatton would have to take place beyond the grave.

Frances rose. In spite of the lateness of the hour, she must summon the servants and send messages to all her surviving half brothers and sisters. Her father had decreed that his funeral should be clear of all manner of pomp and superfluities, but there would nonetheless still be much to arrange.

This final act of filial duty to Sir Edward would mark the end of a major chapter in her life. The Duke of Buckingham and the Countess of Buckingham were both gone from the earth. Her slate had been wiped clean with her father before his end. Her mother would now presumably resume possession of Stoke, and Frances felt ready to return in safety to London, where her heart lay. With so many obstacles cleared from her path, she had every reason to anticipate a clear and tranquil future together for Robin, Sir Robert Howard and herself.

But life does not always unfold according to reason.

CHAPTER THIRTY-SEVEN

California

"I guess this is the last time I'll be seeing you here, Antony."

"Yes, I'm off in a few days. I can't quite take it in. I know it's only been weeks, but I feel as if I have been here an eternity."

We were seated on our usual bench in the garden of Dream Canyon.

"And how are you feeling now about leaving?"

"Scared."

"Are you staying on in the States or will you go back to England?"

"I'm going home, at least for now. I've heard from the boys in the band. They're eager to start rehearsals as soon as I'm up for it. And I've composed some new songs while I've been here, to try out with them."

"Moonlight Jax?"

"Yes. I haven't had contact with any of the guys from Road Agents or Toe-bee Men since I've been in here. And Robert has probably ruined any chance of me putting Nights of the Road back on the road."

"Why would Bob do that?"

"Because he doesn't like me, Sarah. I can't say I blame him. I have not been likeable for a long time. Nobody dislikes me more than me."

"Antony, I haven't come out here today for the last time just to listen to you run down Bob or beat yourself up."

He gave me a sharp stare. "Why *have* you bothered to come here today at all?" The harsh note in his voice hit me in the solar plexus. I breathed deliberately and steeled myself.

"I wanted to say goodbye and wish you well. But I also came for a selfish reason. I felt it might be my last chance to check out something with you. First, though, I have something for you."

I brought out the package that I had concealed in my shoulder bag. Makepeace stared at the Jiffy bag, as I asked, "How much detail do you remember about your life in the seventeenth century as John Clavell, highwayman? Or rather, how much do you remember about what happened after your highwayman days were over?"

"What do you mean, what happened after?"

"Do you remember what happened *after* John Clavell was caught and imprisoned?"

Makepeace shrugged. "I get stuck there. I was probably executed and went straight to hell. That could be why it's such a block, each time I try that silly *Embrace your Death* game. Hell fire and brimstone. All too awful for me to want to remember."

He shook himself and shifted on the bench. I could feel his discomfort, but I persisted. "What happened to John Clavell when he came out of prison?"

He looked at me long and hard, then shook his head. "I don't know."

I removed the book from its envelope. "I've brought you a leaving present that may help to fill in some gaps. It's the life story of a highwayman called John Clavell. He may or may not have known Frances Coke, but he definitely lived in Dorset as a boy. His uncle lived not far from Corfe Castle and owned property and enterprises around Kimmeridge. He was his uncle's heir, so he may have spent time at his home."

Makepeace sat rigid, looking at the book.

I continued. "He stole college silver when he went up to Oxford, yet he was let off without penalty. He didn't get away so easily as a highwayman. He was caught and sentenced to be executed. But then he received a full pardon from King Charles the First. When he came out of jail, he went on to become a successful lawyer and doctor. He wrote books and poetry, and made what may have been a happy marriage to a very young girl."

Makepeace's jaw had dropped open. He continued to stare at the book in my hand, as if it might bite him.

I held it out. "Take it, Antony. Read it. The person you believe yourself to have been back in the seventeenth century recreated his life successfully when he came out of jail. I look forward to hearing what kind of a life you recreate for yourself."

Makepeace took the book, gingerly, as if it was contaminated. After staring at the cover for several minutes in silence, he looked up at me again. "So you believe my story now?"

It was my turn to fall silent. When I spoke again I could hear that my voice sounded strained. "I don't know what I believe. I get nowhere if I try to think things through with my mind. I feel divided about the subject of reincarnation. Part of me is open to the idea and another part is as sceptical as Bob. Although maybe not as extreme in dismissing it as him."

"Do you at least believe it possible that you are Frances Coke?"

I shrugged. "I don't know, Antony. Over the years I have come to rely on the signals I get from my body."

"What signals does your body give you about this?"

"It's a feeling thing – hard to put into words. Not so much that I was Frances Coke in a former life exactly. More that I understand her intimately and that many of her experiences feel familiar. Some things in her story trigger me. And certain things have made me wonder if it is possible that I am her."

"What kind of things?"

"You told me when you first arrived here about your childhood dreams. Well, I never remember my dreams, but I used to have strange dizzy spells when I was a kid. They started again recently. The first came just after I received a postcard of Corfe Castle from Bob. The next happened just after I talked to you and Bob when you were at Corfe Castle."

Makepeace leaned forward and stared at me intently as I continued, "Each time I came round from these spells, it felt as if I was returning from another time and place. They ended when I was with you in the cabin, after you told Bob and me your story about John Clavell and the others. I haven't had a dizzy moment since and somehow that doesn't feel like an accident."

I stared up at the mountains. "Now I spend hours each day wondering about Frances and feeling myself into her life and situation. I do research on her whenever I have time. Often, when I read something new about her life, I get a sense of being told stuff that some part of me already knows."

To my surprise, Makepeace challenged me. "What if it is all autosuggestion? What if I planted this whole idea in your mind, and you are now identifying with something that has nothing to do with you?"

I laughed. "Perhaps it is. Suddenly you sound more like Bob Howard than Johnny Clavylle. Look, I'm not trying to prove anything to anyone else. I just want to make sense of all this for me. But there is one thing I want to ask you. Something happened at the cabin, that I could not make sense of at the time. It was when you handcuffed me to the bed."

Makepeace looked sheepish. "I hope you know how sorry I am now about all that. I must have been totally out of my skull. Drunk as a skunk. Please say you forgive me."

I laughed again. "Yes, I know you're sorry. And yes, I forgive you."

He breathed deeply. "Thank you, Sarah. That means a lot to me."

It did not seem useful to add, "But I can't yet trust you." I debated whether to drop my question, but this might be the last time I saw Antony Makepeace, so I went on, "I don't know if you remember, but at one point, I became half-crazed with terror. When you handcuffed me to the bed, my body started screaming. I felt as if I had been beaten. Do you remember?"

Makepeace nodded. "I'll say I do. You suddenly went hysterical on me, and you begged me not to hit you again, although I hadn't done so."

"Right. When I read more about Frances Coke, I found out that she was coerced into marriage with Sir John Villiers as a young teenager. Gossips at the time suggested that her father may have tied her to her bed and tried to beat her into submission. Coke had a reputation for behaving brutally when he lost his temper, so it would not have been surprising if he used violence when she resisted him."

I shuddered involuntarily. "I had a visceral reaction, when I read this part of her story. My back started burning." Even as I spoke, I could feel myself begin to shake and burn again at the memory. Makepeace stared at me and then began making patterns with his toe on the ground. He said nothing.

I cleared my throat, but my voice still sounded strained. "I called my mother in England, to ask if she remembered me getting beaten in my youth. She swears my father never laid a hand on me. Nor did anyone, as far as she and I know. No teachers, no school bullies. Yet I have this deep memory of having once been tied up and beaten. As if it was imprinted in me. It's a mystery."

Makepeace shrugged. "I can't help you. I do remember thinking your reaction was quite bizarre. But I know I didn't beat you, in any lifetime." He laughed without humour. "So welcome to my world, Sarah. This has been a bloody mystery to me since that regression workshop. The only way I can make sense of it is to accept that I have lived before."

I glanced at my watch. "Oh no." I stood up. "I'm sorry, Antony. This has been such a quick visit, but I have to get back to L.A. for an evening meeting. It's a long drive and I can't afford to get caught up in rush hour traffic."

Makepeace rose. He caught one of my hands in his and looked down at it, colouring under his tan as he spoke. "Sarah, I owe you more than I can say. I'm grateful, even if I haven't shown it. I'd like to think I could be half as good a friend to you as you to me. Please, let's keep in touch, and let me know if there's ever anything I can do for you."

We hugged and I stood on tiptoe to kiss Makepeace on the cheek. I touched a dimple that had appeared with his smile.

"Yes, there's something you can do for me. Take care of yourself, Antony Makepeace AKA Johnny Clavylle. And take care of that dimple."

My heart beat fast and my eyes became misty as I walked back to my car.

CHAPTER THIRTY-EIGHT

England 1635

"It can't be true." Frances sat in her Westminster apartment by the river, her face ashen at Sir Robert's news.

"I fear it is, my love. Ridiculous as it seems, your persecution did not go to the grave with the Buckinghams. That wretch Laud has been whispering in the King's ear about resurrecting your penance. My brother Edward gave me the tip today. We must get you and Robin out of Town immediately."

"I can't believe it. And I won't leave you again, Robert. My trial was years ago. Why would the Archbishop bring it up now? And why should Charles be willing to listen to him?"

"Why does Laud do anything? We're pawns in a much bigger game, Frances. The rumour the Archbishop has set about is that His Majesty is disgusted with us both for flaunting our sinful life together here in Town."

"That's preposterous. I've been living here in Lambeth ever since Papa died, quiet as a mouse in my own lodgings with Robin. You maintain your apartment at Suffolk House to fulfil your Parliamentary duties. We are so rarely seen in the same company together and even then we are modest in our behaviour. For that, Charles accuses us of flaunting ourselves? Why should he care, as long as we are not hurting anybody? Purbeck has never raised any objections about our situation."

"The King may not care about us, but he is increasingly concerned about his public image. Giving Laud agreement to pursue your penance offers a soft option for him. It shows support for the English Church, and helps send an indirect message that his wife's Catholicism has no—"

Robert's sentence remained unfinished. Outside the withdrawing room, a loud knocking was followed by audible protests from Lady Purbeck's manservant. A sergeant-at-arms entered the room with two constables.

"Is this woman Viscountess Purbeck?" The sergeant ignored Frances and addressed his question to Sir Robert. She rose and moved between them. "I am Lady Purbeck and these are my lodgings. How dare you enter in this unseemly manner, when I am entertaining a visitor?"

The sergeant-at-arms stared at Frances, then looked over her shoulder to Robert. "My Lord, I hold a warrant for the arrest of Viscountess Purbeck, by order of the Council. I ask you not to obstruct me or my men in the pursuance of our duty."

Robert responded, "If you wish me not to obstruct you, then start by addressing this lady with the respect she deserves." He moved in front of Frances to confront the officer. "What is your name, Sergeant, and where are you proposing to take Lady Purbeck?"

"My name is of no concern. I have orders to escort her to the Gatehouse."

"I shall find out your name, Sergeant. And be assured that, if you or your men upset Lady Purbeck in any way, I will learn of it and your lives will cease to be worth living."

Frances interrupted them. "What of my son? What are your orders for him? Surely a child of ten is not to be committed to the Gatehouse?"

"I have no orders concerning any son."

Robert turned to Frances and took her hands in his. "This matter shall be straightened out immediately, my dear. I will take care of Robin and send word to you before the day is done. Don't fear for the boy."

But no word reached Frances that day, and the only information she received on the morrow was that Sir Robert had also been seized on his return to Suffolk House. She could not ascertain where he had been taken and of Robin she heard nothing until after her first visitor appeared. He was the last person she expected to see in the Gatehouse, for they had not spoken to each other for years.

"What a dreadful business. Are they treating you well, Frances?"

The years were not treating Viscount Purbeck well, but the smile he gave his wife was warm and he manifested no symptoms of mania or melancholy. He took her hand and kissed it tenderly. "I never thought to see you detained here. I would have come before, but I only heard about your situation this morning, directly from His Majesty. What can I do for you, my dear wife?"

Frances blushed. "You still address me thus, in spite of our separation?"

"It is how I always think of you, my dear. And, even if I did not, we are still man and wife."

"After the sentence was brought for which I am apparently now detained, I sought to overset it through claiming my rank as your wife.

At that time, I was advised by their Lordships that you had denied me that privilege." The challenge in her voice was clear and Purbeck coloured.

"Frances, you know that my brother did many things in my name when he was alive, with which I was not in full agreement."

"I do indeed, my Lord. But I was told that their Lordships had received a letter specifically signed by you that Buckingham had acted to block my petition with your privity and assent. You were reported as having declared that according me privilege as your wife would go against your will and you protested against it."

He looked wretched. "But you surely also know I had previously spoken up for you, Frances. My brother removed me from Town, so I could not speak to their Lordships to explain our situation. He also swore the King would declare me mad and I would be kept away from Court permanently unless I signed."

Purbeck came forward and took her hand again. "I do remember that George assured me also at that time that you wished to leave London with Howard and the boy. He told me that, by declaring you free of privilege as my wife, I would actually be granting you the freedom you most desired."

She pulled her hand away. "Purbeck, you surely knew I would have stood a better long-term chance of freedom if the case had been dismissed on grounds of privilege? I would certainly not be here today, with no idea of what has happened to my son."

He went down on one knee. "Forgive me please, my dear. I was so unhappy and confused then, Frances. My head is not always clear, as you know. But you know I would never have done anything intentionally to allow you to be detained like this, especially so long afterwards and in such rude circumstances. That is why I have come here today. To offer you my help."

"You can help me most by telling me what do you know concerning Robin? And Sir Robert?" Purbeck shook his head. "I know nothing of either of them. I was indeed myself going to inquire of you about the boy's current whereabouts and welfare, to see if I might be of service to him."

"Then please, my Lord, I beg of you to go now and find out whatever you can concerning Robin *and* Robert, and send me word, any word at all. As quickly as you can. It is an agony not to know if my boy is safe."

"I will return as soon as I have any information."

After Purbeck's departure, Frances sat in some discomfiture. His comments concerning Buckingham's intervention in her privilege case rang true. Purbeck had never dissembled with her. It had felt indelicate to ask the husband from whom she was long separated to inquire after the well being of her lover as well as their son.

The speed with which he reacted to her request spoke to John's generosity of spirit. Efficient too, when not in his distempers, Viscount Purbeck was back within the hour. "My dear, you must not fret. The news is good. Well, that is to say, it is not all bad. At least, concerning Robin. As for your – that is to say – um, well – Howard is still being held close prisoner, but I am assured he is shown every courtesy due to his rank. I also hear that his brothers are strenuously engaged to secure his release from the Fleet."

At the word Fleet, Frances gave a small cry. John Villiers put out his hand. "No, no, you must not be afraid, my dear. It can only be a short time before Howard will be set free. And my other news is good. The boy is safe and well. It was judged better that I do not know the details. I am committed to help in any way I can, but a quite reasonable fear among Howard's friends who are guarding him was expressed that, if I were to have one of my episodes, I might not keep a close guard on my tongue."

"Oh, John."

His limp hand had fastened on hers and Frances clung to it, as tears that had been welling in her eyes overflowed and spilled down her cheeks.

"There, there, my pretty maid, don't cry. We shall soon make everything right. Many who love you are already engaged to find a way to release you from here." Purbeck clasped Frances to him in an awkward embrace. This time she did not fight it.

Sir John released her and drew a white lace handkerchief from his doublet. "Let me dry these tears." Frances allowed her husband to wipe her face as if she were a child. She gave a shaky smile when he had finished.

He stepped back to view his handiwork. "That's better. Now, my dear, I can ask about for further information, but I also have to be cautious about what I learn and whom I ask, for Laud has spies everywhere. I am a marked man in his eyes for having converted. I must not arouse the King's ill will, but get you out of Laud's clutches we somehow must and shall."

Her lip trembled. "Where shall I go when I am released? I can't go back to my old lodgings, since Laud is determined to continue hounding me. That monster has so much power throughout the land as Archbishop that I don't know where I can be safe from him. With Robert in the Fleet, it is impractical for me to go back to Shropshire. Mama cannot want me at Stoke, for she has made no effort to visit me since I have been incarcerated. What can I do, my Lord?"

Purbeck looked serious. "You would not be safe with me either. I believe you must steel yourself to leave the country for a time, Frances. Once you're out of harm's way, I can find the best moment to talk with the King and ask him to pardon you. Dragging out this demand for your public penance over so many years is unkind and unjust. In softer mood, His Majesty may listen to me. Only one as petty as Laud would ever have pressed him to insist on it. That man is dreadful and he is attacking me indirectly by imprisoning you."

He sat and encouraged Frances to do the same. "There are other options. If necessary, I can ask their Lordships to get their old decision against your privilege reversed. I can explain that at the time my thoughts were disordered and my brother misled me. God knows, such a plea will surprise none who know me and knew him. But that will take more time than you currently have. Your penance is already set for St Clement Danes, a week on Sunday. Have you thought about doing it?"

Frances looked shocked. "I've not stood out so long against an unjust sentence in order to give in now. I will never do penance for something of which I am not guilty. You and I agreed years back, when you nursed me through smallpox, that I need feel no shame about anything I have done. So for me it is a matter of principle. What pains me most is that the King should behave thus. Charles has become so cold toward me."

"No, no. He is still a loyal and kind man at heart and he has taken great care of our family. It's not him, my dear. It's Laud who is making trouble."

"John, the King of England need not to pander to his Archbishop of Canterbury, any more than he need always have followed your brother's lead during the years that George hounded me. You say Charles has taken care of our family, but he does not take care of me. Instead, he has ordered my public humiliation. If you do not chastise me for anything, why should our King, who was my dear childhood friend?"

"My dear, you must not let the King's behaviour upset you like this. He is under pressure from so many quarters, but things will come right in the end and you shall be free."

Frances doubted this and continued to persecute herself with fears until two days later, she received a nocturnal visitor. Already prepared for bed, she searched for a garment to cover herself more fully, when she heard the sound of a key turn in her locked door.

Unusually, that door remained ajar after her visitor had entered.

"Lady Purbeck, do you recognise me? We should not mention names since walls have ears, but we have a mutual friend. You and I met once, many years ago, at his uncle's manor in Staines."

Frances remembered a gangling, genial youth who had accompanied Robert to visit the Knyvetts during her brief time with them in Staines.

That youth had grown into a genial sounding, much larger and thickset man. She relaxed. "Yes, indeed I do. I was a prisoner then too, but under much less austere conditions."

The man looked around him. "I must agree with you. But even if these conditions compare unfavourably with Stanwell Manor, my Lady, you are fortunate in having at least one here at the Gatehouse who is willing to help you leave them behind."

"What do you mean?"

"If you are ready to trust me, let's not waste valuable moments in explanation. I need you to put on these clothes. You must also arrange your hair under this hat." He looked at Frances who, in night attire, had left her long dark mane to fall free over her shoulders and down her back.

"My, you do have a lot of hair, don't you? Fortunate that we men wear ours long as well. Please dress quickly. I cannot risk leaving your cell, yet you may rely upon me to keep my back turned while you change."

Frances looked at the garments he held out to her. "These are boys' clothes."

"That is how we shall enable you to escape. Nobody will remark a man and a youth leaving the Gatehouse, but we have only a small window of time before the turnkey must do his next rounds. My carriage is outside and my horses are fresh. We must be quick and quiet."

Frances dressed at speed. For the first time since her detention, she giggled. "Did Robert ever tell you about how I avoided my penance once before?"

The man spoke over his shoulder. "No, my Lady."

"On that occasion I was obliged to flee from York House. The Savoy Ambassador, Abbé Scaglia, lived next door at the time. His servants dressed his page up as a young lady, and the boy acted as my decoy. So we will be righting the balance tonight, when I leave dressed as a boy. There. How do I look?"

Her visitor turned and whistled softy. "Perfect. As if to the manner born, my Lady."

"Oh, I am indeed entirely accustomed, sir. And for that I can thank Mama. She enjoyed shocking my nurse and Polite Society by allowing me to dress as a boy often during my childhood."

CHAPTER THIRTY-NINE

California

"Holy Dooley, Sarah, what were you thinking of to let the bloke go free? Don't tell me a few weeks in an expensive rehab summer camp will have straightened a nutter like him out. I'm amazed Bob allowed it."

I laughed. "Bob was amazed too, at the time."

Jane and I were lunching back at Figtree's on the Boardwalk. She had been flying a different Qantas route to Asia for several weeks, and had only just resumed the Sydney-Los Angeles connection. It was our first conversation since my abduction and also the first time I had spoken about my kidnapping with anyone other than Makepeace and Bob. I had sworn Jane to secrecy before telling her what happened.

She still looked askance. "So why *did* he? Allow it, I mean."

"I suspect Bob thought he stood little chance of making anything stick on his own, if I was not willing to bring a case. He's a pragmatist. But he did also say that in the past he's always ended up giving in to Johnny Clavylle – which is what he calls Antony Makepeace – because the man is such a brilliant musician."

"So your gullibility and Bob's love of musical genius hacked it over common sense? What a pair of mugs. I reckon you both need to see a shrink."

"There was more to it than that. We thought rehab should be given a try."

"If you ask me, this Makepeace bloke really had a lend of you both. I might have guessed it of you, with all your weird ways, but I'd have expected different from Bob. I think he deserves a medal, though. Most men I know would have wanted their pound of flesh. Bob had as hard a time of it as you, in a way. He didn't know what was happening and had to find you with so little to go on."

"Yes, it must have been awful for him. But Bob likes harmony in life as well as music, and I've not known him bear a grudge against anyone for long. He's tough and he hates people getting the better of him. He vents often and loud. Then he just seems to drop his frustration and moves on. Doesn't waste energy nursing grievances."

"Whereas your crazy highwayman was obviously tortured and twisted up in his own past. Probably still is, even after drying out. He's lucky you gave him a fair go. So what do you make of all this past life stuff he believes in?"

I pushed a solitary shrimp around the rim of my plate with my fork. "Just thinking about it presses my buttons."

"Forget your buttons. I don't want to hear about them. *Are* you this lost love of his, reincarnated, or not?"

As Jane pressed me, I stabbed vigorously at the shrimp. It fell off my plate and I let it sit, staining the paper tablecloth, while I stared back at her.

"I can't tell. It's not that simple. My feelings fight with my head. My head says I am Sarah James, living in twenty-first-century California. My body says something strange is going on that I can't explain away rationally. And, since I started the research, I seem to have become obsessed with a period in history about which I knew nothing, until Antony opened the door."

She did not let go. "Do you *feel* that you are Frances?"

I skewered the shrimp and returned it to my plate. "Remember those dizzy spells I was getting?"

Jane nodded. "Yes, I meant to ask you. Did you get them checked out?"

"No, but they must be connected with all this, because they stopped as soon as Antony shared his story. I have thought of trying hypnosis to see if I can find out what's going on, but something prevents me. I don't like the idea of putting myself in someone else's power."

Jane shook her head. "Hypnosis doesn't attract me either, although a friend of mine in Sydney found it helped him give up smoking."

I shrugged. "Anyway, I really don't have a simple answer to your question, Jane. But Frances and her story do feel familiar, and certain events seem to resonate. My strongest physical reaction came when I was handcuffed to the bed in the cabin."

"Say more about that."

"What more can I say? It was horrible." I trembled again. "My flesh aches even now when I speak of it. Perhaps I'm tapping into a collective memory pool of women beaten through the ages."

Jane looked sceptical and shook her head. "That sounds too convoluted."

"Well then, why don't you tell me what *you* think is going on? Your guess is as good as mine about what it all means."

"I didn't *have* the experience. You did. Your guess *must* be better than mine. And I bet you actually do prefer one of your theories over another."

"I don't, but I know that seventeenth-century Frances Coke was pursued, attacked and detained over and again by people and institutions all the way up to the King of England. If I am Frances reincarnated, at least I've escaped the violation and persecution she suffered."

Jane pursed her lips. "Makepeace kidnapping you and holding you against your will was a violation, Sarah, however much you may deny it and even if you have forgiven him. Your ex used physical violence against you before that, remember? It took you quite a while to get away from him and his highfalutin family. And, from all you've told me, there was plenty of pressure on you to put up with things and stay married."

I preferred not to be reminded of such things, and protested, "But look at me now, Jane. I lead a liberated life in California that no woman in seventeenth-century England could possibly have done. I know I'm privileged, if I compare my situation with millions of women around the world, but so was Frances, in relative terms, in her own day. Think about it. I have economic, religious and social independence. I can think what I want, say what I want and go pretty much wherever I like."

Jane looked thoughtful. "Yeah, I guess that *is* true. Laws and attitudes have changed, at least in some countries and for some of us. But globally power and wealth remains in the hands of a relative few, and millions of women do still live in poverty and subjugation. You suffered too, to get clear of your own old-world system. You've had to work hard to claim your own freedom. Your road has been a lot tougher than mine. Maybe that's why you identify with Frances."

"There are plenty of reasons why I may identify with Frances. Perhaps I've blocked out some event in my childhood that triggered a somatic reaction. Perhaps I saw a kidnapping movie at an early age that got lodged in my subconscious. Perhaps I had a history lesson about Frances and have completely forgotten."

"When you've done yabbering, give me your number one theory."

"I've already said I don't know. Why does it matter to you, anyway?"

Jane sat back in her seat. "That's a good question." She thought for a while, then said, "I want to know what happens to us when we die. I like the idea that I may get another chance at life, if I screw things up this time round. And I want some proof positive before signing up to believe in reincarnation."

I chuckled. "You mean 'promise me certainty so I can surrender to the unknown'?"

Jane grinned. "Yeah, something like that. I always wanted the insurance papers signed in triplicate before buying into any religion."

"Let me ask *you* the question then. You're good at reading people, Jane. How do you explain Antony Makepeace's story?"

Jane stared at her plate, then looked up with a laugh. "OK, you've got me. I don't know either. I do really want to believe that you *are* Frances, and that you've come back to life to make a better deal for yourself and others this time round. Including getting married to Bob."

I giggled. "You romantic old softy!"

"Right on. I guess it is romantic and also quite comforting to believe that we've lived before and will live again and things can go on getting better. And yes, I'm still rooting for you to marry Bob. I happen to think he's a great bloke and that you're a good match for each other."

"Oh, Jane. Let's not get back on that old refrain. You've just put the cause of women's freedom in the West back a hundred years. Woman is only complete when spliced to a great bloke, eh?"

We both laughed. Jane waved her empty wine glass hopefully at the waiter. "After all this serious talk, I need another drink."

After he refilled her glass, I continued, "All our explanations are based in our present understanding of the universe. We try to reduce things to what we can understand. Frances lived then. Sarah lives now. Sarah feels what Frances felt. *Ipso facto* Sarah is Frances reincarnated. But what if, in trying to reduce things like that, something gets lost?"

"Like what?"

"I don't know. I feel there's some kind of truth over the horizon that can't be spoken. It concerns why we are here and what our lives and deaths are about."

Jane's brow furrowed. "Uh-oh, are you going cosmic on me, girl?"

"Not really, so let's leave our questions out in the cosmos, where they perhaps belong."

"That's fine by me."

Jane stared across toward the ocean and then back at me with a gleam in her eye. "Oh, one other thing. What's happened to the drunken musician? Has he gone back to Europe? Is he drinking again or have his forty days in the desert taken him beyond temptation? I wonder if Bob will help bad-boy Johnny back on stage to twang his guitar in public, dressed in sackcloth and ashes or bushranger's gear. If he does, I hope I'm in the front row seat for his gig."

"He's back in England. To know more, you'll have to watch this space, like me. But I promise you one thing. If Antony Makepeace AKA Johnny Clavylle ever plays music again in the USA, I'll do my level best to ensure he doesn't have to do it in sackcloth and ashes. Frances never did appear in the Chapel of the Savoy or St Clements Danes barefoot and in a white shift, so I don't see why Johnny Clavylle should have to do public penance."

CHAPTER FORTY

England 1635

Henry Danvers, Earl of Danby, was awakened from his slumbers, to be advised that a youth had just been admitted, who urgently begged a late night audience with his Cousin Henry.

"Admit him to my library, stoke up the fire there, and tell him to wait on my pleasure."

Danvers clambered out of bed, donned a long velvet dressing robe and descended the staircase of his recently enlarged country home at Cornbury Park, in Oxfordshire. The sixty-two-year-old Earl had known drama in many guises while serving kings of France and England on land and at sea. Yet he was still capable of being surprised, and his astonishment was complete when the slim, dark-haired boy standing before him in his library revealed herself as Frances, Lady Purbeck, dressed in male attire.

"Frances, dear girl, what a surprise. I received word to expect a visit, but not that I must receive you at an advanced hour, in fancy dress. This is a rare to-do."

"Cousin, you are good to receive me at all. I do not wish to put you in an embarrassing position. Especially since you have done so much on my behalf in the past. That's why it seemed wiser to arrive under cover of darkness."

"I've done little enough for you, child, apart from lending my signature occasionally to ensure you received your marriage portion, as is your due. But I fancy you may now be in search of more robust aid than that. Are you still on the run, m'dear?"

"Yes. And I do need some immediate advice, as well as practical help on how to get to Paris, if you are able to offer either. Perhaps you have some experience in the matter?"

Her innocent-sounding question went home.

"Hah! Who told you that story, child? You weren't even born when the duel took place. I was hardly more than a boy myself. It was Eliza,

I'll be bound. Your mother has never been able to resist repeating a juicy tale. And what an adventure it turned out to be. You know, but for killing Henry Long, I'd never have joined the French army."

The Earl's eyes gleamed, as his mind travelled back forty years and more. "I did receive a full pardon from His Majesty before the turn of the century."

"But not before you had been obliged to spend years abroad as an outlaw, Cousin. Your experience can be invaluable to me now. You've travelled a path I find myself obliged to take."

"Obliged?" Sir Henry sounded suddenly sceptical.

Frances strove to prevent her voice shaking as she replied, "I would not choose voluntarily to leave my family and the land of my birth. Unfortunately, Archbishop Laud has poisoned His Majesty against me."

"Hmm. Yes, I heard about that. But exile is a lonely path, child. Why not swallow your pride and serve your penance? Humbling, I grant you, but discomfort for a single hour may be a small enough price to pay for the peace you'll then enjoy, as long as you can behave with discretion thereafter."

"It's not a question of discomfort, which I have known in full measure. Or of discretion, which I possess in abundance. I simply will not give in to an injustice." Frances swayed in exhaustion. "May I sit, Cousin?"

"Oh, please excuse me, m'dear." Lord Danvers drew a chair forward. He rang to call for refreshment as Frances sat down. She blinked, yawned and removed her hat, then untied and removed her over cloak. The tight-fitting male clothes beneath accentuated her figure.

She found herself looking up into appreciative eyes as the Earl surveyed her. It occurred to her that her mother's first cousin might be advancing in years and still single, but he was evidently not immune to female charm. He was also a man of influence, and still involved in administering her marriage portion, received from Buckingham's estate. She needed him on her side.

"You know I have a son called Robin, Cousin Henry. He is a fine boy. Honest and brave. He will be ten years old this year. I want my son to be able to stand tall when he reaches manhood. The world may call him a bastard, but Robin shall know that his parents were proud of him, and never cowed nor broken by petty tyrants."

"Hmm. Easier for his father than you to bear up against petty tyrants, m'dear. But there is something I don't understand. Why did young Howard show such an appalling lack of judgment as to have lodged you in Westminster, right under the nose of those who might still wish you harm? You were snug enough for years, tucked away in your Shropshire love-nest with him, and then afterward with your father. Might you not have stayed on at Stow with Eliza, when your mother reclaimed the property?"

"Mama is unhappy with me about certain things. But please don't pin lack of judgment on Sir Robert alone. I was totally complicit in our decision, when Robin and I moved to Westminster to be near him."

"So why the devil did *you* not have the good sense to keep yourself and your boy out of harm's way?"

"Robert and I love each other, Cousin. We have neither of us ever loved anyone else, although we cannot hope to marry, because Purbeck won't divorce me. Robert and I have known so much separation over the years, including those two years I was at Stow. Surely you can understand that we wanted to be together again after my father died?"

"So why not go back to Shropshire?"

"With Buckingham and his mother both dead, we assumed I had nothing more to fear. And, Robert has been obliged to spend more time than ever in Town engaged in political affairs, since he was elected to Bishops Castle, although I don't entirely understand how that can be, since the King has prorogued Parliament. As for me, well, have you ever spent extended time in the depths of rural Shropshire, with only a child for company?"

"Never had a child nor even a wife, m'dear. But you were tactless in your choice of London residence. Living right under Laud's nose. So now, if you truly mean to head for Paris, you and Howard will be obliged to live further apart than ever. Unless he is willing to share exile with you, when he gets out of the Fleet."

Frances sighed. "That may be true. All I can say is that it is easy to be wise after the event."

"Well, it has never been my habit to mince words, even to a lovely young woman in distress. You are in a tight spot, Frances. You're much more exposed than Howard. He'll get out of the Fleet soon enough. A Member of Parliament can stand on his privilege and the Suffolk clan still has pull in the land, even if the present Earl is an even bigger spendthrift than his parents, and may yet ruin the whole Howard family before he's done." Danvers shook his head and puffed out his cheeks. "You, however, are an easy target, for any one of a mind to score religious or legal points, or settle an old personal score."

The Earl reflected awhile, then added, "You do appear to have consistently attracted the ill will of some mighty powerful men, Cousin. I wonder why?"

"We both know I can thank Papa for setting me on that particular path, by selling me into high places for his own political ends. Yet, in fairness, my father did try to use the power restored to him in the interest of the country he served." Frances gave a despondent sigh.

"What you say about people settling old scores is so accurate. I've been the butt of other people's squabbles since my childhood. Mama once said I've inherited all her misfortune, yet I'm barred from enjoying her fortune. She also said I'm her Achilles' heel, and her many enemies like to use me against her."

Danvers barked with laughter. "Your mother was never a shrinking violet, even as a girl. For sure she has enemies aplenty. Haven't seen much of her lately, but she was ever a quarrelsome and calculating minx, utterly absorbed in herself. Beautiful, though. Still able to wrap men around her little finger and keep 'em dangling for as long as it suits her, I'll be bound. Led your father a dreadful dance. Always humiliating him."

Frances shook her head. "Be fair, Cousin Henry. You know Papa was not always kind to her, either. Mama is her own woman. She makes enemies in part because she will not give in to authority. I take after her in that. Sadly, we are not as close as we were. She didn't like me living with Robert in Shropshire, and felt it a great disloyalty to her that I went to my father at the end."

"Hmm. I've also heard some say that she prefers to keep her distance from a daughter who eclipses her own beauty."

"Oh, that's unkind. And untrue. I've never held a candle to Mama in looks. She's always told me I have too much of my father about my countenance."

Frances stood up and went to warm herself by the fire. In male attire, she had already begun to assume the informal habits of a man. She turned and smiled at the Earl.

"I don't regret these last two years with Papa, Cousin, even though Mama and Robert were both so set against it. I've created my own fate by always following my heart. It is one reason why I will never do public penance. I've done nothing of which I need repent. Above all, I will not have my son think I have ever felt one moment's shame about the circumstances in which he came into this world."

She swayed and sat down again. "Thank you for listening so patiently to my story. I am sorry to have disturbed you at so late an hour and to have kept you out of your bed. It was inappropriate of me to presume upon our relationship. If you need me to leave immediately, I understand. If you can but allow me and my escort to rest our horses and our heads for a night, we'll leave discreetly at first light and cause you no further embarrassment."

The Earl of Danby coloured. "Cousin, even were we not related, it is not my practice to turn a lady in need out of my home. Albeit one dressed up in boy's garments. You shall stay, and tomorrow I will see what I can arrange. Did you know that, thanks to his Majesty's peculiar sense of humour, I'm the Governor of Guernsey?"

Frances nodded.

Danvers grimaced. "It's a ridiculous job for an active soldier. I've never enjoyed shutting myself away in an old Channel Island castle to keep watch for non-existent invaders, but it is probably time I visited my responsibilities in person there again. I fancy that may serve you well."

Frances blenched. "Guernsey? I would prefer not to have to take up residence in Guernsey, Cousin."

The Earl looked amused. "Don't blame you. Can't stand it myself, which is why I spend as little time there as possible. No, Guernsey offers you no long-term solution as a bolthole. You would be noticed immediately and you would still be subject to English law. But it may prove a convenient stepping stone for one wishing to travel on to France. If Laud means to arrest you again – and I would guess the small-minded fellow does – he'll have men posted to keep watch for you at all the usual Channel ports."

Henry Danvers chuckled as another thought struck him. "Someone I know has recently arrived in Paris. His company may serve you well. He likes tilting at windmills, so he'll be ready to take you under his wing. Likes a pretty face too. Digby. Young Kenelm Digby. Have you ever met him? He must know Purbeck and Howard."

"By reputation, but curiously our paths have never crossed. Robert must know Sir Kenelm, for his late wife's family lived some miles north of Clun. I never met Venetia, but I heard often of her beauty and… unusual character. And you're right, Purbeck and Sir Kenelm also know each other. They both served the King when he was Prince of Wales and they share the same faith."

The Earl of Danby spoke hastily. "Yes, well, the less said about their shared faith the better, Cousin. Your husband's religion can't have helped your case with Laud. It may be one of the principal reasons the Archbishop hounds you."

"Robert and Purbeck have both said much the same."

"It would also account for why the King lets Laud make a public example of you, child. His Majesty has to be so careful, with that Catholic wife of his stirring up religious trouble whenever she can. No doubt about it, you're caught up in all this Church turmoil, whether you like it or not. Mark my words, religious differences and these incessant power struggles between the King and Parliament will end by splitting our nation in two. Perilous times we live in. But I'm only an old war dog. What do I know about anything?"

Henry Danvers rose and rang again on the bell pull. "Where is that man of mine? You must eat something and I must make sleeping arrangements for you and your escort. Tomorrow we'll plan on how we can leave for Guernsey, without creating a stir. Maybe we'll keep you in boy's attire and you can travel as my page. We'll get you away safely first and then we can think about how to get your son to you. I'm far too old to risk exile again myself, so we must find a means that keeps my nose clean with His Majesty."

As he bent to offer his cousin his arm to rise, the nose in question shone and the firelight accentuated the shadow cast by a large scar on the left of Sir Henry's face. The Earl of Danby was unlikely to admit to Frances that a spot of masquerade, in the company of an intelligent and lovely woman half his age, was just what he needed to enliven an ageing, single soldier's existence.

CHAPTER FORTY-ONE

California & England

"He swears he hasn't touched a drop, Bob, and he said that you can check that out with all his friends."

"I already have. I've spoken with all the other guys in the band."

"What did they say?"

"The same as Johnny. No interest in alcohol, at least in their presence. Easy to be with. He hasn't missed a rehearsal. His new compositions are brilliant and his playing is crisper than in years. All the guys are curious about some new Wonder Woman in his life. Johnny tells them she's saved him from himself."

"Oh, has he got a new girlfriend? He didn't say anything about that when he called me. I wonder why he was so secretive. Perhaps he's feeling shy. I must ask him about her, next time we speak."

Bob looked disbelieving. "Are you being deliberately obtuse, Sarah? Johnny's spreading the word that you're his guardian angel and the unrequited love of his life."

My heart skipped. "You are kidding, aren't you?"

Bob grinned. "Don't worry. I've told the band members it has nothing to do with you personally. It's just that living in the City of Angels has given you wings. It's a well-known phenomenon. Every woman in L.A. who's not a native-born Angeleno floats around with her feet off the ground and her head in the clouds. Some even play harps."

"So I'm Antony's Wonder Woman? Oh dear. He threatened to start that theme with me when he was in rehab, but I wasn't having any of it. He flipped too quickly from demonising into idealising. But you should know he's talked about you in glowing terms to me as well, Bob. We had better spread our wings and fly over to England quickly, just to remind him how wonderful we are not. Which reminds me, did you book our tickets today?"

"Yes, and I traded in so many air miles that you are travelling first class with me, ma'am. And none of your European socialist complaints about elitism, please."

I fought and lost a brief internal battle between my indignation that people can be treated differently on the basis of how much they can pay and relief at the prospect of comfort on our trans-Atlantic flight.

Bob had already moved on to another topic. "Johnny won't idealise me for long when I tell him what's needed if a US tour is gonna work. And you'd better remember I'll be keeping my eye on you two when you're together. Johnny Clavylle is not going to woo you away from me. I can spill the beans on what a little shrew you can be when you lose your temper and I'll also tell him how high maintenance you are."

That comment surprised me, even in jest. "What makes you say I'm high maintenance? I think I'm quite frugal in lifestyle, especially by comparison with most of the women you are said to have dated."

"Ah, but I have to buy you a new halo and set of wings almost every week, because you wear the old ones out so quickly with your Wonder Woman do-gooding. Luckily, they're on *special* just now in the Beverly Center, so I'll stock up on spares for you before we leave for England."

"You're an idiot, Bob Howard. And you can save your breath. Antony had enough opportunity to see me in all my shrewishness as well as my angelic glory, while I was tied up at Joshua Tree."

I had responded in kind to his teasing, but Bob stiffened and I detected an edge in his voice, when he replied. "Oh, did he see you in *all* your glory? You told me you kept your clothes on."

"Are you still wondering whether anything sexual went on between us?"

He denied it. "I was only joking."

"Uh-huh."

"Come here, woman."

"Is that an order?"

"When have I ever succeeded in ordering you to do anything? Will you come here, please?"

I allowed myself to be pulled gently into Bob Howard's arms, but tension about the place of Antony Makepeace in our life was still dogging our relationship. Since we had returned from the desert, it had felt as if Bob and I were walking around on a dormant but live volcano. Would it blow or die out naturally over time?

As I was asking myself the question, Bob's lips found mine and his hands began to caress my breast. He must have felt my resistance, for he stopped immediately, pulled back and looked down at me. "What is it? Don't you want me?"

"Yes, I want you. I also want you to trust that I have told you everything that went on between Antony and me."

"Oh forget it, Sarah. I do trust you. I'm just cautious where he's concerned. It's not you and Antony Makepeace that I worry about, but Johnny Clavylle. I lost several girlfriends to him, remember? And saw him drop them. I've watched his seductive routine at work too often for comfort. Most women don't withstand it."

"I'm not most women. Your namesake in the seventeenth century was willing to trust his Frances, even when they were forced to live apart. Can't you trust me?"

The volcano blew without warning as Bob erupted. "You don't know a blind thing about who or what some four-hundred-year-old namesake of mine may or may not have trusted. You've picked up some garbled stories and scraps of pseudo-historical fact. For all you know, the original Robert Howard was an untrusting and untrustworthy brute. He could have been another corrupt nobleman and woman-beater, but the people who wrote the books found it more exciting to paint him as a hero."

I reacted hotly. "Frances was a beautiful and a desirable woman. She would have had many opportunities for other liaisons, yet she remained true to Robert Howard and he to her through thick and thin. I know that in my essence. Why did she do so? I'll tell you why, Bob. Because she loved and felt safe with him. Someone as sensitive and honest as her could not have done so, if Robert hadn't been inherently trustworthy."

Bob looked disconcerted. "I'm not sure why you're suddenly telling me all this. It feels very heavy."

"I'm not sure either. It seemed to erupt out of what we were just saying to each other. Yes, Antony Makepeace can be seductive when he turns on the charm. I've felt that at first hand and at close quarters. Yes, I find him attractive. But I doubt I'd ever trust him. Not unless he can shed his stage image and address something much deeper. Something erupts in Antony from time to time, just like this fight did now between us, when we talked about him. Except, unlike with you and me, he turns mean and vengeful when he erupts."

"I can be pretty mean and vengeful too."

I laughed. "Sure!"

Apparently missing the irony, Bob asked seriously, "Do you trust me, Sarah?"

Faced with the question, I answered without hesitation. "Yes."

"Why?"

"It's a mystery to me. Just like the mystery that seems to have existed between Frances and her Robert."

His expression changed and he relaxed. "Well, here's another mystery then. I want to make love with you right now. Since I'm not allowed to force you, I'm mysteriously hoping you want to make love with me too."

I laughed and began to strip off my clothes. As I made for the bedroom of Bob's apartment, I heard him follow me in noisy and appreciative pursuit.

But ten days later, we were in a hotel room in Knightsbridge, fighting again. Jet lag and tiredness had loosened both our tongues and tension had been mounting between us since the phone message arrived from Makepeace, inviting us both down to Kimmeridge for the weekend.

"Sarah, I know what I said. I do want to visit Corfe Castle with you, but I'm going down to see Johnny on my own first, to get this whole thing sorted out. This is purely business. I need to judge whether he's fit to do a tour or whether I'm best not wasting my time. I've decided to go down to Dorset alone and that's all there is to it."

I flushed as I repeated myself. "Antony has invited *both* of us to Kimmeridge. Why are you so determined to separate things out? Life doesn't always fit into neat boxes marked business and personal."

Bob's face closed. "Whether you like it or not, that's how I run my life. And that's how I intend it to stay. You're not going to dictate to me how I run my business."

I flared. "I feel mad when I hear you say that. I don't have any interest in dictating how you running your business. But you may like to remember that the reason I got kidnapped was because of what you call your business. And while you were in the middle of that business, you must have talked personally to Antony about me. You even required me to speak personally with him on the phone, right in the middle of your business."

"That was completely different."

"I don't see why. You're trying to shut me out now, but I was a prime mover in getting him to go into rehab. If I hadn't been involved, Antony Makepeace might not even be sober enough for you to contemplate organising a tour for Johnny Clavylle and his band at this moment. I find your logic highly illogical. You're just out to try and control us all."

"I'm only trying to protect you."

"Excuse me then for saying that your protection of me with Johnny Clavylle comes a little late in the day. And I don't need that kind of protection anyway, Bob. How dare you decide what is best for me, without even consulting me? How dare you try and decide what is best for Antony without consulting him either? Why can't you treat us both like adults, capable of making up our own minds together?"

"I'm not trying to decide anything for anyone else, although Johnny long ago gave up the right to be treated as an adult by the stupid way he behaved."

"You *are* trying to decide for everyone. If you weren't, you would do us both the courtesy of discussing things first, rather than announcing unilaterally that you've decided to go alone down to Corfe. You could have explained that you want to keep things from the past separate from your discussions about the proposed tour. You could have been open to what either of us might say in response. Instead you present me with a *fait accompli* and plan on doing the same with Antony. I don't know about him, but it doesn't work for me. If that's how it's going to be between us, I'm getting on the next plane back to L.A.."

Bob's lips were tight. He folded his arms. "Anything else you'd like to put me right about?"

"Since you ask, yes. Just because you bought my ticket with your air miles doesn't mean you've bought the right to decide for us both what happens while we're here. And there's another thing. You're setting Antony Makepeace up to fail all over again, if you call his past behaviour stupid to his face. It will put him straight back on the defensive. I've heard pretty wild tales about Bob Howard and what he got up to on the road with his band. Were you born so incredibly superior to Antony or did you just get lucky?"

We glared at each other.

"Oh, fuck it. I knew I should never have brought you with me to England. I'm going out."

Howard picked up his wallet and the keys of our rental car. He left the hotel room without another word.

I stared in frustration at the slammed door. Returning to the bed, I picked up the note containing Antony's telephone message. I reread it and lifted the phone. On the point of dialling his Kimmeridge number to accept his invitation for myself, I stopped and replaced the receiver.

As I did so, the hotel room door opened again. I looked up to see Bob standing in the doorway. He came inside and closed the door quietly behind him. "I'm sorry, honey. You're right. I *was* trying to control things."

He breathed deeply, sat down on the other side of the bed and gave me a shamefaced smile. "I guess I'm jealous of how close you seemed to get with Johnny, especially while he was in rehab. And I'm scared of not knowing what may happen if the three of us are all together in one place again. Especially in that particular place, since that old castle seems to be significant to you both."

I got up and went across the room. I put my arms around Bob and hugged him. "Thanks for coming back. And for explaining how you feel."

He sighed. "I really don't want to find myself getting sucked into doing something business-wise for Johnny, just to please you."

I released him and asked, "Is that what it felt like last time the three of us were together? That you were sucked into agreeing to let him go into rehab?"

He shrugged. "Not exactly, but your behaviour did influence me. Quite strongly. If I'd been alone, I would have called the cops."

"If you'd been alone, you never would have needed to. We're all connected in this story. Antony kidnapped me in part because he saw me as your Achilles' heel. He was trying to get at you through me."

Bob laughed suddenly. "He got more than he bargained for then. Kidnapping you led him into doing exactly what I had failed to persuade him to do. You're tough, Sarah. Tougher than me, when you choose to be."

It was a new way for me to think about myself and particularly in terms of our relationship. "I don't know if that's true. But if I am, aren't you glad I am? Surely getting Antony to go through rehab was a win-win situation for us all, even if we've had to go through some pain together along the way?"

"Don't count on a happy ending until it happens, Sarah."

"I don't. I don't have hopes or expectations, concerning this or most other things these days. But the reports are good on Antony's sobriety for the moment. And remember, if he had been locked up in jail, there'd have been no chance of Johnny Clavylle making another stage appearance."

"I remember. Do *you* remember what one is supposed to do when a fight is over?"

I went into his arms willingly. My voice was muffled as I spoke into his chest. "Thanks again for coming back."

"You're lucky I did!" His reply was made in such a provocative tone that I could only laugh. I beat Bob's chest in mock anger, then confessed, "I was so hurt and angry after you walked out that I was on the point of calling Antony to say I'd come down on my own. Then I realised I would be doing exactly what I had just been mad with you about."

We kissed, long and slow. Bob released me. "So what *are* we going to do about Johnny's invitation?"

"How about suggesting he comes up to London first, and we meet somewhere near the hotel? We could have dinner together and then I'll leave you with him to talk business. It might be best for us to meet on neutral ground initially, instead of in Antony's own back yard. I do still want to go to Corfe Castle, but let's do that after you and he decide about the tour. And let's stay in the hotel you ate at, rather than at his place."

"Good idea, babe. Especially since it means we can spend more time in this large and extremely comfortable hotel bed first. They do say that sex is so much better after a fight."

"Who is the 'they'?"

"Do you need names? I thought you trusted me. Here's your chance to prove it." Bob nudged me laughing onto the bed.

CHAPTER FORTY-TWO

France 1636

"What a fool I was to imagine I would be safe in Paris, Kenelm. Can you believe that Lord Scudamore bribed the sister of one of my servants to make sure that the King's wretched writ was served on me?"

"You didn't accept it though, did you, Frances?"

"I refused to receive it into my hands. But the girl can testify that I was in the house and aware of its delivery. That's partly why I fled back to the convent. Also because it took so long for Cousin Henry to arrange the transfer of my funds."

Frances spoke with unusual bitterness. "Kenelm, does Lord Scudamore really have nothing better to do than harass me? It's difficult enough being a pauper here in Paris, without being actively pursued by the King's Ambassador."

Her visitor looked sympathetic. "I know it's frustrating, but try not to take it to heart. Scudamore is trying to fulfil what he sees as his responsibility. Unfortunately he's a long-time friend of the Archbishop and Laud must be pressuring him to serve you up as a church plate offering for the Puritans. You can be sure there's nothing personal in the Ambassador's own behaviour."

"On the receiving end, I can tell you that it feels very personal."

"If I know Scudamore, he's feeling torn 'twixt the devil and the deep blue sea. It's shocking luck that your arrival in Paris should have coincided with that of an Ambassador who is also so cosy with Laud. But you must not despair. The Archbishop is my old tutor. I'm trying to use my own relationship with him on your behalf. Even though he looks askance at my religious allegiance, I may yet prevail upon his humanity."

"If he has any. Please do keep trying, Kenelm. I fear arrest again, every time I hear a knock on the door. If this pressure from Lord Scudamore continues, I may be obliged to join the convent. But the Mother Superior has made it abundantly clear I cannot keep Robin with me. I can't give up my son. And to renounce Robert altogether would be more than I can bear."

Digby chuckled. "I can't quite see you donning a nun's habit." He changed his laugh to a cough when Frances looked at him with reproach. "Be sure I'll write to Laud again, and to Lord Conway and a couple of other fellows in high places as well. This situation is too hypocritical for words. Countless relationships like yours and Howard's go on behind closed doors. Although that may not be the best line to take in pleading your case."

The laugh threatened to return, as Digby added, "I will instead speak of your sweetness, beauty and virtue and end by reminding my friends that creating a scandal for your extradition makes a mockery of our nation here. Our Gallic neighbours find our public prudery beyond comprehension."

Frances returned to her underlying grievance. "I can't understand the King's attitude. It hurts me more than anything. Charles and I were such close friends. You know him intimately. Why do you think he's changed?"

"His Majesty is a difficult man, m'dear. I put it down to the combination of Henry's death and parental over-anxiety. Once he was the heir, they encouraged Charles to believe himself the most precious being on God's earth, not excepting God."

Kenelm Digby grimaced, as he continued, "He also came in contact with Buckingham at an impressionable age, which was a disaster. I remember the two of them in Madrid, when they were trying to get Charles hitched to the Infanta. Their behaviour was embarrassing. George was always a master at egging the Prince on. And the aftermath of the Spanish business showed how, when Charles feels rejected, he can turn vengeful."

Frances protested, "I've never rejected Charles. He's the one who has driven me away. Now he's ordering me back to do my penance."

Digby shrugged. "I'm sure first Buckingham and then Laud have long encouraged the King to believe that you are wilfully rejecting his authority. He's too challenged in that domain to be able to bear it in those he loves. Cheer up, dear lady. I'll do what I can with my English connections. I also have influence here in France. Let us see what Cardinal Richelieu can do on your behalf. Perhaps we can get the King and Queen to put pressure on Charles through his busy little wife."

Digby beamed at Frances. "In that regard, it's providential that you are intending to convert. I'm thrilled to hear your decision. And I'm convinced the Cardinal and their Majesties will now lend you their full support. One way or another, sweet Frances, we'll find a way for you to return to England without being forced to stand barefoot in your shift in the Chapel of the Savoy or St Clement Danes."

Sir Kenelm Digby was continuing to put himself about on her behalf, with notable success among the French although with none at all from across the Channel, when Frances received another knock on the door of her modest Parisian lodgings.

She peeped around her morning parlour door, fearful yet anxious to see who was demanding admittance of her French maid. As she recognised him, apprehension converted into ecstasy. "My darling! I'd begun to lose all hope of seeing you again."

Frances ignored her servant as she leaped into Robert's arms. His grip tightened around her, but neither spoke as they both savoured the warmth of bodily contact after so long a separation. The presence of the maid as well as a need to know at once what had been happening with her lover during their many months apart trumped the physical desire that rose in Frances.

She checked his face. "Was it very dreadful for you, Robert? They kept you in the Fleet so much longer than we expected."

Sir Robert Howard loosened his grip with evident reluctance. "They wanted to ensure I could not aid your escape, my love. No, it was not dreadful, but they did fine me and order me not to come near you again. Oh, and I'm expected to make myself immediately available whenever His Majesty wishes my presence at Court."

"Oh no! How can we ever manage to see each other?"

He laughed. "Don't worry. It is all arranged. The King cannot object to me staying with my own brother. It's to our advantage that Theophilus took over the Wardenship of the Cinque Ports from George. Apart from augmenting Theo's income, of which my expensive brother is ever in need, Dover is but a hop, skip and jump from Paris, my love. So a message can always be got to me by one of Theo's men, and I can be back in London with His Majesty in a twinkling of the proverbial eye."

Frances thought instantly how the challenges of Channel crossings on leaky vessels in intemperate weather might hinder such a plan, but Howard's reference to the King diverted her to speak of other things.

"I'm receiving such kindness from their Majesties and the Cardinal, Robert. Dear Kenelm Digby spoke to Cardinal Richelieu on my behalf, and he arranged a guard with a troop of horse around our lodgings, until Scudamore got the message to stop bothering me. Then Kenelm spoke with the French Queen on my behalf. You may have heard that Anne has approached her sister to intercede directly with Charles?"

Robert nodded. "I heard a rumour. But has she had any success?"

Frances pursed her lips and shook her head. "Sadly, from all I can tell, Henrietta Maria makes no progress. The King's love for me must have turned to hatred, if the wife he adores cannot soften his attitude toward me."

Howard tightened his hold on her as he responded, "Beloved, you must not take any of it personally. I promise you the King's present behaviour has little or nothing to do with you. Now let us find a place to sit, and I will bring you up to date with all that is happening in England."

He removed his travelling coat and hat and Frances led him into the morning parlour, where they sat with their arms entwined around each other.

Robert continued, "The King is totally preoccupied with his own problems and, believe me, they are getting bigger by the day. He's embarked on a path of religious reform with Laud so extreme that now the Scots are up in arms. They've never forgiven him for insisting the Anglican service be used for his coronation there. Now there's talk of imposing a new Prayer Book in Scotland to encourage the spread of Anglicanism. The Scots won't stand for that. If Charles tries it, they'll revolt. Meanwhile, there's a heated rebellion building against Strafford in Ireland."

Frances frowned. "Isn't that just Scotland and Ireland? The Scots and the Irish have so often felt resentment against the English Crown."

He shook his head vigorously. "No, it's much more than that. And religion is only part of it. We're facing an all-out struggle for who's in charge of the country. Charles took a high-risk course in ignoring Parliament for so long. For the moment, the judges continue to rule that Royal Prerogative gives him the right to commandeer ship money direct from Customs, but I don't believe they can hold the line. Opposition to His Majesty grows stronger as his demands to supply his confounded military campaigns spiral."

"Things are really bad, then?"

Robert looked grave. "I tell you, Frances, in the whole of my life I cannot remember more tension and division. The country is like a powder keg. If the King will not moderate his behaviour and demands, we'll end with a conflagration. I hate to say it, but you and the boy may be safer here."

She pulled back a little and studied his face. "I'm sorry to hear all this. I was so hoping we might soon return. I know my personal situation must matter little in the wider order. Still, I can't believe it would cost Charles anything to show a little kindness toward one who has loved him so loyally all her life."

Howard shrugged. "He still listens to Laud, my dear. And the whisper is already abroad that you converted. That gives the Archbishop fresh ammunition to use against you. You are even seen to be compounding your sin by leading others into the ways of your Catholic wickedness."

"That's untrue." Frances wrenched herself out of his arms. "My relationship with my God is *my* affair. I would never seek to force it on anyone else. Not even you."

Howard chuckled. "Seek it or not, I might not be converting myself without your influence."

Delight fought with consternation in Frances's eyes. "I didn't know."

"I'm telling you now."

"I'm astonished. I would never have dreamed of trying to encourage you to convert, Robert. You aren't truly affected by me, are you?"

Robert Howard laughed outright. "You make a poor religious zealot. Are you not pleased that I have decided to embrace the True Faith?"

"Yes, but our relationship with Our Lord is such a personal thing. We must search for our own answers. If we borrow from others we can't call it a True Faith."

"I agree. But, by choosing to return to the old religion, we also acknowledge God's representatives here on earth, that we may be guided by their word. A human embodiment of His Presence on Earth is an essential piece of our doctrine. And our faith *is* meant to act as a beacon for others. I freely admit that you *do* influence me in my decision, although so also perhaps in a curious way has Charles, by following Laud's punitive lead, as well as by setting himself above God in the way he rules. However, my conversion also comes from my heart, so you need not fear."

A frown creased Frances's face and deepened. "I fear something more painful. Our conversion faces us with a moral dilemma. How can we honour our religious vows and live together again outside the sanctity of marriage?"

Sir Robert Howard's features registered a range of emotions as he stared over her head, but serenity filled his grey eyes by the time they lowered to meet her distressed blue gaze.

"The God I worship is a God of love. He smiles on all unions founded in love. Your vows to Purbeck were given in an Anglican service and the marriage was never fully consummated. John and you are both Catholics, so the ceremony that joined you has no standing in our Church. We are still bound by the law of our land, which will prevent our legal union in England unless Purbeck divorces you. God understands that we would be married if we could. And I believe that is enough for him."

Frances looked at him. "Robert, do you truly believe this?"

"Have you ever known me lie to you?"

A gurgle escaped her. "I have known you be extremely sparing with the truth on occasion. Especially when trying to pull me out of the dismals."

"But not over questions of conscience and my relationship with our Maker." Robert spoke quietly.

She reached out a hand and touched his face. "Sometimes, my love, you quite take my breath away."

He blushed. "Why do you say that?"

"Because you see to the heart of things. I've been agonising over our situation. Rehearsing all kinds of arguments. I even discussed taking the veil with the Mother Superior, in the convent that gave me shelter when I arrived, and again when I was hiding from Lord Scudamore and his wretched writ."

Robert looked thunderstruck. "Taking the veil? You're not serious?"

"I was, for a while. Then I saw it was impossible. But I felt shame that I could not relinquish my dream of making a home again with you and Robin. I scolded myself for my weakness of the flesh. Now my fears are dispelled."

Her eyes became moist. Robert's mouth sought and found hers. Their kiss was long and passionate, yet it also transcended physical desire.

They drew apart. Frances spoke softly. "Forgive me for having doubted things could come right for us, Robert. But now we must call our boy. Robin has grown so fast you will not recognise him. He has missed you beyond words."

"The boy has indeed grown. He and I have already established that he is catching me up in height, if fortunately not in girth. And he's awaiting the signal that his mother and father are ready for him to join us."

Frances exclaimed, "You've seen Robin already! Why did you not tell me sooner?"

"He was outside when I arrived, playing in the courtyard, with a couple of young ragamuffins who don't appear to have a word of English between them. He, on the other hand, seems to be doing a creditable job of mastering French. Especially the language of the streets, if I mistake me not."

"Why didn't he come in with you?"

"I wanted a few moments alone with you first. Robin anticipated it, without me even asking him. But he also begged us not to be too long."

Frances burst into tears. As Howard folded her back in his arms, physical desire sprang between them again. They looked at each other and smiled ruefully. After months apart, in the interests of an eager eleven-year-old, they must wait a little longer to satiate their hunger.

CHAPTER FORTY-THREE

England

"No, Johnny. It won't work to open up with either Toe-bee Men or Road Agents. And Nights of the Road on the bill as well is pushing it too far."

"Why?"

Bob Howard looked at Antony Makepeace across the table of the Mayfair restaurant in which we were dining.

"There's no upside. Nights of the Road doesn't fit. A different era. Not well enough known in the USA. And a bigger line-up doesn't make sense. It spreads the marketing focus thin and adds to overheads. You risk keeping away more people than you attract. The gig will be expensive and long. Apart from anything else, it's too much to ask of you physically."

Makepeace wore a mulish expression. "Nonsense. I'm in better condition than I've been for years. Ask the guys. The highwayman theme links all the bands together. And so do I. You want to keep Nights of the Road off the bill for your own reasons. Admit it, Bob. You never could stand that I was more successful than you. It would hurt your pride to see the band perform without you."

I held my breath. The atmosphere at our table had begun to sour, from the moment Antony Makepeace tried to force the pace, by insisting on talking about the possibility of a tour in front of me.

Bob became cool. "Think what you like, Johnny. I know what I'm willing to offer. I know my market and I trust my own judgement."

He resumed his positive tone. "My recommendation is that we run with Moonlight Jax. I think Jax can sell enough tickets in its own right, if we position and promote the tour correctly. We can open with an up-and-coming American group that complements Jax and pulls in the young crowd. Maybe a female band."

Bob pushed his chair back, and continued, "I'll put something in an email for you later this evening. Then it's for you and the guys to decide if you want to run with my proposal. You can talk it over with the others and let me know if you agree the concept by Monday. If you do, I'll put some opening band suggestions together and send you a list of names with websites and YouTube links, so we can make a choice. Sarah, are you having a dessert?"

With his question to me, Bob was making it clear that for him the tour discussion was now closed. Makepeace turned to me. "Do you have any influence with this jerk? Can you make him see sense? The highwayman theme is perfect. Nights of the Road would be an essential part of that. *The* essential part. It's the foundation on which my whole career was built."

I shook my head. "I can't teach Bob his trade. I know nothing about the music business and I've lived in the States less than two years. What he said earlier to you about the highwayman theme not going over well makes sense: 9/11; wars in so many parts of the world; all this has created a particular climate. Bob must be a better judge of all that for the USA than you and me."

Makepeace persisted. "But the highwayman theme is strong visually and in every other way. It's got nothing to do with war. It's romantic, for God's sake. Everybody gets off on the bad boys working for a common good stuff. It brings out the Robin Hood in us all."

I shrugged. "Robin Hood is an English myth. For all I know, stealing from the rich to pay the poor is a nightmare for many people, in the number one capitalist nation on earth."

"You're just being stupid." Antony's irritation lashed me.

I responded in kind. "Maybe. But perhaps it's not so smart to glamorise highway robbery by labelling it romantic. It obscures the sordid reality of a world ruled by force. I don't find the image of people stealing what belongs to others romantic, whether to survive, help people or for personal greed."

My words must have hit a nerve. Makepeace grew suddenly red in the face. "You disappoint me, Frances. I thought you'd understand."

I started at his reversion to my middle name. It took me straight back to the California cabin, where Makepeace had last used it to me. I spoke softly. "My name is Sarah. I live in the twenty-first century. A century that has already known enough violence of every kind."

Makepeace sat and scowled. I changed tone. "Antony, you asked if I had any influence. If I have, I'd like to influence *you* to trust Bob about this tour. I love your new music that he played for me. Why not concentrate on playing music that you are so brilliant at creating and leave packaging and promoting the tour to him?"

"As if I have any choice." He had become the victim again.

I stood up. "I need to leave. My Australian friend, Jane, flew into London today from Sydney. I've promised to meet her for a drink in half an hour."

I leaned down and kissed Makepeace on his cheek.

"It's good to see you. I'm thrilled that things are going well with your music and the band. And I hope we can get down to Dorset before flying back. I'd love to see Corfe Castle again."

As I entered and shut the door of our hotel room later that evening, Bob spoke out of the shadows. "So what did you think of Johnny tonight?"

I turned on a light and walked over to him. "I didn't know what to make of him. He looked well. He drank Perrier and seemed relaxed in doing so. He was fun to be with, until he pushed you to talk about a tour. Once he started arguing with you about which bands to include and even called me Frances, all that threw me." I dropped my purse on the floor and sat beside him.

Bob nodded. "I thought you left abruptly. Things were calmer after you'd gone. We stayed off sensitive issues and just talked about the music and getting the right record deal. I think he's cleared his drinking problem, at least for now. But my guess is that Johnny Clavylle remains a loose cannon."

"So what are you planning to do?"

Bob sighed and chewed his lip. "I dunno. He's a great musician and his stage charisma has always been incredible. But something is still gnawing away at Johnny from the inside and rehab didn't clear it. Maybe nothing can."

"Will you go ahead with the tour?"

"I'm willing to risk it, if we can agree on the right line-up. America will still love Johnny, as long as he doesn't shoot his mouth off about sensitive political issues on the talk shows. Those new songs of his are quite remarkable and the business can do with an injection of originality and quality just now. A tour in support of a solid record deal could work well for everybody."

"Has the band already got a record deal lined up?"

"Nothing definite, but there are plenty of nibbles. All the guys know they'll get a better deal if they can use my name and the prospect of a US tour. I've just emailed Johnny and the band members my proposal. The next steps are with him to talk things over with the others, let me know their response by Monday, and then follow up with the record companies. I'd be surprised if they turn me down. So how about we concentrate on us now, sweetie? Do you still want to go down to that old castle before we leave?"

"I need to find out which day I can visit my parents, and I've agreed to meet John at the solicitor's office to sign the divorce papers together tomorrow. That should only take an hour. But yes, I'd love to see Corfe Castle again, especially with you. Will Antony join us while we are there?"

"How about we hang loose and get his response on my proposal before we decide? I'll call that hotel where Johnny and I ate dinner, to book us a room for Thursday night. In the meantime, let's enjoy London. It's so rare to have the luxury of free time together like this. That reminds me, how was Jane? Do you expect to see more of her while she's here?"

"She looks wonderful and sounds happy. She's leaving again in a couple of days, but she wants us both to have lunch with her and meet her new man tomorrow if we're free. I said I'd check with you first."

"Let's do it. I like Jane. She has her feet on the ground."

"That's funny, since she works in the air! Actually, all the flight attendants I know are down to earth."

"And all the ones I know are extremely sexy."

"Bob Howard, are you trying to make me jealous?"

"No. Just trying to get your mind working in a particular direction."

"Well, you don't need to be so indirect, if what you're trying to do is score with me tonight."

"OK, woman, would you take your clothes off now please?"

"I thought you'd never ask."

CHAPTER FORTY-FOUR

France & England 1640

"Charles is offering a full pardon, Frances. You must consider taking it."

Frances's face was pale and drawn. She said nothing, but doubt was written in her eyes.

Sir Kenelm Digby elaborated. "The King will waive the fine and the penance, if you return to Purbeck. The Viscount will declare Robin officially as his son and heir."

"I can't go through all that again!"

"Frances, if you do, the King will wipe the slate clean. Don't you owe it to Robin? Howard can never recognise the boy in England. You cannot keep him in France indefinitely, since he has no estate to inherit here. Letting Robin take your husband's name will make him Viscount Purbeck someday. Don't you think he may thank you for that?"

She shook her head. "Kenelm, Robin has been so happy to live under his father's name here in France. He may not wish to give that up. And I mistrust what is being offered. Why does Charles do this now?"

"In part because so many of us have petitioned so hard on your behalf, dear friend. But also, I would guess, because the Long Parliament has the upper hand. Laud is in the Tower and Strafford with him. The King has lost key advisers, and is under pressure such as he has never known. Charles needs to be seen to compromise over many things. Your public pardon serves as one tiny offering."

"So it's because he no longer has Laud to lean on, rather than out of personal concern for me?"

"Who knows? You must be delighted that Robert turned the tables on Laud. The Archbishop is already fined for Robert's unlawful imprisonment in the Fleet and there'll be more charges before Parliament has done with him. Many are baying for his blood."

"Robert sued Laud in order to clear our names, not for money or vengeance. He's also demanding reparations for the sorcery charges brought against me by Buckingham. Since Laud *is* in the Tower, I don't feel I should have to bargain with Charles."

"I doubt you will get any reparation for those sorcery charges, since they were dropped before going to court. Accepting the King's olive branch offers the best prospect for Robin and it means you can both return home. You won't have to stop seeing Robert, as long as you do so quietly. Laud won't dare come against you again, even if he is released."

"Now you're recommending me to indulge in hole-in-the-corner behaviour you have previously labelled hypocritical. How can you, Kenelm?"

"My sweet friend, let me try and say this in a different way. The Puritans are gaining power every day in the land. You will stand utterly condemned by them for loose living. To the Puritans, Charles already shows weakness in offering you clemency. You could consider him your protector against them."

"So the Puritans are my real enemy?"

"They always have been. But it's not just the Puritans. You know England as well as I. For many in His Majesty's Court you committed a sin far worse than adultery. You not only gave birth to a love child in an extra-marital relationship, but you also show no penitence for having done so. The Polite World in England doesn't like its secrets exposed so blatantly. You haven't played by Society's rules. And you're a woman. Didn't your mother warn you of that long ago? She has only got away with so much herself through having been left a fabulously wealthy young widow."

"I long ago stopped listening to Mama, given her comportment with certain men outside her own marriage. If I understand you, I am to be condemned for being honest, poor and faithful. Oh yes, and a woman."

Digby laughed and the sound was bitter. "Yes, and a woman. Look at how the world condemned my beloved Venetia and called her a courtesan, even after our marriage. Face it, my dear. There will always be a double standard between how men and women are judged. Robert can continue to claim immunity and move freely in Society, but you have no protection, unless you can reclaim your privilege as Purbeck's wife, which was denied you at the time of your appeal. Now do you see how Charles protects you?"

"I shouldn't need that sort of protection. I don't like pandering to hypocrisy and I made that clear enough long ago at my trial when I called out my persecutors as cuckolds. You said that these double standards make our nation a laughing stock."

Kenelm's own laugh was mirthless. "You don't make friends by calling men cuckolds, particularly when it is true. And I don't hear many people laughing about England at present, since a civil war would destabilise the whole of Europe. Listen to me, sweet friend. You're virtuous and faithful to Robert. I of all people have reason to know that you are not for tempting. But you have had the double misfortune to be born a woman and into a nest of vipers."

Frances continued to shake her head. Digby took her hands. "The Suffolks and your parents shared a talent for making enemies with long memories. Your personal beauty and charm have not helped. They turned many a woman and spurned would-be lover at Court against you."

"I haven't been near the English Court in years, Kenelm."

"But you are not forgotten. There isn't a woman at that Court today who can equal your record. How many can boast desirable and constant lovers, willing continually to risk and suffer imprisonment for them? How many can say that their husbands have never allowed a word spoken against them? How many can say that countless men in England and France would fight to be first in the liaison line, if they would only give us the least encouragement?" Digby shook his head. "Dear friend, you might be shocked how many would turn out to spit on you from jealousy, if Charles ever obliged you to make that barefoot walk in your white shift."

"Believe me, Kenelm, I learned that from a Great Hall packed with jealous souls at my wedding, when I was only fourteen. That memory has me ready to remain exiled here in poverty, rather than endure public humiliation again. I can scrape by in Paris a little longer. Cousin Henry was able to raise additional funds through the action to get my jewellery and clothes repossessed from Isabel Peel. But why does the King no longer show me the trust we knew as children? And why are you recommending I give in now to hypocrisy that you have always spoken out against."

"You would have to ask His Majesty his reasons yourself. As for me, it's probably because I've become more pessimistic about the big picture. Your case must be seen within a wider purview. In the present climate you will never get the justice you seek and your individual case is tiny, by comparison with all that is presently at stake in England."

"My individual case is based in issues of principle that feed many other and larger causes in England. A father should have no right to coerce his daughter into a lifetime of misery to suit his own ends. A brother-in-law should have no right to steal a woman's dowry and separate her from her husband for his own ends. A King may have the inherited right to govern our realm, but he should then take responsibility to be just to all subjects, not only the men. And he is not above God. He has no right to dictate with whom I should live or whose name my son should take. Our Lord will judge me and my relationship with my lover more kindly than the Court and my King."

Kenelm Digby looked beaten. "Very well then, Frances, leave judgment of your affairs to God, but remember that Our Lord is not known for encouraging men and women to live together outside marriage. And be clear that no man in Parliament or the Court will support you publicly, except perhaps your Robert and that husband who wants you back. There are few mad eccentrics around like me. That's why I live in France."

Digby squeezed her hands. "Think of Robert as well as Robin. You place Howard in an awkward position, if he has to continue fighting battles on your behalf when he needs to keep all his Parliamentary wits about him. Leave Parliament to wage battle with the King on his Royal Prerogative. Concentrate on your son and securing the best terms for a return to England."

Her chin came up. "That's exactly what I plan to do. My husband judges me more kindly than the rest of the world."

"In that case, write to your husband and ask him to demonstrate his kindness by divorcing you for non-consummation of the marriage. Only then will you be free to marry Robert, and only then can Howard claim Robin as his son and heir in his native land."

"That is exactly what I intend. Except I shall visit Purbeck in person."

Digby whistled. "You run a risk by returning to England before being sanctioned by your King."

"It's a risk I will take, to speak directly with Purbeck myself. Such delicate matters cannot be discussed in writing."

"Then I wish you good luck and God speed, my dear. Paris will miss you."

Several weeks and a choppy Channel crossing later, Frances stood before her husband. It was the first time she had been in England for five years.

Viscount Purbeck listened to her request and sighed. "No, I cannot give you a divorce, my pretty maid."

"Why not?"

"You ask too much of me, Frances. I talked things over with Charles, just as I promised you. It took much longer than I hoped, but His Majesty has now stipulated terms for your pardon. Surely they are not difficult for you to accept? The boy is my heir. Your mother and I have agreed that Robin will eventually inherit all her estate."

He patted her hands. "Don't worry, my dear. You may continue to see Howard with my blessing, as long as you are discreet. I cannot let His Majesty be embarrassed by you both, when he has been so gracious to us. I want the boy and you to be seen with me occasionally in public. That is all."

"John, our marriage was never truly consummated. And it was not a Catholic ceremony. We are not married in the eyes of God."

"Robin is living proof that our marriage was consummated. And our marriage was conducted according to the laws of this land."

Frances steeled herself, and then, "John, Robin is not your son."

"Who says he is not?" His gaze was bland.

She faltered. "People have always said he is not your child."

"You and I never have."

"John dear, you do know as well as I that our marriage was never–" Frances stopped, at the stricken look that flashed through Purbeck's eyes.

It cleared instantly, as he said, "I know many people said I am impotent. Including some who were dear to me. You and I knew differently. And the boy proved the gossips wrong."

Frances stared in frustration at the Viscount.

He smiled sadly. "My dear, it can really be quite comfortable for all concerned. You shall stay married to me and can still see Howard when you wish. Robin lives officially with me, yet may also visit his mother's friends as frequently as he desires. Everybody wins."

"But–"

"Frances, I have never insisted on anything with you in the whole of our married life, but understand that I will not move on this."

Hours later Frances was in Suffolk House describing the outcome of her meeting with her husband. "I suppose it must be his pride at issue, concerning Robin's paternity and our marriage."

Sir Robert Howard showed no surprise. "It's not only his pride, although how he is seen in the world must matter to him. Remember also that the terms of his mother and brother's estate left Purbeck with very little. The King took responsibility for him after Buckingham died, but Charles is desperately strapped for cash. The Hatton fortune still speaks as loud as ever it did in your affairs."

"The Hatton fortune? Must it always come back to that? Well, Mama writes me that her financial affairs are in a total mess. I'm not sure what's left in the way of her fortune, except Stoke, Hatton House and a few manors. For all I know she has mortgaged all of those too. She sold off the armaments at Corfe and then the castle itself to Sir John Bankes. She's scrabbling around now to pay off huge debts. All these years on, she still spits venom for her lost income from Hatton House, when the Duchess of Richmond threw the lease back at her."

"You know she shot herself in the foot over that, by telling any who would listen that she had been cheated."

Frances nodded. "I know. Mama shoots herself in the foot often, yet she usually comes about. Still, she swears now that the upkeep of her properties is milking her dry. I suspect she is missing the sage advice of Holles, as well as his companionship and constancy, since his passing."

Sir Robert Howard looked sceptical. "I notice Eliza still lives as extravagantly as ever. I've never heard her satisfied with a property deal. She complained about the price she got for Corfe, yet John Bankes is the last man in the world to do her down. She was forever screaming how your father cheated her. I held no brief for Sir Edward, given his prosecution of my own kin and his treatment of you, but Coke did try to bring Eliza's affairs into order and manage them wisely on her behalf. If your mother's affairs are in a mess now, she has herself to blame."

Frances frowned. "Papa also grabbed many of her properties and bestowed them on his own children without her consent. It was deeply offensive to Mama how he overrode her wishes in his control of her estate. But perhaps I would have done the same in his place. He may have had more to bear with from her than I understood. I so wish they had been reconciled before he died." She fell into sombre reflection, then emerged with a start. "All this is a red herring in terms of Purbeck. Why would Mama's fortune still speak loud with him?"

Robert looked pained. "Wake up, Frances. If Purbeck divorces you, he will be bypassed from all living claim on your Mama's estate."

She gasped. "So even Purbeck's love for me has only ever been about my inheritance?"

Robert Howard shrugged. "Purbeck has demonstrated his love for you many times. Remember how he nursed you with the pox? But the Hatton holdings are colouring his response to you now, I'll be bound."

Frances blanched. "If that is true, I feel more uncomfortable than ever about this proposed pardon. And how will our son react?"

Howard shrugged again. "Our son's interests could be well served, if Purbeck keeps his word that you and the boy are free to come to me. Robin will have an assured place in English society and he'll be your mother's heir. I will make over my own properties for Robin's lifetime use, via long-term peppercorn leases. He'll face neither the stigma of bastardy nor the weight of living as a poor man. And he'll have us, Frances. He knows we've never wavered in our love for each other and him."

"How much do you think worldly matters will weigh with Robin?"

"I predict that what will weigh most with Robin is his mother's well-being. He's a loyal son to you, my love, and he adores you. You have been the only constant in his sixteen years of turbulent and itinerant life. If you accept, Robin will accept."

"What do *you* think I should say to Purbeck?"

"Frances, it is not for me to tell you what to do. All I can say is that, if you accept Purbeck's terms and the King's pardon, I will do everything in my power to care for you during such life as we can share. We'll have to let our dreams of marriage go, until and unless Purbeck dies, and neither of us can wish that upon the poor fellow. It changes nothing between you and me."

"So you say I should agree?"

"I say you must, as always, do whatever is in your heart, Frances."

Frances looked at Sir Robert Howard for a long moment. Then, "What is in my heart today has been in it since I was fourteen years old. You are a blessing in my life. I love you and I am yours. And if it is truly best for Robin, I will agree to the King's terms."

CHAPTER FORTY-FIVE

England

"Everyone agrees it's a strong proposal."

Makepeace's voice sounded flat. We were lunching with him on a sunny Thursday in the tiny village of Corfe Castle. Thanks to its conservation area status, the historic core of the village had changed little since I was a child and we were visiting on a quiet weekday out of season. The castle ruins were visible from our table and I was awash in childhood memories.

Bob nodded. "I've had calls from the other guys. But what about you, Johnny? Are you up for it? I get the feeling that you aren't too enthusiastic. If not, you need to level with me now, before we go any further."

Antony spread his long and fine-boned fingers out toward Bob in a gesture of reluctant acceptance. "I guess we should do it. I want to play the States again. I want to get out on stage with the new songs. And the record company is falling over itself to do a deal with the one-and-only great Bob Howard. Someone – I wonder who? – had already talked with them. They had a hard copy of your proposal to the band on the desk when I met them yesterday."

Bob looked surprised. "Not me. One of the boys from the band must have forwarded it. And that someone was out of order, if they agreed to let you deal with the company on their behalf."

Makepeace shrugged. "Whatever. It's a done deal. The company said your proposal was the clincher for them. The guys are happy and hungry to work. Loads of our mates have failed to get signed for a record or a tour this year."

Bob probed. "What are your reservations, Johnny?"

Makepeace shrugged again and turned to stare at me. "Hard to say. General disillusionment, I suppose. I had a romantic dream about a woman, who I wanted to marry me. Turns out she doesn't share my dream. Then I had a romantic dream about the highwayman tour that I want to do in the USA. Turns out nobody shares that dream either. Romance is yesterday's news. Reality is the new god. What to do? Get real, I suppose. Grin and bear it."

He smiled sadly across at me. I stayed silent.

"Sticking with what is real makes more sense than kidnapping people at knife point and trying to coerce them into a dream that isn't theirs." Bob spoke dryly. My heart sank.

Antony Makepeace slowly returned his gaze to Bob. His face became a mask. "I've been wondering when that would be thrown in my face. I knew it was only a matter of time. Why are you proposing this tour, Bob? So you can take every opportunity to prove how smart and successful you are? Wanting to look better than me, in your woman's eyes?"

My body ached as it began to soak up the negativity between them. Overtly, Bob was unaffected by Johnny's retort, but I knew he had realised his own error.

He responded neutrally. "I've asked myself the same question. I guess I'm proposing it because you are a great musician and I'm a great promoter. It's a chance for us both to do what we are good at, while making a buck and giving the public good value for money."

Bob's eyes softened and he smiled at the man sitting opposite him. "For what it is worth, I'm also impressed. You went into rehab and came out a winner. You've composed a brilliant batch of new songs out of your recent experiences. I know how much willpower it takes to turn away from the demon drink and so much of the other shit that's killed so many of us. Johnny, you've not only succeeded where a lot of people failed. You've turned what could have been a disaster into a creative triumph. That's the bottom line on why I'm eager to go on the road with you again."

Makepeace looked astonished. An uncertain smile flirted with his lips.

Bob had more to say. "That said, we need to find a way to let bygones be bygones. If not, we're better going our separate ways. Maybe that's why I bring up the past now. Not to throw it in your face, in the way I just did. That was a cheap shot and I apologize. But we need to recognise and accept what happened between us, if we are to lay it to rest and move on."

Bob looked round the hotel dining room. It was early and we were the only people eating. He spoke again. "This seems as good a place as any to exorcise any ghosts. This is the table at which I was foolish enough to pass you my damned phone, so you could speak to Sarah. I've learned my lesson about that. Sarah will be pleased. She's always hated me dropping her into conversations with unknown people that she doesn't want to have."

"But this is not where your Sarah and I first met, old chap." Antony smiled.

"Where did we first meet?" My voice sounded constricted to my ears.

"Up there." Makepeace twisted round and we followed the direction of his pointing finger. Above us, the ruins of the castle lay bathed in soft sunlight.

"If we've all finished lunch, I'll show you the exact spot. How about it? Shall we all go up together and listen to what the old stones have to say? Perhaps some ghosts from the past are hanging around up there, waiting to greet us." Makepeace pushed his chair back and stood up. "Ready to go?"

Birds swooped and soared in the air above us, soon afterward, as we stood facing each other on the hill. Makepeace had led us up at a brisk trot, looking neither to left nor right, to a grassy spot between the ruins of what he named as the Buttevant Tower and the castle's Old Hall. I was still trying to catch my breath, when he grabbed my shoulder.

"Just here. Do you remember now? This was the exact spot. And this was where we always came afterwards, each time you returned to the castle. It was our ritual, to remind us about the day we met. The place was not in ruins then."

I looked around, then turned to study the vista from where we were standing. I had no recall of meeting Antony before, on this or any other part of the hill. My strongest memory was of wandering the extensive castle ruins with my father as a child. I looked at the two men and became aware of unspoken tension in Bob.

"I'm going to explore the view further up. I'll see you both in a while." As if he did not want his anxiety to be seen, or perhaps to give Makepeace and me space to talk alone, Bob wandered on up the steep hill. Antony stayed facing me, with an expectant look on his face.

It had been easy for me to discern what was bothering Bob. Against his own reason, he must be afraid that some alchemy of place would combine with the personality of his former band member to undermine our own relationship and drive a wedge between us. And now, as I looked at Antony, I became aware of an unvoiced question emanating from him: *which of us will you choose today?*

I turned my head to watch Bob's broad back and strong legs make easy work of his climb. I wanted to call out and reassure him; to say, Hey wait for me, I'm with you. Yet in this moment, in my heart, I could not detect an answer to the question the two men were posing. Instead, I felt dislocated and disorientated, as if the pieces of my life had been thrown in the air by an unseen hand. I could not yet see what pattern they would form when they fell again to earth.

"Do you remember now, Frances?" As he used my middle name and Antony Makepeace's eyes bored into me, I felt an urgent need to distance myself from him, physically and psychologically.

"My name is Sarah," I muttered and dropped to the ground, where I sat and began to pull at the short tufted grass.

"But I was John and you were Frances then. You know it now, don't you? That's why you're getting upset. There's really no need. It can all be so simple, if you will just open up and be honest with yourself and me. It's not too late. We can still turn the clock back."

I became distracted, as I noticed that the hem of my long skirt had unravelled. I must have snagged it during our climb. Now I felt irritated at myself, for not having changed, before leaving the hotel, into something more suitable for clambering around the castle ruins. I pulled and pushed at the snagged thread to try and work it back into the fabric without creating a hole.

As I did, I heard a girl's voice echo down the slope: "Oh no! This must have happened when you were pulling me up the hill. Now Nurse will be cross and she'll complain again that I behave like a hoyden when I'm in the country." My head jerked up as I sought the direction of the child's voice.

"What are you looking for? What are you thinking about?" Antony squatted beside me. He pulled a blade of grass and sucked it between his teeth. His closeness and the intensity of his presence confused me.

"Please let me have some space. I'd like to be on my own, Antony. This is a special place for me, because it has memories of my own childhood. I came here often with my father. Why don't you go up and chat with Bob? Show him the layout of the castle as it used to be."

"I didn't come up here to be with Bob, but to be with you."

"Antony, please go away. Go anywhere. Do anything. Just leave me alone for a while." I must have raised my voice, for Bob swung round to look down at me. Even at the distance between us, I could read a new question in his eyes: *do you need help?*

I shook my head, smiled and waved to reassure him. Then I leaned over and gave Makepeace a slight push. He almost overbalanced. "Go on," I said.

"For God's sake, woman. You've made your point. I'm going." He stood up and moved away but, instead of heading after Bob, he took a sideways direction around the hill and disappeared from view at a half jog.

I was alone. For the first time since leaving the hotel, I felt able to breathe and think my own thoughts again, free of disturbance from either Bob or Antony. I lay back on the grassy slope and stretched out, luxuriating in my solitude. The sky was a soft blue and the day was warm.

I began to drowse as my eyes traced the passage of the birds. They appeared to be playing whistling games of catch and tag. I mused on the enduring fascination of birds, as a symbol of freedom and in terms of their instinctive wisdom and relationship to the elements. They seemed to have an unerring ability to gauge the seasons, to judge their flights over long and short distances, and to know where in the world they should make their home and when. If only we humans could tune in so easily to our ancient homing instincts, I said to myself.

I thought then of Frances Coke who became Frances Purbeck.

Did you ever lie daydreaming here like me, on the hillside of your mother's castle as a child, Frances, or was your life so circumscribed by nurses and guards that you were never free to wander out alone?

I was forever escaping my nurse as a small child. The guards here were my friends but I spent much of my later life escaping from other people who wanted to curtail my freedom.

Clear and strong as a single matins bell came her answer to my question. Surprised and fascinated, I tried another.

Why have you entered and become so much a part of my life at this time, Frances?

To help you stand on my shoulders, see further and go further for us all than I was able to, during my own earthly existence.

It was as if she was lying at my side, staring up into the sky with me, chatting with me like girlhood friends. I tried again.

Why me?

You are the blood of my blood, dear one. And we know the same need to free ourselves from fear and follow the messages of our hearts, however uncomfortable that may be.

Did you find that freedom here on earth before your end, Frances, or were you always pursued and denied the liberty to live your life as you wanted?

"Sarah, who are you talking to?"

"Frances, who are you talking to?"

Absorbed as I was in dialogue with a being that had lived four hundred years before me, I had seen neither Bob nor Antony approach, until both were standing almost on top of me again. They had arrived from different directions, but came upon me in the same moment. And spoke the same question to me in unison, except that each used a different name to address me.

I listened for Frances but, even as I did so, I knew the magic of our moment together had been broken. I sat up hastily. Then stood. I felt interrupted and embarrassed, as if I had been caught with my hand in the cookie jar. I found it difficult to focus immediately on Bob or Antony. Once I did, I observed them from a place of detachment, as if they were strangers.

I looked at each in turn. Both were very tall but any resemblance ended there. The one was fair, fine-featured, and almost ethereally slight of frame; the other was chestnut-haired and brawny, with shoulders that might have been made for an American football field.

I still had not responded when one of them moved toward me, and my hand shot out in an automatic warning gesture. I stared without smiling at Antony Makepeace. He stopped but his body crackled with an electric charge. He grinned at me. I could feel and almost taste the eroticism of his aura. I wondered idly how many women had been sucked within its vibrant spell.

In a split-second, his mood shifted. The birds that had earlier captured my attention must have caught his, for his head went back and he stared up into the sky. Now I saw again the same bright blue-eyed gaze, with its innocence and sweetness of expression, that I had witnessed before at Joshua Tree.

Even as I watched, his features changed again. His head came down, his eyes focused back on me and they held a lost, forlorn look. I felt the same desire that I had known before in Dream Canyon, to wrap my arms around him, to shield and help the child within him to heal.

Was Antony Makepeace messing with my mind, or did these mood switches of his occur autonomously? I had no way of knowing, but I knew I needed to free myself in this moment from his energy field. I broke our eye contact deliberately, by staring down at the ground. A small piece of green Purbeck marble that I had not noticed before lay winking up at me in the flattened grass, where I had been lying. I bent over to pick it up and, as I turned it in my hand, it occurred to me that the lovely and irregular stone had as many bright facets and raw edges as Antony Makepeace had moods. In the space of a minute, he had offered me a few of the more appealing ones.

But, since my time in the Californian desert, I had seen darker features also etched into the walls of Antony Makepeace's soul. When pressed and stressed, I had known him attack, if only to defend. A malignant worm still lay buried within his psyche: furtive, guilty or ashamed to show itself to the world. It had the power to trigger fear between us. I could not tell if the fear originated in me or in the man. All I knew was that it had reared its head between us too often for me to trust him, or me when with him.

Bob cleared his throat. "So what are we doing now?"

His words released me from my reflections. I turned my gaze from the stone and looked up into Bob's large and open featured face.

Behind his apparently imperturbable gaze, I read unspoken thoughts and feelings. In this man, much lay beyond my reach. His extraverted and apparently uncomplicated exterior cloaked a more complex being. Bob Howard owned secret recesses to which I was not yet privy. Perhaps I never would be. I sensed an artist's impressionability in Bob and, from time to time, I also glimpsed the remnants of slights from his youth and traces of a lost innocence. Yet, whatever his early disappointments in this life or any other had been, they had not left him fragile, flawed and unpredictable.

In Bob, sensitivity and an appreciation of beauty seemed to mix more or less harmoniously with pragmatism and equanimity. As I looked at him, I understood that beyond his earthy physical appeal, I also valued his capacity to deal with the world as it is, while still retaining hopes and dreams of what it might become.

By now I had seen enough of Bob to know that he was not to be taken advantage of, that he was capable of feeling anxious, hurt and even being hurtful in the moment. I did not doubt that he could play hardball when challenged. But, under threat, he did not typically lash out. Instead he withdrew inside his inner sanctum, until he had found the necessary control to act with intention. By that time, generosity and open-heartedness had been given a chance to breathe again. In Bob Howard's company, I trusted myself. I felt safe as well as loved and desired. And I could not remember when, before knowing Bob, I had felt safe, truly safe and desired, by any man.

Here on this English hillside amidst the ruins of Corfe Castle, Antony Makepeace's unfinished business with his internal demons stood revealed in striking contrast to Bob's balanced being. Self-persecution would make Antony an unpredictable companion until and unless he could work his issues through.

I had lived long enough alongside such demons in this island of England, during my marriage. They had attacked my physical and psychological well-being, from within as well as without. My physical move to West Coast America had put me beyond their reach, until the day I allowed Antony Makepeace to pierce my defences and enter my life.

It came to me in that moment that I still needed to learn some new form of self-protection. I felt the air rustle as if in agreement.

"Well? Are you coming or not?" Makepeace sounded sulky.

"Where?"

"I just said. Back up to the place where we used to look over to Kimmeridge."

I shook my head. "I've seen all I need to see today, thanks, Antony. Here. This is for you." I handed him the piece of Purbeck marble, then walked across and put my hand in Bob's. He gave me a sideways smile but said nothing.

Antony scowled down at the stone then looked at me. "Come on. You know the view is great from higher up. Come on, Bob. Let's go."

Now Bob spoke. "It's up to Sarah. I'm easy. I've already been higher up and seen the view. And I've already stayed at Kimmeridge. You two decide. This is your territory, not mine."

"You're right, Howard. This *is* our territory. You don't belong here. You never did. You've no place trying to come between Frances and me."

My heart sank again, but I felt Bob squeeze my hand as he turned his slow and lazy smile upon the other man. "You may not feel I belong, but I am here now. And, in case you hadn't noticed, this woman likes to be called Sarah. And she's with me."

He let go of my hand and walked across to Makepeace. He stopped inches away from him and looked Antony in the eye. His tone remained light, but there was also challenge in his words. "Speaking personally, Johnny, I've had enough of going round in circles, and this old castle feels like a good place to stop the world. It's decision time, dude. Shall we bury the past and let any old ghosts associated with past lives and this place rest in peace? Can you and I take to the road again and let the world hear some great new music? Or shall we drop the whole idea of a tour and go our separate ways? It's time to stand and deliver your answer, my friend."

CHAPTER FORTY-SIX

England 1642

"My Lady, there is a gentleman to see you. He will not give his name, but he says he is known to you and that you will wish to give him audience."

Frances frowned at her servant. "Why the mystery, I wonder? Does he look to you the sort of gentleman to whom I would wish to give audience?"

The footman smiled at his mistress. "My Lady, it is not for me to judge, but he does not look a dangerous type."

"Bid him enter then, but stay close by, in case I have urgent need of you."

Frances laid her sewing aside as the servant ushered in a tall and slender figure clad in expensive clothes.

She gasped. "John! John Clavell, where have you sprung from? Oh my goodness, I have not heard news of you in years. Come here, dear John, and let me see you clearly."

The footman withdrew as Frances rose and took the man's hand. She turned him toward the light, and observed his lined and pallid countenance. "Why, you are looking… prosperous. What a wonderful surprise, to see you after all this time."

John Clavell kissed her hand and bowed low.

Straightening again, he gazed into her face. "My health is indifferent, but my spirit is strong. What of you, Frances, are *you* well? I must say you look to be in fairly fine fettle. You may not have heard of me, but I have kept track of your movements. What a busy life you have led. When I heard you had returned from Paris and received the King's pardon, I decided that I must make a special effort to see you."

Frances chose not to remark that she had been back in England for nearly two years. Instead, she said, "Where is your home now, John? I have been imagining you back in Dorset, living out your life at Glanville's Wootton or at Kimmeridge perhaps, progressing your uncle's projects for opening up the Isle of Purbeck. Did he ever get that harbour enlarged to his satisfaction?"

Clavell laughed but it was not a happy sound. "I am not particularly welcome in Dorset. My father died. My mother, who never showed interest in me, has remarried several times. My uncle did not appreciate my student escapades, and liked me even less once I turned highwayman."

John Clavell sat without invitation and stretched out his long legs. He continued, "Can you believe that the old fool still throws my past in my face, even all these years after my pardon, although I have expended much energy on his behalf, in progressing his legal affairs in Ireland?"

"That must feel hurtful to you, John."

He shrugged. "I long since gave up caring a fig for him and his opinion of me, and so I made my own way instead. A successful one at that."

Frances raised her eyebrows. The boaster was back.

John Clavell coloured. "I assure you, I have done well. I made a fine reputation for myself across the water in Ireland as a lawyer and latterly as a doctor."

"You live in Ireland. That must be why I heard nothing of you after your release. Is life dangerous there now, with all the recent unrest?"

Clavell responded elliptically. "I stayed well clear of political and religious disputes while in Ireland. And I still try to do so, now I am re-established in London. Before you ask, I no longer hold people up on the King's Highway. I wrote a full recantation of my former ways while still in prison. It has been published several times since I produced it, at the time of my confinement. You own a copy?"

"No, John. But I did indeed hear that you had written something while in prison."

"Oh? I confess myself a little surprised that you should not have a copy of your own. I will see if I can locate one for you. It may be difficult to obtain because it is so popular that it sells out very quickly at each reprinting. Yes, my Recantations were published with the full approval of His Majesty and at the encouragement of his lovely Queen. Perhaps you missed that, through being so out of favour with monarchy yourself at the time? You've kept up with my play and other literary works since, though, I expect?"

Frances shook her head and Clavell looked put out. "That *is* disappointing."

She chose diplomacy. "You know I have never been much of a reader. And I go very little to see plays these days. But it does not surprise me that you should enjoy success as an author, John dear. Your letters, when we were children, always were a joy to receive."

John Clavell puffed out his chest. "Yes, you see before you a man of many talents and much success."

"I am glad. I have so often wondered how you were. I did write to you once myself. My... a friend procured your address for me at the time you were still engaged in holding people up, and I sent a letter to you. Did you receive it?"

John Clavell looked momentarily disconcerted. "I don't remember receiving any letter from you at that time." He waved his hands in a gesture of dismissal as he said, "But it's all so long ago that memory escapes me. I prosper now, as you have remarked. I have another wife too. Younger than my first wife or you, my dear. An adorable girl. And very pretty." He said the last with special emphasis, looking at Frances from beneath his long blond lashes.

If John Clavell had been hoping for jealousy, he must have been disappointed by her reaction, for Frances clapped her hands in unfeigned delight. "Oh, John. It pleases me so much to hear that you have found happiness of the heart, as well as worldly recognition. I have wished both for you, these many years, while I was overseas–" She broke off, as the footman announced another arrival.

"Why, Robert, my dear, I did not expect a visit from you now. This day is proving full of surprises. I have a guest here who will interest you, though. Someone of whom we have spoken together many times."

Howard had stopped short at sight of the man sprawled in the chair.

He bowed. "John Clavell. Your servant sir."

Clavell stood and returned the bow in exaggerated form. "Your servant, Sir Robert."

"You two have met each other?" Frances's surprise showed in her voice.

John Clavell turned back to her: "Your... your... hmm, now exactly *what* should I call Sir Robert in relation to you these days, Frances?" He paused long enough to make his point but not to await an answer. "No matter. Sir Robert here was indeed good enough to come and see me in person, when I was so unreasonably detained long after my pardon. You did not know? Secrets between lovers, eh?"

Frances ignored the sly undertone. "You're right. I knew nothing of any meeting, although I knew all about Robert working to try and secure your release. I was so grateful to him. He had insisted that I must not intervene in your affairs directly myself, for fear I would be arrested again. Your sentencing came only months after I was myself charged and detained, so that was a difficult time for me. I did however write confidentially to the Queen, John. She promised to take up your case herself."

John Clavell's eyes widened. He bowed elaborately, a third time.

"Then I must thank you, as well as Sir Robert here, for having possibly aided my release. I do believe Her Majesty did indeed much influence the King. It was her gracious intervention that ultimately secured my freedom. Of that I am certain."

Frances smiled. "No need for thanks, dear friend. It is reward enough that you were freed and have since made a fulfilling life for yourself. Robert, did you know that John has become a lawyer and doctor, as well as a man of letters? He has been living in Ireland and latterly taken up residence in London. He is married too. Oh, is your wife with you here, John?"

"Isabel plagues me to take her everywhere with me, so I send her home to her doting and *very* wealthy father from time to time, in order that I may pursue my affairs and especially my writing, uninterrupted. However, things have been so unsettled in Ireland that I have considered bringing her to London permanently. It is hard for a man of peace like myself to be sure where to be safe these days."

"Isabel? That's her name? How pretty. I hope you'll bring your wife to meet me when she is next in England."

Robert Howard spoke. "Clavell, you must be aware that it isn't only Ireland that is unsettled. Depending on your allegiance, you may be removing your wife from the frying pan into the fire, if you bring her to London just now."

Frances turned quickly. "What is the latest news, Robert?"

"Things go from bad to worse, my dear. Parliament is hopelessly split. Charles will likely head north and my guess is that all who declare for the King will be obliged to quit London, just as his own family already has."

Their visitor was momentarily ignored, as Frances considered the implications of this. "What of your Parliamentary duties, Robert?"

"I can no longer hope to remain neutral within the House, if Parliament insists on pushing through its Militia Ordinance without Royal Assent."

"So what does all this signify for a peace-loving and law-abiding fellow like myself, Howard?" John Clavell spoke languidly.

Robert turned back to him. "It means a dangerous tug-of-war is taking place between King and Parliament to establish who controls the army in our land. I fear you will soon be obliged to decide your camp, if you have not done so."

"Interesting. And when you are forced to choose, upon whose side do you both come down, I wonder?" John Clavell's voice now held a mocking note.

Robert surveyed the much lighter man. His face revealed nothing of his feelings, and his voice was level as he replied. "I can never take arms against my King. Frances will, as always, make her own decision, but my guess is that she will remain loyal to His Majesty."

"What about it, Frances? Do you intend to remain faithful to a King who drove you into exile?"

Frances refused to rise to the goading. "I made a pact with myself on my wedding day, to love and be loyal to Charles forever, John. That pact holds today."

"*Very* interesting. So, with some people at least, you remember the value of loyalty?" John Clavell's delivery matched the content of his question.

Frances moved instinctively to Sir Robert's side and put a hand on his sleeve. Her signal had its effect. Howard addressed their visitor in neutral voice. "I predict that many families throughout this land will soon be split in two, Clavell, my own included. Few, if any, will be spared painful choices. Civil war is a dreadful prospect, in which the only certain winners are those who make profit out of gunpowder and the sale of arms."

"My, you do sound melodramatic. Are things really that desperate?" Clavell's drawl had not provoked Robert Howard sufficiently for him to lose his temper, but Frances felt his rising tension through her hand.

"Time will prove me right or wrong but, yes, I really believe they are. So, Clavell, on which side will *you* come down?"

"Oh, you can count me out of your little Parliamentary frays. I'm just a humble lawyer, Sir Robert. A lawyer, a physician, and a writer of renown. I leave politics to those who have a penchant for squabbles, and a stronger stomach than myself for fighting their fellow men."

The tone of self-satisfaction induced a dry response from Robert Howard. "Your stomach was strong enough for fighting when you held up your fellow men – some women too, I seem to remember – with pistols on the King's highway. To each their choice of battles and battlegrounds, sir."

Howard turned and looked down at Frances. He smiled. "Forgive me, my dear, but I must return to the House. I only came to breathe in a little fresh air and to check that all is well with you. I expect to be kept late, so you should not expect to see me again this day. Give my greetings to Robin. I'll see myself out."

Sir Robert kissed Frances on both cheeks. He bowed to John Clavell, and left. John's face flushed as the door closed. "Goddamn it, Frances. There was no need for him to take that patronising tone with me. I wonder at Purbeck allowing Sir Robert entry to your apartments. What a smug fellow your Howard is. How can you bear having him around you? But then, I suppose anything must seem better than the madman's company."

Still she kept her temper. "My Lord and Sir Robert have a perfect understanding. You were happy enough for Robert to use his patronage to help secure your release, John. He put himself out on your behalf then. If he is short-tempered now, you may be sure he has reason. He is desperately concerned for our country."

"Well, he need not take out his desperate concerns on me."

Frances looked at John and saw the sulky, wilful and irresponsible boy lurking behind Clavell's self-satisfied and sophisticated exterior. The air of defiance that had so often seemed amusing in their youth sat less attractively upon a middle-aged braggart.

For the briefest of moments she was drawn back into other memories of their childhood together and knew mild pangs of grief for their time of innocence gone forever. Her mood must have been contagious. Clavell moved to seize her hand and the gleam in his eyes had her momentarily back with him on a grassy hillside in Dorset.

"Frances, do you ever think about how things might have turned out differently for us? Do you remember our dreams? Imagine if you and I had married and were living now at Corfe Castle. We would have defended the castle against all comers."

She pulled her hand away. "Children's dreams have little place in what is likely to unfold in Dorset soon. Our beloved Corfe Castle may find itself under siege, if King and Parliament declare war. And I'm not sure that you and I will find ourselves on the same side."

"If we had married, I would decide which side we are to support and you would be loyal to me."

"Your wife follows you in all your persuasions, I collect."

"Certainly she does. We're married seven years, but the dear child is still only sixteen years old. A good girl, Isabel. Very biddable. And very pretty."

Frances stared open-mouthed at John Clavell. Then she found herself chuckling. "Yes, I'm sure she is. A biddable young wife must suit you perfectly, John. So please do extend to your very pretty Isabel my warmest wishes for her happiness. I hope your choices keep her and you safe."

She moved across to pull the bell. "Now, I'm afraid you really must excuse me if I do not offer you refreshment. I have some mundane domestic duties, which cannot be put off, since my own household may shortly be obliged to quit London."

CHAPTER FORTY-SEVEN

California

I felt furious with Jane and did not trouble to hide it. "Why did you share my story with a total stranger? You swore you would not tell another living soul."

Jane responded aggressively. "Don't get your knickers in a knot, Sarah. I didn't tell her any details, well nothing that could have identified you. I didn't mention names. We simply got talking together on the flight, when she couldn't sleep. She came back in the galley, had a drink and told me about some workshops she had just been running in Australia on past life regression. It sounded useful for you and I thought you would want to know about her."

"But you asked her if anyone ever remembered their past lives as far as back as the seventeenth century in England, didn't you?" I tried to rein myself in as I spoke, but was still feeling upset and exposed.

"Yes, like I said before. And she said yes, people often remember lives much further back than that."

"And then you asked her if people ever came across other people who had lived at the same time as them in the past, and if one person might remember it and the other not." I knew I still sounded accusatory.

Jane was defensive. "Yes, but that was as detailed as it got. I didn't name you or the highwayman. Just mentioned that someone who believed he'd lived before had come on heavy with a friend of mine, telling her she was his reincarnated love. I didn't even mention the kidnapping." She wriggled in her chair. "Strewth, Sarah, I thought you'd be pleased I got the woman's details. I didn't expect to get my head bitten off. Do you want her name and number or not?"

My anger faded and I could see Jane was feeling hurt and huffy. "Yes, thank you. I accept you meant it for the best. Sorry I reacted so negatively at first."

She passed me the paper on which the woman had written her address, email and phone number, and I glanced at it. Catrin Morgan lived in Santa Monica. Too close for comfort. I put the paper in my purse and did nothing about it.

But my mind kept circling around the thought of making contact with Jane's airborne acquaintance. Finally, on a Saturday morning when I had nothing planned for the weekend and Bob was out of town, I began to compose an email, then stopped and picked up the phone. I was rehearsing the message I would leave, when she spoke in my ear. "Hello, this is Catrin Morgan."

I stammered, "Oh, hello. Sorry, you surprised me. I always expect people to let their calls go straight to voice mail in this city."

Her throaty Welsh laugh warmed my heart and I felt myself relax, as she replied, "Isn't that the truth of it? Who am I speaking with?"

"My name is Sarah James. You met a friend of mine, a flight attendant called Jane Barry, when you flew back from Sydney last month, and you told her I could contact you. I'd like to learn about the work you do with past life regression."

She was free the next day, and I offered her Sunday brunch in Shutters, in return for an hour of her time. Catrin had walked over from her apartment and was standing outside when I arrived and handed my car keys to the valet. The hotel was cheerful and noisy, as always at weekends, but she had reserved us a quiet corner overlooking the ocean, where we could hear ourselves talk and not be overheard.

For a while, as we ate, our talk was general. We swapped life stories, impressions and experiences, as two expatriates living in L.A.. Then Catrin asked me a question: "What would you like to know about my work?"

I felt tongue-tied, but she proved an empathetic listener and I found myself sharing my story without reservation. Whenever I lost the thread, Catrin prompted me with a well-chosen word or phrase. She was clearly an expert facilitator.

"So what do you think, Catrin?"

"About what?"

I became flustered. "Does what I've told you have anything to do with past lives, or is it just a case of a couple of over-active imaginations?"

She laughed. "I'm not offering up my response-to-the-sceptics routine here, although you might like to ask yourself sometime where you think the feelings and sights and sounds of your imagination come from. I've heard what seem to me some interesting pointers in your story, but I'm not sure how helpful it would be to offer you an analysis on the basis of what I've heard."

She paused, stared at the ocean, and then continued, "If you want as a threesome to try and unravel together whatever has been going on between you, it could be important for you to work with someone who's experienced in deep memory process. It could be particularly useful for your rock singer to get some support, although I'm not certain he'll want to receive it."

"Catrin, I understand your reservations about offering an analysis. I'm a therapist myself, remember? But, to encourage either Antony or Bob to explore further, I'd need to better understand and become more detached about what is going on between the three of us. Please offer the analyst in me some crumbs from the table to chew on."

She made a face. "Are you sure about your own motives in wanting to encourage either of them to go any further?"

"I would like to clear the air between us, whether that involves them directly or not."

She hesitated, then, "Very well, for what it is worth, here are some impressions."

Catrin took a sip of water and then began. "Let's start with your boyfriend, Bob. He sounds like a man looking to get on and enjoy his work and the woman he loves. So, it would appear, did his namesake. I see them as down-to-earth and practical men, energetic and not prone to spend over long in self reflection." She looked at me and, when I nodded, continued. "Not too many personal weevils. Loyal, straightforward. Answering a challenge when needed. I didn't notice Bob digging deep for answers about past lives."

I nodded again. "You've judged him right."

She paused and I waited for her to say more. "The coincidence in names is obviously interesting, and that long-term charge in the relationship between him and the other man speaks to possible past life involvement. They may have tangled together in several past lives." Again what she said rang true for me.

Catrin ordered another coffee and we both sat in silence, looking out toward the ocean until it arrived. Then she resumed. "Your friend Antony almost certainly accessed a past life in his workshop. But he did not process the unfinished issues surrounding that lifetime. So an unresolved life, probably already affecting him unconsciously, re-awoke to create waves in this one."

"Is that a typical experience from a workshop?" I asked.

She grimaced and I understood she did not want to criticise a fellow professional. She said, "Sometimes it's enough just to access a past life and shine a light on it for any existing disturbance to dissolve. But with difficult lifetimes, especially any that were interrupted or ended badly, the process may need help to complete itself, or it continues to cycle and haunt the present life. If he came to me, I would want to work with

Antony experientially and have him focus particularly on how he died in that lifetime. Help him flesh out what remains unfinished in his history."

"I think his therapist may have tried to do something of the sort, when he was in rehab, but he told me he kept getting stuck. And he was also approaching things from the perspective of Antony today, rather than as John Clavell then."

She agreed. "Yes, there are many ways to work with the moment of past life death, but you do need to enter the lifetime itself to process it. Antony may not find resolution, unless he opens up his Pandora's box of the past again."

"Should I suggest it?"

Catrin looked equivocal. "Do you think he wants to? I'm wondering if a part of him has become addicted to the drama. It may make him feel special and fit his stage image. From experience, I've observed that artists sometimes dabble and then shy away from treading too far along the path of self-awareness. In some there's a fear of demystifying and losing the muse that fuels their creativity."

"Is it a bad thing if he shies away?"

Catrin shrugged. "It's his right to do so. I don't think it is a particularly good thing, if it means he abuses others like he did you."

"I never felt Antony would hurt me intentionally."

She was immediate and direct in response. "Stop kidding yourself, Sarah. He took you and tied you up against your will. He did hurt you and those scars I can see on your wrists should remind you, if ever you are in danger of forgetting. He played with a knife and a loaded gun. He could have killed you."

I fell silent. Her words had struck home. I looked at my plate and my half-eaten croissant. I drank the dregs of my cold coffee. Then I looked up at her and nodded. "You're right. I guess I have been hiding from admitting this to myself."

She smiled warmly. "Yes, it feels to me as if you've been using a type of child's 'magical protection' to pretend you are safe, haven't you? I won't see and admit the problem, so it won't see me. If I stay very still, it won't even know I'm here."

The truth felt uncomfortable. "I need to find a different way to arm myself in future, against Antony and any other Antonys, if I'm to be useful to them and me."

Catrin responded, "And maybe that's why Frances emerged in your life at this time. You told me earlier your immigration lawyer said you have a guardian angel. My feeling is that Frances is one of them."

"So I'm not Frances Coke or Frances Purbeck herself, come back to life?"

"Look, I would need to have a session with you for us to be definitive about the relationship, but Frances told you explicitly, when you were on that hillside in England, that she is a blood ancestor of yours and she is in your life to help you know the freedom she could not enjoy in her own lifetime. She said she wants you to go further. It sounds to me that she's encouraging you to mature and evolve."

Catrin looked at the ocean then turned back to me again. "I also get a sense that she became a symbol for her age, and occupied a position in society that she may not have been fully aware of, while still alive. She may not have seen herself as a trail blazer, yet she challenged the mores of her time quite dramatically, given the weight of powers that ranged themselves against her. Many of the underlying issues her story highlights are still current today, even if their surface shape has morphed and changed."

"But do you really think she's an *angel?*"

Catrin laughed at my incredulous expression. "There are at least three types of ancestral spirits that I've encountered in my work. One type is earth bound and very attached to earthly things. They hang around and reincarnate as soon as possible after their death. They typically lead mundane lives, and little about Frances sounds as if her life was mundane."

I agreed. "No, from all I have read, she lived a life of style and privilege, even though she also knew personal privation and abuse. There is a tale that she left a French convent in a hurry because she did not enjoy the primitive conditions. It may have been unkind gossip or she may have been attached to her creature comforts. These must have been relatively great, given her class. But I'm sure that possessions mattered less to Frances than following her heart."

Catrin moved on. "There's another type of ancestral spirit that is confused. Still caught in a complex that needs to be resolved, and not sure necessarily whether they are dead or alive. Your conversation with Frances was cut short, but it sounded anything but confused on her part. She knew she was dead and she told you immediately why she was with you."

"That's two types of ancestor you think she isn't. What's the third?"

"The third are the enlightened ones, including those from the angelic realms. They come from the past and the future, and they're here to help us evolve and grow, personally and collectively."

"You think Frances is an enlightened being?"

"Sounds like she learned wisdom in that one lifetime. She may have learned more in others. She said she is here to help you see further and go further. My hunch is she had been signalling to you for a while. You got a strong body signal in that cabin when you felt your back was on fire. Ancestral memories are carried in our blood and encoded in our DNA. Disembodied spirits and ancestors can both make themselves known at cellular level, through somatic signals. I'd love a chance to facilitate a session with you to find out more about Frances."

I felt myself withdraw and contract. "I'll think about it, Catrin. To be honest, I've always felt leery of hypnosis."

She picked up on my energy. "Me too. I don't hypnotise clients. It's simple to help people access ancestral spirits and past lives, if they want to. I'm speaking only out of professional curiosity. You don't *need* me, Sarah. You connected spontaneously with Frances. You can do all the rest yourself. If you want technical guidance, you could read the work of a marvellous man who was wise in the ways of ancestral spirits and past lives. His name was Roger Woolger and his books and audios are still available."

I found a pen and made a note of the name. "Thanks. I'll follow that up. Unlike Frances, I love reading, and I could benefit from knowing more about this whole field you're involved in."

Catrin nodded. "I think you'll find it fascinating. If you're into astrology, you may also enjoy a book by someone who worked as Roger's partner for years. She shows how our charts reveal karmic complexes we're working on in this lifetime. As a matter of interest, would you be willing to tell me your birth details?"

I laughed. "That seems a minor confidence, by comparison with what I've already shared with you."

She pulled out her iPad and entered my birth data into an astrology program. Then she smiled and showed me my natal chart. "I thought so. Leo-Aquarius 5th/11th house nodal axis. Hmm. Look at those 11th and 12th house planets in Cancer and Leo, including your Sun and Pluto. There's that Sagittarius nomad influence sitting in your south node. I've a lot of Sag in my own chart."

"What you're saying resonates but I don't know why."

Catrin grinned. "I've another suggestion for your reading list, then: *Understanding Karmic Complexes*, by Patricia Walsh. I thoroughly recommend it and I'm betting you'll learn a lot about yourself from that. It's a pity we can't determine Frances's natal chart, since we have no birth date for her."

She put her iPad away and said, "I thought I heard echoes of Gemini karmic issues echoing in your musician friend's story. That's the other end of your Sagittarius axis. It would make sense of why you two have connected. It suggests there are ways in which he might help you too, if he could just get over himself."

The language Catrin had spoken was incomprehensible to me, as were the hieroglyphics on the chart she had shown me, but I felt an inner *aha* as she talked, and a visceral surge of interest to learn more. That led me to say, "I *would* like to attend one of your workshops, Catrin. Perhaps this can open a new door for me. I've felt I'm just treading water on the work front. I sense there is so much more to wake up to, for clients and me. I can't see the bigger picture, yet I know it's there. I yearn to explore the whole cosmos."

Catrin was suddenly glowing. "I'd love having you on a workshop. Give me your email address and I'll put you on my mailing list for upcoming events. I'll send you the link to Patricia's website as well, in case you are interested to do something with her."

I wrote my address down and, as she put it in her purse, Catrin added, "If you really want to push your boat out on the cosmic ocean, connect in with the work of a woman called Lisa Renee, here in L.A.. I'm not sure she gives individual sessions any more, but she has a website and Internet community, called Energetic Synthesis. I was going to suggest it anyway, since she offers training in psychic self-defence. Her work could be useful, given how psychically open you are."

She chuckled and added, "Prepare to be surprised by Lisa though, unless you are already conversant with all matters extra-terrestrial."

"You mean aliens? I don't know anything about them, but I must be half way there already myself, since I'm a registered alien here in the USA."

"Me too. What a crazy label they gave us. Just asking to be lived into as an identity, isn't it?" We laughed together and I felt joyful, knowing I had met another kindred soul in the City of Angels.

Catrin and I parted, after agreeing to do brunch again some time soon and, if possible, make it a threesome with Jane. As I drove back to the Marina, I reflected that I owed Jane a lot for creating such a promising new connection. I would have to give her a more graceful apology than I had managed at the time. Standing her brunch at Shutters with Catrin might be a perfect peace offering, and would also make a change from Figtree's.

CHAPTER FORTY-EIGHT

England 1643

"Thanks be to God! Robin came to tell me that you had survived the battle and said to expect you any day. But, with so many dead and wounded men still being brought back here from Newbury, I could not help but wonder if he might be keeping bad news from me, my love. Oh, but you are exhausted, I can see. What can I get you?"

Sir Robert sank into a chair and shook his head. "Nothing, my dear. I can only stay a short while, for I must see that my men and their horses are safely billeted. I had to see you briefly, to reassure you that I am well. And I will return tonight, if I may. If you have space for me, that is? You have little enough room to swing a cat here, it would seem." He looked around the cramped cottage that Frances had succeeded in securing, just to the south of Holywell Street.

Frances laughed, as much in relief that Robert was alive as at his pained expression at her living conditions. She searched for evidence of wounds in him, of which none were visible, and saying, "I assure you this is a veritable palace, by comparison with the lodgings that many have been forced to take here in Oxford. The Queen offered me rooms with her at Merton College, but I preferred to put a little distance between us. Charles is relaxed in attitude toward me these days, but I do not mean to give him unnecessary offence."

Frances took Robert's hand. "I know the cottage is small, but you can come to me here at any time of day or night without hindrance. I assume that, as a Member of Parliament as well as a military officer, you will be offered your own rooms with or near the King in Christchurch? Or will you billet with your men? Is it true, as Robin says, that you are to be part of the Oxford army? I hardly dared to hope for that."

"Quite true. I don't know what living arrangements are to be offered me, although I do know the King continues to say he does not wish to disturb any Oxford scholars at their studies through our presence. But

Frances, you are looking pale and very thin. Are you quite well, my dear?"

She tossed her head. "Now I have you again, I will go on famously. Before, I was in some danger of pining away. It has been so many months since we were together. And after all those early successes that kept us buoyed up, the news reaching here since the siege of Gloucester ended has been so dreary that it has been hard to keep our spirits high. Although I have to say that the Queen's arrival in July brightened all our lives. She is a rare tonic, Robert. A perfect companion for the King in these challenging times. Oh, and you may be astonished to hear that I have made my peace with Su Denbigh."

"Your sister-in-law? You're right, that does astonish me. Whatever can have wrought such a transformation? I expected the Dowager Countess would be in mourning for her husband, but still capable of spitting blood toward you, especially after we named her in your petition to recover your lands and goods."

"I doubt we can ever be bosom friends, but we are cordial. We must be, for we live so much on top of each other here. Everybody is in straightened circumstances and we feel united by a common foe. So we find a blessing in extending forgiveness wherever we can, and there is what my young friend Anne Harrison calls a kind of cheerfulness between martyrs that binds us."

"I am glad if it means that the likes of Su Denbigh are treating you more kindly, Frances."

"Su had apparently begun to feel more favourably toward me from the moment she heard I had converted. She was also impressed that Queen Anne spoke for me to Henrietta Maria. She understands that I brought the petition to furnish Robin with his needs. She acknowledges she would have done the same for her son."

Frances moved to sit, and patted the worn sofa, but Robert remained rooted in his chair as if he might never rise again. She continued. "Su is particularly amiable toward Robin, because he fights so valiantly for the King. Perhaps it was the influence of George and their mother that made her frown on me so for all those years. I do feel for Su's loss and I cannot imagine what it must be like to be so torn apart."

"Why torn apart?"

"Robert, you must know that her own son fights for Parliament? She adores Basil and cannot bear that he has taken arms against the King."

Robert nodded. "Denbigh has gained a well-deserved reputation as a courageous and intelligent soldier. He is an immense asset to Parliament, and he can also be the same for us, if we can persuade the King to take peace talks seriously. Basil served years overseas as a diplomat, and he will help reconcile our two sides, if given the chance."

"It's good to hear you speak generously of a man who at least nominally is our enemy. I wish you will talk with Su. She may take solace from what you say, for she cannot yet come to terms with what she regards as his defection. I try not to gloat about Robin's success, but I found it hard to stay silent when the King granted his patent to be Governor of Oswestry."

"Yes." Robert did not sound as though he felt like gloating. "I hope that won't turn out to be a mistake."

"Mistake, whatever can you mean? Surely you are proud that Robin has been honoured with such an important appointment, and in Shropshire too?"

Robert grimaced. "My love, it is indeed an honour, but he is very young. To take on the governorship of an important military centre at the age of nineteen is a heavy responsibility. I fear Robin may have problems keeping order between his men and the townsfolk."

Frances bristled. "I am astonished to hear you speak so of your own son. Robin is well travelled and wise beyond his years, after the life he has led. Fortunately he does not entertain such qualms as you. He is very excited."

Sir Robert Howard laughed. "Yes, my dear, I know. I have already seen him once today, supervising the distribution of muskets and pikes among his men. He is in high spirits."

"As well he should be, with three hundred men under his command."

Robert looked serious again. "Yes, and there's the rub. That's a lot of armed men for a nineteen-year-old to keep in order. Especially in the coming winter months, when there is likely to be little or no campaigning. Men defect or get up to mischief easily when they are idle and, Royalist though Shropshire still declares itself to be, there are some contumacious characters in and around Oswestry."

"Robert, am I to understand that you would have preferred our son to remain a private volunteer throughout this war, as when he fought at Edgehill last year? I thought Purbeck, you and I were all agreed that I should purchase him his commission? The only concern I have heard from Robin himself is that he would have preferred to have raised a cavalry regiment or dragoons, like his father. But he understood that I could not afford that and does not reproach me for it."

The grey of exhaustion showed across Robert Howard's face as he shook his head. "Frances, my dear sweet love, I have not returned from months of raising a regiment, laying sieges and storming cities, in order to cross swords with you on the subject of the son we both adore. Yes, I am very proud of Robin and his commission. But I simply wish he had been made a captain rather than a colonel first, and given enough time under an experienced commander to develop the maturity he will need in his new appointment. Enough. You were telling me that you and Su Denbigh are now friends, and you also hinted that the same may be true for you with his Majesty?"

In spite of her pallor, Frances looked radiant at Robert's reference to the King. "Such a good talk we had. I wish you could have been there to hear. His Majesty explained to me how difficult things have been for him these many years, with all the growing challenge to his right to rule in Parliament, as well as the rise of such virulent Puritan feeling against us Catholics."

She leaned back and blinked before continuing, "I actually felt quite tearful when Charles told me how bereft he had felt at the loss of his father and then Buckingham. How it had stirred up old memories of losing Henry and feeling fearful and not up to the weight of being King someday. Oh, but I'm sorry, Robert. This must be tiring you further, to hear me prattle so. You probably want to leave?"

"No, my dear. You cannot know how much the prospect of sitting down in a comfortable chair again, to listen to you prattle, as you call it, has kept me alive and hopeful through many dreary moments in the field. My men have had me for months. They can spare me a few moments longer to you now."

Frances beamed. "Then I will continue. Yes, he came as near an apology to me as it is possible to expect from one's King, when he admitted, just between us, that he had allowed himself to be led on too extreme a path of religious affairs by Laud. He did not want to be seen by the country to be favouring Henrietta Maria's religion over the Anglican Church, so he overcompensated. But the Puritans' extremism eventually sickened him."

She spread her hands wide. "Once I understood his position, I could no longer feel upset toward Charles. And the sweetest moment came when he acknowledged privately that I have had much to bear in my marriage. He had taken note that all these years Purbeck has only had kind words to say of me. Charles said that my husband is often disturbed, yet very far from a fool, so he takes it as a fine character reference for me."

"To be vindicated, after all your years of being out in the cold with the King, is wonderful. I am so glad for you, my darling. It also makes my own struggles the more worthwhile, to hear that you and Charles are at last reconciled."

"If that were not enough, His Majesty told me that I have reason to be proud of how I have reared my son. He wishes he had a thousand young men as brave as Robin Villiers in his army. He also declared his gratitude to you, for your many acts of uncomplaining service, in Parliament and in the field. He said that it is noblemen like you and the loyal men of Shropshire that encourage him in his darkest moments to stand firm in his fight against evil. You fuel his determination to do what is needed to restore order and goodness to this country. When he said that, I thought I should burst with pride for you and Robin. Our talk reminded me of the many times that Charles and I would share sad and happy thoughts, long ago, when we were children together."

Frances rose from her seat beside Robert and went to a plain wooden dresser, on which stood a single bottle filled with ruby-coloured wine. "I have been keeping this for you. I hope it is still good. It is the very last bottle from our cellar in Paris. Saving the best until last. Would you like to try a glass, my love?"

Robert whistled. "You little squirrel. I thought our French loot was all gone, long since. No, let us keep it for the moment when we can toast our son's appointment with him, perhaps this very night. I promise you that listening to you is all the food and drink of which I have need just now. What more news do you have for me?"

Frances sat down again, this time on the arm of his chair. "Where to begin? Well, one sad piece of news came to me at mid-year. I heard it through a casual conversation with a tradesman, whose family hailed from Purbeck and who remembered Corfe Castle well from when he was a lad. He said John Clavell died in February. He could tell me nothing of how he died or what happened to John's young wife. He received the information quite by accident himself, when he was making a delivery to Brasenose College. Two porters were discussing the death and the long ago theft. My own inquiries have as yet yielded nothing."

"Did the news much sadden you?"

"Yes, but in that wistful way in which one hears that a piece of one's distant past has broken off and disappeared, like an iceberg swallowed by melting waters. John and I had travelled such different paths since we were young. I don't know if he ever dropped his resentment. It was eating him against us still, even on his last visit. I wish his soul at peace."

Robert grunted. "And what of Purbeck? Where is he at the moment?"

"I am not sure. Oxford does not agree with him. It is too cramped, and all the tension that swirls around the town whenever we hear of battles going badly makes him nervous. His sister Su gets very irritated by him and says she has too much to do for her Majesty to be able to have him under her feet here. I think he may return to Oxford now the King will winter here but, the last I heard of him, he was at the family home in Brooksby. The country is better for him, as long as he does not get caught up in any fighting. Mama declared he is welcome to live at Stoke, since she has no further need of it to entertain her Parliamentarians."

"Ah, dear Eliza. I'm surprised it has taken this long for her to appear in your narrative. I don't suppose that cryptic comment is to be taken to mean she has prostrated herself before the King and embraced the Royalist cause?"

Frances chortled. "Far from it. It simply means that Parliament has returned Hatton House to her, and she has gone back to London. Which will be a good thing for all of us in Oxford, since her welcoming so many of our enemies at Stoke, almost under his Majesty's nose, was a continuing source of irritation to Charles during last winter and spring. Did you not hear of the cheeky letter Mama wrote to Prince Rupert when she left Stoke?"

"No. Prince Rupert and I have lately confined our remarks largely to giving and responding to battle orders. Him giving; me responding. And sometimes regretting it afterward."

"Are you and Rupert on bad terms now?" Frances broke off her story.

"No, my dear. The Prince is a daring and gallant commander and much to be admired. My loyalty to him, as to His Majesty, remains absolute. But Rupert is impetuous at times, and occasionally prone to order a cavalry charge when sitting tight might better do the business. He also tends to use my dragoons as cavalry, rather than in the tasks of mounted infantry for which we are intended. But military talk has no place here. Continue with your story of Eliza. Love her or loathe her, she always goes her own way."

"I have little to report about Mama. She disapproved of me joining the King's Court here in Oxford, and did not shrink from telling me so in a long letter, written in her idiosyncratic style. She said I have made my poor father ashamed and he is turning in his grave, which is ripe, coming from her. She also said that she could not imagine why I deprive myself of my creature comforts in Oxford, when I could be staying comfortably in London with her, if I would change my allegiance. After that, she declared that she is now all but penniless, with having to entertain so many Roundheads with prodigious appetites. Oh, and she is planning to bring a petition to Parliament."

"Another one? What this time? Don't tell me she's fighting the Bishop of Ely again."

"Lord, no. The last one retired hurt, poor man. His fight to get full rights to the Holborn property restored to the Bishops was decided permanently in Mama's favour a couple of years back. No, a carpenter called Johnson has erected a cottage against one wall of Hatton House, during Mama's absence, and plans to use it as an alehouse. She wants the offending structure removed."

"The woman is indefatigable. Nearly seventy and still picking fights. If they have given her back Hatton House, Parliament must have decided to hold her as a secret weapon to launch from London, if we look like carrying the day militarily."

"And do we, my dear? How are we doing? Or do you prefer not to say?"

Robert Howard stretched and stood up, rubbing stiff limbs. "I prefer at this moment to go and tuck my men and horses in, then return to bore you all evening and night, with the details of every event in which Sir Robert Howard's Regiment of Dragoons has engaged, while we were apart. That bottle you have saved will aid the telling, especially if Robin joins us. If you can muster some broth or dried biscuit to accompany it, I will be in heaven."

"I'll do better than that. I'll go and visit the butcher, the baker and the candlestick maker. I know just who to talk with here, to furnish a feast fit for a returning hero and his son."

"Don't tell me you have dispensed with servants altogether since I saw you last, Frances? Surely you still have at least one maid to shop for you, and a cook? You do have a kitchen?" Sir Robert looked around.

Frances laughed. "I am not yet reduced to a life without servants or any means of cooking. But I have a magic touch with victuallers and tradesmen. My life's more challenging experiences equipped me better than most to live under restrictions and forage successfully in a garrison town. My friends here are frequently furious that I can always find the best cuts, even meat itself, when they have just been told there is naught but bread and water available and precious little of that. Please, never inquire too closely of my methods, but I assure you they are legal. Well, almost."

CHAPTER FORTY-NINE

California

"This is ace, Sarah! I never thought I'd be sitting in a centre front box at the Hollywood Bowl. What a shame Catrin is out of town. She so wanted to come with us. She'd have enjoyed being a tall poppy too. All those folk up there are jealous of us."

We were sitting together during the intermission, after the opening band had played. Jane had twisted round and was looking over her shoulder, up through an almost full amphitheatre, which was currently abuzz with anticipation for the headline band to come.

I laughed. "You may not feel so superior to those folk up there once Midnight Jax starts. Bob has warned me it will be very loud at times. Much louder than the women who just played. So maybe those higher up know a thing or two about where to sit during rock concerts at the Bowl."

"Don't you believe it. I can see a whole bunch of them up there, shaking their fists at me now. Green with envy they are."

I looked round. "Personally, I feel quite exposed sitting here. I actually prefer sitting up toward the back in the Bowl."

"You're kidding me."

"No. I love it up high. I find it easier to breathe. I can look down over the huge crowd. Be in and out, part of it and not part of it at the same time. The stage is like a puppet theatre from up at the back but the large screens and the sound system still keep you connected in with whatever is happening. The Bowl really is a bowl, too, so it feels as if the land is cradling everybody at once. And you can see the giant cross, which isn't visible from here."

"Very mystical. But don't go religious on me now, and spoil my fun, girl. I'm here to feel special for one night. That includes knowing that everyone behind me wishes they were sitting in *my* seat."

Jane craned her neck around again and then smirked at me. "After all, this is Hollywood, babe. And we're talking Moonlight Jax, Hollywood style. Vulgar ostentation and filthy hedonism for the rest of the night, I hope."

I threw up my hands in mock defeat. "Very well. Enjoy your filthy hedonism. Just don't blame me, if you find yourself wishing you'd accepted those earplugs Bob offered you. And don't expect me to sympathise and stay around, if your desire to be a focal point of envy attracts the Evil Eye. We'll be screaming for a blessing from my mystic cross then. Oh, here we go."

While I was speaking, the lights dimmed. The high-pitched clamour of the crowd slowly died away, as people settled in their seats. Gradually, all movement and noise from the audience ceased. For an extended moment after the crowd had stilled, the darkness vibrated around us. Then lightning flashed and a gigantic clap of simulated thunder reverberated through the Hollywood Bowl. Spots blazed white-lit intensity upon four black-clad figures and their instruments at the back of the stage.

When the musicians had bowed and waved, their four spots moved forward to coalesce in a single concentrated beam at the front of the stage. It shone down upon a tall, slender blond-haired man, clad from head to toe in skin-tight black leather, trimmed with glittering gold. His head was bowed.

Jane nudged me. "We've avoided the sackcloth and ashes, I see. Good on you, girl."

I grinned as I gazed up at the figure standing so straight and motionless. In slow motion, Johnny Clavylle raised his head and stared unsmiling into the crowd. Watching him, I could see the man was in his element. He was born to stand on a stage and command the attention of thousands. Johnny lifted his arms wide in greeting and spoke two words, "'Ello 'Ollywood." The audience erupted into laughter and applause. Johnny Clavylle grinned, waved and brought his left hand down into crashing contact with the strings of his guitar.

Music exploded around us and the show was on.

Beside me, Jane was clearly in heaven. The louder and more insistent the beat, the more she enjoyed it and, by the time the concert was halfway through, I had relaxed enough to enjoy myself too. The set list was a well-chosen mix of Johnny's older and newer compositions. At the tail end of a twelve-gig tour, it was obvious that Bob's hard work in promotion and coordination had paid off. Johnny had reportedly behaved himself impeccably throughout, and played to critical acclaim around the country. This final performance at the Bowl was polished and a fitting culmination to a tour that had almost never happened.

The members of Moonlight Jax were musicians of calibre. Each had the chance to show off his talents, but the man in centre stage drew and kept eyes upon him throughout the show. For nearly an hour, Johnny Clavylle held seventeen thousand people in his sensual sway as easily and lightly as if the crowd itself were made of feather down.

"And now for something none of you will have heard before. I'd like to sing you a song I composed recently. I've been keeping it specially for tonight's show and this audience."

Johnny took off his electric guitar and replaced it with an acoustic one, brought to him by a stagehand, who was also carrying a high stool. Johnny spent a few moments adjusting the shoulder strap and settling on the stool. The he looked up again.

"The song is called *Betrayal*. It is written for and dedicated to a woman I have loved." He paused for dramatic effect. Then, "For Frances."

The two words pierced me in the solar plexus. Nauseous suddenly and gasping for air, I reached for the water bottle at my side, but the music had me in its grip before I had taken a sip. The tempo and mood of this song was different from all that went before. The melody was mournful, the lyrics stark and bitter. John Clavylle sang to his own accompaniment. Behind him, the band had blended silently into the black of night.

Red and white spots circled the front of the stage and caught the singer in their occasional flickering beam. He sat on the three-legged stool, with his head bent to obscure his face, and those long, shapely fingers the only moving part of his body visible to his audience. The crowd sat as still and silent as statues and Johnny Clavylle sang:

You were my childhood inspiration
Your hair, your eyes, your face
Were my delight
My life was cause for celebration
And then you left
And day turned into night

My world since then is one long struggle
To pull your dagger
From my heart
Each time I've hoped the wound is healing
I hear again
Your words that we must part

You left and found a joy denied me
You took a lover
Bore his son
Hate is the crippled child you left me

The only child
I'll know 'til life is done

Each time I've hoped the wound is healing
You say again
Those words that we must part

His audience stayed silent for a long moment after Johnny's elegant fingers had ceased to move. When he raised his head, he stared straight at and through me, unsmiling, and I read the hatred he had sung of in his eyes.

Applause, when it came, was appreciative and sustained, yet curiously muted by comparison with what had gone before. Of the virtuosity of the music and its musician there could be no doubt. But the singer's energy had shifted the collective mood of the crowd. The bleak message of his lyrics was reflected on the faces of many.

I dared not move while Johnny stared at me. It had taken all my willpower to remain present and conscious during his performance and I still hovered on the edge of fainting. I knew intense relief when he broke our gaze, half turned and walked back toward his musicians, and I had to struggle even now in order to stand.

My world was swimming around me as I spoke to Jane. My voice sounded strained and far way. "I need some fresh air. I'll see you at the after party. You've got your ticket, haven't you? And you know where the Museum Terrace is?"

"Yes, love. Don't worry about me. I'm fine. Do you want me to come with you? Did that song get to you? The man's a bloody genius to create such tragedy out of thin air. But what a prick, to aim it at you. I'll have some things to say to him later, if I get the chance." Jane half rose.

I shook my head. "Please stay, Jane. I'm OK, really. I just need air."

I felt my way haltingly toward the nearest exit. The crowd was still clapping Johnny's solo, as I went through the turnstile. Out in the plaza, I wandered blindly. My heart beat unevenly and my skin felt clammy. Crowds were ambling in the grounds outside the amphitheatre. Around me, people wandered nowhere in particular, apparently enjoying not getting anywhere. Usually, I loved the laid-back atmosphere outside the Bowl auditorium. Tonight, its aimlessness only exacerbated my disorientation and discomfort.

I took the long outdoor escalator up to the higher level. Crowds thronged thickly here too. Slowly, the atmosphere of cheerful good humour seeped into me by osmosis. My physical pain and nausea had eased. I felt numb in my solar plexus, but my tunnel vision had cleared and I no longer felt in danger of fainting.

After some songs went by me unheard, I moved back into the main amphitheatre and made my way down to the front row of W section. By now, vacant seats were plentiful, since people were dancing in the aisles to an up-tempo rock number. Up in the high reaches of the Hollywood Bowl, the crowd was mixed in age, socioeconomic group and racial composition, but a heterogeneous audience had bonded in mutual appreciation of Moonlight Jax and Johnny Clavylle.

The air was warm and humid. Marijuana smoke swirled in the lights. The cloying smell of weed caught in my throat. I had never liked pot, whether ingested directly or second-hand. But I found myself smiling. People are becoming collectively stoned, I thought and wondered how many people were getting mildly high, who had never taken an intentional drag on a joint in their life.

Now, for the first time since rejoining the concert, I felt ready to look down toward the stage and the performers. From this distance, the black-and-gold-clad figure at the front looked tiny. The enormous screens on either side of the stage enabled me to see Johnny's face in close-up, but even these magnified images were distant enough for me to feel safe in my body again.

I breathed more easily and tuned back in to the music. This time I would be vigilant for whatever Johnny Clavylle might have in mind.

CHAPTER FIFTY

England 1645

All who knew her understood she would be leaving soon.

The Catholic priest smuggled in to the cottage had administered the viaticum. Frances had confessed her sins and received absolution. Lady Hatton pursed her lips at sight and sound of a papish sacrament, but refrained from derogatory comment.

Eliza had been coming and going from the cottage daily, frail but upright and walking without aid of a stick, for several weeks. Nobody understood how she had entered the beleaguered city or, once inside, had found the best lodgings in town. It was generally assumed that one of her Parliamentarian friends had passed the word to General Fairfax, commanding the siege from Marston, so that he would let her through unchallenged. Once she was within the city walls, perhaps one of her old Royalist flames had provided assistance. Or maybe it was the son-out-law, Sir Robert Howard, with whom she was reported to be recently reconciled.

These days, Eliza Hatton was mostly silent and sad; a circumstance all but unheard of by those who had known her during any of her seventy years. In an era when few saw fifty, Eliza had survived the death of most of her contemporaries and too many family members. Some, like her first husband and her elder daughter, she had loved. Some, like her second husband, she had loathed. But no leave-taking had accorded her such grief as that which she was experiencing in slow motion, through watching the last child of her womb take a protracted and inexorable leave taking.

Frances did not share her mother's sadness about her situation, although she too was silent. Day after day, she lay in bed, outwardly immobile, yet inwardly journeying through many dimensions: drifting, dancing and returning. The pains bothered her less each time she travelled ever further beyond the frail confines of her nearly spent body.

There were moments when she knew herself back again, lucid and firmly anchored in the room with Robert, Robin or Eliza. Then Frances would seek to show her earthly companions with her eyes how much their devoted attention and presence meant to her. But soon the mundane world would dim again and lose its momentary meaning, as other realms opened and beckoned her beyond.

Frances travelled to the past. She journeyed to the future. Fragments of crystalline memory and disconnected impressions of lives to come streamed through her awareness, like passing clouds and birds on the wing. The threads of the tapestry that had been her present lifetime's journey unravelled slowly, as she dreamed and gazed on giant looms, loaded with the warp and weft of future lives.

She knew and cared little of what was happening immediately outside her Oxford cottage door. She knew the current siege would be lifted but she had also seen the end of things in this tragic Civil War and so many other collective conflicts still to come.

The King and Queen had both departed Oxford already, leaving a dispirited Court and garrison to try and hold out against an implacable Parliamentarian siege. Henrietta Maria had left more than a year before, the reason given at the time that her baby needed to be born in a safer place than Oxford. But safe places anywhere in England proved difficult to find for the Queen and her faithful Su Denbigh. The women finally braved the seas at Falmouth, to take up permanent residence in Paris, less than a month after baby Henrietta entered the troubled island kingdom over which her father's grip was loosening.

Frances had still been well enough at the time to walk to Merton College and bid farewell to the Queen and her sister-in-law. By the following January, she was unable to leave her bed. When the King sent word that he would come in person to the tiny cottage to make his adieux to Frances, Lady Hatton displayed rare diplomacy, by absenting herself for the afternoon.

As Charles gave Frances the royal hand to kiss, she felt him shudder. She squeezed his fingers and sought to shape her cracked lips into a farewell smile. The effect was to send him from the room in haste, that none present should be obliged to witness their monarch's tears. Charles left Oxford with his personal troop the next day, riding through blossoming wisteria trees of early May toward Woodstock.

The fortunes of the King and his troops thereafter were little talked of in the sickroom. Defence of Oxford itself was uppermost in the mind and conversation of the town's occupants but, if any of her immediate family had felt inclined to weigh a dying woman's days down with dismal reports of war, political differences within the family must have given them pause concerning what they might share.

Occasionally, when they thought Frances was asleep, Robin and his grandmother would talk together. Since Eliza Hatton had never seen need to lower her voice when speaking, Frances then received firsthand confirmation of what she had already observed during some of her scouting missions forward in time. Robin would resign his commission and tender his services to Cromwell and Parliament, as soon as his mother was buried.

Frances loved her son for keeping his silence with her, to protect her from his decision. If she had been told, she might have found words to explain to Robin that his defection from the King did not distress her. She had long since made her own peace with Charles, but she understood her son's resentment for the years during which his Majesty had kept their family in exile. And Robin was not the only man who had fought on the Royalist side to be feeling deep frustration now at the intransigence of the King, in the face of all efforts by Lord Denbigh and others to act as peacemakers.

Frances also knew how hurt Robin had felt at his dismissal from Oswestry last year by Prince Rupert, after purportedly failing to keep order in the town. It had only restored her son's pride a little to learn that the older, supposedly more experienced, officer chosen by Rupert to succeed him had made a far worse showing than young Colonel Villiers.

In joining Parliament, Robin would be on the side of history, at least for a time, and Frances had already seen enough to know that he and his father would never have to face each other on the field in opposing armies, which was the only circumstance that she could not have borne.

Thanks again to Eliza's clarion clear voice, Frances heard full details of her mother's intentions for her will. She would leave Hatton House to grandson Robin, during his official father's lifetime. After Purbeck's death, Stoke Manor would come to Robin and Hatton House would then be passed to one of several possible relatives, according to provisions in the testament, whereby Eliza would seek to mould lives long after her demise.

Mama, what a remarkable woman you are. Quarrelsome, yes; manipulative, certainly; narcissistic, indeed. All of these difficult things and more. Yet enchanting and beautiful to look upon still, in spite of your advancing years; amusing and entertaining too, even now in the grip of your obvious sadness.

Mama, you have let me down often in life, and I know that I have also disappointed you. But it was you who taught me by example to be willing to betray another, in order to be true to myself. Mama, please get that will written and signed quickly. You are not long for this world, and

Robin must have material security, if he is to surmount his own challenges.

Robin remained her prime concern, in her approaching death, as he had been throughout her life as a mother. Frances wanted to alert her son to another name change. One might have expected that three surnames – Wright, Howard, and Villiers – would be sufficient for any one man in a single lifetime. But Frances foresaw how Lord Purbeck's rejection, under the influence of a new wife, would finally tip her son over the edge and into disgust of the Villiers name and all its associations.

At least Robin would have the sense to await the Viscount's death before seeking an official change, by which time his own inheritance would be safe. She understood Robin's logic in seeking an alternative name from within his own marriage. How ironical, then, that this fourth one, albeit briefly brimming with political expediency, would weigh him down with baggage of a different kind.

A certain justice lay in her child adopting the surname of cousin Henry, thanks to whose support Frances had escaped through Guernsey to Paris and continued to receive the funds that kept Robin and her alive. But Robin would fail in his bid for the title and estates of the Earl of Danby. And the prospect of her son marrying the daughter of a regicide saddened Frances, even if the personal performance of Elizabeth as a loving wife would be all that she could wish for.

Robert would inevitably hate that match at first. Who could blame a man who would continue so doggedly in his Majesty's service, and end his military career in staunch defence of the last castle in Shropshire to hold out for the Royalists, for recoiling when asked to welcome as daughter-in-law the child of Sir John Danvers? One of fifty-nine men who would sign the execution papers for their King, may God rest his and all their misguided souls...

Frances took joy that the birth and christening of her granddaughter and namesake, Robin's own baby Frances, would present a future occasion for mending bridges between father and son. By then, there would be still more personal hurts to heal between Robert and Robin, and her son would have opted out of the Church in which his father still worshipped.

Frances wished more than anything that she might find a way to shield Robin from his dual sense of abandonment when, already rejected by his official father on Purbeck's remarriage, his birth father would marry. She yearned for her son to understand that Robert did not intend his late union in life to be a cancellation of all they had known and shared together. For herself, Frances felt profound relief that her lover would enjoy the sanctioned comfort of a decent woman at his side for his last five years on earth. Of all men she knew, he deserved it.

If Frances could have intervened at all in Robert's marriage, she would have simply sought to deter the said decent woman, as his widow, from attempting to dislodge Robin's claims to lifetime leases of certain properties his father had left him in lieu of his name. Then again, Frances understood from first hand experience what any mother might be willing do for her children, to assure their future security. Katherine Neville Howard might not bear her husband's love child any personal animosity, but she would have her own family's needs to care about, left with two small sons and the baby girl that Robert would sire, before taking his leave of life.

Forewarning of all these events to come, and many more, Frances would have liked to share with her son, during their last days together on earth. But there are matters that the dying may not speak of to the living. And so Frances kept her silence, along with her sorrow at the suffering she saw Robin would endure.

Because the next twenty years would generate so much unhappiness within their family and the nation, Frances preferred to journey far into the future, as her earthly end drew close. She observed lives in future generations that she would seek – and fail – to enlighten from her spirit state. So much hatred, so much violence, so much brutality still to unfold on the world stage, fuelled always by greed, and manipulated through fear. Frances would need to be active for her messages of love and liberty to take root in the parched soil of collective affairs. She would also have to accept that germination would be soul-achingly slow.

Yet, one day, many hundreds of years hence, a young girl would come to visit the ruins of a castle that Mama had once owned. The child would not yet be awake to their connection, but Frances would recognize instantly a descendant of her granddaughter's line. Blood of her blood. And that blood link would give her authority and a special responsibility to intervene as needed in the child's field, although divine right order also dictated that Frances must do nothing against the girl's own free will.

The matrix of mind control operating over the world at the close of the second millennium would still be dense. Most of humanity would remain blind and deaf to multi-dimensionality, as the girl grew toward womanhood. Frances would have to be so patient, and experimental too, in her efforts to connect and communicate. The girl would have to be the one to open a direct line between them. In the meantime, her ancestor could offer only subliminal protection, as the child stumbled and struggled through life lessons.

Frances knew that they would eventually establish a direct connection on that same ruined castle hillside, and it would be a grail encounter for them both. But she must not get ahead of herself now, nor of the loved ones who were devoting themselves daily to tending her wasting body, in this cramped and threadbare cottage that destiny had dictated would be her last living abode.

Robert had stayed on with the Oxford army, even though he longed to head west with the King and back toward Shropshire. Stalwart, self-sacrificing, self-sufficient Robert. How best might Frances serve her beloved Robert in these last moments? Her very thoughts had conjured his presence. Here he was now, entering the room in his dusty and faded red uniform with its pink sash, which had already seen too many days of war. Frances could feel that Robert was tired and anxious. Was it because there was someone with him?

"Frances, my dear, can you hear me? You have a visitor. The siege is lifting today and people begin to be free to enter and leave the town. One has come just to be with you."

The man beside Robert came forward. He hovered at her bedside, looking down upon what she knew must be a pallid face. With a jerky movement, he knelt and she felt him kiss her quickly on the lips.

Frances did not stir. Her eyes remained closed. She had no words to offer Viscount Purbeck. All that had been between them in the past had been said, and she did not feel quite ready to exonerate John's future rejection of her boy, even though she would forgive her husband freely enough when the time came.

Beneath her lids, Frances watched as Lord Purbeck stood again, turned, gave Robert an embarrassed half-smile, muttered something inaudible to the man he yet claimed as his son, bowed to Eliza Hatton and hurried out of the room. Goodbye, earthly husband. You have been kind when you could. I wish you well.

To her quiet joy, Sir Robert did not leave with Purbeck. Released by the lifting of the siege, he stayed at her side throughout the dimming of the day. She noted how he waved aside all offers of refreshment, and she sensed he also understood that these were their last precious living hours together. She felt silent gratitude that he shook his head emphatically, when Lady Hatton begged to take his place, that he might go to his own lodgings for much-needed rest.

Mama, you can leave now. You do not need to be with me at the end. We will not be separated long. Yes, Robin, please accompany your grandmother, and escort her back to her lodgings. I need some private moments with your father. You understand. You always did.

The door had closed on Lady Hatton and their son, and they were alone together at last. Robert was sitting in the chair he had placed beside her bed.

"Oh my love, my love. How will I go on without you?"

She heard the anguish in his voice, felt him sink his head upon his chest and allowed his grieving presence fully into her field of light. She held him in his sadness and envisioned them enveloped together in a cloud of gossamer light devotion. She sensed his spirit lighten and felt him enter dreamtime with her. In this dimension, she could be his guide and offer him a brief taste of the sweetness to come, when they would again be free to travel together in the unity of lighter realms.

So tempting to want to take Robert with her now, to speak the spell and whisper the words that might encourage him to accompany her. But his time to leave had not yet come. Frances was granted grace, in their last shared moments, to infuse Robert with spiritual strength to sustain him through his earthly loss, but she must not tamper with divine right timing.

The door hung so crookedly on its hinges that Robin could not enter the room quietly. He looked inquiringly at his father, who was rubbing his eyes as if emerging from a deep sleep. "Not long now," Robert mouthed.

Robin went past his father and around his mother's bed. "Mama, I am back." His voice was low and gruff.

I know, my son. Thank you for this blessed interval you granted me with your father. Even as a child you were sensitive to our needs for time alone. You deserve so much more kindness from this lifetime than you will receive.

Frances remained motionless, lying between the two men, with her eyes shut. Robin knelt. He picked up her all but bloodless hand and pressed it to his lips. His father stood, pulled up a chair for him and then returned to his seat on the other side of the bed. The two men sat watching her for any sign of movement. She lay like a sleeping log between them, aware of their joint presence, content to float peacefully, misting them gently with her love.

"Papa, will she endure like this for long?"

As Robin spoke the question, Frances opened her eyes. Parchment pale and delicately fine of feature, she had never appeared more beautiful to the men in her life than in this moment.

"Robin."

"I am here, Mama."

"Robert."

"I'm here, my love."

With an immense effort of will, Frances turned her head and brought her focus upon each of the men in turn. Her Royalist lover and Roundhead son each gazed without blinking back at her. She saw the love they shared for her eclipsing all their political differences, and prayed that the unity they were experiencing now might sustain them long after she had gone.

Frances struggled to form her words. "They are at Corfe Castle."

Her voice was so low that it was hard to distinguish her speech, but Robin may have thought he had divined his mother's intention, for he responded with tact. "Mama, you may rest easy. There is no fighting currently at Corfe Castle."

Her eyes closed and fluttered open again. "John is at Corfe Castle."

Robin looked questioningly at his father, who shrugged. Her son spoke again. "Sir John Bankes? No, Mama. He died here in Oxford last Christmas, remember? It is Lady Bankes who still heads the resistance at Corfe Castle. And she leads it most valiantly, Mama."

A frown creased the marble-like smoothness of France's brow. She knew what Robin could not, that feminine fortitude would prove unequal in the final assault, and that the fine and beautiful castle – so long at the heart of inheritance disputes between their family and the Villiers – would be demolished by Parliamentary order within less than a year.

It was an effort to speak and try to be understood. She summoned the energy to whisper again. "Not Bankes. My own John."

Robin stiffened. "Do you mean John Villiers? Lord Purbeck was here with us earlier today, Mama."

"*My* John. My friend, John Clavell."

This time Frances spoke clearly. Sir Robert took her hand and spoke gently. "My love, John Clavell is also dead. Don't you remember? He died more than two years ago."

Frances opened her eyes wide, but their far-away expression revealed that she no longer saw what was before her in the room. She nodded. "Yes, I remember. John is at Corfe Castle. He loves birds. We played together there when we were children. Before the world became an unkind place."

She closed her eyes. For a while, the three figures remained as still and silent as a painted tableau.

"Frances is at Corfe Castle with John now." Robert or Robin may have heard her words correctly. If they did, they could no make sense of them.

"You are here with us and we love you, Mama." Robin's voice broke.

Frances spoke again with unexpected strength. "Yes. Promise me that, out of love for me, you two will never fight each other."

"We promise." They responded instantly in unison. Unwept tears gave weight to their words and both heads bowed in emotion.

Her voice at the last was clear as a reed: slender, pure and upright. "You have both been my joy and guiding stars in this life. Take care of each other always. I love you."

Frances left Oxford quietly, on the same day that its second siege of the Civil War was lifted. Unlike so many other weary inhabitants, free at last to move in and out of the town, she had no need to use the city gate.

CHAPTER FIFTY-ONE

California

With the closing chords of the last song and the dimming of the lights, the concert had come to an end. I remained seated. Around me, early leavers rushed for the exit, perhaps hoping in vain to avoid the scramble to exit the Bowl's stacked parking lot.

I felt in no hurry to move. I envisioned the scene on the Museum Terrace once the after-show party began. Would Bob be there already, making sure all was prepared? Before joining him, I needed to find a way to armour myself. I wanted to be clear about how I would respond to Antony, if he asked for my reaction to Johnny Clavylle's performance tonight.

How could I protect myself against his hurtful cut-and-thrusts? I stared toward the giant Hollywood Cross, still hazy through the marijuana mist. Hey Frances, if you're here, tell me how I stop this man piercing my defences, as he did tonight with that song of hate.

Her response was immediate and unequivocal:

Nobody can hurt you unless some part of you is in agreement with being hurt. You create your own reality and your own demons with your fears. Command and protect your space, Sarah. Decide who and what you let into your life. Drop your denial and face the truth within you. Observe the world as it is, from a neutral place, instead of judging how you think it should be. Think with your heart, my dear. You do this already with your clients. Now do it in your life.

I sat, stunned not only at the clarity of her message but that it matched advice from a class I had recently attended on Catrin Morgan's recommendation. Seventeenth-century-lived-and-learned wisdom from Frances synthesised with twenty-first-century methods of psychic self-defence.

Yes, that's exactly right, I said to myself.

"What did you say, luv?"

I looked sideways.

A woman of indeterminate age had remained seated, while others in our row were leaving. She moved closer and I noticed she wore a large *I Love Johnny - I Love Jax* pin on a gaudy sweater overprinted with a winking black and gold moon. The sweater did not quite cover her bulging midriff.

"Thought you might be talking to me, luv." She had a Cockney accent.

"Excuse me. I must have spoken my thoughts aloud."

"Do that meself, sometimes. You're English, ain't you? Been a fan of Johnny fer long?"

"Not really. I've known his music for about a year."

"You 'ad real a treat tonight then. I been following 'im since 'e was a lad, with his first band. Nights of the Road, that was. Loved 'em all. But this lot? Brilliant. Best gig of Johnny's I been to. And I been to a few, I can tell you. Came six thousand miles fer this. Like you must of too, I suppose. Cost me an arm and a leg. Worf ev'ry penny."

"I live here in L.A., so I didn't have to travel like you. That's real dedication, to come six thousand miles for a concert. I'm glad you feel it was worth the trip."

"I'll say. 'E's a genius, you know, luv. Gets better wiv age. They're stupid, this lot that are leaving. 'T'ain't over yet. There'll be an encore. 'E never leaves without one. And 'e always saves summat reelly good for last. E's a luvly lad. A real gent. Makes you proud to be British. Not often I feel that way, these days."

I sat and pondered her words. This long-time fan could have no inkling of the complexity behind the black-and-gold façade that was Johnny Clavylle's on-stage persona. What an invitation to addiction it must be for a man like Antony to have fans idolise him, and for as long as she and others like her had been following him. The incompleteness of the woman's perspective jarred on me, but then I asked myself who was I to judge her, or wish to strip away Johnny Clavylle's mystique?

Down in the auditorium, the Jax band members had trooped back onstage. As Johnny acknowledged them individually, each took a bow. Amid casual waves, the musicians left and Johnny was the last to exit. At the side of the stage, he turned and blew two-handed kisses to the crowd. Calls for an encore rose and rippled through the Bowl.

For a while, as I stared down at the darkened stage, I wondered if fans would be disappointed. More people begin to drift toward the exits. "Are you sure there *will* be an encore?" I asked the woman on my left.

She was emphatic. "E *never* lets us down, luv." As she spoke, lights went on again and the black-and-gold figure walked back on stage, alone. Whistles, yells and screams rose to a new crescendo.

Johnny Clavylle raised the hand that was not holding his acoustic guitar, asking for silence. The crowd obeyed.

"You've been an incredible audience tonight. Thank you all so much."

People clapped and stamped their feet.

Again Johnny held up his hand and again the crowd fell silent.

"This is the last gig of our North American tour. It's been such an honour to play for you here in this amazing setting. We want to thank everyone who made it possible. I've dreamed since I was a kid of playing the Hollywood Bowl. Thanks for making that dream come true for the band and me tonight."

More foot stamping, clapping and cheers. I noticed there was no trace of Cockney in Johnny's voice as he continued, "It takes an army to create and produce a successful rock music tour. If I were to name everyone that the band and I are indebted to, we'd still be here at dawn. But I do want to ask you to join me in saying a special thank you to everyone who works at the Bowl, as well as to the guys who've been on tour with us, the ones you never see, working away like beavers backstage."

The crowd yelled its enthusiastic thanks.

"And I need to name two people without whom this tour would never have happened." Johnny paused and drew breath. Then, "Bob Howard and I played together in a band that a few of you here tonight may be old enough to remember, called Nights of the Road."

Fresh screams broke out, as the name of the band and its original singer registered. The woman beside me nudged me. "That's the one I was telling you about, luv."

I nodded and tried to smile but my heart was thudding too hard.

Johnny Clavylle spoke again. "This tour couldn't have happened without Bob's genius, organization and hard work. Robert, my old mate. It's been good hitting the road with you again." He half turned, and looked to the side of the stage as he spoke. "Ready to join me?"

Bob walked on stage. Casually dressed in a summer-blue-sky silk shirt and jeans, he looked a million dollars, but it was not his clothes that took what remained of my breath away. He was carrying an acoustic guitar. Was Bob about to break a near thirty-year musical silence to perform with Johnny Clavylle? Was Johnny ready to share the limelight again with his long-time rival?

The men shook hands, then clasped each other in exaggerated, show business style. Cameras zeroed in. The giant screens showed a frontal view of Johnny looking quizzically into Bob's eyes, then the image switched to Bob, who quickly turned away, to face and acknowledge the excited audience.

The woman beside me squealed. "Look at 'im. Bob 'Oward. 'E was my first pinup. 'E was a dish, back then. Ain't seen him fer years. Looks good fer 'is age. Must be going to sing. What a treat. Wait 'til I tell 'em back 'ome."

The woman leaned forward and hugged her arms tightly around her middle, as Johnny spoke again. "Bob and I haven't sung together in public for more years than either of us cares to remember. We'd like to do so now for you. We're going to sing you another new song never performed in public. We wrote it after I met an incredible woman with whom I fell hopelessly in love. Only trouble was that Bob got there first. That's been the story of my life with Bob Howard. I guess he's what you call an early bird; the one who finds the juiciest worms."

Johnny Clavylle clapped Bob on the back and made such a droll face that the crowd roared with laughter. Then his voice dropped. "This woman *is* special to both of us. Without her, I would not be alive, much less standing here tonight. Bob and I wrote this song together for her, while we've been on tour. It's by way of saying thank you, for all she's done and been and still is in both our lives. This song's for you, Sarah. It's called *Yours* – and we still are, sweetheart."

The lights dimmed but for two golden spots on the two men. Johnny and Bob took up their guitars, swung round to look at each other, then faced forward again and began to play. I thanked the stars that I had exchanged my front-front box seat for W-section anonymity. Even so, each time the two men stared up into the audience, I watched their eyes on the giant screens, and felt that both Bob and Johnny knew where I was sitting.

The song itself started soft and smoky. Key changes were unexpected and the men's harmonies delicate and dancing. Two masters of their profession and art serenaded the Hollywood Bowl and me:

You walked the shore on sands of sweetness
We tramped our night roads of decay
You took our hearts
Grown tired and jaded
And gave them strength to face the day

You gave back our faith in living
Your gift means more than we can say
You put the love into living
When we met I blessed the day

Yours is the voice that speaks forgiveness
Yours is the voice that sings of trust

Yours is the voice that offers blessings
When all around turns to dust

And somewhere in the future
The story will unfold
On resurrection road

Tears misted my vision, spilled over and began to soak my face. My Cockney neighbour turned to whisper something to me. I felt rather than saw her register my wet cheeks, open then close her mouth, and turn back to watch the stage.

The music was on a slow burn and build. A bass drum came in and lights revealed that the other band members were now back on stage. With Johnny and Bob's voices intertwining, I no longer distinguished between which of them was singing and when, as I surrendered to what felt like a growing anthemic mood and meaning of the lyrics:

We took the line of least resistance
Rode our rock steeds into night
Tangled in a past existence
Lost the sense of wrong and right

In that moment of darkness
I saw the sunlight in your hair
And I found where my heart is
When I saw you standing there

Yours is the voice that speaks forgiveness
Yours is the voice that sings of trust
Yours is the love that lasts forever
Your truth renews, removes our rust
I'm yours….I'm yours

And out there in the distance
The story will unfold
On resurrection road
Resurrection road

After all the years of searching
You gave my love a face
Just when I thought I'd lost it all
You are my saving grace

Yours…
Yours… I'm yours
Yours…
I'm Yours

Yours is the voice that speaks forgiveness
Yours is the voice that sings of trust
Yours is the voice that offers blessings
When all around turns to dust

And one day in the future
The secret will be told
We know you'll be waiting
On resurrection road

Johnny and Bob stood motionless. They laid aside their guitars. They stared at each other, then moved to hug and hug again. This time, through my tears, I knew that their embraces were heart-felt and I felt healed and whole.

Tumultuous applause filled the Hollywood Bowl. People around me were standing, stamping and cheering. I could not move.

"Ain't they jus' brilliant?"

I had no words for the Cockney woman who leaned over toward me. I could only smile and nod. She stood beside me with a broad grin on her face for several minutes after the applause died. Then she sighed, wished me good night and a safe journey home, and made her bulky way toward the exit.

After the entire area around me had emptied, I sat on, staring up at the stars. The air was heavy high up into the night sky, but pinpricks of light were visible beyond the haze. Questions tumbled through my mind. Had jealousy and the desire for retribution run their course in these two men, as all things must with time? Or had marijuana in the air enveloped performers and crowd in some benign brume of benevolence that would dissipate once it encountered bustling streets of Hollywood and beyond?

I had no way of gauging whether the chaotic career of Johnny Clavylle and his rivalry with Bob Howard was experiencing a temporary respite or a total transformation. Time alone would tell whether angels had helped to orchestrate some lasting symphony of reconciliation between Johnny and Bob on the stage of the Hollywood Bowl.

Perhaps the man called Antony Makepeace had found, through his art, an alchemical path to exorcise his demons and transmute his troubled past.

Perhaps some miracle had just occurred for us all on this road to resurrection.

Perhaps…

I wiped my cheeks, which were still moist, with the back of my hand. As I did so, my eyes were drawn again to one of the large screens. The cameras had been left on and showed the two men still standing with their arms around each other's shoulders. They talked to each other and acknowledged members of the crowd who had lingered after the show to approach the stage and call up to them and other band members.

Johnny looked every inch the megastar, glowing and transformed. Bob appeared the confident and enthusiastic man I knew and loved. I felt great warmth and affection for both men as I watched them from my perch on high.

Are you there, Frances?

Yes, I'm here.

You were quite right.

About what?

That nobody has the power to hurt me, unless some part of me is in agreement that they should.

Ah, so you understand that now. I'm glad.

I know something else too.

What else?

I'm done with watching and wanting others to behave in particular ways in order for me to feel OK. I must stop giving away my power by waiting for the world to change. I have to learn to accept things as they are and embody in my life what I want the world to be. If that means losing friends or dropping relationships with certain people, so be it. I've waited long enough on the sidelines for my life to begin. Thank you for the lesson, Frances.

A gentle breeze stirred the night air as Frances released her breath. I felt rather than saw her smile of recognition that her task with me was done. In that same moment, I realised also that she would now feel free to leave. I knew a pang of grief tinged with fear that we might part so soon after connecting. Then I recollected a truth that I had once known but then forgotten: in a realm beyond time and space, Frances and I were one. Separation was illusory.

As above, so below.

Within time and space, the spirit and wisdom of Frances had anchored and activated in me.

Perhaps it was my imagination, or simply that the air had cleared with the departure of the Bowl's pot smokers but, as my gaze drifted skyward again, the stars seemed to be shining twice as bright.

It was time to join the party.

At an elevator, I bumped into my Cockney companion of earlier. She was huffing and puffing and red in the face. " Are you OK?" I asked.

"Left me 'andbag in the ladies loo up 'ere, din't I. Got it now, stupid cow that I am. But I missed me lift. I'll 'ave to get a taxi."

"Where are you staying?"

"A little 'otel just off 'Ollywood Boulevard."

My heart went out to her. "I can give you a ride on my way home, but not for a few hours. I wonder, would you like to come to a party with me?"

She looked doubtful. "I'm not dressed for anything posh, luv. Is it far? What kind of people will be there? I don't want to be a nuisance or nuffink."

"It's right here in the Bowl. Come as you are. You're dressed just right, and I can guarantee you'll like meeting at least two people at this party. I have a hunch they'll like you too."

We chatted together as we took the elevator down to the Museum Terrace. I did a double take when I learned my newfound friend was called Fran Cook. You can't make this stuff up if you try, I thought.

I was soon smiling and feeling rewarded by the expression on Fran's face, when I introduced her to Johnny Clavylle and Bob Howard. Within minutes she and the two men were lost in reminiscing together about the good old days of Nights of the Road. I felt deep contentment as I stood back and watched their animated faces.

"What a character. Where did you find her?" Jane came up beside me.

I grinned. "I think she found me. But that's Los Angeles, isn't it? You no sooner say goodbye to someone than another person pops up to take her place. Life is just one long game of musical chairs in this city."

Jane looked confused. "I'm not sure what you're talking about. I'm glad to see you happier than when I last saw you, but who did you just say goodbye to?"

I laughed. "That's a story for another time. I seem to remember that when we last saw each other, you were wishing us a night of filthy hedonism. Come on, girl. Let's dance."

And we did, until dawn and beyond.

THE END

All the seventeenth-century characters of Nights of the Road actually lived and I have tried throughout to stay true to such facts about them as are known. None of the twenty-first-century characters did or do live, even though some may bear a passing resemblance to people you and I know.

No birth record has yet been found for Frances Coke. References to her age at marriage range from fourteen to sixteen. Her marriage licence declares her as sixteen in August 1617, but her age may have been overstated, given the coercive circumstances in which Frances was bound to a much older man. I have opted to place her birth at the later date of 1603.

The marriage of Mistress Frances Coke to Sir John Villiers, later Viscount Baron Villiers of Stoke and Viscount Purbeck of Dorset, created a huge stir in the upper echelons of British society. The King of England and his favourite, Buckingham, orchestrated events from afar during negotiations, and played prominent roles at the wedding.

This was the most formidable single battle of many between Sir Edward Coke and his wife Lady Elizabeth Hatton (nee Cecil) that enlivened seventeenth-century gossip. It was also another battleground for two remarkable rivals of their day, Coke and Bacon. Francis Bacon became embroiled in the story, from the moment of the schism between Coke and Lady Hatton over Frances. Elizabeth sought Bacon's aid to return their daughter to her custody and one letter of the time sent to Coke's daughter, Ann Sadler, suggested she might even have pulled him out of his slumbers to do so.

Bacon may have seen the dispute not only as a chance to help his much-loved friend and cousin*, but also as an opportunity to do Coke further mischief. If so, he would have done better to rest content with his rival's recent fall from royal grace and his own ascendancy to the role of Lord Keeper of the Great Seal. He was out of touch with the prevailing social tide, for he seems not to have recognised that Buckingham and his mother were as eager for the match as Coke. Perhaps he could not pass up an opportunity to stir the pot. He certainly underestimated Buckingham's position in the affections of James the First.

Bacon wrote first to Buckingham, itemising reasons why the match was 'very inconvenient for your mother, your brother and yourself.' These included the inadvisability of marrying into a disgraced house, in which a husband and wife at odds were behaving in an Un-Christian fashion, and the likelihood that Buckingham would lose all his friends as a result of such an association. Suggesting the latter to a man with an ego the size of a house was not the wisest of moves.

Having received a curt put-down from Buckingham, Bacon committed a greater gaffe, by intimating his concerns about the proposed marriage to the King. In the second message he sent to James, Bacon presumed to suggest that Buckingham might be feeling too secure in his 'height of fortune.' Bricks of royal wrath rained down on him from afar – James was visiting Scotland for the first time in fourteen years on the English throne – for daring to criticise the King's favourite, as well as for attempting to obstruct a marriage to which the monarch declared himself warmly disposed.

Bacon shared Coke's view of the world in at least one regard: he was terrified of royal disapprobation. His awkward *volte-face* required him to distance himself from Lady Hatton and Frances for a time. Meanwhile the Coke-Villiers match occupied Society's mouths and pens for months, and many a gentleman of letters opined on it in private correspondence. The views and positions expressed depended much on the writer's relationships with the principal players. Inconsistencies abound between the accounts of the day; much like media coverage of events in modern times.

Some did express a passing sympathy for Frances, particularly when a rumour went viral that Coke had confined and beaten his daughter into submission, with the complicity of Buckingham's unpopular mother. But Buckingham's ascendancy with his King was already such that none who wrote about it appears to have sought to influence the outcome of the marriage negotiation, whatever their private opinion. For some, recounting the tale was as much about proving their pride of place in the political and social swim, or showcasing their wit, as passing on useful and accurate information.

Descriptions of the wedding also varied. Some wrote about how pretty Frances looked in her white or ivory dress, with her hair hanging long and loose down her back. Others presented the sorry picture of a tearful and unwilling child.

For years thereafter, Frances was rarely out of Court news, except when she lived with Robert Howard out of sight in Shropshire. But, from the beginning of the 1640s, writers of the day became increasingly preoccupied with the dangerous divisions that were leading to Civil War. We find little mention from this time on about Frances, other than a few brief glimpses in legal records concerning her property appropriation, her continuing efforts in law to recover this and her personal possessions, and the final simple record of her burial, as Viscountess Frances Purbecke, in the register of St Mary's the Virgin in Oxford.

For all that has been said and written of her during or since her lifetime, Frances remains remarkably elusive. Everything we know of her, even including those dictated letters from her parents that she copied out and signed before her marriage, originates from those living with and around her rather than from Frances herself. If she set out deliberately to avoid attention, it would not be surprising, given the extent to which she was pursued and persecuted by the powerful during so much of her life.

There is no epitaph to Frances in the Oxford church in which she was buried on 4th June 1645, although the seventeenth-century Oxford antiquarian Anthony Wood referred to a floor plaque in the church of St Mary the Virgin, which has long since disappeared. Perhaps the two most touching artefacts of her life are the lovelock that flows down over Sir Robert Howard's left shoulder in his portrait painted by Antony van Dyck, believed to date from the late 1630s, and the evidence that Sir Robert – eligible bachelor as he was, and surely comely enough of countenance to attract the ladies – remained unmarried until entering his sixth decade of life, three years after Frances died.

In one instance, I may have strayed from the path of known facts. John Clavell did live and love, steal college silver and rob people on the highways of seventeenth-century England. He also served time, escaped execution, recanted his former criminal lifestyle and became known thereafter as an author, a lawyer and a doctor. Whether Frances met John at Corfe Castle during her childhood or had any dealings with him in her adult life is unknown. I have found no proof that she did and none that she did not.

I have asked Frances directly if she enjoyed a relationship with John Clavell. She says nothing but gives me that enigmatic look captured so powerfully in her portrait of 1623, by Michiel Jansz van Miereveld, which hangs today in Ashdown House, Oxfordshire. So it must rest with you, dear reader, to decide whether the story of Frances Coke and John Clavell's meeting is fact and/or fiction, as well as to draw your own conclusions about its place in the lives of the present-day characters in Nights of the Road. Whatever you conclude, I hope you may have enjoyed reading as much as I have enjoyed the writing.

Midi Berry. January, 2015. Agoura Hills. California. USA.

* Francis Bacon was nephew to Lord Burleigh, Elizabeth Cecil Hatton's grandfather.

ACKNOWLEDGMENTS

My thanks go first to the ancestors and especially my father, **Lloyd Hughes-Owens**. You infused me with a love of words, history and research that made learning a pleasure. You encouraged me to believe that all things were possible for your daughter. You inspired me to stand on your shoulders and go further, by showing me how much the world lost when you kept your poet soul under wraps and published only the serious stuff. I know you are smiling and enjoying the read, as Nights of the Road rides onto the public stage.

I thank spirits of place and three special locations. **Corfe Castle**: my blood thrilled when I visited you first as an eight-year-old. Thank you for requiring me to write about you. I'm not sure we are done with each other yet. **Corsica**: thank you for teaching me to turn inward from an extraverted lifestyle. Thank you for reminding me that storytelling runs in my blood. And thank you for your granite strength and beauty that resonates with stories still to come. **California and the City of Angels**: thank you for the sunshine and the crazy spirit of optimism that makes every one of us living here think we have a great book or film script inside us, and every other one of us try to write it.

For an Oxfordshire born-and-bred girl, a special place also exists for some **Oxford** thanks. A couple of kind people checked out details of Frances Coke's burial at the University Church of St Mary the Virgin in Oxford: **Penny Boxall**, thank you for checking the survey records for a plaque. **Alan Simpson**, thank you for providing the exact register entry.

A batch of thanks is due to providers of book cover images. **Burke Wallace**: thank you for being good to look at, on my book cover and in real life. And thanks for musical fun in the Why Lie days. **Tracy Cianflone**: thank you for spending hours on a hotter than hot day with your artist's eye and camera to capture the picture needed to bring rock music and highwayman elements of Night of the Road to life. **The National Trust**: thank you for preserving the portrait of Frances Coke, Viscountess Purbeck, for making her accessible for the public to enjoy at Ashdown House, and for your charming and efficient service when providing me with the licence for image use. **Mike Kempsey,** thanks for your photography skills, for your fine work on the book cover and for your generosity in sharing your image of Corfe Castle, which matches the spirit of ancient stones in Nights of the Road. Thanks for proof-reading and for your endless patience and moral support.

Then there are friends, who helped with the heavy lifting. **Madeleine Kingsley**, writer and book reviewer, journalist, counsellor and friend of fifty years: you have been there to share, celebrate and enrich the journey at so many milestone moments of our life. Thank you for being with me for this latest adventure, for shining the light of your wisdom and for sharing the warmth of your heart. **Nicola Cornick**: you're one of the unexpected gems and gifts that this ride with Nights of the Road has already yielded by way of new friends from afar. Thank you for your encouragement, for inspiring me through your own writing journey and for volunteering at Ashdown House, as well as writing a wonderful blog about the National Trust property that cares for Frances Coke's portrait. **Will Keyser**: thank you for giving me practical feedback and ideas on self-publishing. Your indefatigable energy to 'bring to market' whatever you start and continuing curiosity to explore new horizons have been a role model for me ever since a job interview one long-ago cold winter's night turned into a twenty-one-year business and family partnership. I feel blessed that our friendship endures as we take our new paths.

And to my far flung family around the USA, Australia, Corsica and Ireland. **Jim, Elena, Alex, Martini, Aron, Lorcan, Tiger Lily, Rebecca, Aebhe, Fran, Ed, Tom and Joe**: you all are the reason I stay around when winds blow chill and the *au dela* beckons. I wish my arms could reach around the world to hug each of you in person daily. Having so many of you stay during some part of this recent Nights of the Road journey has leavened my writing days and kept me anchored in the world that exists beyond my pen. Watching you grow and go and follow your individual stars is my great joy and delight. My son, **Mark**: thank you for being a gracious website host and for holding the lantern as I waded through the intricacies of WordPress. Thank you too for sharing a great Nights of the California Road trip. My granddaughter, **Sienna**: thank you for being, and for being the reason I write for the world. And **Mark Singer**, last and also first, my beloved drummer man and life partner: thank you for your enthusiasm and whole-hearted support for me, even when you have no idea what I am doing. Thank you for giving me space to reflect, write and roam, and for always being there to come home to. Thank you quite simply for being the love of my life. And for feeding **OJ the cat**, who deserves thanks, in his own right.

AUTHOR'S PAGE

Hello! I was born in England of Welsh origin, but I have lived and worked in five continents as a management and development consultant, before returning recently to my early love of story-telling.

Nights of the Road is my first published historical novel. I have several unpublished manuscripts and I'm currently researching and writing *The Corsican Trilogy*, a series of novels that follow the lives of three generations in a family caught up in eighteenth-century revolution in Corsica, America and Australia.

I have children and grandchildren living around the world in Australia, Corsica and Ireland. I live mid-way between them all in the beautiful Santa Monica Mountains of Southern California, with my exuberant rock drummer partner and a charming orange cat called OJ.

My passions are nature, indigenous cultures, history, music, reading, art, family and friends.

Do visit Nights of the Road and me at our websites and pages, and please feel free to leave a comment at Midi's blog. I'd love to hear from you:

> www.nightsoftheroad.com/blog
> www.nightsoftheroad.com
> https://www.facebook.com/midi.berry
> https://www.facebook.com/nightsoftheroad
> www.linkedin.com/pub/midi-berry/2421/598

Thank you so much for reading Nights of the Road. If you enjoyed it, please spread the news among your friends. And, if you can spare the time, do give me a review at your favourite retailer and/or on your blog. For inquiries about guest posts and interviews, contact me at nightsoftheroad@icloud.com.